W9-ABW-152

The Demon's Daughter

The Demon's Daughter

EMMA HOLLY

BERKLEY SENSATION, NEW YORK

THE BERKLEY PUBLISHING GROUP
Published by the Penguin Group
Penguin Group (USA) Inc.
375 Hudson Street, New York, New York 10014, USA
Penguin Group (Canada), 10 Alcorn Avenue, Toronto, Ontario M4V 3B2, Canada
(a division of Pearson Penguin Canada Inc.)
Penguin Books Ltd., 80 Strand, London WC2R 0RL, England
Penguin Group Ireland, 25 St. Stephen's Green, Dublin 2, Ireland (a division of Penguin Books Ltd.)
Penguin Group (Australia), 250 Camberwell Road, Camberwell, Victoria 3124, Australia
(a division of Pearson Australia Group Pty. Ltd.)
Penguin Books India Pvt. Ltd., 11 Community Centre, Panchsheel Park, New Delhi—110 017, India
Penguin Group (NZ), Cnr. Airborne and Rosedale Roads, Albany, Auckland 1310, New Zealand
(a division of Pearson New Zealand Ltd.)
Penguin Books (South Africa) (Pty.) Ltd., 24 Sturdee Avenue, Rosebank, Johannesburg 2196, South Africa

Penguin Books Ltd., Registered Offices: 80 Strand, London WC2R 0RL, England

This is a work of fiction. Names, characters, places, and incidents either are the product of the author's imagination or are used fictitiously, and any resemblance to actual persons, living or dead, business establishments, events, or locales is entirely coincidental.

THE DEMON'S DAUGHTER

A Berkley Sensation Book / published by arrangement with the author

ISBN: 0-7394-4678-9

BERKLEY® SENSATION
Berkley Sensation Books are published by The Berkley Publishing Group,
a division of Penguin Group (USA) Inc.,
375 Hudson Street, New York, New York 10014.
BERKLEY SENSATION and the "B" design
are trademarks belonging to Penguin Group (USA) Inc.

PRINTED IN THE UNITED STATES OF AMERICA

To Susan Ilene Johnson.
Because once upon a time,
while at a very boring job,
two women became lifelong friends.

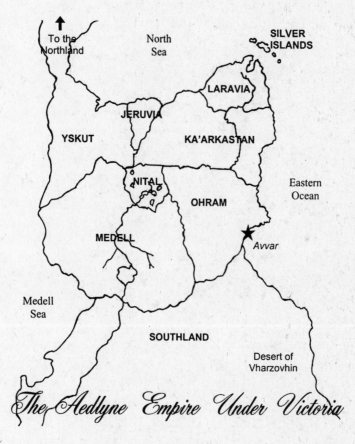

The Aedlyne Empire Under Victoria

Chapter 1

The first human expedition to the icy wastes of the north was not for exploration, as your teachers would have you believe. No, it was for gold, tantalizing veins of which had been discovered in the bordering mountains of Yskut. What triumphs might have belonged to our fair empire had we claimed the Northland's vast reserves for ourselves are best left to the drunken ramblings of old men. Hoping only for filthy lucre, and perhaps a knighthood, the leader of the expedition, one Captain DuBarry, had his team lower him by rope into a promising crevasse. Instead of gold, he found the hidden city of Narikerr—the city and the demons who lived within.

Not true demons, of course. The Yama are our allies, and I must be sensitive. It is only their alien appearance that makes us give their species that name.

So DuBarry found the Yama and their wondrous technology. Understandably, perhaps, since they had been living in scrupulous isolation for thousands of years, the Yama did not find the excitable captain quite as wondrous as he found them. The discovery of the

health enhancing effects of human etheric-force on Yamish-kind
was all that allowed the intrepid captain to escape alive.

                               —*The True and Irreverent History of Avvar*

~~~⌒~~~

Take a holiday, *his superintendent had said.*
You're working far too hard.

Eight hours later, Inspector Adrian Philips was fleeing
for his life through Avvar's fog-shrouded slums. He could
have activated his implants, the tiny devices the Yamish
doctor had tucked so cleverly beneath the tendons of his
wrists. His muscles would gain power then, as much power
as the demons it was his dubious honor to police. Unfortunately, the surge of artificial strength wouldn't last and,
once past, would leave him drained. That he couldn't
afford—even if those who chased him were only humans.
Better to save the advantage for when he truly needed it.

He tried to run faster on his own, but the soiled overcoat
he'd donned as camouflage in this seedy section of the capitol flapped about his legs. Though the hem threatened to
trip him, he dared not break stride long enough to discard
it. His pursuers were too close. Even now he heard them
splashing through the lake yesterday's rain had made at the
intersection of Fifth and Heaven's Gate.

Heaven's Gate.

Despite his fear, a laugh rasped in his throat. Call him a
Bedlamite, but he'd rather be here, running from a gang of
slumboys, than home with nothing to do but contemplate
the mess he'd made of his life.

"There's the bloody peeler!" cried a voice not nearly far
enough behind him. It was a young man's tenor, the dialect
pure dockside—like an irreverent bully trying to swallow a
bag of marbles.

The clatter of hobnailed boots accelerated. All too soon,
a shoulder slammed the small of Adrian's back, throwing
him forward. His right cheekbone hit the stoop of a shuttered harness shop.

Stunned, he gasped in pain as they flung him onto his

back and began kicking him—kidneys, stomach, wherever they could reach.

He couldn't see them. The thick marine mist obscured their features, though their voices rang clear enough. He knew what he'd find in any case: bodies gone lean from feeding the demons with their life force; honed faces; pale, perfect skin. Those who served the Yama came to share a bit of their alien beauty. Not their strength, not their cleverness, just a reason for the shallowest vanity. He'd heard the latest fashion among the gangs was to have their tongues tattooed to match their employers' natural forked markings.

Too ignorant to see how cheaply they had sold themselves, his attackers cursed as they pounded him, telling him to keep his nose where it belonged. He wasn't wanted there, and they'd better not see him in Harborside again.

Part of him wanted to laugh. These young men must have been demonbait once themselves. Yet here they were, defending the exploitation of their fellows.

All he'd wanted was to find one lost boy.

Adrian dodged one kick and rolled into another. A foot pinned his arm and ground down until his bones threatened to part company. With a grunt of pain, he wrenched free. He had to get a new hobby. Searching for missing youngsters was not a one-man job. Too bad his department figured the children of the poor were destined for a bad end anyway, so why waste the man hours? Adrian Philips, however inadequate, was their best hope.

Judging it more than time, he tightened his fingers in the pattern the Yamish doctor had taught him to activate the implants. A flash of heat streaked up the veins that led from his wrists. His heart pumped harder, and a frighteningly wonderful feeling swelled in his breast, as if one sweep of his arm could smash the world.

Gritting his teeth to maintain control of his impulses, he threw the nearest slumboy off him, the body flying off as if it weighed no more than a cat. One opponent taken care of, he drove his heel into the shin that wore the sharpest pair of boots. Bones snapped at the blow, and he wondered if he was sorry. Even if he was, he didn't have time for regrets. Exclamations of surprise and anger met his success. A fist drove toward his face. He stopped it dead with the flat of his palm. This time he strove to be more careful. He'd pull the attacker over with his own momentum.

The boy stumbled as he yanked. *Choke hold him,* Adrian thought. He didn't have to kill him. He could threaten his life to force the others to back off. Before he could pursue this strategy, the largest of his attackers barked a sharp order. As suddenly as they'd set after him, they disappeared. Their footsteps reverberated off the gritty cobbles, at least one of them limping. Perhaps seeing the fight come back to him had ruined their sport. Certainly, they'd not been cowed by his being a member of the law. The inhabitants of Harborside were in much more danger from each other than from the police.

There weren't, after all, many officers willing to compromise their humanity as Adrian had. The prejudice he faced for accepting his implants, no matter how practical they were, was no small thing.

Numb with shock, he lay panting by the curb, trying to figure where he'd gone wrong. Adrian was no green recruit. He knew how to judge when a situation was about to turn dangerous. But there'd been no warning today. No strange looks from the people—demon or human—who he'd questioned about the Bainbridge boy. No sign that he'd been fingered for Securité.

Harborside. Just when he thought he understood it, it started speaking in tongues.

He tensed as a woman shrieked somewhere in the distance, either in laughter or pain. Perhaps her Yamish keeper had laid his hand on her heart. Perhaps he was even then drinking from the well of her vitality.

Etheric-force, a subtle form of electricity that some called animal magnetism, had always been transferrable in small amounts—a natural result of interaction between living beings. As far as Adrian knew, only the Yama could draw it off deliberately. To them, human energy, slightly different from but compatible with their own, was a cross between miracle elixir and spiked coffee. It strengthened their already-formidable constitutions and made them, by all accounts, feel both relaxed and alert. No such benefits redounded on their human donors, but they recovered after a day or so of sleep. As long as the exchange was voluntary, it was all perfectly legal.

Sighing, Adrian struggled to sit up, feeling a thousand years old now that the implant's unnatural boost of well-being had passed. Thunder rumbled ominously, a sure sign of winter's approach. He couldn't stay here. If he did, others would sniff out his weakness.

With a groan he got to his feet, blinking dazedly through wisps of blue-gray fog: half coal smoke, half moisture. The halos of the street lamps, their glass wired in diamond patterns against breakage, expanded and contracted before his eyes.

This was demon science, Queen Victoria's reward for allowing some of the Yama to settle in her slums. A devil's bargain, many said, but what was the spinster queen to do with the Medell army nipping at her border? Their neighbors to the west had been fighting Aedlyne rule for centuries. Nor were they any less belligerent under their own kings. To fend them off once and for all, Victoria decided to accept the Yama's offer of superior technology. She couldn't have known the settlers who arrived would be the Yama's own outcasts, low-born rebels who couldn't, or wouldn't, live within their homeland's strict hierarchical system. The aristocratic Yama—the *daimyo,* as they called themselves—didn't want to be tainted with their presence any more than they'd wanted to be tainted with humankind's.

Not one to waste an advantage, regardless of what it had cost, Queen Victoria, High Lady of the Aedlyne Empire, had ordained that every street in every subject nation be lit against the night. Not for the first time, Adrian blessed her fear of the dark, even if the swimming lamplight did make him dizzy.

At least the illumination told him which way to go.

He began to walk, not toward his base station in Little Barking—that was too far—but inland, away from the harbor, the quickest route to safety.

He stumbled repeatedly as he navigated the crooked, foul-smelling streets. He couldn't blame the stench on the city's newest immigrants. Even demon riffraff were fastidious. Built by humans a century ago, these rickety wooden houses, their gargoyles splintered and stained, listed dangerously over his head. Some of the upper stories hung so far over the street, their inhabitants could have tapped the opposite side's windows. He didn't relish walking beneath these arches; they were too well suited for concealing threats.

He knew he must be gone from here by nightfall. It was more than dark enough already under the fog.

Cursing, he clapped a hand to a persistent stitch in his side. His palm came away wet. He blinked at the shiny red, barely comprehending what it meant. Apparently, one of the slumboys had used a blade. The beating he'd been taking must have distracted him from feeling the injury, but seeing it gave it power. Without warning, his legs folded.

Get up, he ordered, shaking his head on hands and knees like a wet dog. He tried to call on the implants again, but it was too soon for them to work. All he got for his attempt was a sickening surge of adrenaline. The sound of childish laughter swelled from a nearby alley—dark laughter, youthful exchanges of mockery. His neck tightened. Here even children were dangerous. Endangered and dangerous.

With so many serving the demons for the sake of a few scarce coins, it was impossible to know which side anyone was on.

Raising his head with an effort, he spied a brick wall up ahead. Brick, not wood. He must have reached the boundary of Harborside. A fire escape hung down the building's side like a ladder to heaven. Though it abutted the poorest section of Avvar, the four-story brick box inhabited another, safer world, a world he was determined to reenter. He eyed the contraption longingly. Too woozy to think straight, he didn't stop to wonder if there was an easier way out than up.

Regaining his feet, he tried to grab the lowest rung to extend the ladder fully. Vexingly, it was too high. He had no strength to jump for it, though he tried. In desperation, he pulled off his overcoat and swung it like a grapple.

The ladder descended with a rusty squeal. Shaking his head in wonder, he began to drag himself up the rungs, about as strong as a starving pup. Up he struggled, one story, two.

Midway through the third, he passed a lighted window. The tableau inside made him stop and gape. A couple was making love on a kitchen table. Both still dressed, the man was cinnamon-brown, the woman as golden as the desert of Vharzovhin.

These were a previous generation's immigrants, when *newcomer* still meant human. The golden woman kissed her lover's neck, her arms and legs tightening in rhythm to his thrusts. Her blouse had fallen away to reveal one perfect breast, and her nipple stood out sharply in arousal. The man ran his hand up under her skirt, baring her calf and thigh. His eyes were closed, his head thrown back as though the woman were killing him with pleasure. Then his thumb slid into the crease at the top of her shapely leg, pressing something that made her back arch like a bow. A sharp female cry struck the glass, unmistakably orgasmic.

Adrian's throat constricted. Turning away, he tried not to compare this scene to his life with Christine. Three months their marriage had lasted. He'd never even coaxed his wife to make love without her nightclothes. She was a decent woman, a model of middle-class Victorian propriety. His consenting to have the implants had been the last straw. After that, she hadn't wanted to touch him at all. Adrian had loved her, but he couldn't live that way; couldn't sire children on a woman who'd been trained to hate the marriage bed, who had come to think of him as a monstrosity.

Monster or not, he didn't think a morsel of warmth was too much to ask.

Two years had passed since he'd left her. He supposed her rejection shouldn't still hurt. It did, though, distracting him from where he was even as he dragged himself upward. Finally, he was able to lever his chest over the ledge of the roof.

Nauseated from loss of blood, he rested his cheek against the rough wet pourstone. Someone had planted a garden on the roof. He heard the rustle of leaves in the first spatter of rain and smelled late-blooming roses. He smiled faintly, then realized he was about to faint. He pushed himself higher, groaning, trying to ensure a fall on the right side of the ledge.

Thunder boomed as he dropped with a thunk into a flowerbed. As though this had been a signal, the skies opened, pummeling his body in hard, silvery sheets. He closed his eyes, feeling the rain pound him clean. His fingers touched something ruffled and smooth—marigold petals, he thought.

He chuckled to himself. How absurd. He'd fallen into the Garden. He, who had been exiled.

He wondered if he'd die here, if his former wife would feel relief at the news. He'd only seen her once since the divorce, at the wedding of a mutual friend. Her eyes had lighted on his face from across the aisle, then flew away like a startled bird. That was all. No words were exchanged. No one else had seen her response, but he'd stayed away from the old neighborhood after that. Why risk tormenting her? He didn't enjoy it, though he knew some men reveled in mastering their wives. He heard their stories at the station house, saw the attitude in every stern-faced male with his fingers tight and white around his woman's arm. *Allow me to know what's best for you, my dear. Allow me to know.*

He didn't understand those men, but sometimes he envied the freedom they claimed—at least with their mistresses. To be able to cry out in the heat of passion, to shed one's inhibitions with one's clothes, to be an utterly sensual creature and to have one's partner be the same . . . that must be paradise. But how could Adrian take joy in a mercenary arrangement? He didn't want a paid sham. He wanted true desire.

If he paid his partners, he *would* be no better than a demon.

Weighed down by more than bodily fatigue, the last of his strength dissolved.

~~≫~~

He woke to the sensation of hands roaming his body. At first, he assumed he was being robbed, but the exclamations of concern that accompanied the search suggested someone was trying to ascertain how badly he'd been hurt. He opened his eyes a slit.

His examiner was a woman. She knelt on the rain-black granite by the flowerbed. Her legs were doubled beneath her like a child's. A hurricane lamp glowed yellow at her side, spitting oily curls of smoke where raindrops struck the heated glass. In its homely light, he saw she wore a thin white gown, muslin, with tiny eyelet straps to hold it at the shoulders.

The gown would have been indecent even if it hadn't been plastered to her by the storm. Her nipples were dark and puckered in the cold, and Adrian told himself it was only his delirium that kept him from looking away. Her breasts had a lovely shape, swaying as she moved. *Beautiful,* he thought. He could see the faint shadow of their veins, blue against white rounded flesh.

"You are awake," she said, startling his eyes to her face.

She was not pretty. That was his first thought. Her mouth was too wide, her eyes too pale—almost as silvery as a demon's. The similarity made him shudder instinctively, though her irises did not cover up her whites. Her hair was a different matter. Long and abundant, it clung to her outrageously naked shoulders like caramel-colored seaweed. Her lack of modesty made him wonder if she was a prostitute. Perhaps he hadn't made it out of Harborside after all.

Straightaway, he rebelled at the possibility. In the lantern's wavering glow, she had the fresh, clean skin of a farm girl; the honest features of someone's sensible maiden aunt. The thought of her selling herself to strangers appalled him, especially if those strangers weren't interested in sex.

"Does anything feel broken?" she asked, her voice pleasing to the ear and surprisingly cultivated. Adrian prided himself on the practiced breeding of his speech, but her dulcet ease put all his care to shame.

When he opened his mouth to speak, nothing came out. He shook his head.

She laughed and squeezed his shoulder reassuringly. Then, to his complete astonishment, she eased her arms under his back and knees and, with no more than a grunt of effort, lifted him like a child.

He was not a small man. Spare of flesh but tall, he was not some stripling boy to be hefted as easily as a sack of flour. That, however, was precisely what she did, striding quickly across the expanse of her rain-swept garden.

For a moment, he was too rattled to struggle. Then, "Are you mad?" he demanded, twisting from her arms. His knees buckled as soon as he got his feet under him.

The prodigy laughed but not mockingly. "Too proud, are we?" Arranging his arm around her shoulders, she hauled him to his feet.

They stood, swaying like drunkards, before a partitioned glass door. The woman elbowed it open, and together they stumbled into a dark room. Adrian received an impression of space, high ceilings, wood floors, and many, many windows. He smelled something that reminded him of the varnish his father used at the shipyard. They turned right to cross the length of the room. Water squelched from his shoes with every lurching step, miles of steps. Finally, they reached a parlor with faded velvet chairs and fringed lamps and, saints be praised, a crackling fire in the grate. A generous heap of clean-burning Northlandic peat glowed blue behind the fretwork screen. It smelled like the country.

The woman settled him on a long gray- and pink-flowered couch, her arms shaking from the strain of supporting him. Even in this light, he could see she was strapping, possibly as tall as him. All the same, he was relieved by the sign of human frailty.

"Better?" she asked, and touched his cheek with the backs of her fingers.

A shock hummed through him when he met her worried gaze, an oddly sensual awareness. Her eyes were just as eerie as they'd seemed before, a pale, pale blue, the color uniform except for a delicate fringe of gold around the rim. In spite of the dangerous comparisons they brought to mind, he couldn't help picturing her eyes half closing with desire as he slid into the softest of moorings. Her lids would flicker shut when he pushed inward to his hilt. They would—

"Thank you," he whispered, disconcerted by the turn of his thoughts.

She smiled briefly and began removing his soggy clothes. Adrian protested, but she ignored him, pushing his limbs this way and that with the impersonal efficiency of an army nurse. Thoroughly embarrassed, he closed his eyes and tried to appear unaffected. He reminded himself he was a grown man, nearly forty. Even with a fire, he couldn't lie there in his wet clothes. If this woman wasn't ashamed to strip him naked, why should he be concerned?

The stab wound behind his right hip inspired a furious exclamation. She grabbed a towel from the stack of folded laundry that sat in one of the wing chairs by the fire. From the way she stuffed it under him and pressed, he guessed he was still bleeding.

"Lord love a duck," she swore, sounding frightened for the first time. He almost laughed. He'd never heard that expression before.

Fluttering a little, she pulled a knitted afghan off the back of the couch and tucked it around him. It was very soft. Lambswool, he thought.

"Stay," she ordered, then pulled a face when his mouth quirked ironically. "Very well, you're not going anywhere."

Unaccountably warmed by the exchange, he closed his eyes as she left the parlor, trying to ignore the pain in his side and the way the floor was tilting like a ship at sea.

He heard her speaking earnestly to someone in the hall. A
sleepy answer came, a boy's voice making some argument.

Her son? he wondered. *Her partner in iniquity?* But, no,
the boy wouldn't be sleeping if that were the case. These
were prime business hours for that sort—at least for human
customers. And come to think of it, the place didn't look
like a brothel, more like a poor but genteel boarding house.
One that couldn't afford a maid.

The woman and boy moved toward the doorway.

"They'll be busy in bed," the boy was saying. "They
haven't been married a week. I don't think Abul cares if he
ever sleeps."

"Pull the eel out of harbor yourself if you have to," the
woman countered. "Just get him up here."

That settled, she returned to Adrian's side. One hip
perched by his, she pressed the towel more firmly to him
and stroked his wet hair back from his brow. The last of his
fear gave way at her touch, and a different tension replaced
it, like a boiler building up a head of steam. Whatever her
occupation, this woman's hands held more erotic power
than anyone he'd met. If drinking energy felt like this, he
understood why the Yama found it addictive.

She spoke. "My downstairs neighbor is a resident at St.
Steffin's. He'll know how to fix you up."

He sighed and nodded. The steady brush of her fingers
was so nice he couldn't bring himself to regret the impro-
priety. The caress filled him with a painful longing, like the
scent of food after a fast. It had been so long—an eternity—
since anyone had touched him kindly. It seemed intolerable
that she was a stranger, that this tenderness was born of
pity rather than any appreciation of who he was.

His forehead tightened under her hand as she leaned
closer, her unbound breasts warming his chest even
through the dampness of her gown.

"I'm sorry you're hurting," she whispered close to his
ear. In spite of everything, he couldn't prevent the heat of
her breath from sending blood sluicing to his groin. The tip
of his cock itched as it stirred against the blanket. "Abul
will be here soon. He's a good doctor, and you'll be fine."

Her thumb swept up the furrow between his brows. "I promise."

"Sweet," he said, without meaning to. He didn't mean to sleep, either. He tried to hold off, to maintain his guard, but between running halfway across Harborside and using his implants in the fight, he was done in.

A moment later, helpless to stop it, he sank like the dead.

Chapter 2

~⌒~

Every so often, one of the *rohn* (the lower class demons who had been banished to Avvar) would go mad from imbibing too much human etheric-force. Alas for those addicted to the habit, along with the inebriating effect of taking another species' energy came the burden of that species' emotion, a burden these lower class Yama were ill-equipped to handle. Only a Yamish aristocrat's mental constitution was sufficiently refined to remain unmoved. Though likewise unused to the fire of human feelings, they could enjoy the benefits without the harm—even if it was considered crass to enjoy them often. The *rohn*, by contrast, were apt to turn violent. From this dilemma was born the practice of medically "enhancing" select members of those humans responsible for maintaining public order, thus allowing them to subdue an offender without resorting to deadly force—a leveling, if you will, of the playing field.

The idea of forbidding etheric drinking to lowborn Yama was not considered by the upper ranks. They reasoned the deportees' lot was hard enough. If they wished to take artificial comfort while forcibly separated from all that was good and pure in Yama life, that was their concern.

My personal theory, with which you are welcome to disagree, is that the *daimyo* secretly approved of their brethren's dissipation. If nothing else, etheric addiction kept the rabble content.

—*The True and Irreverent History of Avvar*

"It's good you heard him moaning when you did, but he'll recover."

Roxanne's neighbor sat calmly on a stool by her couch, his instruments returned to his battered leather satchel. Twelve stitches had been required to seal the gash in the man's lower back. With a compassion to match his competence, Abul's long brown hand smoothed the muslin pad he'd taped over the wound.

Watching, Roxanne felt a pang that was more reflex than regret. She didn't blame Abul for falling in love with Linia. She was pretty and sweet, and she'd adored Abul right back. A fellow emigre from Jeruvia, Linia had also pleased his parents. Roxanne couldn't claim any of these attributes. Her regret lay in having grown used to being Abul's best friend. She didn't desire him precisely, but she'd liked having that "what if?" in the back of her mind.

For as long as she could remember, she'd wanted to be safe and loved. When she was young, she'd dreamed a man would make her so, someone strong and kind and handsome, someone who would respect her for who she was— not the scandalous bastard of a famous singer, but a good woman. As the years passed and no such paragon appeared, she realized she wasn't wild enough for a bad man, nor conservative enough for one who was respectable. Caught between worlds, she resolved to make her own safety. As for love—the sort that put stars in a woman's eyes and a ring on her finger—well, plenty of people needed her love. She would take comfort in offering haven to someone else.

Stifling a sigh, she watched Abul fold back the daisy-link afghan to bare a mottled abrasion on the man's outer flank. Without warning, a flush of sensual awareness curled through her belly. Except for the bruises, the invalid's skin was a perfect creamy olive. Abul squeezed some ointment from a tube and spread it across the discoloration. The man was thin, but rather than detract from his beauty, the spareness emphasized the grace of his naked hip. Roxanne's fingers twitched with a desire to appropriate the job of salving it herself.

"The blade just grazed his muscle," her neighbor continued. "Lucky for your friend, he's hard as a rock."

Roxanne heard the suspicion in his voice, but only paid attention to the words. She eyed the definition of the man's broad back. If he was a rock, he was a battered one. He was all over black and blue. Her cheeks warmed at the thought of soothing each tender abrasion. Kissing it. Licking it.

She shook her head. She was being ridiculous. How many naked men had posed in her studio these last few years? For that matter, how many had paraded through the hostels and boarding houses of her youth? She thought she'd grown immune to the sight of bare male flesh. Apparently not. The rhythm of arousal pulsed between her legs. She couldn't remember feeling this goading a desire before.

Abul was staring up at her, a question in his eyes. "He'll be out for a while. You should get some sleep yourself. You look almost as bad as he does."

"I'm all right."

He stood and took her hands in his own. "You be careful," he said. "This man is strong."

"I'm strong," she countered with a rueful smile. Her unusual sturdiness was part of what drove romantic prospects away.

"He doesn't have an ounce of fat on him." Abul gestured toward the sleeping man. "That level of muscularity is possible to achieve with effort, but few humans go to the trouble. To me, he looks drained."

"No," Roxanne protested. "His skin is too dark for him to have been Taken."

"If he'd started serving the Yama recently, he might not show many signs."

"I'm not jumping to conclusions," she said. "It isn't fair."

"Being fair doesn't always keep you safe."

His words surprised her. He was a doctor, sworn to aid all who asked. From comments he'd made in the past, she knew he wasn't entirely comfortable treating the occasional injured demon, though most healed too fast to need help. Nor was he overjoyed with the arrangement Queen Victoria had made to have visiting Yamish doctors teach advanced techniques to the staff at St. Steffin's. How could demons know more than they did about human physiology? So what if the species were similar? Thank God they weren't identical. Despite these attitudes, she hadn't expected to hear him speak in favor of prejudice.

"Should I not have called you?" she asked, feeling unaccountably forlorn.

The hardness melted from Abul's face. "Of course you should have. He was hurt."

She smiled at him in relief, glad their friendship was intact. Though they'd never been lovers, they'd been through a lot together—lean times and lonely. But Abul had Linia now. Roxanne had Charles and little Max. And her work. And a roof over all their heads.

Abul's dark eyes warmed with kindred awareness. He spoke more professionally. "The worst is the blood loss and the knock on the head. But his pupils are responding appropriately. Have him rest for a few days, and get him to drink as much as you can: soup, tea, some of that expensive Medell orange juice you like, if he can stomach it. He might feel queasy once the narcophane wears off."

Roxanne nodded, refraining from pointing out that the useful painkiller was a Yamish invention.

Her friend's capable hand smoothed her hair from her face. "You sure you're all right, Roxie? You look shaken."

"It's not every night I wake to find a man nearly bleeding to death on my roof." When his brows pulled together, she patted his arm. "No, no, I'm fine. And speaking of going to bed, don't you think you should return to yours? Linia will be wondering what happened to you."

Abul flushed and grinned. After giving her a few more instructions and categorically refusing payment, he moved to the door and opened it.

"I'll knock it off your rent," she insisted as he paused on the threshold.

"Slumlord," he teased.

She waved him away with a laugh. She knew she ought to go to bed, but the stranger sleeping in the parlor drew her like a lodestone.

She pulled the low, tasseled stool toward his shoulders and sat down. He'd turned himself over on the couch. His chest was lightly furred, his shoulders broad, his waist narrow. His face could only be called compelling. She studied it in the firelight. Stern but very handsome, with good strong bones. Not starving bones, like demon servants got, but clean and dramatic. Dark hair framed his features, black as ink. It brushed his shoulders, a popular length among human males. Banished demons wore theirs very short, while the few aristocrats she'd seen in Avvar let theirs fall to their waists, a mark of honor they forbade their inferiors. It seemed that class distinctions were universal to both species. Indulging a private grin at the observation, she noted that his nose was thin, proud and sensitive at the same time. A wide mouth stretched beneath it, the lips narrow and grim even in sleep. Lines of tension scored its corners.

Unable to resist, she touched one scarlike mark with the tip of her finger. The rasp of stubble made her shiver. His lips moved in response, disturbed by her touch, but she couldn't make herself pull back. She stroked the valley beneath his lower lip with her knuckle, then jumped when he uttered a throaty sound. She would have left him alone then, but his head turned and his lips captured her knuckle. She froze. His tongue curled around her finger, wet and warm.

Waves of startled heat flowed across her body as her nipples pebbled beneath her gown, chilled by the damp muslin. Deep within her, tiny embers flared. His suckling reminded her of a kitten, and a knot of tenderness closed her throat. It would have been easier if tenderness was all her reaction was. Unfortunately, she would have welcomed those tugging lips anywhere. Everywhere, come to that.

Who was this man? Why did he move her so strongly? Surely the reason was more than his vulnerability, more even than his harsh beauty. She had seen those qualities before. But then why? Was it, as Yamish doctors claimed, a trick of invisible chemicals?

I don't know a thing about him, she thought as his mouth finally released her finger.

The dark fans of his lashes twitched. When they lifted, his eyes were a startling gray, dark as thunderclouds. Pain tinged them, even through the daze of narcophane. Something else was there as well, stronger than pain. Staring into his eyes was like opening the door to a secret furnace of sexual desire, as if he'd gone without a woman for quite some time. *Amazing.* Flat on his back, barely able to move, and the sight of this man's yearning made her weak. Now that was chemistry.

She leaned closer instinctively. His breath fanned her lips, hot and ragged.

"Hush," she said. "You're safe now." But it was not pity that drew her to kiss his unmarred cheek.

She must have hoped it would happen. Emboldened by her gesture, his lips turned toward hers, searching for connection. She didn't let herself wonder if it was wise, but cradled his jaw in her palm and lowered her mouth. He was strong enough to kiss her, parting his lips to invite her in. More than invite her. His cheeks hollowed as he tried to entice her deeper. She held such power in that moment, her skin ran with thrills, and her heart raced with excitement. She had kissed men but not many. To be wanted, to be the one to say "yes" or "no" was a unique delight. When she ventured farther, he released a long, liquid sigh.

He stilled beneath her. She thought he'd fallen asleep again. When she tried to pull back, though, the soft inner flesh of his mouth closed round her again, sucking in quick

little contractions. Gradually they slowed, his tongue playing languidly with hers as he began to trust she'd stay. The
sounds he made, hungry, pleased, flew straight from her ear
to her loins.

Few as they'd been, no kiss had ever made her feel like
this, sleepy and achy and swept almost out of herself. She
knew she didn't want it to end.

She didn't think he did, either. His hand touched her
chest, fingers curling blindly against the curve of her
breast. His skin was hot. Damp. Acting on impulse, and
maybe in defiance against Abul, she took his hand and eased
it inside the neck of her gown, pressing his palm against
her warm, swollen peak.

Drowsy as he was, his body recognized the intimacy. He
exhaled silently, a brush of air against her cheek, and then
his body stretched in a long undulation. His fingers tightened on her breast as the wave rolled up him. Sighing herself, she noticed a hummock forming between his thighs,
his organ lifting the wool forcefully. He shifted. Groaned.
And then his free hand fumbled for his genitals, cupping
shaft and balls together and rubbing the whole in a slow,
hard circle against his pelvic bone.

The massage seemed so primitive, so unthinking, she
wondered if he knew he was doing it. Maybe he thought
this kiss was a dream? Regardless, she went hot and cold at
the sight. He released himself with a shiver, his penis prodding even higher than before. Then his tongue moved into
her mouth for the first time, curling around her own and
stroking.

Her insides liquefied. She sensed how dangerous he
might be with all his strength at his disposal, just as dangerous as Abul warned, though in a different way. No harm-
less invalid, this man would have the power to make a
woman beg. She was both relieved and sorry when his lips
drew on her one more time, then fell away.

She pulled back from him, shaken as she'd never been
in her rather eventful life. His eyes were closed, and he was
breathing evenly in sleep. Was there truth in half-sleep,
as they said there was in wine? Did a man become more

himself or less? Trembling, she tucked his hand under the blanket. She kissed his forehead lightly, the same as she'd kiss Charles or Max but not the same at all. She suspected she'd never kiss this man without wanting more.

Most outrageous of all, she didn't yet know his name.

Chapter 3

In the days of Victoria's reign, there were two levels of association with demons: Touched and Taken. If you were Touched, you
served the Yama as a menial, sweeping their floors or clerking
behind the counters of their clean, dark shops. This was suspect
but understood. If you were Taken, however, you fed them from
the swirl of etheric energy above your heart. You gave them the
basic substance of your life in return for coin. You might not ape
your masters as the gangboys tried to do, nor take their side in
disputes, but every human who saw the Yama's mark upon you
knew you were a traitor to your own kind.

—*The True and Irreverent History of Avvar*

Charles woke at dawn. The man was sleeping in
Roxie's parlor. That had never happened before. Never
mind it wasn't a social call, the mere presence of a stranger
disrupted his usually leaden sleep. Usual now, that is; if

he'd been such a heavy sleeper when he was living on the street, he wouldn't have lasted long.

Sighing, he threw off his smooth but carefully mended secondhand sheets. They were dearer to him than the newest silks. Each time he pulled the satin-stitched monogram over his chest, he remembered nights by the fire watching Roxie repair them. She understood his hunger for beautiful things, for care spent on him alone. She made him believe she meant to let him stay.

"I used to keep up my mother's costumes," she'd said, drawing the thread in and out. She told him about living like a gypsy with La Belle Yvonne, voice of the century, mistress to kings. Her stories brought the adventure to life: the excitement, the marvels, the thousand thoughtless hurts. He shared her ironic laughter when she told him how the Great One really died, killed by the wife of an old lover while busy in bed with a new one. She'd been stabbed in the heart with a butcher's knife—not a gold-plated rapier like they'd said in the daily rags.

"At least she died happy," Roxanne had said.

She'd also died penniless, leaving her fourteen-year-old daughter to fend for herself.

Charles cried himself to sleep the night she told him the tale, not because her story was so pitiful—he'd heard worse—but because what he'd come to feel for her terrified him. Roxie could be lost to him at any time. An accident. An unfortunate love affair. Nothing was sure in this world, not since the demons came thirty years before. It was dangerous to get too attached to anything.

Grimacing at his thoughts, he padded in his pajama bottoms down the hall. The wide, pedimented parlor entrance was a remnant of this tired old neighborhood's glory days. The pocket doors were slid back. Peering inside, he saw the stranger slept, snoring softly, one hand dangling to the floor. He laughed through his nose at the sight of his clothes in a sodden pile by the grate. Roxanne was no domestic.

Quiet as a dockside mouse, he crossed the Jeruvian rug's swirl of ivy and roses. Time had faded its mosses and pinks, though the wool still smelled faintly of foreign sheep. He frowned as he gathered up the clothes. The overcoat was pure Harborside, rank with ancient grime, but the rest . . . He fingered the finely woven fabric of the jacket and the smooth, starched cotton of the shirt. Better than average working class, these, though they weren't custom-made.

He squinted suspiciously at the invalid. Unlike Abul, Charles was experienced enough to spot humans who'd fed the Yama, even if they'd only been Taken once. This man didn't have the look, though that didn't mean he should be trusted. The morning light revealed a violent discoloration on the right side of his face, the skin taut and shiny from swelling.

Poor sod, he thought in spite of himself, then took the clothes to the laundry room where he could poke through them without fear of interruption. All too soon, he was glad he had.

His face was grim by the time he climbed back upstairs to begin breakfast. Roxanne would want coffee, toast, and eggs for Maxie, and soup for the stranger. Charles filled a big pot under the hand pump and set it to heat on the stove.

It hadn't taken him long to catch Roxie's love of Yamish conveniences, despite his distaste for their origins. Old though it was, her building had everything: indoor plumbing, gas, an electric generator on the roof. The thing sucked power right out of the air. Ambient energy, they called it. The lights, the icebox, and the clothing mangle were the only things powered by it now, but he wouldn't be surprised if she converted the heat soon, too. Sometimes people stood in the street marveling at their windows, shining so brightly at all hours. It gave him a strange feeling to be on the inside for once.

He shook off his thoughts as Max pattered in, still in his underclothes, awakened by the smell of the strong Bhamjrishi coffee Roxie loved so much. Rubbing his eyes with a fist, he clambered without speaking onto one of the mismatched kitchen chairs. Max was only five, but Charles poured him a cup, cutting it liberally with hot milk. Roxie had never tried to stop him, just raised an eyebrow occasionally. Fact was, Roxie rarely scolded them for anything. She'd said right out of port she wouldn't try to mother them. She'd try to make a place they'd like to be, try to make it easier for them to live right, but any policing they'd have to do themselves.

Charles had promptly abandoned all thought of stealing the silverplate.

"Who's in the parlor?" Max asked, slurping his steaming cup.

"Don't know. Roxie found him lying beat up in the garden last night. She thinks he's running from someone in Harborside."

"He ain't from there."

Charles didn't have to wonder where a five-year-old gained such savvy; he knew only too well where.

Max's brow puckered. "Abul fixed him, didn't he? Bet he was all bloody. How come you didn't wake me up?"

"Roxanne said not to." Charles handed the boy a plate of buttered cinnamon toast and eggs, hoping that answer would do. It seemed to. Max fell silent and began eating with concentrated attention.

Watching Max polish off his food as quick and neat as a cat, Charles remembered how he'd found him in an alley the previous fall, tipping over rubbish containers because he was too short to paw through them any other way.

Charles had no idea where he'd come from. He'd tried to find out before he resigned himself to being stuck with him, but nobody would claim the spike-haired boy. Max was no help because he hadn't talked then at all. Charles had assumed he was mute. Even the demon's procurers, humans who convinced parents to sell their children into service, kept their distance. Considering that what they did was illegal—pandering any human under the age of twelve was punishable by hanging—they shouldn't have scrupled to leave Max alone. They did though, probably because Max had a scary look in his button-brown eyes, like he'd seen things so evil they'd twisted him inside.

Charles wasn't remotely certain he wanted to know what those things were.

Max had fought all Charles's attempts to help him. Food didn't soften him, or clothes, or friendly words. He was a fierce little city rat, his face bereft of the slightest human emotion. Then, one cold night after Charles had dragged him into the shelter of a moldy basement, he'd woken to hear Max crying, harsh, tearless sobs, curled in a ball with his back to him.

Charles didn't have much experience with physical affection, but it seemed impossible not to pull the boy into his arms. He'd held him that way all night, rubbing his bony little back and murmuring unkeepable promises. After that, Max still had the wary eyes of a streetkid, but the crazy glitter was gone.

Two weeks later they'd met Roxanne. She was coming down Front Street when Charles spotted her, her arms laden with secondhand cooking utensils, her breath puffing white with the vigor of her stride. Max and he were huddled in a doorway, storing up their energy before making a noontime run on The Laughing Crow. Charles knew one of the chef's assistants there. Sometimes he'd sneak them things when the head cook was busy, though he got angry if they came every day.

Roxie had seemed a creature from a different world: clean, well fed, rosy with health. Her hair in the winter sun was the most amazing goldy-orange Charles had ever seen, a brilliant, happy color. Her walk was as quick and sure as a man's.

He didn't think a woman like that would give them anything, but he wanted so badly for her to stop and see him, to turn her face if only for a second, that he called after her and asked if she could spare a few pence. At first she kept walking like they all did, but then two agonizing heartbeats later she turned, met his eyes dead on, and retraced her steps.

She set her packages down and hunkered in front of them, heedless of the trash that brushed the hem of her clean green skirt. Charles couldn't look away from her eyes, though the effort of holding the contact made him wince. He couldn't remember when he'd last met the gaze of another soul. Finally, her glance flicked over to Max, who was leaning half-asleep against his shoulder. He saw her taking in his youth, his bluish pallor, the dangerous prominence of his bones.

Max was starving the old-fashioned way, simply because his growing body didn't have enough to eat.

Her lips thinned as she got to her feet, sweeping her hands angrily down her full skirts.

"Can you come with me?" Her voice was gruff, not kind at all. With one gloved hand, she retrieved her bag handles while extending the other toward him. Charles could only gape in astonishment.

"I can make a home for you if you want," she said, reaching stubbornly. "I have a place of my own, free and clear. I've got the room."

He hadn't believed her, hadn't expected more than a meal and possibly some strange proposition. Maybe she was a missionary or a new breed of procurer. It had taken a week of plentiful meals and baths and clean clothes and crackling fires and, above all, her prickly kindness before he realized she'd meant exactly what she said. As for Max, he made up his mind in an hour, ignoring Charles's warnings not to get too comfortable. The very first night he'd climbed into Roxie's lap as they sat before the fire and rubbed his face in her bright hair until she laughed musically and looked for a moment quite painfully beautiful.

And now this man was here. Charles had seen the way she looked at him, touched him: as if he'd drugged her, as if she wanted to climb his maypole and do a jig. Roxie might be odd and reclusive, but she was still a woman.

Scowling, he hacked up a carrot and tossed it into the roiling soup pot. His straight, fair hair tapped his forehead with the force of his movements. The copper panel behind the stove threw his image back at him as if in accusation.

Even flushed with anger, his face looked angelic. Now and then, because he was so pretty, demons would mistake him for one of their own and would try talking their jabber to him. Sometimes, some of them bowed. When his hair had been long, he supposed he resembled their upper-class *daimyo.* Before he'd run off from the crib, where he'd gone because he thought it would be better than having his life force sucked, his looks had made a lot of money for other humans. Now he was beyond vanity.

He wished he were beyond pity as well, but that feat he hadn't quite achieved.

Mustn't grudge the invalid his broth, he thought as he stirred. After all, the sooner the stranger recovered, the sooner he'd be gone.

Chapter 4

Love is a madness sweeter than wine.
Love is a rusty blade that tears instead of cuts.
Give me love as human as a child's first cry.
Give me love, I say, or give me death.

—Ohramese translation,
"Song of the Love–Mad *Rohn*"

Adrian sometimes spoke to the Yamish woman who ran the food stall across from Little Barking Station. She was an older demon, as pretty as a bisque porcelein doll. Gray streaked her short black hair, and fine, thin lines arced from her eyes. From her tiny kitchen on wheels, she sold delicious coffee and tea, far better than the foul station brew. By some miracle, she always served it piping hot.

"Two pence," the woman would say as she handed his steaming cup across the wooden counter.

When he said thank you, she always bowed her head and smiled—a habit few *rohn* took up. To smile was to display the imperfection in their makeup, to admit they were not as emotionally disciplined as *daimyo*. If a *rohn* did attempt to smile, it usually looked more like a grimace. Not this woman, though. She gave him, however shyly, a true smile, one that felt like a gift of trust.

The day he'd walked out of Little Barking Station with the Yamish doctor who was going to install his implants, her eyes had widened like silver coins, following them all the way from the station's door to the waiting diplomatic coach. Her mouth had hung open as if in horror, revealing the dark coloration that made all Yamish tongues appear forked. Aware of human sensibilities, Yama almost never exposed the mark.

"Do you know her?" Adrian had felt compelled to ask the doctor.

"Who?"

"The Yama who runs that stall."

His companion didn't deign to look or break his stride. He smoothed his long sable-brown hair around his nobly shaped skull. His elegant face was as motionless as a mask. "Many people know me," he said. "My medical skills are what you would call famous."

As Adrian opened and held the lacquered coach door, *infamous* was the word that came to mind instead.

They'd driven to the cleanest medical facility—hell, the cleanest place Adrian had ever seen in his life—the converted wing of an otherwise closed-up mansion in Kensington. The walls and most of the furnishings were pale blue, as cold and spotless as Northern ice. The doctor's manner had been the same.

It's just their way, Adrian had told himself, but when the doctor's assistants strapped him to the shining metal table, it had taken all his will not to struggle.

"Twenty minutes," the doctor said, "and you will be as strong as one of us."

One of the assistants made some comment in his native

tongue. Though none of them betrayed the slightest hint of humor, Adrian sensed they were mocking him.

"Twenty minutes," the doctor repeated, and with the tiniest prick of a needle, he put him out.

Now, for reasons Adrian could not fathom, the food stall's owner perched on the edge of the couch where he lay. Her fingertips, cool and slightly wrinkled, rested against his bare breastbone. Her hands were longer than a human's, just different enough to notice. Beneath the nearly weightless touch, his heart beat a fraction faster than it should.

It was strange to know that without his enhancements, this slender old lady was stronger than he was.

"You don't know what he took from us before they exiled us to Avvar," she said, her words thickly accented. "You can't imagine how much our little rebellions cost."

Her presence was so vivid, Adrian didn't realize he'd been dreaming until he shuddered himself awake. His own cold hand lay atop his breast. For a second, he imagined his wrist was still wrapped in bandages. Lord, what had he done to have such a dream?

Fortunately, the world he woke to was more pleasant. The sun was warming his face, and his nose twitched to the heavenly smell of something edible. His stomach rumbled in anticipation, but full consciousness also brought an awareness of the battering he'd taken. Wincing, he opened his eyes.

A slim, fair-haired boy stood above him, fourteen or fifteen by the looks of him. He was astoundingly beautiful, more than most humans could dream of being. He was also quite angry.

"Doc says you need soup," he snapped, and thrust a rough blue bowl at him.

The contents of the handcrafted ceramic steamed in the cool morning air. A draft blew wisps of its rousing fragrance toward Adrian. His mouth watered, but as soon as he tried to rise on his elbows, a hammerblow of pain split his skull. Sweat popped out on his forehead from the effort not to groan. Sinking back, he closed his eyes and tried to breathe again.

"Goodness, Charles," said a sweet familiar voice. "The man's not ready to feed himself."

His pulse quickened at her approach. His strange morning dream was supplanted by a very different memory. He recalled her touch on his face and, yes, kissing her until his head reeled with pleasure. Was it possible he'd cupped her breast? His palm seemed to remember a warm, silken weight. But maybe he'd dreamt that, too? He studied her expression, the faint blush beneath her freckles. She was staring at his mouth. No dream then.

But how different she looked all dried out! Two high windows bordered the fireplace, and the light pouring through them caught fire in her orange locks, loose around her shoulders now, long and thick and flyaway curly. He pictured himself rubbing those electric strands against his cock. Without thinking, his hand lifted toward the blazing cloud, like a child reaching for a toy.

Misreading his desire, she took his hand in hers and sat next to him on a stool. Given the edge on which his rather ridiculous arousal was poised, he was glad she wore a silk wrapper over her nightgown. It wasn't what he'd call a modest covering, but it was better than nothing. He narrowed his good eye at the cigar pocket draping her breast. *Ballocks.* She was wearing a *man's* silk robe.

"How do you feel?" she asked, her forehead pleating at his sudden scowl. "Do you think you can talk?"

"I—Who are you?"

"I'm Roxanne McAllister, and this is Charles Watkins." She tipped her head at the angry blond boy. "Max is in the kitchen finishing breakfast, but I imagine you'll meet him soon. I found you lying in my garden last night. Do you remember what happened?"

"Yes." He spoke softly, the word unconsciously libidinous. "I remember."

She blushed again. It made the freckles on her cheeks blend together.

His mind ran backward. *Max,* she'd said. Was that her husband?

"My name is Adrian Phelps," he said before he could blush himself. She didn't seem as plain as she had last night. In the morning light, with her hair flaming around her, she was almost pretty.

"Well, Adrian." She sounded flustered, but her informality pleased him. He didn't want her calling him Mr. Phelps. Especially since Phelps wasn't really his name. "Let's see if we can get some of Charles's famous carrot-potato soup into you before you keel over again."

Careful not to jar him, she eased him forward and began tucking a mountain of velvet pillows behind him. In complete defiance of his wishes, his cock lurched upward each time her body brushed his. By the time she finished, he was fully erect and light-headed from the flight of his already-denuded blood supply. She smelled good. Spicy. The scent mingled enticingly with the steam from the soup. To his relief, he could manage the spoon himself as long as she held the bowl, though he was grateful for the napkin she'd draped across his chest.

He was very hungry, and the soup was wonderful. The only way he'd have enjoyed it more was if the young chef hadn't been glaring at him as he ate.

He told himself to be glad for the warning. No point letting his guard get too low, no matter how alluring the boy's what—aunt? sister? guardian?—seemed. He knew nothing about these people. Even in the most law-abiding households, policemen weren't welcome guests, so how much more so in the shadow of Harborside? By the time the bowl and spoon were set aside, his instincts of self-preservation were back in place.

"Now." The woman braced her hands on silk-clad knees. "Can you tell us what happened? Who did this to you?"

Adrian allowed a brush of the docks to color his voice. "Nothing to concern yourself with, ma'am. Merely a disagreement between two gentlemen of business."

"And we know what business that is, don't we?" The boy spoke for the first time since he'd thrust the soup in Adrian's face. Out of nowhere, a packet of stiff white papers struck his lap.

Adrian flinched. The packet had been thrown hard, aimed spitefully and, regrettably, he had nothing between his privates and the blow but the knitted blanket.

Roxanne raised her eyebrows at the boy but didn't take him to task.

"What is it?" She scooped the papers off his lap. For an instant, the warmth of her fingers brushed one stinging testicle. His cock stretched another half-inch at the inadvertent intimacy, but he was too anxious about her reaction to the pictures to worry over that.

He knew them by heart. Sketches of his lost boys, five in all, though Tommy Bainbridge was the only one gone missing recently enough to offer hope. He'd paid the police artist out of his own pocket to make them, and he didn't have copies. From Charles's reaction, he realized the sketches must have been taken for a panderers' catalogue.

There were few lower occupations to which a human could sink.

Roxanne refolded the packet and placed it on the cushion by his thigh. Her body was stiff with tension. The intensity of his desire to reassure her shocked him.

"This is what you do? Find boys to offer to the demons?"

"No, ma'am," he said. "I was looking for one of the kids. For a friend. He had a misunderstanding with his wife. She took off with the boy, then dumped him dockside. My friend said he'd pay good to get the tyke out of there. Don't get me wrong. I'm not saying everything I do is strictly up and up, but I don't hold with pandering."

Roxanne's unsettling silver-blue eyes searched his. He met them gladly. He was enjoying, perversely perhaps, her attempts to penetrate his inner world.

"Never," he said softly, firmly. "You can take my word on that."

After a moment, her shoulders relaxed. Her smile

quirked the corners of her mouth. Though she didn't actually say she was glad to believe him, he knew she was. A different kind of warmth spread through his body, far more dangerous than lust.

The boy cursed, disgusted by the exchange. This time Roxanne did scold him, sharply enough to send him from the parlor in a huff.

To Adrian's disappointment, a few minutes later she stood as if she, too, meant to leave.

"What's wrong?" she asked, attuned to his change of expression. "Is there something else you need?"

Another kiss, he wanted to say, but there *was* something more pressing . . .

She slapped her brow in sudden understanding. "Sorry. Didn't think. I'll be back in a flash."

She returned with a freshly washed milk carafe. Cows decorated its side, black and white, green grass, blue sky. It had been handcrafted with the same rough charm as his soup bowl, probably by the same artisan.

She grinned sheepishly. "Sorry I haven't got anything more appropriate."

Then she started to lift the blanket.

"No!" he said sharply, automatically. "I mean, I can do it, ma'am."

She looked him in the eye, not teasing now. "You're not strong enough to turn yourself yet. You want to pull out your stitches? Or ruin my favorite couch? Besides"—she winked—"I saw it all last night. There's no need to 'ma'am' me to death, either. The name's Roxanne."

Adrian groaned, more in embarrassment than pain, as she rolled him gently onto his side.

"Thank you," he said thinly, trying to mask the awkward pause. "You've been very kind."

The woman snorted out a startled laugh. "I'm not helping, am I? Why don't I come back in a few minutes?"

"Tell me you're a nurse," he pleaded when she returned to collect the bottle.

She laughed. "'Fraid not, but I've been something much more horrifying: the only hand with a needle on a

ship full of fractious old salts. The things I've had to sew
up! You'd faint dead away if you knew."

"You were a sailor?"

"Oh, yes. With Captain Rilke and the all-female crew of
the *Ka'arkastan Queen.* Max thinks it's very glamorous.
He can tell you every port we hit."

Max again, Adrian thought. Blast the man. "You didn't
like it?"

"I was young when I signed up. And penniless. The idea
of three squares a day and a couple dozen brawny women
to look out for me was exceedingly appealing."

"They say Rilke's crew doesn't like men."

Roxie grinned. "No, they don't. And don't appreciate
debate on the subject, either. I don't see it myself. Men
might be different, but they aren't worse. Common sense
says you have to take people one at a time."

"Women always seem like people to me."

"Well, I should hope so!" Her eyes danced merrily.

"I mean, when men say women are this or women do
that, I can always think of one who doesn't. I guess . . ." He
slowed as he thought about it. "I guess maybe the same is
true of demons." Since she didn't seem shocked by this
idea, he struggled onto his elbow and cocked his head at
her. "You know, I never have conversations like this."

"Don't you?" She pulled the blanket farther up his
body. Her gaze was on the muscles of his chest, and he had
the distinct impression that she was admiring his build. "I
do, all the time. The product of an irregular childhood, I
suppose."

He could see that. Rules fell away in her presence. She
had created a world apart here, not Harborside, not proper
society. He wondered how far her liberality might go.
Could he ask her anything, tell her anything, and have the
confidence kept safe? Years of habit—professional and
personal—kept him from testing her, but the prospect
thrilled him deep inside. Anything might happen with this
woman. No dream, even his dream of sensual freedom,
seemed too outrageous to contemplate. In a matter of
hours, she'd granted him more liberties than his wife had

in three months of marriage. If he tread carefully, he might earn more.

Assuming this Max person wasn't her protector. Assuming she didn't treat every man who crossed her path this way. Her behavior was so far from what he knew, he found it impossible to judge.

His ears perked when he heard her speak to someone in the hall. The kitchen, apparently, was just across the way.

"Hey, pipsqueak. Don't you think it's time you put some clothes on?"

"No-o," said a voice both gravelly and babyish, the mysterious Max, he presumed. His shoulders relaxed. That voice couldn't belong to the owner of a smoking robe.

"No?" said Roxie. "Better watch out then. 'Cause you're that much easier to tickle in your underwear."

Two flashes hurtled past the open pocket doors, one howling with delighted terror while the other growled, "Better watch out. The Tickle Monster's coming."

His eyes pricked. *Children.* He remembered how badly he'd wanted them when he married Christine. He'd seen too many children in pain since then. It was hard to believe in happy homes.

Much more comfortable and fatigued by the morning's events, he drifted back to sleep. He woke to the sound of voices in the big windowed room between the parlor and garden, an old ballroom, he imagined. One of the voices was Roxanne's, already familiar and disturbingly stirring to his senses. The other belonged to a soft-spoken young woman. He heard Harborside in it and something foreign. Maybe Nital.

Curious, he turned his head on the stack of pillows. A large open archway connected the two rooms. His present line of sight revealed a slice of polished floor and, in the distance, the partitioned patio door through which Roxanne had dragged him last night. Stymied, he closed his eyes and concentrated on eavesdropping. What he heard did not reassure him.

Roxanne was speaking. "Up on the platform, ducks. I want you lounging on that divan."

"Is this enough leg, Miss McAllister? I can pull the robe up more."

"No, that's fine, sweetie, but let's have a bit more bosom. Good, good. You'll knock the old geezer's eyes out. Now here's the scenario: You're Lilith, secret lover of the great king, Alphonsus Aurelius. He's been off fighting those pesky Medell marauders for two long years and, as you might imagine, he's feeling frisky now that he's back."

The other voice giggled. "Oh, Miss McAllister, I love it when you get historical."

"Culture, Miss Randle. Culture is what gets us out of the tavern and into the gentlemen's club."

"And doubles our fee?"

Roxanne laughed and, in spite of Adrian's horror, the beauty of the sound sent a delightful chill down his spine.

"With a thin veneer of historical significance, I can charge twenty times what I used to. And speaking of which, I think you're due for a raise, Miss Randle, seeing as how my clients are beginning to ask for you by name."

"Oh, Miss McAllister," gushed her willing victim. "That would be lovely. I could put the boys in private school."

A mother. His rescuer was coaching an innocent young mother in the tricks of the trade. Roxanne must be a madam. Only to humans, it sounded like, but still—! He might have to arrest her! Unless he'd misunderstood . . . but he didn't see how. All that talk of clients and fees. And bosoms. What else was an officer of the law to think?

Hard as he strained his ears, all he heard after that was the occasional stage direction and, now and again, the sound of something pinging against a metal container.

Mystified, but too disturbed to examine the situation further, Adrian shut his eyes and slept.

Night had fallen by the time he roused again. The pretty fringed lamps had been lit. Electric lamps, he realized with a start. And where did the money for *that* come from? One of the shades had fat pink roses on it, the other green and gold dragons. The blue peat fire had been lit again, and the warmth and color mingled together like a seductive dream of home and hearth.

Roxanne was leaning over him with her lips curved sweetly in greeting. Caught unguarded from its rest, his cock jumped to attention like a hunting dog. His body didn't care if she was a criminal. It just wanted what it wanted. A little petting, a lot of pumping. Her silky skin. Her honeyed welcome. Lord, it had been too long. He felt as if he were about to burst. Her hair smelled of ginger and lemons. Plaited now, it curled over the swell of her breast in a thick orange rope. All he could do was stare at it, at her, his doubts meaningless in the face of the sheer physical pleasure her presence inspired.

The sleeves of her loose white shirt had been rolled to her elbows. Though he tried, he couldn't resist the temptation to brush his thumbs across the bare flesh of her forearms. Her pale eyes warmed, but she didn't move away from the caress. Did that mean she wanted him to touch her? Had her kiss the night before been more than kindness? If what he suspected about her was true, he was insane to care. Insane or not, he couldn't deny he did.

His breathing deepened as the moment spun out. He was so hard the ache blotted out his other pains. His balls pulsed with eagerness. Bad enough he'd been this long without a woman, but she was more woman than most. He wished— oh, how he wished—he could justify making her his. She wasn't some well-bred miss to cringe at his advances, nor some sad-eyed widow to smother him in gratitude.

Roxanne was, oh, he didn't know what she was. A siren. A goddess. A—

"Oh!" A green smudge on her chin sparked his memory. Finally, he identified the smell that lingered around her studio. "You're a painter."

"That's right." Her pale eyes twinkled. "What did you think we were doing in there?"

Heat flooded his face. "I . . . I wasn't sure."

"Liar. You thought I was some sort of madam."

"But I didn't *want* to think it."

She laughed at his protest, a happy, sexy sound. How different she was from the women of his class, how uninhibited. Which raised another question. Now that he knew he wouldn't have to arrest her, did he have what it took to seduce her? The impatient pounding of his cock told him it wouldn't wait long for answers.

❧

Paintings bought and sold, said the gold-leaf lettering on the door of McAllister's Fine Art Supply. Esconced behind the counter, Roxanne pushed her admirably-in-the-black ledger aside. A demon couldn't have balanced it more neatly, even if they were quicker than humans at ciphering. Pleased with more than her business success, she was too euphoric to heed the suspicions Charles had come here to share.

"Don't tell me you still think he's a criminal," she said. "Not everyone who lives in dockside is, you know. I think he's just a decent working-class fellow who's trying to help a friend find his son."

"If he's so decent, why hasn't he mentioned a job he needs to get back to?"

"Does every decent person have a job? Anyway, maybe finding lost things is how he makes his living. Plenty of people would be willing to pay not to have to go prowling around Harborside, even people who live there."

Charles pushed his hair back in disgust. "He hasn't offered to pay you for taking him in, has he?"

"I wouldn't let him if he did. Be fair, Charles. Accept the fact that he's just a regular person who happens to be more uptight about certain things than you."

"And you're making it your mission to loosen him up, aren't you?"

Roxie knew he was upset, but she couldn't contain her laugh of agreement. The prospect of seducing her guest seemed so wonderfully achievable. Every time she came near him, his blanket tented up. She'd had men react to her before, but not like this. His shyness made flirting with him terribly entertaining. She was going to enjoy every minute of this, every second.

Charles propped his hands on his hips. "I never thought I'd see the day when you, of all people, would go in for a meaningless, sordid—"

Clearly, he couldn't think of a word he could utter in her presence. "Who says it will be meaningless?" she teased. "Or sordid? And even so, perhaps I'm tired of self-restraint."

"What self-restraint?" His handsome face purpled in outrage. "You're not the sort of woman who has those sort of—"

"Charles." She cut him off before he could choke on his splutters. "Don't mistake me for a saint. Most women want a man now and then, whether they care to admit it or not. Maybe I simply never wanted one enough. In any case"— she reached across the counter to pat his shoulder—"I'm an adult. Even if I were your mother, sweetie, I'd be entitled to a private life."

"Fine," he surrendered. "Just don't come crying to me when he leaves you out in the cold."

Chapter 5

"Those people can't sing," Seamus Connell, proprietor of the Running Bull, was heard to say. "Can't sing. Can't dance. Can't so much as beat time on the bar. Personally, I think it ought to be against the law for them to try."

—*Illustrated Times* account of the "Hawk's Day brawl," in which three humans and two Yama died as a result of their injuries

On the second day of Adrian's convalescence, Charles caught him leafing through the packet of lost boys. He'd recovered sufficiently to be propped in the wing chair by the fire, but not enough to resume his search for Tommy Bainbridge. Adrian hated letting the matter drop, even for a few days. For a young boy, a few days in Harborside could last a lifetime. He considered taking his sometime partner, Farsi Ross, into his confidence. The sergeant was game and good-hearted, and one of the few officers who hadn't drawn back from Adrian after he'd been "enhanced." Unfortunately, Farsi had moved here from the islands a few short years ago. The twists and turns of Harborside would be a bigger mystery to him than they were to Adrian, who'd lived in or near the city all his life.

"Give me those," Charles ordered, snatching the sketches from his hand.

Slow out of the gate, but not that slow, Adrian shot out his hand to manacle the boy's wrist. It wasn't his implants that allowed him to do this, but a rigorous physical training schedule he followed on his own. Pride was part of the reason he kept it up. He refused to depend on Yamish technology alone. Thanks to his discipline, Charles tried to escape his grip but could not, obviously surprised an invalid could muster so much strength. Adrian might be breathing hard, but it would be a sad day when he let a fifteen-year-old get the better of him.

"I told you what those were, and I wasn't lying," he said. "And they're my only copy. I'm not giving them up."

Careful not to hurt the boy, he gave one more sharp twist. The papers dropped. Charles rubbed his smarting wrists.

"I was going to give them back," he said, his face sullen. To his credit, he didn't whine or call Roxie for reinforcement. "I wanted to take them around Harborside myself. I know where the streetboys hang out. Maybe I can learn something you couldn't."

"I don't think Roxanne would want you out there."

"Roxanne is not my mother."

This simple statement carried an assortment of warnings. Adrian studied the defiant young face, measuring—as he often had to do—not just honesty but spine. Charles had more of the second than the first, but Adrian judged he was telling the truth about wanting to help.

Why, he's got a crush on her, he thought. The discovery gave him more tolerance for the boy's bad temper, though he felt obliged to object to his plan all the same.

"There are demons in Harborside who don't pay the

slightest heed to the law. A boy like you, as pretty as a *daimyo,* they'd snatch you up like candy lying in the street— and worry about 'consensuality' later."

"I know how to steer clear of them," Charles said, his lip curling in contempt.

"You *think* you know."

"I *know,* old man. Things you wouldn't want to see in your worst nightmare."

Adrian considered the boy's anger-flushed features, aware of how close hostility could rub with tears. Roxanne might not have sold herself to live, but it came to him that this boy had. Maybe to the Yama or maybe not. Demons, after all, had not cornered the market on exploitation.

Who failed you? Adrian wondered. *Parents? The Children's Ministry? Or did anyone ever look out for you?*

Knowing better than to let his compassion show, he bent down with a muffled groan, collected the fallen papers, and handed them to Charles.

"Very well," he said. "I'd appreciate the help."

The boy's eyes flashed with a surprise he quickly hid. Nodding sharply, he tucked the packet under his arm and left.

〜

Max and Adrian stood side by side on the roof. It was almost dawn. Roxie's house was taller than most, and they could see clear across Harborside to the docks, though from this distance they couldn't make out more than the pennants on the topmost masts.

To Adrian's delight, Max's welcome for the stranger in his household was warm, especially when he discovered Adrian's talent for making floatable ships out of waxed grocer's paper. Each evening while the others read or rested, he would spread his flotilla across the parlor and growl them back and forth around the claw-footed chairs. Constructing them for the boy gave Adrian a precarious sense of belonging, one he'd rarely felt in his own family.

Max was the only boy he knew who didn't make wars with everything. Adrian had eight nephews. At Max's age, they'd all been able to see an army in a bowl of grape pits. They would have sunk half his ships by now.

Of course, the glory of battle was a common Ohramese obsession. Here in Avvar, they considered themselves the center of a grand empire. The center, in fact, of all the world worth knowing. Any insecurity they might have harbored at knowing Yamish weapons had saved their bacon from the fire, they compensated for with belligerence. In their hearts, naturally, they knew that if Victoria hadn't made her devil's bargain, the Medell might have been only the first of their subject nations to win back home rule.

Caught up in these thoughts, Adrian dropped his hand to Max's dark, spiky hair and absently smoothed its tangles. He scanned the horizon. They were waiting for the sun to rise so Max could sail his new schooner in the birdbath. The day before, Adrian had made the mistake of telling him a ship always began its maiden voyage at sunrise.

Yawning so mightily his single crutch trembled, he shifted within his "new" secondhand clothes. Charles had bought and laundered and, Adrian suspected, even pressed the outfit. The young man might feel threatened by their guest, but he was too fastidious to leave a job half done.

Roxanne certainly hadn't ironed them. Her own clothes, a shocking collection of loose silk shirts and snug men's trousers, were always a little less than crisp.

The day Charles produced the outfit, she'd teased Adrian about the shame of covering up his body. She'd said she was tempted to keep him her naked slave. He'd grown so aroused at her playful words, he'd thought he'd leap off his chair and tumble her to the floor.

He'd wanted to touch her, but he'd held back.

Deciding he wished to seduce her proved easier than getting himself off the mark. He didn't want to offend her by moving too fast. Just because her sort talked bawdy didn't mean she'd tolerate being treated with disrespect. Whatever "her sort" was. He'd been here four days, and he still hadn't deciphered that.

"What in the world—" he said, noticing what he had under his hand. "Boy, you've got a cowlick that won't quit."

Max went as still as a little statue. Had Adrian frightened him? But he relaxed a second later and leaned into Adrian's leg, hugging it just above the knee. Even with the crutch, Adrian was almost too weak to keep his footing. Funny how he could be so long recovering from damage that had taken, at most, ten minutes to inflict.

"Roxie says my hair just grows that way," the boy volunteered indistinctly.

Adrian realized he had his thumb in his mouth.

"Is that so? Then I suppose I'd better not interfere with it."

"You can." The boy removed his thumb. "I don't mind."

Adrian smiled in the gathering light and patted his cheek.

The launching successfully achieved, the *Ka'arkastan Queen* was sailing between rock and reed when Max looked up and said in his endearing, gravelly voice, "Are you staying?"

Knowing instantly what he meant, Adrian's heart squeezed tight.

"No, Max." He tweaked the boy's pug nose. "I have a house of my own. I'll be going back there as soon as I'm well."

"Oh." Max's gaze returned to the birdbath, to the troop of white clamshells that formed up around its edge. He reached for the *Queen* and pushed her in a new direction. The water wrinkled like silk under the young sun. "Is your house very far?"

Adrian steeled himself. It would be cruel to lead the boy on.

"Far enough," he said, his voice very low, very gentle. And then he couldn't help relenting. "But it's not the other side of the world."

The boy looked up briefly, his hard young face unreadable. Did Max realize what Adrian had implied? For that matter, did he? Where the hell was the boy's father anyway? He'd like to tell that blackguard a thing or two, abandoning Roxie and Max like that. If Max was Roxie's. Up until then, he hadn't found the nerve to ask.

The failure was ironic. He was a policeman. He poked his nose into other people's business for a living. Just because a woman made him jump in his drawers didn't mean he had to turn into a tongue-tied idiot.

I'm done with that, he told himself. *From now on, I'll find out everything I need to know.*

~~~~~~

His chance came later that day.

Roxanne was running errands, the boys were out, and Adrian decided to do some detecting. Within the hour, he'd searched most of the rooms on the floor, finding little of interest. The tiny storeroom behind the kitchen, however, was unturned soil.

Longer than it was broad, the storeroom overlooked the roof garden. There was no access to the outside, just two round windows of rippled green glass. Art supplies crammed the wall of metal shelving opposite. His eyes widened at the monstrous cans of dry pigment. Exotic names were stenciled on their sides: Thalocyline Blue, Southern Yellow. Beside the paint lay heaps of brushes still wrapped in tissue, tins of turpentine, and giant rolls of canvas.

Fascinating as all that was, it didn't seem likely he'd find anything concerning Max here. He didn't leave, though. He felt her here, among the tools of her art. He touched the brushes and the tins. His skin shivered with wonder. From such homely artifacts, her paintings came.

He found the portrait almost by accident. It was wedged in a corner, covered against the dust with a paint-stained sheet. Curious, he lifted the cloth, surprised to find the picture side facing the wall. As he turned it, he noticed what a nice frame it had: stained oak, carved elaborately and picked out in gilt.

He stared at the finished canvas. It showed a beautiful woman at her toilette, looking back over her shoulder at the viewer. Her upper lip was rouged, her lower bare, and her graceful hand held a red-tipped brush, poised forever in a moment of nearly completed cosmetic perfection.

The picture was different from the paintings in Roxie's studio. Those were vivid and quick, bursting with juicy life. This displayed no less technical skill but was darker and more detailed. Adrian could count each facet of each gem in the sparkling rings, each lash that fringed the glowing eyes. Instinctively, he knew it was an earlier work.

He recognized the subject, of course: La Belle Yvonne. He doubted anyone who'd ever seen her would forget.

He heard her sing when he was just thirteen. A big, sobby historical. If he closed his eyes he could see her voluptuous figure in the huge bell-skirted, cloth-of-gold gown. The décolleté had seemed to plunge to her navel, though it was probably banded behind with flesh-colored silk.

When she opened her mouth and that voice like liquid gold poured out, she seemed to embody the power of a female unrestrained by society. One of the Yamish diplomats, attending out of politeness, had fainted in his box. None of the Yama, *daimyo* or *rohn,* were used to the arts. The idea of wanting to express emotion was alien. Adrian's reaction to the performance wasn't quite that intense, but being the age he was, just discovering his sexuality, her figure had loomed large on his symbolic horizon—mysterious but significant.

At the least, he could understand why the demon swooned. There *was* something frightening about La Belle Yvonne. Her charisma overwhelmed, like a creature from a world whose sun was too bright, whose night was too dark.

And she made him sad.

That mystified him most of all. When the opera was over and she stood on stage alone, beaming, taking her bows and collecting the heaps of crimson roses that were her trademark, she seemed somehow more tragic than the ill-starred heroine she'd just portrayed: surrounded by all that adulation and still bereft.

His father had sensed something was troubling him. He'd knuckled Adrian's head and pulled him more tightly into his shoulder. But Adrian knew his father had spent a week's salary on those tickets, a special birthday treat for his eldest boy.

His father didn't even like opera. He'd had to ask the Jeruvian grocer down the street who was good, who was the best for his boy who had music in him.

His father wasn't one for bragging, but, as he consulted that shopkeeper, Adrian could see the secret fairly bursting to come out. Isaac Philips had discovered it only by chance. He'd walked into the church basement one evening to find Adrian practicing on the old choir-practice spinet, making music that could be recognized as music and, even then, a little more. His boy, the son of a callused shipmaker, could make magic. Surprised as he was, Adrian's father never stopped to ask why Adrian had slunk in the dark to do this thing. And he never did tell the secret, not even to Adrian's mother, not until his son was ready to tell her himself.

Isaac was proud of Adrian. Proud of a son too ashamed to admit he wanted to be more refined than his father.

Adrian knew only a beast would spoil this gift, so he smiled up from his tenth row center seat and said, "Wasn't it wonderful, Father? Wasn't she amazing?"

He hadn't gone to see the diva a second time, not even when he could afford the price of a seat himself. He was in his twenties when Yvonne died, but for a moment, when he heard a newsboy call the headline, he was thirteen. The busy capitol street had disappeared, and in the place of smoke and horses he smelled the perfumed heat of the crowd, heard the shuffling silken murmur, and once again thrilled to the belling note.

He almost jumped out of his skin when Roxie touched his shoulder.

"My mother," she said quietly.

He shivered under the warmth of her hand. "Your mother was La Belle Yvonne?"

She nodded. She was looking at the picture, her expression intent and, to him, cryptic.

"I didn't know her last name was McAllister."

"It wasn't. I made that up. As far as I know she didn't have a last name. She was a bastard, you see, just like me."

She smiled at her mother's image, a smile of mingled
bitterness and acceptance. In that moment, he realized she
was beautiful. Very beautiful. And no one knew it. Especially not Roxanne. But she ought to know. She needed to
know.

"Your mother was beautiful," he began. His heart was
pounding, as though he stood on the brink of some crucial
turning point.

She nodded, still not looking at him, then laughed. "Unlike her daughter."

He could tell she'd used those words before.

"No," he said, "you're—"

"Oh, stop." Her hand cut the air. "I hate that. Anyway,
being beautiful didn't make her happy. She'd spend hours
peering into the mirror, terrified of getting old. And then
she'd take a new lover, someone younger and prettier
than the last one. Toward the end, she didn't even care
if they were rich. She . . ." Roxanne swallowed. "People
used to whisper that she was feeding demons on the sly.
That this was how she kept her looks. It might have been
true. Sometimes she'd sleep all day through, just like
demon servants do."

He stared at her. He felt as if he were gazing through a
lighted window at something he wasn't entitled to see, but
from which he couldn't turn, pretending he hadn't meant to
look while knowing in his heart he had. As abruptly as a
curtain being swept aside, Roxanne had become real to
him. She had thoughts, feelings, an entire history that pre-
dated him. She was still a stranger, but she was real.

The pleasure this inspired was perturbing.

"So you, um, traveled with her?" He shifted his crutch to
a more comfortable position. "All over the world?"

She nodded distractedly. "Until she died."

And then she did look at him. Her uncanny eyes seemed
to glow, but to him they were as lovely as the rest of her. In
the light from the rippled green windows, her lashes
gleamed like spikes of gold. They were surprisingly thick.
Adrian imagined them fluttering against his cheek as she
climaxed and couldn't contain a blush.

Lord, he was a bloody schoolboy around her.

"I'm sorry I snapped at you," she said with an apologetic smile. Her lips were full and sensual, the upper peaks sharp, the lower curve slightly bowed—her mother's mouth, he now saw. "I know you were trying to be kind."

"Roxanne," he blurted before he could think better of it. "Is Max yours?"

Her head jerked back, and she stiffened. "Max and Charles are my cousins. Their parents died, and now I'm taking care of them."

He knew she was lying. Fear was shaking through her limbs. He touched the side of her face, smoothing a curl of orange-gold off her temple. "It doesn't matter. I don't care who they are."

"They're my cousins," she insisted.

He pulled her into his arms and tucked her head beside the crook of his neck. Though he didn't hold her tightly, the contact was instantly erotic. To his gratification, he found he was a few inches taller than she was. Immensely happy, he stroked her back and rubbed his jaw across her hair, not thinking about his job or her secrets, just holding her, just soaking up her essence. Her tremors began to ease.

"You don't have to be afraid of me," he said, and she squeezed his waist. His pulse jumped another notch.

She leaned back far enough to see his face, her hips resting lightly against his. She must have felt the strong, rhythmic leap of his arousal, but he couldn't make himself move away.

"Does this mean you'll stop poking through my things?" she said. "Give up searching for signs of some absent protector?"

For a moment he was too befuddled by desire to follow her meaning. When he did, he locked his arms behind her back and hitched her closer. She didn't protest. In fact, her eyes gleamed with excitement.

His chest rose and fell more deeply.

"So there aren't any cigar stubs?" He dared to punctuate the question with a slow forward roll of his hips.

Her breath caught. Then she shook her head.

"No razor strops?" His hands raked down the firm swell of her bottom, tilting her to him. He paused, giving her time to refuse him, steeling himself to stop if she asked.

"No," she whispered, and instantly sent his pulse slamming through his veins.

Her lips parted, her tongue glistening pink between them. He thought if he didn't kiss her he might expire. She licked her delectable upper lip, and he heard himself begin to pant.

He moaned her name, his mouth already there.

Slowly, slowly, their lips closed on each other, their tongues soft, then hard, then soft again. Her muscles melted against him, conforming to his shape. She pushed away the crutch, and then he was leaning back against the cold metal shelf, a roll of canvas digging unheeded into his shoulder.

He widened his stance, and she rubbed her mound against his erection like a love-starved cat, prolonging the motion until he thought he'd go insane. God, it was good. Root to tip, she went, as if measuring him for insertion. The roll of her hips pressed the head of his cock against his abdomen, scraping the delicate skin against his hair. Famished for a more enveloping touch, he sighed as she shifted closer. Beneath her fitted cotton trousers, the softness of her sexual lips compressed his straining arch. The blood pounded there like a third, shared heart.

He turned his head to deepen the kiss, thrusting his hands into the crisp, cool waves of her hair. He filled her mouth with his tongue and met nothing but acceptance. She kissed with the boldness of a man and the subtlety of a woman. Surrender and engagement. Brass and flirtation. A groan of pure male lust rumbled in his chest. He drew her tongue into his mouth and suckled it.

This is your bud of pleasure, he thought, his lips imprisoning the soft flesh as his tongue circled and flicked. As if the thought had indeed been willed to her mind, she shuddered and pressed closer.

Her hands ironed the back of his shirt, up and down, left and right. He wanted them on his skin. Cursing, he yanked the shirt out of his trousers and urged her arms under the cloth. Yes, that was better. Her hold was strong and warm, her hands wonderfully curious.

But it was becoming difficult to breathe.

He broke free to gasp for air, then kissed her again, harder than before. Surely breathing wasn't that important. In his delight, a moment passed before he realized she was kissing him back just as greedily. The revelation was heartstopping. She wanted him. She was as hungry for this as he was.

Her hands touched his spine beneath his waistband, an intimate touch, the touch of a soon-to-be lover. He froze at the implication, and so did she.

"Yes," he whispered against her lips. "Please put your hands on me."

This was the encouragement she needed. Her palms drifted lower, under his linen. Her fingers cupped his buttocks, her thumbs parting the cleft. The sensation was unexpectedly arousing. It raised an itch her fingers moved to soothe, following the curve of his cheeks. His head dropped back and hit the shelf with a clang. The tips of her fingers sent sparks skittering across his nerves, a strange heat that coursed through the darkest reaches of his body. He could hardly believe she was doing this. It struck him that she wasn't afraid of anything. She would touch him anywhere he asked. But he wouldn't be able to stand it. As it was, he trembled on the edge of climax, his balls knotting in preparation. He should stop her before he embarrassed himself, but he wanted—he sucked a quick, hard breath—he wanted to know what she'd do next.

His teeth ground together as her hands advanced. Her fingers curled between his inner thighs. She hesitated.

"Yes," he urged again, opening his legs still wider so she could brush his scrotum from behind, her height just allowing it. The loose skin moved beneath her gentle tugging, making its fullness sway.

"Adrian," she whispered, a rasp of sound. "You're so heavy. Can you feel what's happening between us? Can you feel what you do to me?"

She squirmed closer, her leg climbing his, her foot braced against the apple of his calf. The seam that covered the tender peach of her sex clung to his erection as if it had been steamed. She was wet. Wet enough to penetrate all the layers of cloth between them.

The realization was more than he could take. Consideration be damned. He had to have her. He couldn't wait another second. He fumbled desperately for the catch of her trousers, shuddering as she shifted around to cup his testicles. Her fingers tightened.

Her name tore from his throat. His head jerked forward.

She lifted her mouth for another kiss, kneading him with such perfect, welcome pressure he feared he'd cry.

And then they heard Max in the hall, calling out their names. Adrian cursed as he drew back. He knew he wasn't going to have her now after all.

Chapter 6

The Yama exchange energy amongst themselves all the time, though they needn't touch to do it, and it doesn't have the same effect on them as when they feed off humans. Fire-talking, as it is known, is integral to their culture—a silent, second language. Messages conveyed run from "I'm tired" to "Good morning" to "You: lower than a worm! Get out of my way." Naturally, only *daimyo*, with their control over the essentially emotional nature of this energy, could send communications so nuanced.

When Captain DuBarry, the human who first discovered demons, appeared on their icy doorstep, he was treated—ostensibly at least—as a guest. Following the dinner thrown in his honor at the residence of Narikerr's head *daimyo*, a lovely Yamish woman was sent to his room. Imagine her surprise when her foreign lover provided quite the extra charge. She had no choice but to abandon her initial orders to kill the man when she was done. Her employer, the prince of the city, had a right to consider this extraordinary, and unexpected, development.

In less official accounts, Yamish witnesses report that

DuBarry was moderately handsome, hung like a horse, and possessed the charm of an energetic puppy. It is possible these traits also influenced the assassin's decision to spare his life.

—*The True and Irreverent History of Avvar*

⌐⊸⌐

Like all Yamish diplomats, Herrington was a spy. His posting in Avvar was a mark of the regard with which the Emperor's inner circle held him, but also a sign that his family, established though it was, did not inhabit the ruling ranks. No one would ask those rarified flowers to interact with lower beings, much less to immerse themselves in the stream of alien life. Apart from a few Yamish necessities one couldn't be expected to live without, Herrington's house was a human house. His clothes, his servants, even his name had been altered to mimic human customs. After thirty-some years in this city, he was— gods help him—beginning to think human thoughts.

His handlers approved of him "going native." Not the thought part, per se; that slow evolution he kept to himself. The rest of his observations, however, provided them with a window both on human life and on how their criminal classes were adjusting to their grand experiment.

That he himself was under equally close scrutiny, Herrington was well aware. He ignored the attention as best he could. To dwell on such things was to write one's feelings about them in one's energy, where other *daimyo* could read them and pass judgment. Herrington saved indulging in annoyance for when he was alone.

The strain wore on him occasionally, especially in the years since he'd lost his sister's company. On the other hand, there really was no point in lamenting one's place in life. Without a place, and a purpose, he'd be no better than a *rohn*.

At the moment, Herrington was not alone, though his companion was just his human footman. They were engaged in one of his continuing quests, the comprehension of human creative arts, an activity that had no equivalent for Yamish-kind.

Fortunately, his butler, Albert, had no trouble locating the woman's gallery. Human or not, Albert was a prize. Herrington wished it had been proper to ask *him* to drive to McAllister's. This silly footman was no use whatsoever with the electric car. Humans had recently developed these contraptions by adapting Yamish generators to the purposes of propulsion—an accomplishment of which Herrington was secretly proud. The vehicles might be inelegant, but they worked. Sadly, they didn't work equally well for everyone. Herrington could have driven better than this man, though it wouldn't do to be seen motoring himself around.

By "native" standards, that would have resulted in a serious loss of face.

Peering out the rattling window and trying to put his head into a human place, he decided this was the sort of street an artist-type would favor. It wasn't a bad area. The different-colored houses were cheerful. Some human peacock had planted a big bronze Dian atop his roof, naked as a jay. Strictly to himself, Herrington decided she looked jaunty.

Suggestive art was all the rage among the human upper class, most especially the males. They called it culture. Herrington called it inspiration for fellows who liked to stick their hands in their pockets and give the family jewels a tug. Herrington didn't know if it was due to being Yamish, but he preferred the real thing. Still, it didn't hurt to investigate the latest fashions. This McAllister seemed the best of the bawdy lot. She knew one end of a brush from the other, at least. Herrington prided himself in being able to tell a good artist from a bad. It was, despite his outsider status, more than some of his human associates could say.

He was jarred from his thoughts by a sudden, lurching halt.

He swallowed back a shockingly unthinking curse. The footman had shorted out the points again. The man was a genius with a matched pair and harness. Why couldn't he keep a simple engine operational?

He tapped the glass partition with his walking stick. The

driver slid it open. Herrington wouldn't have had to say anything to a Yamish servant, but he'd learned that humans needed things spelled out.

"I'm getting out of here, Keane," he said. "Have the car running by the time I get back."

"Yes, sir!" The footman's face was red with embarrassment and little expectation of success.

Sighing, another human habit he'd picked up, Herrington handed Keane a few of the coins his valet always tucked into his waistcoat. "Call the tow service if you have to. And Keane—" The man looked up warily. "Next week you'll be attending those demonstrations of electrical mechanics at the town hall."

"Yes, sir. Sorry, sir." Unable to hide his feelings decently, the man looked thoroughly miserable.

Herrington rapped his footman's shoulder with his stick in what he hoped was a bracing manner. "Don't mope, man! Only women mope."

"Yes, my lord," Keane said, a little more sturdily as he realized he wasn't being sacked.

"Good man," Herrington muttered and heaved himself out of the car. Of all the things that wearied him, babying human sensibilities had to be at the top of the list.

Stepping onto the brick sidewalk, he glanced up to mark the street numbers, then strode decisively toward the correct one: 424. *Fancy that.* 424 was the number of the honeymoon suite where he'd taken his first human female. Her giggles when she discovered that all their parts were compatible had nearly rendered him impotent. He'd recovered, thankfully, the length of time it had been since he'd enjoyed any release at all helping him out, along with the necessity to his mission of overcoming that particular hurdle. His handlers required reports on every aspect of human life.

In the end, he'd enjoyed himself more than he expected. Humans gave off a lovely, glowing burst of energy when they came. You didn't even have to try to feed from them. He'd gone all night, as he recalled, making the woman climax until she screamed. What was her name? Daisy?

Dorie? He remembered she'd had large breasts—like a ruddy pair of melons, as the humans said. Perhaps he ought to tell McAllister to find a nice buxom model for his picture. Then he could see if studying it had a similar erotic effect.

Arriving at his goal, Herrington pulled McAllister's street door open and stepped inside to a melodious jingle. Ka'arkish wind chimes. He looked up to see the prisms flashing in the noontime sun. There was no one behind the counter.

"With you in a minute," said a breathless voice.

He looked for its source and saw a slender young human righting a stack of fallen cans at the end of one aisle. He was wearing the silliest fuchsia waistcoat Herrington had ever seen. A *poofter,* he thought, dredging up the term. Definitely not who he was looking for.

Dismissing the practitioner of alternate sexuality, he proceeded to the entrance of the consignment gallery. There, under the velvet-swagged archway, he froze.

A woman, whom he knew by her air of authority to be McAllister, was elaborating the selling points of a large and rather threatening still life to two very small old ladies. Every few sentences, the pearl-draped biddies would put their feathered hats together and whisper furiously to each other. It was not the sight of this oddity, however, that had rooted Herrington to the floor.

It was the woman herself.

His heart convulsed in a way it shouldn't have been able to, its motion so violent he couldn't help but recall an incident from his boyhood when a rival cousin had tried to poison him and actually stopped his breathing for a few minutes.

Alas, the only poison here was emotional.

Louise, he thought.

The woman was the spitting image of his dead sister. Louise had died in an accident two years before, but this woman, this *human,* had the same glorious curly hair, the same strong bones, and the same regal bosom. Oh, what a fine-looking Yamish Louise had been—a subtle and rare beauty. His grief rose in his throat as if her death had befallen her yesterday. Damn her human lover, that bastard Quinceton, for daring her to race his curricle. Not that Louise had needed much convincing. She'd thrown herself into their assignment with a passion that inspired awe. She'd understood humans far better than he, yet never once, despite her involvement, had she lost her true Yamish core.

Numb with remembrance, Herrington moved toward his sister's double as if someone had tied a string to his sternum.

She was wearing trousers. Louise had done that, too, declaring herself to be studying the phenomenon of the human female rebel. Herrington took another somnolent step. Did this woman have Louise's deep, strong voice, as well?

But she didn't.

She had a voice like honeyed burgundy, sweet and penetrating and just the slightest bit smoky.

La Belle Yvonne's voice.

The room dissolved without warning. Of all his human lovers, Yvonne had threatened his control the most. Now he smelled again the musty velvets of the Avvar Opera House, Yvonne's thick facepaint and musk, the discarded orange peels on the floor of the pit so far below his private box. He felt her incomparable derriere slapping his maddeningly swollen loins, her flesh hot as fire, her energy roiling over him as he pressed her even farther over the back of the gilded couch. His lust for her drove him beyond good sense. He'd been rough with her in ways no Yamish female would allow, forcing her beringed little hands to grasp the plump seat cushions.

The purple drapes at the front of the box were closed for interval, but the thought of all the people out there, chattering unawares, waiting for the return of this woman whose clinging quim he was delving had set his arousal to a knife-edge pitch.

That and the fact that she'd made love to someone else no more than an hour before. The vital energy of the stranger's seed still tingled in her sex. She must have hoped Herrington would feel it. She was always trying to stir him to emotion—anger, jealousy, whatever would prove her power. She couldn't have known the lingering fire of the other man would act as a purely physical aphrodisiac. He was harder than stone, desperate with it, and knew he couldn't have stopped himself to save his life.

Regardless of whether she understood, she certainly sensed the unusual intensity of his need. Mewls of pleasure caught in her throat as she fought for silence, a silence that was hopeless to begin with. The couch creaked with their swift copulatory rhythm, the sound echoed by the rustle of her heavy costume, hiked up around her waist mere moments after she'd snuck into his box.

She'd been naked beneath those voluminous skirts and petticoats, as she'd promised she would be, as he'd known she was all through the first act, singing—or claiming to sing—for him alone. She worked his poor Yamish soul into such an unexpected fever he'd hardly kept his seat.

Up the acres of cloth had gone when she'd finally, finally arrived, gathered slowly by her teasing hands, first wine red satin, then snow white lace. She watched him over her shoulder, eyes knowing, confidant with the conquests of many years. He'd tried to resist her. He knew she was trouble, but her sly insinuations, her hot, speaking looks had dragged him irresistibly into her human web. This was her moment. His first surrender. Their first sexual intercourse. He'd thought making her wait had proved his superiority, but now he knew it had only made him more crazed.

Disgusted with himself but too lustful to care, he'd unfastened the placket of his black dress trousers and drew out his furious prick.

Even for his height he was big. Yvonne's eyes had widened at the organ twitching eagerly in his fist. Humans liked to believe only they came in such a size. Sadly, his victory was cheap and brief. Licking her lips and smiling, she lifted her skirts to her waist. Stockings of patterned silk had sheathed her perfectly formed legs, their lacy garters begging to be snapped. Straddling her feet a good span apart, she bent herself forward over the back of the couch. Her sex beckoned like a ruby set between pale white moons. Perfect. Pristine. Except for the goading scent of another man.

"Bitch," he'd said, a word he'd never used in his life.

Yvonne's only response was a creamy smile.

Squeezing his massiveness inside her had proved a challenge. They'd managed, though, both of them reckless with their hunger. She'd groaned as he hilted, groaned and drenched him with arousal. At that moment, he'd been able to read her fire just a bit. He'd known she liked the edge of pain his overendowment brought to the act.

"All for you," he'd mocked, dragging back and shoving in again, hard enough to make her cry out.

He'd meant to go slowly, meant to make her beg, but his body wouldn't have it. Faster and faster it drove him, pouring all that pent-up, forbidden lust into her lushness, harder and deeper, climbing toward glory, never hearing the soft click of the latch turning until, like the ringing of a deathknell, he heard the other sound, the sliding ching of the door curtain being shoved aside on its brass hoops. Cargrove and Hastings had bumbled into the box half drunk to say "hullo," and he couldn't stop, couldn't, no matter how it betrayed his soul.

Yvonne had looked straight at the two gaping humans and wriggled her succulent fanny against him, pink now from his driving blows, her secret muscles pulling him deeper as she convulsed with pleasure. The surge of orgasmic energy had destroyed him. It was immense, deeper somehow than any woman had fed to him before, perhaps because of the human she'd taken first. His climax had surged up from his balls like a stream of brandy with a match to it. He had to, had to, *oh, gods,* he'd clutched her naked hips in a grip of steel and let those drunken human louts watch the bitch reduce him to tears of ecstasy.

In all his life, he'd never cried before.

How she'd smiled when he'd struggled off her, trembling and dripping with his own juices—and still damnably hard. He could have gone at her again, could have fucked her until he fainted. She knew she'd defeated him then, if only for a time. She didn't seem to care that the scandal of being caught *en flagrante* with a demon might damage her career. He'd heard, in fact, that she'd gone on to sing the second act. As for Herrington, that night's indiscretion had cost him his superior's trust. For years afterward, his every sneeze had been watched.

Hearing Yvonne's voice now, issuing so bizarrely from the mouth of his dead sister's twin, made Herrington gasp for breath. This girl, she was his. She had to be. His daughter. Blood of his blood. Fruit of his seed.

His and that bitch's.

It shouldn't have been possible. Yama and humans were, genetically speaking, far enough apart not to breed. He could only conclude that the man Yvonne took before him had influenced the result, perhaps interacting with his emission in some manner that allowed it to germinate.

If his handlers knew . . . His heart clenched with dread. He couldn't begin to predict how they would react.

But now the old biddies had reached a decision on the still life. His daughter smiled at them, starting to turn. In a second, she would see him. In a second, she would know.

He panicked. Only his long association with humans allowed him to identify the response. Helpless to control it, Herrington spun away. He was halfway out the door, his fist pressed tight to his aching breastbone, before he forced himself to stop.

He was *daimyo,* by the gods. He wouldn't quail before a human.

<hr>

Roxie saw the demon sag against the threshold as if he couldn't go another step. Yama didn't often patronize her shop, but she knew the behavior was unusual. Assuming he was ill, she hurried to offer assistance.

The demon lifted his head, and she fell back. He had the Yama's characteristic pale eyes, silver from rim to rim without any white. Seeing those alien eyes was always a shock, but the shock she felt today had a new and extremely disturbing twist. She couldn't have been more startled if she'd run across her twin. The demon had her hair, her scattered freckles, her sturdier than normal build. His mouth didn't match, but his cheekbones were the same, as was his stubborn jaw and nose. The biggest difference between them was that he was older.

Old enough to be her father.

Her hand slapped the base of her throat.

The uncanny resemblance had to be happenstance. Demons and humans didn't procreate. And yet . . . how could she deny the evidence of her eyes? Hadn't she been wondering all her life if this day would come: when she'd meet the man who must have sired her? If that man was a demon, it would account for her mother's unaccustomed silence concerning his identity. Had Roxanne's father been anyone Yvonne could claim, Yvonne would have demanded a generous allowance for support. Roxanne had always assumed her father was poor, but now she saw a darker possibility.

"Sorry to disturb you," the demon said in the clipped tones of a purely human aristocrat. If he had an accent, it was indiscernible. "I'm Lord Herrington of Herrington Downs. The Yamish envoy? Blast. I know I've got a card somewhere."

"I recognize you." How cold she sounded, how distant. She might have been one of *them.* At that frightening thought, her mind stuttered to a halt.

The demon stopped digging in his expensive coat. His hand came out slowly. "Of course you do. My picture's in the paper all the time. Black and white, though, so maybe you didn't *know*?"

She didn't like the emphasis he put on the word. "I don't know now," she said coolly. She told herself she didn't, at least not any more than that they looked alike. Amazingly, her answer seemed to take him aback.

"No. Well." For a demon, he appeared positively awkward. With an effort, he went on. "But you're Yvonne's daughter, aren't you? You'd have to be. That voice. Not another voice like that anywhere." The demon—Herrington— was puffed up like a pigeon, from discomfort was her guess, though procreative pride seemed an option, too. He gave his lapels a vigorous tug, then leaned closer.

"You've got to be my daughter," he said in confidential tones. "Not being a scientist, I couldn't say how it happened, but there's no other way to explain who you look and sound like. Your mother and I certainly were on familiar terms."

"It can't be," she snapped. "It's physically impossible."

"Impossible things have happened before. You're mine, my dear. I advise you to reconcile yourself to that fact."

Roxanne drew a deep, calming breath. She let two hansoms rattle by the door before she spoke. "I don't see why I should reconcile myself to anything. Begging your pardon, Lord Herrington, but as far as I'm concerned, any connection between us is strictly accidental. I have my own life here, my own independence. I don't need that complicated by a stranger who thinks five minutes of *familiarity* with my late mother gives him some sort of proprietary interest."

Herrington blinked at her. It wasn't much of a reaction, but if forced to guess, she would have said he was stupefied. "You wish to deny your connection to me, to one of the oldest families in Narikerr?"

"You bet your demon eyes I do."

Herrington scratched his jaw. Demons were renowned for their greater-than-human intelligence, but his expression was childlike in its lack of comprehension. Roxanne ignored a twinge of pity. He had some nerve, expecting her to turn cartwheels at the prospect of being related to him.

"A true *daimyo* would respect my wishes," she said in a silkier voice.

Fortunately, she'd judged the right tack. Her words recalled him to his dignity. He settled his coat and threw back his shoulders. "I'll leave my card," he said. "Just in case. You never know when a fa—, er, envoy can do a person a service."

She was a mass of quivering jelly by the time he left. Her father. She'd met her demon father.

God help her, she wished she could convince herself it

wasn't true, but many things she'd wondered about were making sense for the first time. Her strength. Her height when her mother had been tiny. The fact that she never, ever got sick. Maybe even her mother's hot and cold treatment could be laid at this door. To bear a demon's child must have been a terrible trial. Roxanne closed her eyes as horror surged over her anew. She could barely take the knowledge into her head.

Shaking herself, she decided she didn't like this Herrington. Used to having his way, she bet, and didn't see why he should stop. She bet he was worse than a human nob. *One of the oldest families in Narikerr,* he'd said—as if she ought to care! It wouldn't be safe to have a man like that nosing around her life, not with the boys. Her arrangement with Charles and Max was strictly informal. The Children's Ministry would never consider an unmarried, illegitimate artist a suitable guardian, and never mind a half-demon. If someone were to tell them, someone ruthless enough to use the information as leverage . . .

Her nails gouged her palms, barely aware of the fluttering concern of the Misses Leventhal, still waiting in the alcove to purchase their ugly but oh-so-fashionable still life.

She couldn't lose Charles and Max. They'd made a home together. They were her family now. She wouldn't endanger that for any amount of blood, no matter what species it came from.

Chapter 7

⁂

I am often asked to speak of Herrington and his daughter, but I refuse to join the ranks of speculating journalists. Suffice to say, their relationship was not unlike that of fathers and daughters everywhere—whatever people might imagine to the contrary.

—*The True and Irreverent History of Avvar*

⁂

Unable to concentrate on serving customers, Roxanne closed the gallery early. She'd planned to return home, only to discover she couldn't bring herself to go.

How was she going to face Charles and Max? The way they'd grown up, on the streets in dockside, demons were true monsters to them. Young as Max was, maybe she could put off telling him, but Charles had a right to know. She'd read stories about Herrington in the rags—mainly because, in addition to being the city's resident Yamish envoy, he was a respected amateur archaeologist. As an artist, she had followed the news of his digs with interest. In the process, she'd also seen accounts of his diplomatic prowess.

People claimed he was a master strategist. Victoria's chief counsel had dubbed him "The Red Fox." Who knew what he might do if Roxanne resisted his wishes?

As to that, who knew what *she* might do if her half-demon side started coming out?

Barely aware of what she was doing, she climbed the steps to the next clanking tram that passed, squeezing into a seat beside a tired-looking maid with a basket of groceries clutched on her lap.

Roxanne's skin was clammy, her shoulders tight. What if, unbeknownst to her, she was even then draining her fellow citizens of etheric-force? Horrified by the thought, she wrapped her arms around her waist, trying her utmost not to touch anyone.

Halfway through its route, the tram's generator stalled. While the driver paid a streetboy to run to the nearest stable to hire a team, Roxanne got out. The clinic Abul volunteered at two days a week was only a few streets away. If he was back to his normal schedule, he'd be there now.

She wasn't eager to confide in him, but she knew she needed professional advice.

The clinic was housed in a converted candy shop. It was cramped inside but well lit by the front windows. Roxanne's expression as she walked in must have been strange, because Abul's eyes widened the moment he saw her.

"Have Doctor Russet finish this case," he said to the nurse who stood at his side.

Leaving his patient behind, he came straight to her and, in front of everyone, took her hands. She couldn't even feel guilty that he wasn't making her wait.

"I need to speak to you privately," she said before he could ask what was wrong.

"Yes. All right." He glanced behind him. "We can talk in the back parlor."

The back parlor was a combination file room, office, and break kitchen for the staff. It had a coal fire and a few sad pieces of furniture. Roxanne sat on a lumpy gray-green couch. Though her eyes were too hot and dry to have been crying, she accepted Abul's offer of a handkerchief. Her friend swung a wooden chair around to face her.

"I need this kept between us," she said.

Abul smiled faintly at her intensity. "You may consider doctor-client privilege to be in effect."

"This isn't a joke. I'm deadly serious."

"As am I," said Abul. "So don't insult my integrity."

Roxanne bit her lip and looked down at her hands, now twisted together in her lap. "I met my father today," she blurted out.

"Did you?" Abul sounded mildly curious.

"He's a demon."

She was looking at him then. She saw how his dark skin paled. His mouth worked for a few seconds before words came out. When they did, they were raspy.

"That isn't possible."

"I'm afraid it is. He showed up at the gallery. I'm his spitting image. And he knew my mother. He recognized that I have her voice. You know I'm stronger and healthier than most people. Plus—" She covered her mouth as another piece of evidence fell into place. "I've always been good with numbers. You know how demons are with math. I need to know, physically, what I have to worry about. I need to find out if . . . if I'm going to start feeding off people."

Abul rose to his feet. Roxanne wasn't sure the move was deliberate, but he put his chair between them, his long brown fingers gripping its slatted back. His hands and nails were scrubbed just as Yamish doctors insisted they should be, and around the collar of his clean white coat hung the silver snake of a Yamish stethoscope. A thought slipped so quickly through her mind it hardly registered.

Was her unsuspected heritage truly a cause for shame?

"I . . . don't believe you will," Abul said, bringing her attention back to the matter at hand. "I've never heard of our species interbreeding, but I do know the Yama begin transferring energy very young. If you were going to develop that ability, I expect you would have noticed it by now. You might . . ." He rubbed his chin uncomfortably. "You might have trouble conceiving a child, but you'd probably need to consult a specialist to be sure, and a Yamish specialist might be best."

Up until then, Roxanne had never heard him refer to his foreign colleagues without a shadow of scorn—or at least resentment. In spite of herself, she smiled. Poor Abul. Discovering his friend was half-demon couldn't be easy.

"I wish I knew more," he said. "I'm afraid I can't predict what effect your mixed blood might have."

Roxanne stood. "Thank you for telling me what you could. You've reassured me just by being calm. I probably panicked more than I needed to. It's not as if I haven't been . . . what I am all along."

"I could attempt to get you a referral."

She tried to conceive of letting a demon examine her. "I'll think about it. For now, I'd like to keep this quiet."

Abul nodded, his face somber. He knew as well as anyone the prejudice she might face. "Will you tell the boys?"

"I'm thinking about that, too. At some point, they'll need to know."

"They'll love you all the same," he said.

Roxanne couldn't help but notice his assurance held a hint of doubt. If she couldn't be certain of Max and Charles, she didn't want to imagine telling Adrian.

⟨≈⟩

By the time the hired cab dropped him home, Herrington's course of action had been decided. Because he couldn't be positive his newly discovered daughter would keep their relationship to herself, he had to be the one to break the news to his handlers, and he had to do it now. Only then could he hope to manipulate their reaction.

With a wordless wave to Albert, who knew better than to approach him uninvited, he proceeded up the stairs to his private, locked study, the one the maids were forbidden to even think about tidying. After picking his way through the unavoidable dust and clutter, he reached his large, marble-topped desk. A secret compartment at the back of one of the drawers hid his one truly indispensable piece of Yamish technology. On the outside, to disguise it from the eyes of unwitting humans, it appeared to be an out-of-date *Farmer's Almanac*. On the inside, a small, flat viewing screen allowed him to speak directly to his superiors in Narikerr.

He opened the false book, laid it on a mahogany stand designed for the purpose, then fit the tiny wireless speaker into his ear. If anyone heard him, they'd think he was talking to himself.

He spared a glance for his favorite framed portrait of Louise. Her resemblance to his daughter startled him anew. He hadn't exaggerated the effect. But he had to push that out of his mind in order to keep calm.

To his surprise, when he punched the code to connect, he reached not the Under-Minister of Foreign Affairs, but the prince of Narikerr himself. A pale shadow of his celebrated father—the man who'd so deftly handled the intrusion of DuBarry—the city's current prince only answered official calls when he was trying to impress a lover, or unconscionably bored. Startled by the sight of the prince's languid, handsome face, Herrington adjusted his strategy accordingly.

"Your highness," he murmured, bowing his head. "You do me great honor."

"Herrington," drawled the prince, the protraction of his speech indicating that boredom was the reason for his presence. "I hope you're calling about something interesting. The city's deadly dull today."

"Only your highness can judge if my news is interesting, but it certainly is unusual."

The prince leaned closer to the screen. One of his thin black eyebrows climbed a fraction higher.

"I have discovered I have a daughter," said Herrington.

To his astonishment, simply saying the word *daughter* set his soul alight with what a human would have called joy. He had a daughter. No matter how infelicitous Roxanne's maternal lineage, Herrington had produced issue. His blood would live into the future. Fortunately, his fierce

blaze of feeling could not be read through the screen. All
that showed in his expression was mild distaste.

"I take it congratulations are not in order," said the
prince. Had it not been extremely lower class, Herrington
suspected the Emperor's nephew would have rubbed his
hands. His royal worthlessness adored being privy to good
gossip.

"Alas, no," Herrington admitted. "My daughter turns
out to be half-human."

The prince was shocked into gasping aloud. "How
could this be?"

As tastefully as he could, Herrington shared his theory
of mixing seed, at which the prince grimaced, then feigned
knowingness.

"Regrettably," Herrington went on, "because she was
born in Avvar to a human mother, she won't be subject to
our laws."

This was debatable, the situation never having come up
before. Herrington knew, however, that if he could get the
prince to agree with him, his interpretation was that much
closer to becoming fact.

"Hmm," said the prince, drawing out the sound unsurely; thankfully, he was not a great legal mind. "Likely
you are correct. I wonder, though, do we want her subject
to our laws?"

"It would be a dire diplomatic mess," Herrington said,
knowing the prince would not like that. It might, after all,
require him to exert himself. "The problem is, this woman
does not wish to acknowledge the tie between us. Truth be
told, she wants nothing to do with me."

"Why on earth not?" demanded the prince.

Herrington pursed his lips sadly. "Humans don't see
us as we see ourselves. I know it is hard to credit, your
highness, but they are barely sophisticated enough to distinguish between *daimyo* and *rohn*. I believe, however, that
I know a way we can lure her into our sphere, so we may
observe any noteworthy peculiarities her breeding may
have created."

"You can't mean to bring this creature to Narikerr!" At

the mere possibility, the prince's well-bred features twisted delicately in horror.

"No, indeed," said Herrington, judging it time to incline his head respectfully again. "That would be most inappropriate—as you yourself have intuited. No, I intend that she should stay in Avvar, under my personal observation, as would be natural were we a normal father and child."

The prince took a moment to absorb this suggestion. Herrington tried not to hold his breath. It was absolutely crucial that Roxanne remain under his protection, under— for that matter—the protection of her own nation's law. If Yamish authorities decided to lay claim to her, especially with her existence essentially unknown, he could not swear she would be treated with the care he'd begun to suspect was due every intelligent being. Not that he'd ever air the view. That would constitute going more "native" than any *daimyo* could approve. In any case, it would be all too easy for his handlers to cause one human woman to disappear.

At last, the prince responded. "I applaud your tolerance," he said. "I am not certain I could remain in the proximity of such a—But she is your daughter. I shall not mention a word."

Most likely, he couldn't come up with one, but Herrington nodded as if in gratitude for his sensitivity. "You are too kind," he said gravely, secretly delighted to have gotten the concession he was hoping for. "It is, as always, my signal honor to serve my prince."

Chapter 8

⚜

The conquering of fear is the highest art.

—The Collected Sayings of the Emperor

Fear no man. Woman is the deadlier of the species.

—Victoria Faen Aedlys,
addressing the troops on the eve of
the Battle of Benworth Vale

⚜

While Roxanne manned the gallery, Adrian dismantled her leaky kitchen hand pump and replaced the worn washers. He figured this was the least he could do. Thanks to Charles's culinary expertise, he'd been eating Roxie's cupboards bare; he'd actually regained some of the weight he'd lost while living on his own. Though part of him would always crave solitude, he knew he'd had too much of a good thing these last few years. The loose bonds of affection that united Roxie's household suited him perfectly. He found his appetite for many things coming back.

The adjustable wrench clanked as he set it by his thigh on the checkerboard floor. In a familiar nervous habit, he rubbed his right wrist with his left hand, unable to feel the implant but conscious that it was there. He'd never experienced such an intense attraction before. Much as he wanted a relationship with Roxanne, he feared her impact on his life. What would his family say? Or his boss? The Securité contract had no morals clause, but it was understood that officers shouldn't fraternize with questionable social types.

Much as he loathed the phrase, he knew it applied to her.

If he wasn't careful to keep his yen for her in check, he could easily jeopardize his career. Since he'd become the station's man for demon-related crime, he didn't have much else. He couldn't afford to muck up the one positive contribution he'd made to the world.

The sound of footsteps approaching snapped him back to the present. Charles stepped into the kitchen's wide doorway. The boy's work apron was damp from a morning spent scrubbing dishes at The Laughing Crow. In spite of this sullying of his attire, excitement sparkled in his eyes.

"I heard something," he said. "Some of the locals think they saw your boy two weeks ago, catching a feed at one of the soup kitchens on Front. He was well, they said, not sick, and not hooked up with anyone dangerous. They don't know what happened to him since, though. He hasn't been around."

"He can't just have disappeared."

Charles cut him a look. Adrian winced at the reminder that of course he could.

Charles's expression softened. "You could talk to Dr. Abul. He works at St. Steffin's. They see a lot of what washes out of the sewers. Not a pleasant thought, I know, but no point putting your neck on the line if the boy isn't around to appreciate it. I'm sure Abul would be happy to check for you. Anything for a friend of Roxie's."

"What's this about a friend of Roxie's?" The woman

herself appeared around the corner with a small brown bag in one hand and an empty casserole dish in the other.

Her cheer sounded forced, but Adrian didn't get a chance to ask why. The sight of the dirty dropcloth between his knees pulled her up short.

"You fixed my faucet," she said, obviously bewildered.

Now that his attention had been drawn, Charles goggled, too.

Well, really, Adrian thought. *Were the people in this household so self-sufficient a guest couldn't pitch in?*

"It was leaking," he said mildly, refusing to defend his actions. "Now it's not."

Roxie's chest lifted on a quick breath, as if she'd meant to speak then thought better of it. Because Charles was present, Adrian fought his compulsion to stare at her breasts. She'd paired her brown moleskin trousers with a romantically flowing man's white shirt. He was ready to swear there was nothing beneath its ruffled front but her.

"Were you talking about me?" she asked with a lightness that didn't seem natural.

Adrian looked to Charles for permission, but his glacial green eyes refused.

"Honestly," Roxie huffed.

Charles put a conciliatory hand on her shoulder. "I was just telling Adrian he needn't worry about paying Dr. Abul for his services."

This appeared to satisfy her, though she eased away from his hold. "I doubt he'd take your money," she said to Adrian, then handed Charles the empty casserole dish. "Linia said your grape leaves were wonderful, and she will trade you her recipe for braised basil chicken."

"I knew I'd get her this time," he crowed and bounded off to claim his prize.

Once he was gone, Adrian wiped his hands on a rag and pulled himself to his feet with the edge of the counter. Roxie resisted at first when he tugged her to him, then gave in with a soundless sigh. His sex began to thicken the moment their hips met, and there was nothing he could do to stop it. That being so, he resigned himself. Tomorrow would take care of tomorrow. Today, he'd enjoy the gift of this warm woman in his arms. To his surprise, when he tried to catch her mouth for a kiss, she twisted her head away.

"We shouldn't," she said, her face averted.

"Shouldn't we?" Wondering what had gotten into her but still hopeful, he nuzzled the delicate softness beneath her ear. "I don't see anyone here but us." Unable to resist, he set his teeth lightly to her neck and gently sucked her skin between.

"Adrian!" she exclaimed, though the sound was more a gasp of pleasure than a complaint.

Despite what her body was telling him, he sensed she was an inch from squirming away. This was definitely a new development. Concerned, he loosened his hold. "What's wrong?"

"Nothing's wrong," she said. "I'm perfectly fine."

"You don't sound fine. First you shrug away from Charles and now from me. That tells me something's happened, something you don't want to talk about."

She looked at him, her eyes so close he could see the tiny rays of silver in her irises. The ring of gold around their outer edges looked molten.

"What do you feel when I touch you?" she asked.

The question perplexed him, especially its intensity. How could she not know what he felt? "I feel good," he said and rubbed her shoulders from behind.

"Just good?" she insisted.

"*Very* good?" he offered back.

She stared at him, then laughed softly under her breath. He wondered if he'd failed some test more sophisticated people knew how to solve.

"It's all right," she said, shaking her head. "Forget I asked."

This didn't seem quite the way to proceed, but because he didn't know what else to do, he slid one hand down her arm. "What's in the bag?"

He felt her reaching a decision. "It's a present for you from Abul. A special sticking plaster so you can have a soak without getting your stitches wet. I thought, perhaps—" She swallowed, for once the one who had to gather her nerve. "I thought you might like me to scrub your back."

Unsophisticated or not, Adrian knew she was offering more than a scrub. Too brilliantly happy to question his luck, he bared every tooth he had in a smile. "I'd like that very much."

Roxanne ducked her head again, but this time the gesture was shyly pleased. "Very well," she said, her voice so smoky it made him squirm. "Let's get wet."

Muscles taut with anticipation, he struggled to keep his footing as they took the narrow back stairs. Her bottom was delectable. He could see the muscles moving in it as she descended ahead of him.

"I hope you're not offended that we didn't shift you down here before," she said. "I figured it would be easier to leave you near the kitchen."

"Nonsense, Roxanne, your parlor is quite comfortable."

She pushed the hall door open. "Bet you'll be glad to get back to your own bed."

He wagered he'd be happier to get into hers.

Grinning at the likelihood of this happening soon, he examined the third floor for the first time since he'd arrived. A wide hall extended the length of the building. Blocks of daylight brightened either end, the effect of two deep-set, decoratively leaded windows. On the far ledge, lavender peonies overflowed a tarnished silver vase. He could smell their heady scent from where he stood.

Seven doors led off the hall, all closed. Her bed lay behind one of them. His chest tightened. He could handle this. He needn't assume he couldn't please her just because she was more experienced.

He glanced at the pictures on the wall. With her fondness for secondhand finery, he didn't expect to find anything valuable, but one canvas jumped out at him, an Andrew Narmis of a girl playing at the water's edge.

No, he thought. A painting like that belonged in a museum. It had to be a reproduction.

"It's real," she said. "Art is an excellent investment."

"You can't just admit things like that. What if I were a thief?"

"You're not." Unperturbed, she opened a door and gestured him inside.

He didn't have time to scold her further, because the bathroom was even more eye-popping than the Andrew Narmis. Tiled in coral and cream, it was almost as big as her parlor. It had one round, rippled window, much like the ones in her storeroom, except this was a rich saffron.

A pedestal sink and vanity were spaced around the walls, along with a flush commode and bidet: an exotic bit of plumbing he could recognize but not operate. A glass-doored armoire stood sentinel to the right of the door, its shelves stacked with thick coral-colored towels. Beyond that a lion-footed divan in cream silk faille offered respite to those wearied by their tour of the facilities. The crowning glory, however, was the bath. Set on a platform in the center of the room, its deep sarcophaguslike tub had been carved from a single block of marble. Pink marble.

Roxanne stepped past his flabbergasted form to open the free-running tap. No hand-pumping here. The faucet looked suspiciously sterling.

"Is that a gas burner?" he exclaimed, bending down to examine the innards of the platform that held the tub. Roxanne admitted it was.

"There's an automatic shutoff. So you can't accidentally stew yourself. Whatever else you might say about demons, you can't deny they invent lovely conveniences."

Her voice held an irony he didn't understand. It reminded him they weren't terribly far from being strangers. And they were alone. He was about to strip naked and take a bath. Their eyes connected. He wondered if his breathing sounded as loud to her as it did to him. The bourgeois in him had a sudden urge to hail a chaperone. His libido might have no conscience, but the boy his mother raised knew he shouldn't be alone with this woman who was not his wife.

Roxanne's courage seemed to falter with his change of mood.

"Well," she said unsurely. "I'll leave you to it."

Adrian could have kicked himself as he watched her pull the door shut behind her. *Idiot.* All he'd had to do was ask her to stay.

By the time he shut off the gas ring, applied his sticking plaster, and lowered himself into the tub, the water was scalding. Fit punishment, he supposed, for his stupidity. Releasing a long, pensive sigh, he decided her leaving was for the best. It saved him from making a fool of himself. Sadly, every word of this was a lie. He was praying she'd come back. Otherwise, why had he shaved so carefully? Why had he scoured his teeth with her mint powder?

When he heard her timid rap, he sat up with a splash, his heart knocking against his ribs. Was it going to happen after all?

At his hoarse answer, she stuck her head around the door. "I, um, thought you might need some help."

"Yes," he said definitely. "Help would be most helpful."

He sounded inane, but better that than letting her go again.

"Would you like me to wash your hair?"

He nodded wordlessly, his energy centered on controlling his reaction. If he was wrong, and she was only being considerate, he didn't want to scare her away. He had nothing to hide behind here, nothing but clear water and steam. His eyes followed her as she opened the armoire and removed a corked indigo bottle. The label was full of flowers. Apparently, she fancied the new scented hair soap from Jeruvia. Rolling her sleeves above her elbows, she dropped a folded towel onto the step beside the tub, lathered her hands, and knelt.

Though she seemed nervous, the first touch of her fingers on his scalp undid him utterly.

"Good?" she asked as he closed his eyes and trembled.

"Mm-hm," was all he could manage. His sex had leapt to full attention in an instant. He knew it would be dark with blood. She had only to look down to see it. He didn't dare check to see if she had.

"When I was little," she said, her voice a trifle high, "I

loved having my hair washed. Once in a while, my mother would do it, and it always made me feel like a spoiled cat."

The scrap of his brain that still functioned wanted to know what else she'd loved as a child—only it seemed wrong to seek confidences when he knew he wouldn't reciprocate. In fairness, all he was prepared to ask of her was more of this obliterating sweetness, more touching, more body-to-body song drowning out all the words but *Yes, now, soon.*

That pleasure he'd be more than happy to turn and turnabout.

Have to stay in control, he thought, but he couldn't remember why. Fighting a groan, he gripped the sides of the tub.

Her chest brushed his arm as she worked more than the soap into a lather.

He was certain then that there was nothing under that ruffled shirt but her. Her nipples were sharp against the linen. She did want him. This was exciting her, too.

She told him to close his eyes while she rinsed his hair with cup after cup of cool water from the sink. The liquid sluiced over his chest and back, warming as it ran down his heated flesh. It swirled into the water, teasing the swollen tip of his sex. When he tried to slouch lower, his legs stuck out of the tub. He had skinny knees like a teenager. He couldn't imagine they'd arouse her, but she cupped one with her dripping palm, lightly squeezing the tendons on either side. Luck or instinct enabled her to tweak the strongest nerve. His leg jerked. The head of his sex broke the surface of the water.

It felt immense, its throb an embarrassment. She'd known how much he wanted her. Now she couldn't help but see. A pause followed during which he knew, absolutely knew, that she was staring.

"Beautiful man," she murmured and then, "don't move."

She needn't have worried. He couldn't have moved to save his life.

Soaping a crisp, golden sea sponge, she rubbed it across his shoulders, then down his back and over the upper curves of his behind. Her strokes were firm and lingering. He leaned back so she could wash his front, letting his arms slide wetly along the rim of the tub. She soaped his arms, his neck, his chest hair. She sent him into a stupor of desire by drawing slow figure eights around his nipples. Then she set the sponge aside and continued the task with her hand. When she finally touched the tiny nubs, his chest arched into her palm. He'd been biting his lip against a moan, but at this he couldn't hold it back, even if it marked him a sexual neophyte, shattered by the simplest trick.

No one had ever touched him with such concentrated attention. If her movements hadn't been so sure, if he hadn't known whose daughter she was, he'd have been tempted to believe she'd never done this before. Her exploration seemed more curious than practiced—as though it were new to her. Fresh.

His wish that this were true was dangerous. If she really was innocent, he had no business playing these games with her.

Her sigh distracted him, a soft, happy sound. Her touch skimmed down his arm, over the back of his hand, and between his knuckles. She braided their fingers together and squeezed. Strangely moved, he squeezed her back, in thanks, in encouragement, and because the energy building inside him demanded expression.

He was sorry when she let go, but only for a moment.

"Here," she said, reaching into the bath to capture his ankle. Droplets tinkled on the water's surface as she lifted his foot to the rim, forcing him to grab the tub for balance. Still on her knees, she shuffled her towel down the platform to get closer, her respiration suddenly shallow.

What now? he wondered, his own breath coming faster in sympathy.

Her palm warmed his ankle. She tilted his foot upward with the sole facing her. One thumb rubbed the tendons of his instep while the other thumb worked the outer curve. Her hands moved in tandem, smooth, deep strokes down the length of his foot. His toes curled. The water sloshed as he squirmed in reaction. What she was doing felt wonderful, strange, and electric, as if a current had been connected between his foot and his cock, shocking him with hot jolts of sensation. Almost embarrassing, how sexual it was. Who'd have thought such a thing was possible?

The gleam in her eye told him she knew what she was doing, and that she was enjoying it. Confident now, she bent closer. She blew softly on his toes, then took one into her mouth and sucked. He cried out, his cock stiffening so forcefully it slapped his belly.

"Enough," he gasped, though he couldn't bring himself to pull free. "I can't take it. It's like a wire attached to my—to my—"

"Sex," she said. The way she drew out the word made his scalp shiver. She surrounded another toe and flicked her tongue along the wrinkled pad. He groaned. He was going to spend. From a woman sucking on his foot. He couldn't allow this to happen.

"Please let go. Please."

"Your wish is my command," she purred.

She set his foot back under the water. Adrian sighed in relief and just a little in regret.

"I don't want you to think I didn't like that," he said, panting a bit to catch his breath. "I was just afraid I'd . . . finish without you even touching my cock."

To his relief, his language did not repel her. Her pupils expanded as she held his gaze, shiny black swallowing up the silver. She scooted closer, then hesitated in a way he found enchanting.

"Do you want me to touch you there?"

"You know I do."

"Then take my hand, Adrian. Show me what you want me to do."

Heart rocketing in his chest, he took her hand and folded it around his shaft. For a second, he thought he'd die then and there.

"Oh, so soft, so hard," she murmured, her eyes closing. He made her fingers tighten around him, and then his own lids drifted as well, grown heavy with the long-awaited heaven of her clasp. "Please tell me it feels all right."

"Wonderful," he groaned. "Oh, God, I think I have to move."

"Do," she said. "I want you to."

He scarcely needed the encouragement. It had been literally years since any hand but his had held him here. He began to thrust through her hold, gritting his teeth against the exquisite sharpness of his pleasure.

The end came quickly. He pushed through the circle of their joined hands, once, twice. Her thumb slid up the side of his cock, rubbed the neck lovingly for a moment, then curled over to circle the head. As soon as she touched him there he was gone, instantly, like throwing a switch. He moaned as the climax ripped through him, his body clenching in a protracted agony of bliss.

He was exhausted when it finished, emptied out and unable to move a finger. When he opened his eyes she was watching him with an extraordinary amount of concern. Quite obviously, she hadn't expected him to lose control. Shame replaced his pleasure.

"I'm sorry," he said. "You didn't—"

But she was talking at the same time. "Forgive me," she said, her fist pressed to her mouth. "I had no right to risk doing that."

Then, to his amazement, she fled the room.

Chapter 9

❧

Love is a storm, sneaking up on us unawares.

— "Song of the Love-Mad *Rohn*"

❧

Roxanne was huddled in her bed, wrapped in her favorite robe. For once, its satiny smoothness didn't comfort her. With the sheets pulled to her chin, she stared at the ceiling mural of Adam having his wicked way with Eve. Half hidden by foliage and firelight, the beasts were procreating, too. Lions and lemurs, birds and bees. Even Snake had a happy, writhing partner. This was her own private historical re-creation, one that had never failed to amuse her until tonight.

When she purchased this building, she'd knocked down a wall to enlarge her bedroom. After a lifetime of being tucked into corners and a year in the hold of the *Queen,* she'd been hungry for space. Now she felt like the wrong-size doll for the dollhouse. The only things big enough to fill this room were her worries.

She told herself Adrian was all right. Probably. Hopefully. She'd been convinced everything was fine, that she hadn't suddenly developed life-sucking powers. She'd adored watching him revel in her touch, but after his body convulsed with bliss, he'd looked completely drained, as if he could sleep for a week exactly where he was.

Though she prided herself on being worldly—or at least well read—the plain truth of the matter was that she didn't know if Adrian's reaction was normal. When push came to shove, she had no advantage over any other stupid virgin.

Any other *half-demon* stupid virgin.

Roxie covered her eyes and groaned. How could she have treated him as an experiment? In her eagerness to enjoy her first serious sexual adventure, she'd completely ignored his well-being. That was unforgivable.

After all, she didn't merely lust after Adrian, she liked him. She liked his comically proper manners, the way he'd blush at the drop of a hat. Max was blooming under the extra attention, and even Charles had betrayed enjoyment at having a man around. He'd always cooked, but now he was cooking up a storm, fantastic concoctions designed for health as much as savor.

If she hadn't known better, she'd have said they were acting like a family.

Too bad she couldn't afford to let herself think that way. Adrian had blown into their lives like sea spume. One of these days, he was bound to blow out again.

Focus on the happiness you have, she ordered. *Don't be like your mother, always wanting what's out of reach.* Except, with a little more patience, maybe she could have it all. This afternoon's embarrassment didn't mean she had to give up the first man she'd wanted who wanted her back.

Assuming, of course, that she hadn't killed him with her demon powers.

She forced herself to sit up. She had to check on him,

even if it would be humiliating, even if the chance that she'd actually hurt him was small.

She didn't know whether to be relieved or fearful when a shadow appeared at the door. It was Adrian.

"Roxanne," he said, soft and imploring. She saw he wore the gray spider-silk pajamas she'd bought to match his eyes. At any rate, he wore the bottoms.

Her heart thudded as she scooched higher in the bed. Did she dare hope—

"Can't we do this right?" He advanced a step. "Can't we make love?"

His voice was so thrillingly low the crackle of the fire almost masked it. She couldn't answer. The air had fled her lungs. With a half-dozen strides, he reached the side of her bed and touched her cheek with the back of his knuckles.

"Can't we?" he repeated.

She wanted desperately to say *yes*. In the end, though, her need to be fair won out. With a sigh of resignation, she folded her knees tailor-fashion beneath the sheets.

"I wish we could," she said.

"You wish?" Adrian took a half-step back. Oh, she knew that defensive look. She'd worn it often enough to memorize.

"I don't want to hurt you," she pleaded.

"How could you hurt me? Roxanne." He sat and gathered her hand to his hard, bare chest. "Did you think you hurt me before?"

"Not exactly, but—"

"I assure you, I enjoyed everything you did."

She had to cut this short before he reminded her how much she'd enjoyed it, too. "I met my father for the first time today."

"Oh." He let her hand fall to the sheets, though his fingers still touched hers. His brow wrinkled in concern. "Was it upsetting? Would you prefer to . . . try this another day?"

Roxanne was at a loss to respond to that. She wished

another day would make a difference. Pressing her lips together, she tried to decide how much to explain. She'd always considered herself a good judge of character, but did she dare trust Adrian with this?

"Did your father hurt you?" he asked softly, reaching to chafe her hand between his own.

The kindness he radiated made her choice.

"He's Welland Herrington," she said. "Lord Herrington. The Yamish envoy to Avvar."

"Goodness," Adrian exclaimed, his eyebrows shooting up. "That's quite a . . . but . . ." He blinked as what she'd told him began to add up. "That would mean—"

"That I'm half demon?"

"Yes." He dropped her hand to rub his right wrist. "I didn't know that was possible."

"Neither did I until today."

He rose, raked his fingers through his hair, and stared blindly at the wall. When he turned back to her, his eyes were still worried. "That's why you wanted to know how I felt when you touched me. You thought you might be stealing my etheric-force."

"Yes, though it seems I didn't inherit that ability."

He laughed, then covered his mouth. "Poor Roxanne. You must have thought I'd expired in truth back in that bath. If I'd known, I'd have attempted to be less violent in my pleasure."

"It's not funny. The guilt was awful. I was about to check on you when you came in."

"Perhaps we should try again," he said with a suggestive lilt. "To ensure you really aren't capable of . . . sucking me dry."

She had to laugh. He didn't make jokes often enough for her to refrain.

"Please," he said with endearing seriousness. "It would be my honor to be intimate with you."

She would have preferred that he declare himself wholly indifferent to who her father was, but at least he wasn't appalled. She needed no more than half her courage to nod shyly. His heartfelt sigh of relief salved a lifetime of rejection.

Tingling with anticipation, she held her breath as he climbed over her onto the big sleighbed. Midway there, he stopped, stepped back, and loosened the drawstring on his sleepwear. His openness touched her. For her, he would overcome his natural modesty. She watched him slide off the garment, not with an artist's eye but a woman's. Despite what they'd done in the bath, his erection was full and high. Recalling what he'd said about sucking him dry, her mouth watered.

Naked now, he held out his hand to her. "I want to see you."

With a mix of fear and excitement, she slipped from the bed. She knew he found her attractive, but her appearance had never been her greatest source of confidence. It was too different from what she'd grown up believing a woman should look like. Luckily, Adrian had his own opinion. Taking her by the shoulders, he turned her to face the illumination of the fire.

His eyes caressed her first, lingering on her belly and breasts. The coffee-and-cream satin of her robe hung heavily from their peaks. His hands rose, drifting like smoke over her curves. Nothing moved but his hands, his eyes, time itself suspended in the hush. She leaned closer.

"Not yet," he whispered. "You're so beautiful. I can't bear to rush this."

His knuckles brushed her nipples for the first time, feathering back and forth until she ached for more. He turned his palms to her, warming her, just barely squeezing. Her toes curled into the rug. She wanted to hold him so badly she hurt. His hands slid beneath the collar of her robe, easing it over her shoulders. The tie was loose already, requiring only the hook of a finger to tug it free. That done, his gaze followed the satin's fluttering passage to the rug, then rose again to her breasts. She wished he would smile but a moment later was glad he did not. His jaw clenched, then his hands. His erection surged noticeably higher.

"Get back in bed," he ordered. His voice sounded angry, but she felt no fear as she obeyed. The intensity of his reactions thrilled her too much for that.

Her skin was humming when he finally lowered his body onto hers. Hot and thick, his sex pounded between their bellies. His hard, furry chest came closer, flattening her breasts. He stilled at the contact, caught his breath, then stretched catlike against her, seeking the perfect melding of soft and hard.

"Ah," he sighed when he'd finished settling himself. "That is so-o much better. You feel so good. We fit well."

A laugh bubbled in her chest. She'd never been this glad of her height before. She squeezed her arms around his muscled back. "My heart's beating so fast I think it's going to explode."

"Are you scared?"

He seemed surprised, but she had to admit she was.

He propped himself up to study her, and she felt compelled to touch his serious face. His cheek was smooth. He'd shaved for her. The unexpected sweetness curved her mouth.

"Don't be afraid," he said. "It's going to be good for us."

"Yes," she agreed, unable to be coy. "I think you're right." She combed her fingers through the silky waves at his nape, enjoying the delicious luxury of touch. This man, this sweetly shaven, handsome man was going to be her first lover.

He shivered, then pressed his lips to her temple. "I'm sorry about this afternoon. I didn't even kiss you."

"Kiss me now."

He smiled, then claimed her mouth, his tongue warm and probing. Weak with desire, she softened for him, melted for him. His tongue curled around hers, sucking until she was drawn just as intimately into his mouth. Even then he wasn't satisfied, but groaned and kissed her harder. Soon they were rolling from side to side on the bed, their arms wrapped around each other, their legs twining and rubbing as they fought to get closer.

She moaned—too loudly, perhaps—but there was nothing she could do to hold it in. He broke free at the sound, his chest heaving.

"Tell me," he panted. "Tell me what you like."

His hand circled her hip, then her belly. She could feel his fingers shaking, feel their damp, shy heat. Tears of want sprang to her eyes. That she could affect him this way!

"I want you to be ready for me," he said.

She was about to assure him she was when his hand brushed the golden curls of her mound. His longest finger slid between her slick, swollen lips.

She stretched up at him with a wordless cry.

He cradled her body closer, barely touching the pulsing heart of her pleasure. His touch was so light she thought he must be as afraid of hurting her as she'd been of him. His gentleness was exquisite. Each nerve fired separately under his delicate strokes, one by tantalizing one, like a St. Steffin's Day sparkler.

"You like that?" he rasped as if he hardly dared hope.

Yes, she said soundlessly, her cheek rubbing his shoulder. Emboldened, he caught her pearl between the pads of his fingers and worked the softer folds around the firm center.

His name became a groan.

"Yes, sweetheart. Yes." He kissed her cheek in praise, his gaze glued to her quivering sex. Quite clearly, he liked the view. In watching her, he seemed oblivious to the throb of his own desire.

"Please." She tugged at his shoulder. "Please. Come inside me. I can't hold off much"—she gasped as he brushed a sensitive spot—"longer."

"Then don't." The ghost of a smile softened his harshly handsome face.

"I want you inside me," she insisted, gliding her hand down his ribs to his waist.

He pushed her onto her back. "Not yet. There's something I want to do first."

It wasn't hard to guess what he had in mind when he slid down her body and coaxed her thighs apart.

"Adrian . . ."

"Please," he said. "I know it's personal, but I want to."

"I didn't do this to you."

He chuckled, a soft confident sound she didn't think she'd heard from him before. Still smiling, he kissed one plump lip. "It isn't a punishment, Roxie, but if it were, it would be just. You saw me at my most vulnerable. Shouldn't I have a chance for the same?"

"Um," she said, because his fingers were drawing teasing patterns on her inner thighs. "I can't think well enough to answer that."

"Roxanne," he said, making her name a laugh before taking her warmest places into his mouth. His hands slid under her buttocks, tilting her toward him. Immediately, she had to squirm. His kiss was tender—and thorough. His tongue opened every fold, explored every crevice. He dipped into her sheath and hummed at her taste. She tensed as he found the swollen center of her pleasure, suckling it, pressing it hard behind his teeth. Her body arched.

"Good?" he whispered.

She couldn't believe he needed reassurance. "Oh!" she gasped as he did the trick with his teeth again. Her hands were clenched in the sheets, but she tried to speak. "Sir, I believe your mouth should require a special license!"

His amusement buzzed against her intimate flesh. He was still chuckling when her convulsions started, sharp and deep. His hands tightened on her bottom, holding her close while she shook, while he devoured each ecstatic tremor.

He let her settle, then moved over her on hands and knees. She expected him to take her at once, but he remained as he was, head hanging, limbs shaking.

When she touched his hip, he shied like a bee-stung horse. "What's wrong?"

He spoke through gritted teeth. "Maybe I shouldn't have done that."

A drop of moisture hit her belly. She touched it with her

finger, tested its slickness against the pad of her thumb. Comprehension dawned. It wasn't sweat.

"I thought I'd be all right after . . . what we did before, but I waited too long. I'm never going to last."

"That doesn't matter."

"Yes, it does. I want this to be perfect. You have me so excited, I want to scream."

As complaints went, it couldn't have been nicer.

"Look at me," she said, stroking his hair back from his anxious face, thinking what a ridiculous pair they made—both of them obviously longer on theory than practice. "Everything you've done, everything you do seems right to me. Let's not worry about our first time being perfect. Besides, if you move fast, you might not have to last longer than a minute or two."

He released a grudging snort of laughter, then positioned himself between her thighs. "A minute or two I might manage."

Her breath hitched as his crown nudged her threshold. He was full and silky and warm. With her flesh twitching at the contact, she knew she hadn't lied when she said she was close. She fought her desire to twist against him, fearing this would destroy his control.

Even if she didn't care what happened, she knew he did.

He wrapped a hand behind her shoulder for leverage, then pressed the tip of his penis inside. Her eyelids drifted at the partial connection. Lord, it felt nice. How could a simple body part be this vital?

He kissed her fluttering lashes. "Beautiful girl. Won't you look at me?"

She opened her eyes at the boyish plea. He was smiling down at her, and suddenly she felt like a child herself, helplessly, hopelessly tender. He pushed, groaning a little, then frowned.

"You're so tight. Are you sure you're ready?"

"Yes." She slid her hands around his tense buttocks. "Please, now."

He searched her gaze an instant longer, then set his

knees and thrust. She flinched when he broke through her barrier. He hesitated, eyes wide, but she wrapped her calves around his waist before he could question her. She needn't have worried; he was lost in the wonder of entry. He shuddered as her body kissed his root, sighed, then rocked a fraction deeper. Pain fading, her body bathed him in arousal.

"Mm, you're warm," he said. "This must be heaven. But I need to move now, sweetheart. Hold on to me."

They were laughably out of sync, two green horses used to a single harness. He set her feet back on the mattress.

"Let me," he said, smiling to ease her embarrassment. His gray eyes shone with laughter and desire. "Let me take you with me."

And so she did.

He set a slow, easy rhythm. It lasted longer than she expected. He was tight all over by the finish, each stroke marked by a low, rough cry of restraint. She didn't tell him to stop. She sensed how her pleasure reassured him, how it filled some need she hadn't suspected was there. She peaked twice more before he let go. The last was the best because, as she did, for the first time in her life she felt inside her the distinctive pulsing spasm of a man's intimate flesh, the sudden spiking heat, the sweet wash of seed.

"Roxanne," he groaned. "Roxanne."

The sound was better than any dream.

⇐∅⇒

She was drunk with pleasure in the aftermath, drunk and reckless. When he laid his head sweetly on her breast, she decided she had to know everything.

"Tell me about your family," she said.

If she hadn't been so attuned to him, she would have missed his momentary stiffening. He tried to cover it by kissing her shoulder. "I have four sisters, three brothers-in-law, and twelve nieces and nephews."

"I bet you're the eldest."

"Yes, I am. How did you guess?"

"Your air of stuffy responsibility gave you away."

He started back and stared at her. "My what! No, never mind. I heard you." He wagged his head. " 'Stuffy!' "

"It's not an insult. I think it's sexy."

"Oh, really? Why don't we see how sexy you think it is."

When he lowered his head to kiss her, she curled her hand agreeably behind his neck. Silence reigned except for the sound of mouths moving lingeringly against and into each other.

"Oh, I do like kissing you!" she exclaimed when they paused for breath.

Laughing, he lifted his hips to make himself comfortable. He was hard again.

"Are you close to your family?" she asked, forestalling another kiss.

He raised his brows at the delay. "I suppose I am. When I was little, I couldn't keep them out of my hair. I don't see them as much as I should now because I . . . work so much."

She bit her lip against the reserve that had entered his voice. "I just want to know something about you."

"I know." His hand caressed her waist. "Can we make love now? Please?"

"We-ell," she drawled, "since you're asking nicely."

He slipped into her so quickly she gasped.

Before she could catch her breath again, he rolled onto his back, taking her with him. His hands slid between them, first covering her breasts, then pushing her upright. His sex flexed inside her.

"You want me to ride you?" she asked, even though the message seemed clear.

He nodded, his eyes glittering up at her. *Well,* she thought. *How hard can it be?* Not overly so, apparently. He was easy enough to please. His jaw clenched against a moan as she began to rise, coming up on her knees and then sinking down. Soon she found a rhythm that seemed to suit. She liked the solidity of his hipbones between her inner thighs. The skin across them was velvety, and they cocked up nicely to meet her downstrokes. She hadn't known this would come so naturally, or maybe it came naturally because she was doing it with him.

"I'm getting close," he warned, his features tensing. "Let me touch you."

She couldn't keep from clutching him when he did. The involuntary tightening broke his restraint. Crying out harshly, his hips snapped off the mattress to magnify her thrusts. Dampened by their mingled perspiration, the sheets clung to his skin.

"Harder," he gasped. "Yes, yes. More."

The sleighbed creaked beneath the jouncing like an un-oiled hinge. She'd never heard anything as sexy as that rising chorus of squeaks and thumps, coming faster and more erratic until—

"Fuck!" he swore, stiffening in orgasm.

She stared in fascination as the spasm traveled up his body, bowing his back, his neck, pebbling his nipples, flushing across his sweating, straining face.

Beautiful, she thought, watching him bare his teeth and quiver.

"Don't you dare apologize," she ordered when he finally collapsed, limp and blinking sweat from his eyes.

He laughed weakly and moved his hands to help her finish.

⚬⚬⚬

Roxanne's side of the bed was empty.

"R-roxie," he growled, a sated, happy beast.

The sun was high behind her lace draperies. Yawning mightily, he scratched his chest and belly. Criminy, he felt good. He wasn't going to think about tomorrow. He was just going to enjoy today.

"Roxie!" he called, louder this time, scarcely caring if the boys heard. Despite last night's occasional awkwardness, it had been better than perfect; it had been real. He hadn't made a fool of himself, and he hadn't scared her away. Roxie inspired responses his occasional partners never had—crazy uninhibited desires.

Best of all, the sex was only going to get better. *He* was only going to get better.

His masculine gloating evaporated the moment he saw her hobbling back from the bathroom. "Oh, no. I hurt you."

She lowered herself into one of the chairs by the fire. "You had help. And it was worth it."

"Poor baby," he exclaimed, half concerned, half amused. Throwing off the covers, he crossed the soft expanse of carpet and put his head in her lap. Not much of a penance, really. He purred as she stroked his hair. Sweet little hoyden. Fresh from her bath, she wore a silk chemise the color of Medell limes. A lace-trimmed slit ran up it to her thigh. He'd never seen such lounging clothes as she wore; there was hardly anything to them! She must import them. They were definitely not Ohramese. As though magnetized, his hand followed the slit up to the place where some undergarment should have been. He stopped in shock. She was naked beneath the gown.

She laughed throatily at his surprise.

Lifting his head to watch, he was struck by an unexpected pain. Her curls blazed like fire in the lace-cut sun, vivid against the blue chair. She was shaking with laughter, her breasts, her shoulders, everything loose, everything warm.

In another world, she would have been perfect for him.

I'm afraid, he realized. He'd thought he could enjoy this diversion for as long as it lasted, that it could stay casual. But she was so beautiful and he . . . He could never . . . Not with her father being who he was. That twist of fate had changed a highly chancy proposition into one that was downright impossible. He'd have to give up everything to keep her, every single thing he had left. Unfortunately, even thinking about leaving made his eyes prick with tears. He had to swallow hard to keep them back.

She quieted abruptly. "What's wrong?"

He pulled her out of the chair and into a fierce embrace. "I like you so very much," he rasped into her hair.

Roxanne had learned a few things from observing her mother's affairs, one of them being that there weren't many reasons for a man to use that particular guilty-regretful tone. In fact, she could only conceive of one.

No, she thought.

Adrian Phelps was married.

Chapter 10

⤞⤝

It is said that *daimyo* are better at communicating messages with
energy, and *rohn* are more skilled at reading them. Some *rohn*
even claim to be able to decipher human auras. This has led to
the lamentable proliferation of Yamish fortune-tellers in Avvar's
slums. Though the existence of charlatans is undeniable, your
humble chronicler cannot dismiss the practice whole-cloth. As
one wise writer said, "Stranger things have passed through
Heaven and Earth than philosophers can dream of."

—*The True and Irreverent History of Avvar*

⤞⤝

No one could fault Roxie's or Adrian's determination to deny the truth. They had two more days of vigorous
and perhaps slightly desperate coupling before they bowed
to the inevitable. Adrian had recovered from his injuries.
More than recovered. It was time that he go home.

They took the front stairs to the street. Wide and white,

the steps circled down the front of the building in a graceful spiral. When they reached the bottom, Adrian looked up through the screw and saw an old brass lantern hanging from a chain. Spokes of rosy evening light angled in from the windows.

The doctor and his pretty golden wife leaned down from the second floor landing to wish him well. Adrian tried to forget he'd seen them making love. After they left, the silence deepened. Adrian and Roxie were alone.

He kissed her, a brief peck, and repeated his undoubtedly empty vow to call on her. Her eyes crinkled wryly, as if she were mocking the promise in her head. But perhaps she was mocking herself for her reluctance to let him go. Even if her reaction was warranted, he couldn't leave her with that expression. Folding his hands around her jaw, he kissed her slowly, savoring the taste of her, the warmth, the sound of her breathing when the kiss began to sink in. Soon he was running his palms across her shoulders and down her strong back, struggling against a craving to take her one last time in the shadow of the stairs.

Years with her wouldn't be enough to sate him.

When he forced himself to release her, she clung for a moment, then set herself back a step. He couldn't read her now; her guards were as effective as a demon's.

"Take care of yourself," she said.

He didn't trust himself to speak. She couldn't know how accustomed he was to doing just that. Instead, he smiled and touched her cheek before pushing through the door to the street.

It was his first sight of the wider world in six days, and a bit of a shock. He spared a glance for Roxanne's gallery, admiring the lettering on the window and the tidy pyramid of paint cans in the display. As if to remind him who he really was, his detective's eye caught on the figure of a tall, well-dressed man standing in a shadowed doorway across the street. A nob waiting for an assignation, he supposed. Since he didn't want to be seen lingering, even by other skulkers, Adrian walked quickly toward the nearest hansom post, a slight stiffness in his side his only souvenir of the last few days.

Well, that and the hot ache in his throat, like the beginning of a bad illness.

Given his somber mood, the timing of his departure was appropriate. Avvar at sunset always made him wistful, as if some forgotten city had been superimposed upon this one, as if he himself were the ghost of a long dead man. Everything he did, everything he felt had been known before. Maybe not the same way, but close enough to cause the ghost city to resonate with the real, its faded vibration hovering beneath the edge of sight.

Berating himself for his morbid fancies, he hailed a passing horse cab.

The nag was an old one, and the ride took longer than he expected. By the time he stepped down in front of the station, an unlovely soot-streaked hulk of pitted red pourstone, he was almost himself again.

Delaying entry a minute more, he stepped to the coffee vendor's neat wooden shack, open despite the hour. As he'd hoped, the usual Yamish woman was there.

"No coffee," she said in her soft, accented voice. "After sunset only tea."

It was a statement, not an apology, at least not that his human ears could hear. "Tea is good," Adrian said, "as long as it's hot."

He watched her brew it in her clever shiny machine, intrigued by her actions as never before. He was almost sorry when she handed him the steaming cup. Ironically, being in her company felt like a small connection to Roxanne.

Annoyed with himself for needing one, he gulped the tea where he stood and set the cup on her counter. She nodded as she drew it away to wash.

"You don't smile at me anymore," he said impulsively.

"*Rohn* don't smile," the vendor asserted.

"You used to, until the day you saw me walking with the Yamish doctor."

She met his gaze directly, doing nothing to obscure her

alien silver eyes. Their color was precisely the same as
Roxie's, though the *rohn*'s had neither Roxie's whites nor
her delicate gold rim. She didn't deny she knew the man he
meant, though whether she knew that he'd installed Adrian's
implants he couldn't guess.

"He *daimyo*," the vendor said at last. "Very bad man."

"Do you think I'm a bad man?" Adrian didn't know
why he was asking, only that he needed to.

The vendor cocked her head slightly. Adrian had left
his hands resting lightly on her wooden counter. Yama
didn't normally touch humans, but now she turned his
hands over and ran her thumbs across his wrists. An eerie
prickle jumped beneath the veins, as if his implants were
about to activate. He fought an urge to snatch away from
her hold.

"You human," she said with an infinitesimal shrug.
"Good. Bad. Up to you." She nodded decisively, though he
hadn't said anything. "You right. I not blame you for doctor. I smile at you again."

And she did, releasing his wrists and baring straight
white teeth many humans would have envied.

"Thank you," Adrian said, unsure what had happened.
"I'll . . . look forward to seeing you tomorrow."

"Good!" said the vendor with an odd, barking laugh.

Unnerved, but feeling as if he'd taken care of a piece of
business he hadn't known he had, he turned back to his station. The windows silvered as the sun sank into oblivion,
their panes mirror-blank. The only exceptions were the
lights shining through the glass on the top floor, where the
superintendent would be working late, plus the two narrow
lintel pieces beside the entrance, behind which the watch
desk sat.

The familiar sight dissolved the last of his inner strange-
ness. He couldn't count the times he'd rushed up these
stairs, buoyed by anticipation at returning to a job that
challenged him, that he did well.

Caught up in his relief, he didn't notice the slim blond
figure who climbed the front steps behind him, who paused

to read the brass plaques on the vestibule's duty roster, who jerked back at the sight of one particular name, then returned to the curb to collect a waiting cab.

⤚✺⤙

So this was how it felt to get blind-sided.

Roxanne had been stretching canvas in the studio when Charles rushed in to break the news. Heart-weary from hearing it, she slumped on her high work stool, head bowed, hands dangling between her knees. In the darkness outside, rain fell, the first downpour since the night she'd found Adrian. Like a storm of regret, it drummed on the roof and poured off the overwhelmed downspouts.

"At least he's not married," she said, pushing her fallen hair from her face.

"I have no idea whether he is or not. They don't put that on the door. 'Inspector Adrian Philips, married, two children.' "

She glowered at him. How could anyone that spiteful look angelic? "If you're so smart, why did you think he was a procurer?"

Charles shrugged and brushed an imaginary speck off his natty teal shirt. She'd made that shirt for him, every elegant pleat, every tidy stitch. Now she could have ripped it off his back and trampled it without a qualm.

She growled and flung herself off the stool to pace. The paint-spattered floorboards creaked beneath her tread. "I can't believe what a fool I made of myself. A policeman! No wonder he blushed every time I said 'boo.' "

Charles studied his well-kept nails. "The fact that you flaunted yourself at every opportunity may have had something to do with that."

"Oh, I see." She turned to poke his sternum. "Give a man a little encouragement, and suddenly I'm a tart."

"I didn't say that. I never even thought it."

Uncomforted, she covered her face. "Who am I fooling? I never thought I'd say this, but by God, I am my mother's daughter—much good as it did me."

"Stop it. There's plenty of men who'd be interested in you besides that one. Good riddance, I say. He didn't deserve you. That's all I meant. That's—"

To her astonishment, he gasped for breath and broke into tears. The outburst startled her from her gloom. She'd never, in all the time she'd known him, seen Charles cry. Frankly, this was the last thing she'd have guessed would set him off.

"Oh, Charlie," she crooned, pulling him stiff and resisting against her. "You were afraid, weren't you?"

"No, no, no," he said, but he went on crying anyway.

Ignoring his attempts to push her off, Roxanne stroked his fair silky head. He seemed so strong and self-possessed most of the time, she tended to forget he was still a boy—and a vulnerable boy at that.

"That's right," she said when his arms finally moved to hold her, awkwardly at first and then with a fierce strength. "Cry it out. I understand. But I'd never put you out. If somebody wants me, I don't care how handsome they are. They have to take you and Max, too."

Of course, there wasn't much chance of that being an issue in this instance. A policeman. She'd almost rather he were a thief. She wondered how she was going to face him now that she knew. As to that, she wondered if she'd have to face him at all.

"So, Adrian. Been slumming, have we?"

Superintendent Atkinson sat behind a glossy mahogany desk. He was a small man, no higher than Adrian's shoulder. Blessed with a noble brow and a pair of brilliant brown eyes, which—according to station rumor—rendered him irresistible to grieving widows, he was older than Adrian by a few years. To offset the retreat of his hairline, he'd cultivated an extravagant auburn mustache. He'd been Adrian's superior for a year now. Though the superintendent was gentle born and a more political creature than Adrian, they viewed the world with a kindred mixture of cynicism and compassion. Despite the formality required by their respective positions, they'd developed a rapport.

Of all the people in this station, he probably understood the ambition that drove Adrian the best.

"Sir?" Adrian responded, his collar tightening uncomfortably around his neck.

The superintendent smiled sardonically. He had a knack for making his men feel like errant schoolboys, even the veterans. "Hear you spent your vacation poking around Harborside. Not my idea of fun."

"It is my time," Adrian pointed out.

"Oh, quite." The superintendent creaked back in his chair and steepled his hands in front of his mouth. "And a laudable way to spend it. Picked up a few bruises, I see. On behalf of the Bainbridge boy?"

Adrian didn't bother to deny the assumption. Though his superior sat behind a desk, he did have eyes and ears on the street. Hopefully not too sharp.

"I know we don't have the personnel to handle missing children cases," Adrian said. "And you know I hate giving up before I've exhausted every avenue."

"Indeed, I do. You're my favorite terrier." Atkinson blew through his mustache. He looked tired. Adrian realized his acerbity might be due in part to wishing he could do more officially. His next words confirmed the guess. "Any leads?"

Adrian grimaced. "A nibble. He was seen alive two weeks ago."

"Did you notify his folks?"

"Not yet. I've got a doctor putting the word out at the local morgues. If nothing turns up there . . ."

"Yes. No use getting their hopes up for nothing."

"I did accomplish one thing. You know the shopkeeper whose car Tommy Bainbridge smashed before he ran off? I convinced him to drop his suit against the family."

"That must have taken some doing."

"Some. But he had left the vehicle unattended with the engine running. I suggested the Bainbridges might want to take *him* before the magistrate."

The superintendent's eyes sparkled. "Quick thinking.

Not to mention sly." Abruptly changing mood, he gnawed his upper lip and tapped the cracked green linoleum with his shoe. "Adrian."

"Yes, sir?"

"You're one of my best officers. More than that. You and I get on. Enough that I could make what could be construed as a personal observation without you taking offense."

Here it came. Had a street constable seen him in the window at Roxie's? With all that electrification, her place was a neighborhood landmark.

"Sir?" he said aloud.

Atkinson fingered his silk cravat, tucked smooth and neat into the V of his waistcoat. "According to your files, you haven't taken a holiday in two years, so I imagine you had a bit of steam to blow off. Lord knows, I'm not one to demand that my men inform me every time they take a piss. You're a senior officer, and I trust you."

"Is there a point here, sir?"

"I'm working up to it." His grin flashed beneath his mustache, but it was not entirely friendly. "The thing is—I want to make sure you're not in danger of going native on us."

"Sir?" He hoped the embarrassment heating his cheeks wasn't visible. Was that how his superior viewed a liaison with a woman like Roxie? As *going native?*

To his dismay, Atkinson spied the blush. "Lord, Adrian, you can be such a daisy. I'd have thought the time you spend policing those demons would have cured your maidenly ways."

Adrian forced a laugh, as his superior no doubt intended.

Atkinson's tone turned more expansive. "It's all right. I've had a few Harborside flings myself. Earthy girls, out there. Makes a nice change as long as you don't take them too seriously. A sharp man like you is bound to go places, maybe into this very chair. I'd hate to see anything catch you up short."

Adrian took this statement as an expression of concern, though it might as easily have been a threat. "I understand, sir. I assure you everything is under control."

"Good, good. Kept me up a few nights, you know, trying

to decide how to handle it. Upset the missus. Hate when that happens." As though it were a ward against further confidences, he yanked the chain of his banker's lamp off and on. As of six months ago, the station had been electrified. The plumbing, sadly, was as unpredictable as ever. "Everyone's entitled to go off the deep end now and then. Suppose you were due."

"I appreciate your tolerance, sir." Despite his respect for the superintendent, Adrian could barely get the words out. He felt disloyal in ways he couldn't explain. Roxanne wasn't a person anyone had to *tolerate*.

The fact that his superior was berating him and didn't even know the worst made him want to grind his teeth. *It shouldn't be this way,* he thought. *It shouldn't be.*

Atkinson stopped flicking the lamp. Something of Adrian's feelings must have shown in his face. "It doesn't matter if you liked her," he said. "Politics rule here. You know that."

"Yes, sir," Adrian conceded. "I know that well."

Chapter 11

From the earliest age, Yamish children learn the value of sub-
terfuge. An efficient network of spies has prevented more than
one untimely youthful death. When vast fortunes lie at stake
among the great families, not to mention powerful hereditary ti-
tles, how can it be otherwise? That Victoria herself was nearly
the victim of such a plot at the hands of her duplicitous cousin,
Mary, created a bond of sympathy between the human queen and
her new allies. Without this sense of kinship, who knows how
the future would have turned out?

—*The True and Irreverent History of Avvar*

Despite Adrian's claim that he had everything un-
der control, the next day found him sitting in his cramped
fourth-floor office, blinking sightlessly at backed-up pa-
perwork, his mind going in circles around all the things he
and Roxanne had done in bed. He remembered the places

her skin could change texture at the lightest touch, places that might have been beneath his fingers or lips, so clear was his memory.

Worse than the things they'd done were the things they had not.

Memories of her agile hands tormented him, her mouth, her tongue . . .

He wanted her all over him. He wanted her doing things he'd been too shy to ask for. Just thinking about the possibilities sent waves of heat prickling over him. He'd hung his jacket on the back of the door and rolled his shirtsleeves to his elbows. Even with that, his waistcoat felt unbearably confining.

It's just physical pleasure, he told himself, undoing a button. No more important than scratching an itch. She was a nice woman and very uninhibited, but it wasn't the end of the world. He'd get over leaving her behind.

His body begged to differ. That morning on the electric tram he'd caught two charwomen staring at his half-swollen crotch, the result of an imprudent erotic daydream. He'd covered himself with his coat, but the reaction still mortified. Short of binding himself in place, he didn't know how to prevent it from happening again.

He blew out his breath and rose. He couldn't think about anything but her. If he continued as he was, he'd go stark raving mad. A stroll to Bow Street was in order. Maybe a runner could discover something he had not.

A decade earlier, the Earl of Rutherford had established the Bow Street Runners to cure a screaming case of ennui. Since then, the private investigative firm had become a by-word among the upper classes for discreet surveillance of straying mistresses and wives, and for clearing up problems Securité's ill-paid employees couldn't always be trusted to keep quiet. More surprisingly perhaps, the Earl's independent breed of agents had earned a reputation for exemplary thoroughness.

Adrian believed they'd have no trouble digging up answers to questions he hadn't been prepared to press Roxie on before. He'd have to find a way to ask that didn't give the game away, but he wanted to know if there was positive proof that Herrington was her father. If so, perhaps the other aspect of her unsuitability—her irregular single lifestyle— was not as bad as it seemed. Maybe the runner would find evidence of especially good citizenship, or the endorsement of someone important in the artistic world. Geniuses, if Roxie was considered one, were expected to lead eccentric lives.

Adrian suspected he was grasping at straws—anything to justify the risk of seeing her again. He couldn't help it. He didn't want the last six days to have been nothing more than a memorable interlude.

⤙⤚

One week after engaging him, Adrian met the private investigator in a seedy, signless pub a dozen blocks from the station.

The floor stuck to his shoes when he stepped inside, despite the sawdust some earnest soul had spread across the floor. Considering the place's ground-in patina of filth, the absence of Yamish patrons came as no surprise. The runner was a pale, sharp-faced man with teeth like a rat. He slouched in a booth in the back corner, one long boot propped on the bench and one long hand dipping a salted chip in his beer. Adrian didn't think he knew he was meeting a policeman, but his grin betrayed his enjoyment at having someone like him for a client.

The upper classes accepted the runners as a necessary evil. Less secure in their superiority, Adrian's peers tended to turn up their noses.

Ignoring the supposed threat to his status, Adrian took the seat opposite the agent, gestured for the tired-looking, pregnant waitress, and ordered corn beef and slaw sandwiches for them both. He wasn't hungry, but he didn't want to lose the ground Charles's cooking had gained him. Surprised by the courtesy—which a toff would have omitted— the runner recovered quickly enough to tell the waitress to put another pint on the tab.

"This one's flat," he said, winking with red-rimmed eyes.

By mutual consent, they held off talking while they ate. The sandwich was good. Adrian was amazed at how easily he got it down. Not finicky himself, the runner wiped his mouth on his sleeve, elbowed his plate aside, and tossed a thick vellum file onto the table.

"Got a good bit o' stuff," he said with professional pride. "Nothing for sure on who fathered her yet. That opera singer, La Belle Yvonne, must have had a dozen lovers in the same month. Kept a bloomin' harem. Not picky, neither. Gossip columns had her doin' the dirty with—as they put it—*very* foreign types."

"A list of possibilities will be sufficient," Adrian said, holding out his hand. "I can rule them in or out on my own."

"Your call," the runner said indifferently, though he seemed disappointed he wasn't going to be paid to pursue this salacious trail to its end. "Why don't I give you an overview o' the rest."

The "rest" was impressive, considering the brief time the runner had been on the case. Most of it was material Adrian knew already or had guessed: Yvonne's profligacy, the lack of proper oversight for the young Roxanne, two inquiries on her behalf by the Children's Ministry—both dismissed. The later of the two had resulted in Roxanne being taken into the Ministry's care, though she'd been released shortly thereafter. He wondered if Yvonne had bribed someone or asked one of her high-born admirers to intervene.

For Roxie's sake, he hoped the dismissals meant Yvonne had wanted her daughter, not that there hadn't been enough evidence to warrant fostering her out. Even giving the Great One the benefit of the doubt, the sheer weight of detail staggered him. He hadn't expected quite so many examples of moral turpitude.

The thing that really rocked him, however, that made him regret every tangy, dripping bite he'd eaten, was discovering how Roxanne had earned the money for her gallery.

"She was a pornographer?" he asked, too shocked to hide his dismay.

"Please." The runner swigged ale and foam. "An erotic artiste. Top drawer, too. Toffs snapped her up like nobody's business. Her early stuff's worth a bundle now that she's switched to drawin' room fair. Here, I scraped these up for you, but don't bend 'em. They're on loan."

He removed a stack of wax-coated cards from his folder. Adrian shuffled through them. Double the size of playing cards, the pictures were not the worst he'd seen but definitely more graphic than her popular *Scenes from History* series.

One in particular burned itself on his retinas. Two men faced each other across the body of a naked woman. Seeming to writhe on the satin sheets, the woman clutched her breast with one hand, while the other tweaked the swollen bud between her legs. The engraving was so fine, Adrian could distinguish the folds of the tiny hood.

The strangest aspect of the picture was that the men seemed oblivious to the lush little voluptuary. They'd reached across her body to fondle each other's genitals, their touch hesitant, their expressions that of horrified fascination. The gloss of high sexual arousal could be seen on each rampant phallus, one of which was long and arched, the other thick and uncircumcised. The details were so individual, and the emotion so sensitively rendered, it was hard to believe this encounter had not occurred, and that Roxie had not witnessed it.

Had she witnessed it? Or had this peculiar scene sprung from her imagination, fleshed out by her knowledge of human nature and the courage to expose it? Whatever the answer, the tableau made his blood rush more heavily in his veins. Nothing was forbidden to her. *Nothing*.

"Classy, huh?" The runner sounded genuinely admiring. "Wonder how she got the models to do that in front of her."

"You don't know that they did," he snapped.

The runner squinted at him. "You interested in this filly?"

Adrian rolled his eyes.

"Hey, no skin off my nose," said the runner. "Bloke's got a right to fancy what he pleases."

"I appreciate the sentiment, but I assure you it's un-called for."

The runner raised his hands in surrender. "Sure, I understand. None o' my concern. Say, before I forget, she had two kids livin' with her. Don't think they were hers. You want me to dig up somethin' on them?"

Adrian hesitated a moment, tempted, then shook his head. Even if he weren't low on funds, the boys' origins weren't his concern.

"All it takes is time," assured the man. "I can get more on her, too, if you like."

"I don't want anymore," he said.

The runner took this for the dismissal it was. He downed the rest of his beer in a single swallow and stood. "Nice doin' business with ya, guv. Call me anytime."

Then he left Adrian to his thoughts.

"Of all the luck," he muttered, propping his head over the remains of his meal. Even without Roxie's connection to Herrington, this material was enough to brand her untouchable.

He had, however, promised to call on her again. He was going to have to break off with her. Formally. Finally. In unmistakable terms. He supposed he could avoid her altogether, but that seemed cowardly—and far less than Roxie deserved. Better he should do it in person. He could take her to a nice restaurant, tell her how much the time they'd spent together meant to him, how he respected and admired her and loved the way her breath caught in her throat just before she—But it wasn't going to work out. He was very sorry, but their lives would never, ever fit together.

Sighing deeply, Adrian called for another beer.

Chapter 12

⤐

When surveying human art, simply opening oneself to the experience is not advised. Far preferable is focusing on the measurable qualities of the piece. Ask yourself how it compares to similar works. Is it well executed? From what traditions might it spring? In this manner, much embarrassment may be avoided.

—*The Emperor's Book of Etiquette*

⤐

Adrian dreamed of Roxie, just as he had every night since leaving her home: hot, tangled scenes of kissing her bare skin, of sliding into her body's slick, tight hold, of stroking endlessly without release.

"Stay," she'd plead in the dream, her arms hugging him close. "Stay inside me and never leave. I love the feel of you moving. I want to come and come all night long."

Her words seemed to take control of him, making it

impossible to do anything but what she asked, no matter how his body strove for release.

"I need to spend," he'd beg as the mural above her bed came alive, the figures sliding from the ceiling onto the wall. Big as life, though still two-dimensional, Adam straddled the headboard. His cock was hard, but no harder than Adrian's. Eve knelt before it, winked coyly at Adrian, then sucked the tip into her mouth.

When her head began to bob on the reddened shaft, the painted Adam groaned as if he'd die with bliss.

Adrian wanted to groan himself, especially when Adam tensed and then exploded.

"I need to spend," he repeated, his hips working desperately.

"No," Roxanne refused. Her long legs slid tormentingly along his, swelling him even further within her hold. "I'd have to paint you first, and that would take much too long."

He shuddered awake before his dream self could argue. His face was smashed against the pillow, his erection flattened between his belly and the sheets. He'd held off pleasuring himself the previous nights, feeling as if giving in would only make matters worse. This time, he couldn't help himself, grinding his hips against the mattress until his climax broke in a hot, white blaze. Even that wasn't enough to let him sleep. Stiffening again moments later, he rolled onto his back and fisted himself to a second wrenching release.

Then he felt better, though his groin still pulsed ominously. Evidently, a dream of Roxie was more exciting than most women in the flesh.

~⇒~

Considering the frustrations of the previous night, Adrian's morning was not cheery. Too restless to stare at the walls of his bachelor quarters, he spent most of Saturday inquiring after Tommy Bainbridge.

The back of his neck tightened as he walked the alleys where Charles's friends had sighted the runaway, but on this day, Harborside tolerated his presence. Rewarded it, as well. Two older boys, sons of a local pieman, swore they'd seen someone who looked like Tommy sneaking into the back of a peat wagon. Adrian hadn't located the peat man yet, but he did discover a cellar where the boy had spent at least one night with a stack of old newspapers for a pillow. "Ancient City Found Under Boral Lake" screamed the top headline. Obligingly enough, Tommy had left a chalk drawing of a motorcar on the damp basement wall. Whatever his circumstances, the boy was still car mad.

That lead run to ground, Sunday found him trudging up the gravel road to his parents' home in Carpenter's End.

Rough gray stone walled the house of Adrian's youth, two stories high except for the tower Isaac had added to stop his wife from declaring she never had an inch of her own. A set of wooden stairs, painted misty heather to complement the wisteria, zigzagged up the outer wall to the open cupola on top. On summer nights when they were children, he and his sisters would creep past their parents' bedroom to the roof, where they'd survey their kingdom through their father's spyglass. The Philipses owned eight quiet acres with an orchard in the back, a nice slice of country.

He remembered the shock of moving from the city. He'd been twelve. His father had just been appointed master carpenter to a nearby shipyard. *Slumrats,* the children at the village school had called them, mocking their clothes, their accents, the food their mother packed for luncheon. More than one hayseed earned a bloody nose for teasing Adrian's sisters. For his own defense, he chose a different course. Let them taunt as they pleased; he'd show their supposed superiority for the lie it was. He resolved to be better spoken, better educated, and more dignified in every way.

Looking back, he knew his marriage to Christine was an outgrowth of that resolve. The daughter of threadbare gentry, her parents had abhorred the idea of a civil servant for a son-in-law. Nonetheless, seeing how firmly Christine's affections were fixed, and knowing three daughters remained to settle after her, they'd lent their reluctant blessing to the match.

Ironically, when the marriage fell apart, their daughter bore the brunt of their disapproval. To their minds, her duty was to obey her husband, whoever he might be, especially when it came to begetting grandchildren. Gentlebred women had suffered this yoke for centuries. Who was she to complain?

If Adrian hadn't taken pity and released her from her vows, his wife would be suffering still.

Of course, if he hadn't decided to gain promotion by accepting his implants, their marriage might not have crumbled so thoroughly. Christine had never gotten over her belief that the demons had tainted him. At the end, she'd confessed that every time he kissed her, she'd feared his tongue would be forked.

Disturbed by the memory, he scrubbed the back of his neck. He hadn't been home in a year, not since the welcome feast for his sister Julie's last baby. Each missed event, each excuse, increased his reluctance to drag himself down the fieldstone path.

He managed, though, and found his mother stuffing grape leaves on the kitchen table—enough to feed an army. Chagrined, he recalled her habit of inviting his sisters' families for Sunday dinner. He knuckled the furrow between his brows. He didn't think he was ready to see them all.

Because Varya hadn't noticed his arrival, he took a moment to get his bearings. The big, old kitchen with its ruffled chintz and its scratched oak table reminded him of Roxanne's house, a place to put your feet up. He suspected his mother would like Roxie, if only because she was a woman of relatively few words and would let Varya jabber to her heart's content.

Not that Varya was going to meet her. Adrian frowned at the reminder, and it was with that dour expression on his face that his mother turned and saw him.

"Adrian!" Leaping out of her chair, she gave him a tight but handless hug, her fingers sticky from her work.

As he bent to return the embrace, he noticed how gray her hair had gotten in the past year, how thin the braid that hung to her waist. She was still beautiful. *Slim as a girl,* his father liked to say. Adrian tried to guess what he'd have said about Roxie if they'd stayed together as long. *Still full of fire,* he thought, then shook the imagining off. Fancies like that would do him no good.

"Oh, my." His mother set him back from her and wiped quick tears from her sun-browned cheeks. "What perfect timing. Pull up a chair and help me with these."

Happy for the distraction, Adrian complied, grabbing a heap of marinated grape leaves and a dish of barley-olive stuffing, the recipe for which Varya's family guarded jealously. In spite of himself, he wondered if Charles would be able to decipher its ingredients.

"I'm glad you came today," she said. Her work-roughened hands moved nimbly at their task. She hadn't worked at the cannery for twenty years, but she still had the calluses and the speed. "I've been all aflutter with no one to talk to except your father, and he's no help about things like this. Little Beth's rejected another suitor. Sometimes I think we ought to post a sign out front: 'Beware the Heartbreaker.' Much as I love Elizabeth, I don't know what they're crazy about. She's not nearly as nice as Alice was, nor as pretty as Marianne. And as I recall, Marianne didn't have a third of her beaus."

"Well, er, Beth's got a nice little figure," Adrian suggested, more because his mother seemed to expect a response than because he wanted to discuss his youngest sister's attractive powers.

"Hmph. As for that, Julie's is better, even after three babies. And Gaspar was the only one who ever called on her. Not that I've got anything against Gaspar, mind you. He's done well by her, the restaurant and all and so good with the children, but it mystifies me why they drop like flies for Beth. Why, she's downright rude to some of her beaus."

Adrian lost his grip on a grape leaf and had to start again. His mother had tucked up six tidy green cylinders in the time it took him to finish one sloppy one.

"She's got spirit," he said distractedly. "Those boys probably think she's a wildcat."

"Adrian!"

"Well, it's true. Beth's got a lot of life in her. Sometimes that appeals to a man."

His mother hummed noncommittally, then peered at him. "Adrian, you have the strangest look on your face. Have you met someone?"

"Not exactly," he mumbled.

"What does 'not exactly' mean?"

"It means it's not exactly working out."

"But you'd like it to, wouldn't you?" She clapped her sticky hands in delight. "How marvelous! It's been ages since you were serious about anyone. Not since, well, you know who. I know you can make it work if you really put your mind to it."

"Mother, please. She's not appropriate."

Without even looking, he could see his mother tilt her head.

" 'Not appropriate.' What does that mean?"

"It means what it means." He strove to keep his temper. He'd come here to forget Roxanne, not to get raked over the coals. "Can't we just drop it?"

"But if she makes you happy . . ."

"Happy!" he scoffed.

"So that's the way the wind blows." Varya nodded sagely. "Makes you miserable, I'll bet."

"I wouldn't go that f—"

"Yes, I can see it in your face. You've got circles under those pretty gray eyes." He flinched as she brushed a gentle knuckle across one mark. "Probably haven't been sleeping much or eating right, from the looks of you. You know I hate when you don't take care of yourself. Maybe you should stay with us a while. Rest. Let us feed you up. Your grandfather hasn't had a decent fishing partner since Jack Crowley died."

"Mother."

"Is she pretty?" she burbled on, clasping her hands in front of her narrow chest. "No, I'll bet she wouldn't be. Christine was pretty, and you wouldn't make that mistake again. I'll bet she's got spirit, though, just like Beth. I'll bet you think she's a wildcat—Oh!" His mother gasped.

"You've . . . you've already been intimate with her, haven't you?"

"Can't you be quiet for one minute!" he exclaimed, coming out of his chair and spilling all five of his badly stuffed grape leaves onto the floor.

His mother's face crumpled, quavered, and then she was crying into her apron, horrid tearing sobs that simultaneously annoyed and wrenched him.

"Damnation," he cursed, watching her for a second before coming around the table and taking her into a loose embrace. "I'm sorry. That was rude of me. No, stop crying. I'm sorry, really. I didn't mean to yell at you. But nothing's going to happen between me and this woman. It simply wouldn't work out."

His mother finally calmed, using her apron to wipe away the last of what he sincerely hoped weren't crocodile tears. With Varya, you could never tell. Giving her the benefit of the doubt, he patted her still-trembling shoulder. She squeezed his hand to show she'd recovered.

"Oh, Adrian," she lamented, her eyes still glistening— gray, stormy eyes she shared with her son. They were sharp now for all their emotion. "Sometimes I think we shouldn't have encouraged you to be such a gentleman. But your father and I wanted you to have more than we did, to be better."

"Mother, I have never in my life been ashamed of either of you."

His mother smiled. "I know, son, but maybe you've been ashamed of yourself. You make your life a good deal harder than it has to be."

He grabbed a dishcloth from the sink and began picking barley stuffing off the floor. "I'm sure I don't know what you mean."

"When you went after that promotion . . ."

He knew she was referring to his implants. He stopped cleaning up the mess. "I've never been ashamed of that," he said, wanting once and for all to be clear. "Accepting Yamish technology may have made my life more difficult, but it made me better at my job. I can handle situations other officers can't, and I do it without resorting to deadly force. I'm sworn to protect demons, too, Mama. I take that oath seriously."

The back of his eyes burned with how much he meant what he said. More to the point, he knew he'd felt this way long before he'd met Roxanne. Unexpectedly, he was proud of himself, no matter what anyone else thought.

"I suppose you do take it seriously," his mother said, the words coming slower with her surprise. "I guess I always thought part of your choice had to do with wanting to be set apart. You always were a solitary boy."

"The family changeling," he said with a laugh to defuse the tension. "But you must know I don't wish I were different."

His mother sighed a rare surrender. "Very well, I'll stop lecturing. I'm glad you came to visit. You're my firstborn, you know. I miss you when you stay away."

"I'm sorry, Mama," he said, quite sincerely. He looked up from his crouch and made a melodramatically sorrowful face.

As he'd hoped, she laughed and waved away his foolishness. "No need to be sorry. I understand better than you think."

〜

Roxanne's father had implied he'd leave her alone. Roxie hadn't counted on his restraint lasting forever, but she hadn't expected his patience to run out this soon.

A card arrived by messenger: an open invitation to view the Boral Lake find, an archaeological treasure Herrington and his team had unearthed last year. At present, it was displayed in his ballroom and accessible to a select and probably undiscerning few. Unless you had a title, human or otherwise, you weren't welcome to intrude. Roxanne had resigned herself to making do with sketches in the rags. The chance to see the find in person, possibly even touch the ancient objects, made her heart beat faster.

Coming from anyone else, the invitation would have thrilled her. Even those who disliked the Yama thought

Herrington's methods of excavation were praiseworthy. He was committed to preserving both the treasures and the context in which they were found—a result, she supposed, of having to distance himself from the emotions his discoveries could stir. The artifacts, a jumble of statues and third-century housewares, were reported to be in excellent condition. Returning a firm, barely civil refusal inspired a terrible pang of regret. She knew, however, that she couldn't afford to show weakness.

If she ceded Herrington a finger, the "Red Fox" was bound to claim an arm.

Chapter 13

Who among us is free? Only those who see their chains know what freedom means.

—Welland Herrington, *A Memoir*

Charles clattered down the front stairs, his body taut with a strong but unspecified anxiety. He should have been looking forward to delivering this message. Who did that bastard think he was, letting Roxie believe his intentions were serious? Even if Adrian Philips hadn't meant to hurt her, he'd hardly done her good. Roxie hadn't been herself since she met him, but had grown increasingly distant and preoccupied. Charles had no trouble deciding where to lay the blame for that.

Rallying his anger, he allowed his nemesis to yank the chime once again before opening the door. The man's expression on finding only him behind it was priceless.

The bastard nodded stiffly. "Charles."

Rather than reply, Charles examined the man's dove-gray, short-tailed dinner suit. The cut of his waistcoat was conservative but classic, his half-boots shone with a recent blacking, and, to his credit, he had forgone the affectation of top hat and gloves. On a man of his class, they would have been ridiculous. The ensemble's fit proclaimed its fine tailoring, as did the greatcoat he'd slung on top.

Likely, these were the only custom clothes he owned. Charles tried to sneer, but it took more effort than he liked. Philips, damn him, looked sympathetically scrubbed and earnest.

"Is she—?" Philips began.

"She ain't."

"Pardon?"

"She ain't . . . She's not coming."

The razor nick on the man's Adam's apple bobbed. "Oh, well, I suppose I could—" He broke off and rubbed his forehead as if it pained him. Moving backward, he took one reluctant step down the front stairs, then another. At the bottom he gripped the flowery wrought-iron railing and frowned at his shiny shoes.

"I have reservations at Astoria House," he said, a combination of enticement and rebuke.

Astoria House! Charles's heart rate spiked. A person could wait six months to get a table at the Astoria, assuming he had the wherewithal to eat there in the first place.

"Well, we wouldn't want those to go to waste."

Roxie's voice brought them both around. She swayed down the last white treads in a curve-hugging, sunshine yellow gown. Its short, swirling train floated just above the ground, revealing a pair of twinkling satin slippers. Flashing a too-bright smile, she tugged a matching pair of gloves up to her elbows. Her breasts jiggled within the low, heart-shaped neckline. The air thickened in Charles's lungs. He'd never seen her look so feminine. Where was the woman who swore she couldn't face the lying scoundrel, who begged him to make an excuse for her?

"It's all right," she said, reading the judgment in his face. "I changed my mind."

Philips's brow furrowed. "Does that mean you're coming?"

"I look like I'm coming, don't I?"

"You look beautiful," he declared. It was harder to hate him than it should have been, especially when Roxie pinkened at his praise.

Hopeless, Charles thought with a mixture of pride for her courage and exasperation at her stupidity. He should have known she couldn't stay away.

⸻

Roxie had spent much of her childhood eating at fancy hotels with her mother, but the Astoria still had the power to charm. It was housed in an old pre-demon mansion near the shore. Entrepreneur Gaspar Ilario had restored the building to its original glory, restricting all modernization to the kitchen. True to period, the huge crystal-rope chandeliers held candles rather than gas. The scent of beeswax layered one more pleasure into the savory atmosphere.

With a nudge, Adrian drew her attention to the arcs of glass that enclosed the entry's atrium on either side. Tropical fish fluttered inside, bright as island flowers. *Astounding.* But how could Adrian afford to take her here? Surely he wasn't a felonious policeman?

"Ah—er, sir, welcome," said the maître d'.

Roxie realized Adrian must have signaled the man not to call him "Inspector." *Good reflexes,* she thought, then: *Goodness, he eats here often enough to be recognized by the staff.*

However he managed the expense, Adrian hadn't made himself unwelcome. The maître d's smile appeared genuine. He took Adrian's coat just long enough to hand it to a waiting girl. Roxie's wrap and gloves followed, and then they were ushered into the main dining room.

Her heels struck cypress floors so old they were almost black. They'd been sanded flat and polished to a glossy shine. Like islands in a placid sea, Ka'arkish rugs lay across the wood, patterned with elaborate indigo- and rust-colored curlicues. Each island supported a white-draped table on which heavy silver plates twinkled. Though full, the place was hushed, as though its perfection awed even the toffs.

"Here we are, sir, madam." The maître d' nodded at a uniformed waiter to pull out their chairs. Their table was more private than most, because it sat in a half-circle of windows overlooking the beach. Now twilight, the sand was empty of all but gulls.

"Is anything wrong?" Adrian asked once they were settled. "You were awfully quiet on the drive over."

She smoothed the soft yellow folds of her skirt. Her hands shook at the prospect of confronting him with his lie, but she managed a steady tone. "I was wondering how a policeman could afford to bring me here."

A stunned silence followed her statement. He pushed his water glass an inch farther from his plate. "But how—?"

"Charles followed you back to the station. He read your name on a plaque outside the door. 'Inspector Adrian Philips.' Impressive. Most men your age would still be sergeants."

"I meant to tell you." His assertion was earnest but not entirely convincing.

"I'm sure you did."

"It's complicated."

"Yes." She let all her scorn imbue the word, all her pride. Adrian winced.

"We probably shouldn't see each other after this," he said in a breathless rush, his expression pleading. "My job . . ."

She simmered under the insult but did not raise her voice. "I understand. In your position, a woman like myself could only be a liability. An illegitimate bawdy artist. A half-demon."

"Those aren't the only reasons."

"Oh, lovely." The heat in her face began to pulse. "What else is wrong with me?"

"Not with you," he said quietly. "Never with you."

The gravity in his voice encouraged her to meet his eyes. To her surprise, their expression was sorrowful.

"I've been enhanced," he said.

She didn't understand him. The term was foreign to her experience. "Enhanced?"

He rubbed his wrist, a habitual gesture that made her think he might have broken it long ago. His next words set her shockingly straight.

"I have implants: advanced Yamish technology. If I activate them, they increase my strength. I got them as part of an experimental program to enable humans to police the *rohn* more effectively. Without them, I would have little choice except to use a weapon on any demon I needed to subdue."

For a moment, all Roxie could do was blink. He had these instruments inside him. He'd let a demon cut him open and put them in. Lord, he must have been dedicated—and ambitious—to allow that!

When she recovered her powers of speech, she reached instinctively for his right hand. "You have them here? In your wrist?"

Light though it was, her touch made his fingers twitch, a quick, sensual reaction both pretended not to notice. Adrian cleared his throat. "In both wrists, actually."

"You know," Roxie said, fighting not to clench her hand as she drew it back, "when I confessed I was half-demon—not an easy decision, by the by—that might have been an appropriate occasion to mention this."

"I would have had to explain why I had them."

"Yes, you would."

"I wasn't certain I could—"

"Trust me?" She cut him off bitterly. "When I'd just told you my bloody damn secret?"

He sucked in a breath as if preparing to argue, then shook his head. "You're right," he said. "You're right. I have nothing to say in my own defense. I didn't tell you because I didn't *want* to be a policeman with you. I wanted to be a man."

His face had colored at the confession, but he leaned

forward and pressed on. "These devices—I agreed to get them to help me in my job and advance my career. They've accomplished both those goals . . ." He toyed with his silver knife.

"But?" she prompted.

"But the people who know I have them look at me differently, as if in some small way I've gone over to the other side. My position isn't as secure as it could be. If I were to show other evidence of untrustworthy behavior . . ."

"Like keeping company with me."

"Yes," he confirmed reluctantly. "Keeping company with you wouldn't help. I assure you this is not my own position. I know you'd never do anything to compromise a case. Sadly, my personal belief in your integrity is unlikely to sway my superiors."

Roxanne pressed her lips together and nodded. A return of her earlier anger would have been welcome now, but she knew what it was like to fear going hungry, to scrounge for any work you could find. She didn't want Adrian to have to face that. Of course, she also couldn't help feeling disappointed that he wouldn't risk everything to be with her.

Twit, she thought. *Why would any man want to do that?*

To her relief, her disillusionment didn't show in her face.

"I must say," Adrian remarked, "you're taking this calmly."

"Why wouldn't I?" She shook out her blossom-folded napkin and laid it across her lap. At the least, she could save her pride. "We had a nice time. Now it's over."

He stared at her. He looked both startled and hurt. "Right. Well, nothing to say we can't enjoy our last meal together?"

"Right," she agreed, coaxing the leather-bound wine list from his side of the table. "I suppose I can order what I like? Since you've gone to the trouble of choosing such a nice place to cast me off."

He laughed. She hadn't meant to make him laugh. The warmth of the sound annoyed her.

"Please, feel free to impoverish me. It's the least I can

do to make up for misleading you." He smiled as warmly as he'd laughed, looking just as fond of her as he could be. A cruel illusion, Roxanne thought. "This place belongs to my brother-in-law. I coordinate security for private events. In return, he stands me the occasional meal."

"I see." The discovery that he was at least professionally honest pleased her—too much, no doubt. "But then, you're related to Gaspar Ilario. Oh, Adrian!" Before she could stop herself, she'd clasped his smooth gray sleeve. "Do you think you could put in a word for Charles, see if they need an extra chopper person in the kitchen, even someone to clear tables? He's very responsible, and I know he'd love the chance to get his foot in the door at a place like this."

"I'm sure I could do that." His eyes crinkled as he shared her excitement. It didn't seem to occur to him that some women would ask this favor as a parting bribe.

Careful, she cautioned herself. She was giving this man's good opinion too much weight. This was good-bye. It was time to stop caring what he thought. All the same, her mother's blood rebelled at the idea of letting him go without a whimper. Roxanne had the power to make him regret his choice, even if she couldn't make him change it.

Giving her bodice a surreptitious downward tug, she leaned forward, then propped her elbow on the table and her chin on her hand. As she'd intended, his eyes strayed toward her overflowing décolletage. She had powdered her bosom tonight, not to obscure her freckles—she'd never been self-conscious on that score—but to highlight her curves with tiny sparkles. Bound by nothing more than her shift, her breasts swelled into the low neckline.

Was he wondering how far the glitter went? Beneath the edge of her gown? To her navel? To the warm, soft folds between her legs?

She remembered how he'd liked to pet her there, even after they'd been sated. The two weeks she'd spent without his touch sharpened her frustration. She didn't just ache for him, she itched to feel his hot, smooth rod pistoning against those neglected nerves, over and over, thick and strong, until they both exploded with relief.

Her longing must have shown in her face. He tugged at his trousers. The tablecloth hid his hand, but she knew from the way he lifted and settled that he was equally uncomfortable. She ducked her head to hide her smile. She was getting to him. *Just wait,* she promised as the waiter came back to take their order.

She made a production of every bite, leaning forward at the slightest excuse, touching the back of his hand to make a point, cradling her glass against her bosom to warm the wine. By the time the final course arrived, he sat rigid in his chair, nervously rubbing his wrist as if it hurt. She was willing to bet his wrist wasn't what he really wished he was rubbing.

In the gentle light of the candles, sweat dotted his upper lip.

"Are you hot?" she cooed when he blotted it with his napkin.

He glared at her. "You know I am. What's more, you know why."

"Do I?" They had returned to her earliest days of teasing him, with all their heady and flattering enjoyment. Slipping off one satin shoe, she stretched her stockinged foot beneath the table and lifted it onto his chair. He must have spread his legs to ease the discomfort of his erection. The ball of her foot hit its ridge dead on. Immediately, he grabbed her ankle.

"Are you mad?" he demanded. Though his grip was iron, she noticed he wasn't shoving her away.

"Why don't you scoot your chair farther in," she purred, "under the tablecloth." She curled her toes and kneaded him like a cat. His cock was as big as she had ever felt it, not to mention delectably bone-hard.

He'd been flushed already, but now a fresh tide of red flowed up from the points of his crisp white collar. One of his fingers absently stroked her heel. "I'm not leaving here with the front of my trousers damp."

"Tut-tut. I thought you had more control. You certainly practiced it often enough with me. I remember how you'd go on and on some nights as if to prove how many times you could make me spend. Was twelve the limit, or fifteen? Of course, I could pretend to drop my fork and crawl under the table. That would save anyone getting wet but me."

Pleased by the way his brows shot up, she licked her lips. Obviously, no one had played this sort of game with him before. When she leaned closer, he did, too, mesmerized by the fantasy she was painting.

"I'd unbutton you, love," she murmured, "button by straining button. I wouldn't take you out straightaway, though. First I'd kiss you through your underclothes, breathe on you until the linen was wet enough to cling. You do have a lovely shape when you're hard. I'm sure I'd have to admire it. Then I'd edge my tongue under the placket and lick whatever I could reach. The base first, I think, and maybe I'd mouth your balls. Would you help me reach them if I couldn't? Would you slip your hand under the table and cup yourself toward my mouth?"

A strangled cough was her only answer. The hand that held her foot had tightened like a vise, and the sweat from his palm dampened her stocking. Whether he knew it or not, he was pulling her foot into his crotch. His erection felt as thick as a constable's baton. Its pulse beat a hard tattoo beneath her arch.

"It would please me if you helped," she whispered, showing no mercy. "Especially if you wanted to ease the head between my lips. We've never done that, have we? But you'd like it if I sucked you. A woman's mouth is soft and warm. She can curl her tongue around a man's tenderest parts. Do you think you'd be able to feel my tastebuds rubbing your skin? I know I'd like to taste you, like to feel you shooting off in my mouth with all these strangers watching. You'd have to be very, very quiet, though. You'd have to—"

"Stop," he croaked, pushing her foot abruptly down his thigh. "You'll push me over the edge just listening."

The waiter chose then to show up.

"Would sir or madam like dessert?" he asked obliviously.

"Madam would," Roxie teased, sending Adrian a wicked wink.

The waiter's appearance didn't disperse the sensual cloud, though it did thin it. Roxie was content to let that be. She'd given Adrian enough to think about for now. They were relaxing over spiced Nitalian coffee when a shadow fell across their table. Roxie's shoulders tensed.

A short, portly man had stepped up to their table. He stood like a schoolmaster, his thumbs crooked into the pockets of his wine-red waistcoat. His liquid eyes fixed solemnly on her dinner partner's face. Adrian half rose from his chair.

"Philips," said the intruder.

"Atkinson." Adrian resumed his seat. His face was guarded but calm. *Resigned,* Roxie thought.

As though he sensed her concern, he met her gaze across the table, a thousand sweet candles shining in his eyes. He smiled, a wry crooking of one corner of his mouth. Whoever their visitor was, his presence did not bode well for Adrian. Her hand inched across the white linen, but before she could betray him with a touch, his arm waved smoothly in introduction.

"Sir, this is my friend—"

The man cut him short. "I'm familiar with Miss McAllister's identity."

His disparaging manner changed Adrian's.

"How fortunate for you," Adrian responded coolly. His knuckles had whitened on the table's edge in a mute and probably unconscious threat. Roxanne had never seen him like this. His reined-in anger was formidable.

The man named Atkinson took a step back before recovering. "I trust I don't need to reiterate my sentiments regarding this situation."

"I would not advise it," Adrian agreed, his eyes as cold as Ka'arkish steel.

His antagonist met the hard look with one of his own, blew dismissively through his mustache, and turned on his heel. Ten feet farther on, a woman slid her arm through his. Slim, young, and quite expensively dressed, she was not, to Roxie's expert eye, his wife.

The moment he was out of earshot, she leaned across her dessert plate. "Who was that?"

Adrian grimaced. "My superintendent."

"Oh, Adrian." She covered her mouth. Gratified as she was by his defense, she didn't want to cost him his job. "Maybe you should go after him."

He shook his head.

"But if he knew you weren't planning to see me again . . ."

"No." He tossed his napkin to the side of his plate, the motion like the period at the end of a long debate.

She knew he wouldn't discuss the matter further.

Chapter 14

⧼⧽

"Save me! Save me!" Princess Hyacinth cried, her soft pink bosom heaving with distress.

The demon peered coolly down at her, his pale eyes glowing like chips of ice in the murky dark. His long demon hands were pincers on her wrists. "No one can save you," he said . . . or perhaps promised. "I have slain your prince. Even now, he lies bleeding in yon alley."

—*The Perils of the Princess,*
as serialized in the *Illustrated Times*

⧼⧽

Adrian escorted Roxie home despite her insistence that she could manage on her own. After the way Atkinson had treated her, he wasn't about to forego this courtesy.

"Nonsense," he said, two fingers summoning the nearest cab. A shiny black affair rattled over, with a loudly buzzing engine in front and an old-fashioned six-seater coach in back. "It's common politeness to see a lady home."

"But you just broke off with me."

"Nonetheless."

He handed her up, gave their direction to the grizzled cabbie, then climbed into the swaying carriage himself. The black leather interior smelled pleasantly of pipe smoke and leaves. Roxanne sat kitty-corner from him on the opposite banquette. Silhouetted against the black in her fancy yellow dress, she looked a picture of elegance. Aloof. Unconquered. He still hadn't shaken off the web she'd spun at dinner.

A woman's mouth is soft and warm . . . I know I'd like to taste you.

She couldn't have known she'd resurrected his oldest fantasy, the one he'd stroke himself to late at night, the one he'd never dared ask any lover to enact. Roxanne spoke as if it were a treat. Excitement pumped through his veins at the thought of her enjoying the experience with him: *her*, not some shadow figure, but a woman he lusted after and— truth be told—respected. Under the double prod, his sex began to lift.

He wished he had the freedom to accept her challenge. Too bad tonight's fiasco with Atkinson proved how poorly Adrian exercised discretion. He'd had to take her to Astoria House, hadn't he? Because he couldn't resist showing off. He'd thought the only risk was being spotted by his brother-in-law—a slim one, given the demands of Gaspar's duties. Instead, they'd run into the one person he could least afford to see.

And Atkinson had belittled Roxie. That he regretted most of all.

Roxie deserved better. She was a talented artist, an independent, warm-hearted woman. Much as he admired Atkinson, Adrian knew his family connections had helped him get where he was. Adrian doubted the superintendent would have made as much of himself in Roxie's shoes. *It's a backward world,* he thought, *when befriending someone like Roxie is considered anything less than a privilege.*

As they traded seaside for city, she faded in and out of darkness with the passing street lamps. Adrian watched her, helpless not to, savoring her full pink lips, the glitter of her golden lashes, her wonderful freckles like a sprinkling of paprika in a bowl of cream. He'd missed her face. He hadn't known how much until he saw her gliding down the stairs in that hourglass dress. She was so lovely. Could this truly be the last time he'd see her?

He sighed. The sound broke her stillness. Sacrificing propriety for comfort, she swung her legs onto the seat next to him and crossed her arms beneath her wrap.

"I know rank hath its privileges," she said, "but why is your superior entitled to squire whomever he pleases to the Astoria? And don't tell me that woman was his wife. Or does adultery not matter as long as she's a well-born woman of low morals? A widow, maybe." She tossed her head. "That always seems to put the Queen's seal on things."

Recalling his own occasional dalliance with the type, Adrian shifted on the seat. "That woman was his wife's sister, I believe."

Roxie snorted. "Well, that's convenient. Keep it all in the family."

"It could be perfectly innocent."

"I'm sure." She resettled the wrap around her shoulders and cut him a speculative look. "You know, Adrian, if you weren't so principled, you could write your ticket with that man."

"You don't really mean that."

Her lips pursed in tandem with her shrug. "Don't I?"

The question disturbed him. It suggested she'd compromised a few morals herself along the way and didn't care tuppence what he thought of it. "Roxanne—"

"No, no." Her hair stirred in the breeze her gloved hand raised by waving. "You're right. What's a scruple worth if you heave it overboard at the first sign of bad weather?"

He squeezed her knee to get her attention. "You are not unscrupulous. You've done what you had to in order to live. I'm certain you don't truly want me to blackmail Atkinson."

She rolled her eyes at him, then shoved the door open as the carriage ground to a halt in front of her building. "Oh, look. Here we are."

Too stubborn to drop the argument, he climbed out after her, shoved a few notes at the driver, and let the man rattle off.

Roxie tipped her head at the disappearing cab. "You're losing your ride."

Her heels were planted like stakes on the herringbone brick of the pavement—a less than welcoming pose.

"I'm not leaving until we settle this," he said.

"Fine. I'm not unscrupulous, or a bad woman, or any of the other awful traits your hypocritical employer would like to ascribe to me. There." She spread her arms on either side of her lightly bustled hips. "Now you can go."

He scrubbed his hair in exasperation. He didn't want to go. He knew he ought to. She had him so tied in knots, he couldn't take a step in any direction without tripping. "I was hoping you'd invite me in," he said, though he knew it wasn't wise. "Just for tonight."

"Why not?" she said, clearly meaning the opposite. "The damage is done, running into your superintendent and all. Might as well collect what you're sure to be asked to pay for. *Just for tonight.* Why should I mind that you handed me my walking papers? A good time is a good time, right?"

"I thought we could talk."

"Talk!" She closed the distance between them with three quick steps, her heels striking the bricks like flint. "Talk," she repeated, in a different, softer voice. Her gloves slid behind his neck, the cotton smooth and warm. She leaned closer. Her lips brushed his ear. He shivered, despite the wave of heat crawling up his thighs. "Talk like we did at the restaurant?"

He was hard as stone, so hard his cock seemed like a separate entity.

"Maybe," he whispered.

Roxie backed off a few inches and wagged her gloved finger. "But you don't know how to play that game, do you? So I don't see how it could be worth my while." She tilted her head to the side, her eyes hooded as she appeared to consider his prospects. In spite of everything, excitement jumped inside him as her gaze lingered on the bulge pushing out the front of his trousers. "But perhaps you believe you could bring yourself up to snuff?"

He caught his breath in indignation.

"Is that a 'no'?" she asked with brittle flippancy. "Fine, then. It's been nice knowing you, Inspector Philips."

She spun away, but he grabbed her arm.

"Don't do this," he said to the back of her neck, unable to miss her trembling. "Don't let it end this way."

"How would you like it to end? With one last meaningful fuck? At least if I hate you—" her breath hitched in her throat "—I'll get over you sooner."

"Oh, sweetheart." With a wrench to his emotions, he realized she was crying. Before she could stop him, he bundled her up the stairs and into the vestibule, dimly lit by the ship's lantern four floors above their heads. She beat weakly at his shoulders as she cried, her head burrowing into the crook of his neck while he stroked her through her wrap and murmured meaningless endearments.

"I'm sorry, Roxie." He kissed the crisp, orange-scented waves of her hair. "Atkinson isn't fit to lick your boots. Neither am I."

She laughed damply into his neck, a small sign of life. "Don't go overboard. You don't know everything there is to know about me."

His heart melted with relief as her arms came shyly around his back. "I am a professional investigator. I might know more about you than you think."

"Goodness, that makes me feel better." She took the handkerchief he offered and blew into it. When she finished, he teased a single, tiny eyelash off her tear-stained cheek. The tip of her nose was red. The sight stirred a devastating tenderness, worse than when his little sisters had laid their heartbreaks on his knee.

You're in trouble, he thought. *You should leave before it's too late.* He ignored the warning. Instead, he pressed his lips to the heated skin of her temple.

She squirmed in his arms and stretched, a delicious readjustment of their fit. "Adrian?"

"Mmn?" He kissed her eyebrow, then ran the tip of his tongue around the strong curve of bone beneath.

"Do you still want to come up?"

He pulled back slightly, his heart abruptly pounding. "Do you want me to?"

When she bit her lower lip, he wanted to bite it, too.

"What if I promise to make it worth your while?" he said coaxingly.

She blushed. "I didn't really mean that about you not knowing how to play the game. You're very good in bed."

"That doesn't mean I know everything."

Easing his heavy coat aside, she smoothed his lapels. Sensation blossomed at her touch, ripples of tingling pleasure. His sudden breath lifted her hands. "Nobody knows everything. The trick is not to be afraid."

He smiled at the top of her lowered head. "Ah, so that's the trick."

"Absolutely." His stomach tightened as her touch slid lower. "You need to be with someone you care about. To know they want you. To know they trust you, and that you'd never do anything to hurt them." She released the single button of his dress jacket. "It makes you dare anything." Her thumbs converged beneath his waistcoat, meeting at his navel, precariously close to the straining jut of his erection. "You do things you wouldn't do with anyone else."

"Really?" He stilled her hands so he could think straight. Her eyes lifted, their color ghostly in the muted light. "So, the things you were talking about at dinner, you've never actually done them?"

"As long as we trust each other, what does it matter?"

His gaze traced the teasing curve of her smile. He could hardly express how arousing he found the possibility. To be the first man she shared that intimacy with made him ache with desire.

"I trust you, Roxie," he said hoarsely. "I'm pretty sure you want me. And I probably care about you more than is good for either of us."

Her smile deepened at his ragged tone. "Is this leading up to something?"

"Are you up for a little game?"

Her eyes glittered with sudden wistfulness. "One last game?"

"I'm sorry. I wish I could offer more."

Her sigh was silent, a movement of her chest against his.

"You're right," she finally whispered. "We shouldn't end this with a fight."

~

They walked upstairs like sweethearts, fingers laced, arms swinging. Her eyes fed on the sight of him beside her, storing it away. He was the one who saw the ungainly brown-paper package sitting by the door.

Roxie read the card while Adrian carefully unstuck the wrappings.

A small token of my esteem—yr F, it said in bold black script.

Her "F" indeed. She cursed Herrington for reminding her of his existence.

"It's a rosebush," Adrian said, examining the potted stick. "At least according to the label. It claims it's going to be a Coral Ghost."

Herrington was a fox alright. A bouquet she could have trashed without a qualm, but a living rose, a gardener like her had no choice but to nurture.

Adrian looked up from his crouch. "Who sent it?"

"A secret admirer," she growled. The shadow of alarm that crossed his face was almost worth her father's intrusion.

They stowed the plant in a warm corner, stuck their heads in the boys' room to ensure all was well, then crept down the back stairs. They took turns in the bathroom, the tension rising with each completed task. By the time Roxie finished freshening up, a small, hot fruit seemed to have taken up residence between her legs. She needed it seen to immediately.

She found Adrian lounging like a pasha on her bed, majestically naked, his back supported by a stack of snowy pillows. He'd pulled the shades. All the electric lights were on. The fire crackled merrily. Bright. Warm. Safe. The perfect atmosphere for lovers' games. Needing no encouragement beyond anticipation, his cock thrust high and straight from the nest of hair at his groin. Her blood pulsed at the inspiring spectacle. He'd missed her, to be sure.

From the coverlet beside his hip he lifted her long yellow gloves. "Take off that shift. I don't want you wearing anything but these."

She blinked. Adrian didn't sound like himself, even accounting for the edge two weeks of stored-up arousal must have honed. He wasn't asking. He was ordering.

"Has the game started?" She slipped one muslin strap off her shoulder, then the other.

He didn't answer, just watched as she peeled herself bare for him. She wore the white eyelet nightgown she'd had on when they first met. She wasn't sure why she chose it. It was her oldest, not her prettiest. His cock bobbed in approval as she shimmied the cloth past her hips. Her skin heated at the silent compliment. She kicked the shift away.

"Come here," he said, holding out the gloves. Again, she was struck by the authority in his voice. Did he think this would be his last chance to live out his fantasies? If so, it seemed he did not intend to waste the opportunity.

She pulled on the gloves, determined to give him what he asked. In this case, obedience held a wealth of power.

"Do you like it?" She skimmed the daffodil-colored gloves down her naked sides.

"I'll tell you what I'd like." The words were nearly inaudible. "I'd like you to make me ready with your mouth."

She smiled at his erection, its girth grown large, its head vibrating with the force of the blood pounding beneath. She'd started something at dinner. Now he wanted her to finish it. "You look ready to me."

"Don't question me." The soft reprimand stung like a velvet lash. Her knees weakened unexpectedly. "I asked you to do as I said. Now, up on the bed on your hands and knees. No, the other way. I want to see how much you like what you're doing. I want to watch the juice drip down from your little quim."

Hiding a grin, she moved as enticingly as possible into position. Adrian talked dirty just fine once he got warmed up.

"Good," he praised. "Now arch your back."

He slid his hands up the back of her thighs and onto her haunches. His thumbs parted her lips, dipping into the inner folds, sliding past the edges of her gate until they reached the apex of her sex. He didn't touch her clitoris, merely stretched the skin on either side. The swollen flesh throbbed in the cooler air, impossibly sensitized. He lifted his head until his breath warmed her.

"You look very beautiful." His words thrummed through her like a touch.

"Thank you," she gasped, her bottom squirming under his fingers.

He sank back onto the mound of pillows. "You may take me in your mouth. Be careful, though. I don't want to come yet. Just prepare me."

She raised one eyebrow at his quivering crown, already shining with pre-ejaculatory moisture. Considering she'd never done this, not pushing him over the edge could prove a trick. Yes, she'd grown familiar with his reactions, but he looked close to going off right now.

Then again, nothing ventured . . .

Propping her forearms on either side of his hips, she gave the head a delicate, experimental lick. His hands tightened spasmodically on her rear.

"In your mouth," he ordered with what sounded like the last of his breath.

Well, if he thought he could stand it, who was she to question him? Carefully, as though he were breakable, she took the rounded cap within the soft warm clasp of her mouth.

They both sighed as she enveloped him. His skin was so sleek here, so hot. Steadying his shaft with one gloved hand, she drew more of him into her mouth, pillowing him with her tongue, tugging at him with the gentlest possible suction. Sweetness tinged her mouth as fluid squeezed slowly from his slit. His thighs shook against her inner arms. She lightened her touch even more, circling him with her tongue, dragging slowly up the pulsing column before bearing lazily down again.

She'd never done anything this intimate in her life. She could hardly believe how exciting it was. Every twitch communicated directly from his sex to hers. And he was watching it happen.

A minute passed in dips and sways. His tremors increased. Tears of desire collected between her legs, flowing over his fingers, which smoothed them into her skin. His legs tightened until they seemed nothing but muscle. She began to find her rhythm, sighed with it, breathed with it. Her mouth grew hot, as though the sun were shining inside. Adrian swelled to seemingly impossible lengths. Groaning like the tug off Pargit Sound, he pulled her off him.

"Enough." He kissed her tender bud as she trembled over him, gentle kisses that teased much more than they satisfied. She wanted to grind herself against his mouth. Her resolution to give him precisely what he asked was all that prevented her.

She knew he wanted to drive them both crazy.

Finally, when she was a hairbreadth from begging for mercy, he turned her around and kissed her mouth. His tongue pressed inside in a single aggressive thrust, mingling the taste of their desire. She hummed with pleasure. His kiss was water in the desert. He let her drink her fill, his arms holding her so close she could barely move. When they both started moaning, he broke free.

"Still up for playing, or have you had enough of this game?"

She tossed her head so her hair spilled down her shoulders. "Oh, no, I haven't had nearly enough of this game."

"Very well, then. Let's continue."

In a move that would have done a village fair's wrestler proud, he rolled her beneath him, kneed her thighs apart and, with a single probing swivel to mark his target, pressed

himself directly home. Hungry as her body was, it offered
no resistance, just melted and stretched to accommodate
his greatly swollen length. Pleased, she locked her ankles
in the small of his back. She could stand anything as long
as she had him inside her.

A fond smile warmed his face as he smoothed the curls
off her forehead. Gone was the furrow of worry between
his brows, gone the scarlike marks of tension at the corners
of his mouth. He looked ten years younger than the man
she'd found bleeding in her garden. *I'm good for him,* she
thought, tears pricking the back of her eyes. *How can he
give me up?*

"What's next?" she prompted, refusing to succumb to
melancholy.

"Next, we lock ourselves together, here." He punctuated
the instruction with a sharp inward jab of his hips. "As
tight and as deep"—with a low grunt, he pushed a fraction
farther—"as we can. And we stay that way."

"We don't move?"

Mischief lit his eyes at her pout. He shook his head.
"Anything else you can move, or touch, or kiss, but not
your sex."

"What if it moves by itself?" she suggested slyly, coaxing a little ripple from the muscles of her sheath. His cock
bucked in response.

"That's allowed," he gasped.

"How do I win?"

He chuckled. "In this game, everybody wins."

~⊱~

Adrian had stacked the deck against himself by telling her
to wear the gloves. The fine cotton barrier transformed her
touch, transformed her. He'd been enthralled ever since he
saw her tug them to her elbows at the start of the evening.
Those gloves radiated gentility and elegance. She stood
like a different woman when she wore them, moved like a
different woman—a woman she had always been, but now
he saw her clearly.

Imbued with her magic, the gloves sleeked his hair

around his skull. The gloves conveyed the heat of her hands to the back of his neck, to his shoulder blades, to the taut, sweaty spaces between his fingers. Even in their concealment, they revealed secrets.

They told him she loved the long, lean muscle of his thigh, that she cherished the cage of bone about his heart, that the wrinkled sac that held his seed both amused and intrigued her. The finely stitched seam caught briefly on his flesh as she reached around his legs to set him swaying.

The gloves hid her. And freed her. He could tell she knew what they did to him. She ran them up his chest and crossed them loosely behind his neck.

"Kiss," she demanded with an irresistible pucker.

He bent to her.

What a shame this night had to end.

Pushing tomorrow from his mind, he trailed his fingers up the delicate underside of her arm, dipping beneath the glove to reach the crease of her elbow. She shivered, and her breasts plumped with a quick inhalation. He ignored the temptation to wander back to familiar ground. This time, this last time, he would explore her mysteries, her hidden vulnerabilities. Perhaps he would find them not so different from his own.

She'd been nibbling on the tendons of his neck. She gasped out loud when he reached behind his back to tickle the soles of her feet.

He remembered the effect this had on him when she did this during his bath.

"Like that?" he teased, repeating the motion. Her thighs twitched against his waist, and a flow of honey bathed his shaft.

If that weren't reassurance enough, her head thrashed on the pillow. "I'm certain that isn't fair."

"No?" Still massaging her arch, he resettled his supporting hand and pushed with his hips, lodging his sex so deep her slippery bud of pleasure flattened against its root. Her sheath tightened dramatically, milking him with tiny flickers of pre-orgasmic motion. He gritted his teeth. She was almost there. If he held on a little longer, he'd have the victory he wanted.

She growled low in her throat. With neat ferocity, she used her strong white teeth to tug off the gloves, first the left hand, then the right. The sight frayed his control. Off came the veneer of civilization. What remained was a creature of passion. As if she'd been waiting all night to touch him, she slapped her now-bare hands onto his back.

Vowing not to be bested, he blew lightly in her ear.

"Don't make me play dirty," she warned.

"Play as dirty as you like." He laughed, then shivered when she dragged her fingertips along his spine, down and down, skidding through the sweat at the small of his back. Her palms spread over the curve of his buttocks. Then she gripped him so hard she almost rocked him off his knees.

"My, what a nice little arse you have." She kneaded its muscles with the strength of an expert masseuse. "So firm and round. Like an apple. Makes a woman want to take a bite."

The way her eyebrows wagged made him laugh. "Any time, love."

She licked her lips.

When she finally released him, his cheeks were tingling. She wasn't done yet, though. Her hands snaked between them to touch the circle of their joining.

He jumped. "Cheater."

"You said I could touch anything as long as I didn't move my sex."

Her fingers brushed back and forth at the base of his penis, first the knuckles, then the pads. He realized she was painting them with the cream his game had called from her body. He groaned at the knowledge, as close to coming and as needful of it as he'd ever been.

"I want to ask a favor," she said seductively.

"Anything," he swore, which made her smile.

He was on his forearms, and she turned her head to kiss his wrist, her tongue flicking his tendons in a way that stirred a dark, uneasy delight. He'd experienced the same prickling leap when the Yamish coffee vendor touched him there, only this time the sensation twined inextricably with desire. He feared her request before it came out.

"I want you to activate your implants."

"Roxanne." The protest would have been more convincing if his body hadn't surged with excitement. "Those devices aren't toys. I could hurt you."

"Could," she said. "But won't. You'll simply have to hold back even harder than you are now." When she licked his wrist again, he shuddered. "It's our last time, Adrian. I want us both to be part-demon."

He moaned as if she were torturing him. In truth, she was: torturing him with temptation.

"I'm strong, too," she whispered. "If I had to, I could fight you off."

"Would you like that?" he whispered back.

"Maybe. Maybe I want to fight you as much as I want to make love."

The confession decided him. He keyed the implants before he could change his mind.

Immediately, a kind of madness swept his body. Sensations overwhelmed him, a hunger no one was going to stop him from indulging. Every scrap of caution was forgotten in his driving need for release. He drew his hips back and began to thrust into her hard. She met him blow for blow, wildly, joyfully, crying out as she crested.

Again and again she peaked, too many times to count, with beautiful guttural sounds he wished he had the presence of mind to memorize.

They rolled in the bed until she was on top. She rode him even harder than he had her. The force of each descent felt incredibly wonderful.

"Come," she urged, her body gripping him wet and tight.

But he couldn't. It was like his dream of the night before. He wanted, he craved, he rose to a screaming pitch of arousal, but the unnatural strength the implants were pouring through his system wouldn't let the climax break. It seemed they couldn't allow him that weakness.

Almost dying with frustration, his body arched beneath

her, lifting her at the hips. Veins stood out in his neck like threads of fire.

"Come," she ordered, her hands squeezing his shoulders.

And then he did. Heat lashed through him, fireworks, soft explosions of red. The hardest orgasm of his life roared through his cock. He was helpless to do anything but ride the pleasure. Drowning in it, his muscles locked in an exquisite rictus of release. Oceans of relief seemed to pour from him.

Despite this prodigious climax, the final quivers hadn't faded before he felt compelled to turn her under him and start again. He was insane with his need to work himself inside her, coming a second time with a teeth-baring growl.

"Yes," she gasped as he hitched her bottom higher and went on. "Oh, God, keep going."

He wasn't certain he could have stopped. Luckily, the fourth time finished him, leaving him drained enough to collapse. The implants had reached their limit. He was as weak as if he'd been in a fight, though a good bit more relaxed.

"My," she murmured, laughing softly in surprise. "I'm not certain how one judges these things, but I'd wager to say you won."

He had strength enough to smile against the silky pillow of her breast. Betraying no inclination to shift him off, she stroked his sweat-dampened hair.

For all the ecstasy that had preceded it, that was the sweetest moment of all.

Chapter 15

⤚⤙

The forbidden will always attract. This doesn't mean we should comport ourselves in the manner of beasts. Yama must not forget they are the higher race.

—*The Emperor's Book of Etiquette*

⤚⤙

Roxie fell into the sleep of the sated and dreamed of Bhamjran, the city where she first experienced the lure of the sensual. She had been fifteen. Until then, sex was simply an annoying activity in which her mother engaged, too often and with too many unlikable men.

But one afternoon in Bhamjran she slipped away from Yvonne's entourage, away from the theater and the pink, palm-shaded hotel. Free of adult constraint, she strolled the market quarter, soaking in the desert city's sun and dust, inhaling the coffee fumes that hung like incense over the sidewalk cafés. Businesswomen in bright silk raiment jostled her as she threaded through the crowds, huge baskets and platters balanced on their heads. When the trumpets of the temple sounded noon, they stopped in their tracks, closed their almond eyes, and murmured a prayer of thanks for being alive. Thousands of women jangled thousands of bracelets as they clapped their hands in unison.

These are women, she remembered thinking, *who answer to no one but their god.* She wanted their independence for herself, not to be less a woman, but to claim the right to be more.

For three-tenths of a silver denar, a turbaned man with a long gray mustache admitted her to an establishment called the Ladies' Lotus. Standing with the others in the perfumed shadows beyond the stage, she watched a nubile young man, not much older than herself, disrobe to the music of a sitar. When not a scrap of cloth remained, he manipulated his sex to climax for the quietly appreciative throng.

He was the first demon she'd seen naked: a *rohn,* to judge by his clipped hair, though no less beautiful for that. He was probably the servant of a traveling merchant, earning his master extra coins with this unusual erotic display. After all, no matter what a culture's prohibitions against mingling with outsiders, business always found a way to be done. As for young people like the dancer, they'd always enjoy breaking the rules.

As he performed, she saw that his body functioned as humans' did, seeming to have the same basic parts. The main difference appeared to be the pale perfection of his skin. Given how fascinated she was, especially compared to the more experienced locals, he couldn't help but notice her staring.

One hour later, she sat in the demon youth's stuffy room, immortalizing his naked glory in her sketchpad. The more intently she examined him, the more aroused he became. His sex was curved, dark against his marble whiteness, as though he'd stained it with berries.

"Make love to me," he'd said in his silky foreign voice. "I am adept at pleasuring human women."

She'd been tempted, but even then she knew he meant to feed from her energy when she came. The thought frightened her. As Yvonne's bastard daughter, she was already far enough beyond the social pale. If anyone found out . . .

"I am too young," she'd said to his blandishments.

His manners were gentle enough that she feared no coercion—certainly less than she would have with human boys. "As you wish," he'd said. "But please allow me to stroke myself in front of you. Being in your presence excites me greatly. My body requires release."

Given her upbringing, Roxanne had heard the sounds of sex before, even caught snippets of the act, but this was the first time anyone had brought themselves to completion for her personal enjoyment.

The effort it had taken him to climax reminded her of Adrian. The dancer had hung on the edge, tense and straining, for long minutes. She'd found the experience riveting, dangerous in any city but the one that had dedicated itself to "civilized sensuality." The memory had haunted her fantasies for years. Now, in a way, she had lived it out. The irony was, Adrian's Yamish implants rendered him more, not less attractive to her.

When she drifted back to wakefulness, the fire had burned down to a ripple behind its brass screen. The bedroom wasn't cold, only damp. A fog had swept in from the harbor while they slept.

Adrian breathed quietly beside her. She studied his sleeping profile in the firelight, marking the bladelike grace of his nose, the finely cut line of his lips. She tried to see him with her artist's eye, but dispassion eluded her. She could not view him as an appealing array of shapes and shadows, the way she'd viewed the Yamish dancing boy. Adrian was more than a handsome male animal. Adrian had emotions she could understand. He was the man who'd kissed her tears away, who built paper boats for Max, who shared her excitement about helping Charles achieve his dream. He was the man she loved.

The realization came as no surprise. Like a shipwreck, she'd seen the rocks from the start. Her only consolation was that their separation had made him unhappy, too. She knew it wouldn't be fair to ask him to choose between his career and her, but if they both cared enough, wouldn't they find a way to surmount the obstacles between them?

She might be no saint, but surely she deserved happiness?

Her mother would have said that if she had to ask, she wasn't sure enough. Yvonne had never asked, merely demanded. She got her way more often than most. When she didn't, she never concluded she was undeserving. The world was against her, that was all, too stupid to fully appreciate the honor she did them by existing.

I could take a page from that book, Roxie thought, then wondered if the world would let her. Troubled by her thoughts, she turned on her side and snuggled closer to Adrian.

⌁

He came awake in an instant. "Your nose is cold," he said, and she covered the offending protrusion with her hand.

"Sorry. You could kiss it and warm it up."

He turned to do it with a smile, happier than he'd been in ages . . . happier and sadder. He'd forgotten how comfortable her bed was, how her house—with all its refurbished finery—wrapped a person in contentment.

"Adrian?" Her finger drew a circle through his chest hair, just skirting his nipple.

"Mm-hm?"

"Will your superintendent really fire you?"

The concern in her voice touched him. "Honestly, I'm not sure. Officers who are willing to do what I've done are in short supply."

"You mean they don't want implants?"

"They don't want to work Harborside at all. They'd rather leave that distasteful duty to the lower ranks. Atkinson might have to keep me on—though I doubt he'll forgive me for defying him to his face. At the least, I can forget about promotion any time soon."

Her sigh warmed his collarbone. "I didn't mean to get you in trouble."

"You didn't. That's just the politics of my job."

"I wish it weren't."

He hugged her closer, breathing her warm woman's scent into his lungs. "I wish that, too."

In the street outside, a constable called an *All's Well*. With a start, Adrian recognized Farsi Ross's voice. They'd worked together on cases in the past. He hoped Ross wasn't the informer who'd reported his whereabouts. The Silver Islander had been one of few who treated him normally. He'd hate to think he'd lost that friendship, too. Whether Atkinson fired him or not, Adrian needed allies at the station. Without them, he seriously doubted he could do his job.

It would be a shame if he had to forfeit the only activity for which he'd never had to apologize. Adrian loved his family, but he knew he'd drawn away from them more than they liked. He'd loved his former wife, and what had he given her but misery? Working for Securité had been his sole undiluted success. Maybe, as his mother said, he gave too much of himself to it, but who would he be if he stopped being an inspector? The fact that the option even crossed his mind showed how close he was to falling for Roxie—if he hadn't fallen already.

Her head shifted under his chin. "Did you ever find that boy you were looking for?"

"Not yet. But I found a peat man who unwittingly gave him a ride. It seems Tommy stowed away under his tarp."

"To where?"

His hand rode the curve of her waist. "Somewhere between here and Downingdale."

"That's a long stretch of coast."

"Yes, but it's mostly villages. Someone ought to remember a strange, smelly boy turning up out of the blue." Unless he'd found shelter right away, in which case Adrian hoped it was nothing more sinister than a farmer needing an extra hand. From what his folks had said, Tommy Bainbridge was sturdy. He liked to climb trees, play alley ball. "I've given his description to the mail carriers up that way. If they hear anything, they'll pass the word."

He'd also told Tommy's mother that her son was, so far as he knew, still alive. She'd been a tangle of emotions, embracing him one moment, sobbing on his shoulder the next. Why was Tommy still running? she'd demanded. Didn't he know he could come home anytime? Did he want to make them lose their minds with worry?

Adrian had stood in that threadbare kitchen with the woman weeping on his coat and tried to see the room as the boy would have. Decent but dull, it had a teakettle warming on the pipestove, cheap curtains, and knickknacks: same as he'd find in working-class homes across the city. When Adrian was little, his mother had owned the same china pattern, white with pink roses, too heavy to crack with anything short of a sledgehammer. Young Tommy had too much imagination and too much youthful energy to feel completely at ease in a house like that.

Instinct told him Tommy would turn toward home when he was ready, and not a moment sooner. The boy had his own agenda. The problem was, fate might not keep him safe long enough to fulfill it.

"I'll tell you one thing, Roxie, I wish I knew what that boy was about."

Humming sympathetically, she insinuated her feet between his calves. He grinned in spite of his worries. Her toes were as cold as her nose.

"If you think it would help, I could make copies of that picture you had," she offered, her pleasure at having such a convenient foot warmer evident in her voice. "You could send it over by messenger if you didn't want to, you know, be seen here again."

"That would be helpful," he said, struggling to treat the subject casually.

None of his family members had ever wanted to discuss his professional life. In a way, Roxanne's interest, and his gratitude for it, justified the superintendent's concern. It wasn't impossible to imagine this woman becoming more important to him than the rules.

Roxanne sensed his thoughts were troubled when the lines returned to his face. "Kiss me," she said, wanting them gone. "The night isn't over yet."

He hardened with gratifying swiftness, his erection strafing her inner thigh. "Just a kiss?"

"Everything," she said. "Give me everything."

Their limbs wound together eagerly, determined not to waste a moment they had left.

"Let me, sweetheart," he said, rolling her beneath him. "I can go deeper when I'm on top."

She hadn't the slightest desire to argue. Deep was precisely where she wanted him to be.

He groaned as he sank inside her. "Lift your knees for me. Yes, like that. Oh, God, you feel so good."

He thrust gently, smoothly, advancing and retreating.

"Don't stop," she said.

"I won't," he promised, kissing her. "I can't."

"Harder," she pleaded, her hands sliding down his back.

"You aren't sore?"

She shook her head and clutched his hips. "I want to know you were there. I want to feel you in me for weeks."

"Oh, God," he said, and closed his eyes tightly. His control was gone then, and so was hers. Banishing restraint, their bodies pounded together. Hard and wet slipped through soft and wet. Sweaty flesh slapped straining muscle. Moans fought with choked instructions.

"There," she said when he touched her sweetest spot. "Yes, you can go faster."

He cursed at this answer to a question he hadn't even known he asked, but his body took her permission with a vengeance. The bed creaked in its hair-fitted joints as they thumped together. Bhamjrishi beds weren't supposed to creak, but this one was, sounding as if any minute it would split apart. Roxie couldn't regret it, secretly relishing every squeal. They raced toward their mutual end as though it could be snatched away. The sensations inspired by their frantic motions were so strong, she thought the tension must break soon. She didn't want it to. She wanted to hang here forever.

He began to say her name differently, his voice holding a new awareness, a new longing. "Please, Roxanne," he said as her body let him deeper. "Yes, yes, oh, *Roxanne.*"

She held him close, hearing his pain, helpless to soothe it. And then she knew.

She wasn't the only one who'd lost her heart.

"Say it," she encouraged, releasing him long enough to cup his need-flushed cheek. His desperate thrusting slowed. "Tell me how you feel."

She watched the blood ebb precipitously from his face, his skin chilling beneath her hand. He set his jaw. She couldn't doubt he knew what she meant.

"Do it, Adrian." She circled him persuasively with her hips. "Say the words."

His breath caught, then rushed back out as he pushed his steely hardness into her. "I can't. I want to, but I can't."

She crossed her ankles just beneath his buttocks. "It won't hurt."

"It might."

"It might make you feel better."

He moaned as she tightened her legs. "I don't have the right."

"I'm giving it to you."

"I can't," he cried, pushing so deep his tip seemed to breach her womb. He throbbed inside her violently. "Roxanne."

"Then I'll say it. Adrian, I love—"

"No." He covered her mouth with one stiff hand, his hips snapping forward as though sensual oblivion could avert the disaster. Instead, he unraveled completely.

"Oh-h, God, I *do* love you," he groaned, then almost disengaged in dismay.

They stared at each other: he regretful, she bitterly amused. Quite obviously, her victory was not the miracle cure she'd been hoping for.

"I'm sorry." His hand drew an oddly comforting circle on her hip. He'd come to a halt half in, half out of her body. Oblivious to his emotional reservations, his cock shuddered rhythmically. "Should I stop?"

"No." She pressed closer. "Let's give each other what we can."

He sighed at that, sighed and swore at the sweetness of moving again.

They were both too close to hold off climax. The peak came quickly, an acute but mournful pleasure. When it was over, he stayed inside her as long as he could, turning his cheek back and forth against her hair, the way Max did when he needed reassurance. Roxanne rubbed his shoulders until he fell asleep but didn't whisper that she loved him. Though the words pressed against her throat, she held them back. They would be a burden to him, and to her, a cause for later regrets. Pride was her best shield now.

She woke once more that night, to a sound she'd never expected to hear, that of a man crying over her. Adrian was curled over the far edge of the bed, gasping softly in his effort not to rouse her. A month ago, a day ago, his tears might have salved her insecurity. Tonight, they stirred only compassion.

To have found a woman he wanted and probably loved, but with whom he dared not enjoy the feast; to know he had the power to hurt his beloved, and most likely would . . . Well, she wouldn't have wanted to be in his shoes.

Not that her shoes were much better. Her nature rebelled at waiting for someone else to decide her future, but what could she do, really, to resolve his dilemma? She couldn't promise her love would be worth whatever he had to sacrifice. She didn't even know for certain what that was.

From the amount of personal time he spent on work, she knew his job was more than a job to him. Avvar needed dedicated law officers, especially ones who could handle their newest immigrants. Maybe one lonely woman didn't have the right to threaten that.

Then again, maybe loving her wasn't a threat at all, merely the door to a different destiny. She didn't know. She couldn't tell him what he should value most, how much he should risk. Only he could decide that.

But they were together tonight, and he was hurting. Pretending to turn in her sleep, she curled her body around his quaking back. He stiffened at first, but soon his shaking eased. His breathing slowed and deepened. He pulled her hand across his chest and tucked it close.

Small though the comfort was, the warmth eased both their hearts.

Chapter 16

As citizens of Ohram, we have a sacred responsibility to share our values with those in our care. If we forget this, we become no better than any other race of conquerors. God willing, we shall always be a nation people are proud to call home.

—Victoria Faen Aedlys, on signing
the Avvar Accord, the first to
allow Yamish immigration

The unaccustomed emotion of the night before must have knocked Adrian out. By the time he opened his eyes the following morning, the sun was high. He looked over his shoulder to the opposite side of the bed. His heart sank. Roxanne was gone.

And the house was unnaturally quiet.

Delaying the inevitable, he washed, then donned his rumpled clothes. He couldn't remember throwing them into

the corner. Fortunately, his coat would hide the damage until he got home.

Rubbing his aching temple with the heel of one palm,
he clumped up the back stairs to the fourth floor. As he'd
feared, the rest of the house was empty.

They'd left a basket of rolls on the kitchen table. For
him, he supposed, though he couldn't bring his unworthy
self to eat them. He'd hurt her. He'd said "I love you" when
he'd had no right. Worse, he'd made it clear he immediately wanted to take it back. No wonder she'd disappeared
without a word.

Sighing heavily, he took one last look around and left.

~~~~

Two days later, Roxie sat by the parlor fire, smiling at
Charles and Max. The pair was squabbling over who
needed a bath more. They'd taken the horse trolley to Fisherman's Wharf this morning. Got their toes wet in the
foamy waves. Ate too many fish and chips. The beach had
shone like a pink pearl beneath the wintry sky. Adrian was
gone, and life went on.

For all her flaws, Roxie's mother had possessed a
wealth of determination. She'd taught her daughter to use
hers. *Don't mope, honey,* she'd say when they had to leave
a place or person Roxie had grown fond of. *If you don't
walk away from spilt milk, you're sure to turn sour.* Roxie
preferred to mop up spills before she walked away, but she
did see the value in moving on.

If only Adrian weren't so hard to forget.

He must have been disappointed to wake to an abandoned house and yet, that very day, he'd arranged for a job
posting to appear on the message board at The Laughing
Crow: *Kitchen assistant wanted, Astoria House.* Charles
was so excited he'd never stopped to wonder why the
Astoria would troll for workers at such a third-rate hole-in-
the-wall.

The interview Charles had obtained for the following
week had him close to incoherent. What should he wear?

Did Roxie think he ought to mention he could cook, or would that look forward? Maybe he should bring a dish for the head chef. His oyster stew always won raves, but might it be too low-brow for the Astoria?

"Just imagine," he'd said, his voice filled with youthful wonder and hope. "This time next week, I could be chopping parsley for Gaspar Ilario."

Adrian certainly knew how to do a favor. If he'd been anywhere nearby, she would have expressed all the gratitude he'd spared Charles from shouldering.

The boy deserved a chance to shine. Sometimes he seemed to think he had nothing to offer beyond his pretty face. Not today, though. They'd strolled for miles down the beach, kicking up shells and swinging an uncharacteristically bubbly Max at the end of their arms. Once, when Max scampered ahead to investigate some seaweed, Charles had taken her hand in both of his and held it against his heart for a long, poignant time.

A knock at the door shook her from her memories.

"I'll get it," she said. It was probably Abul's wife bringing the fancy fabric she'd ordered from her parents' cooperative weavers society. Sapphire blue, Linia had promised, embroidered with flying snowbirds. Roxie was going to upholster Max's secondhand rocking chair in the material and maybe make curtains when she got time. The boy was big enough to appreciate a room that matched.

But it wasn't Abul's wife who'd knocked. It was Herrington.

Roxanne immediately stepped into the hall and shut the door behind her. She hadn't told the boys about her father yet. The way they'd grown up, on the streets, demons were real monsters to them. On top of everything else, Roxie hadn't been able to face the possibility of them looking at her with mistrust.

"What are you doing here?" she demanded. "In my home!"

Herrington's hands were in the pockets of his overcoat. Though his expression didn't change, she thought he might be clenching his fists. "I hoped to ascertain if you received my gift."

"I got it," she snapped. "It was horribly thoughtful. Now go away."

"I can't go away," he said with infuriating calm. "You and I share a heritage—"

"Half a heritage."

"As you wish." He inclined his head. However spurious, the gesture of respect was oddly affecting. When he looked up again, she'd forgotten not to meet his eyes.

"Whatever your reluctance to face the truth," he said, holding her angry gaze with his cool one, "it stands to reason I might have useful information about your nature."

"What information could you have? You didn't even know our species could breed. Anyway, if I were going to develop any weird demon traits, I would have done it by now."

"Certain of that, are you?"

"What do you want from me?" she said, resisting an urge to curse him to hell.

"What any father would: the chance to know a bit about the child he sired."

She couldn't tell if he was sincere. His face didn't show the kind of expressions she was used to. In fact, it didn't show any expression at all. If she really did have demon powers, shouldn't she be able to sense what he was feeling? She'd heard about that nonverbal communication they used, that "fire-talk."

"How about this?" she said. "If I have any questions in the future, I'll bring them straight to you."

"If you got to know me a little now, it would be easier to approach me then."

Suddenly, she did feel something: a subtle awareness of amusement, as if he were enjoying matching wits with her. Shivers crept up her neck. She shook them off. No doubt her imagination was playing tricks on her.

"I don't want to know you," she said childishly.

The skin beside his all-silver eyes tightened a fraction,

perhaps the demon version of a flinch. She told herself feeling sorry for him would be sheer folly.

"Tea," he said, confusing her for a moment. "At an establishment of your choosing. Neutral territory, as it were. For the duration of half an hour."

"You want me to have tea with you?"

"I enjoy tea, but coffee is also acceptable." The right side of his mouth curled in a tentative smile. It looked surprisingly human. "Bring the boys, if you like."

So he knew about her boys. At least that they existed. Roxie's brow pleated. Whatever he knew was too much.

She loved those boys with all her heart. She'd never dreamed she'd experience such contentment as she'd found with them. The saints bless whatever instinct had sent her back to speak to two ragged urchins. She'd known the moment she looked into Charles's guarded eyes that they belonged with her, that there was nothing to fear by taking them in.

Until Herrington had mentioned them, he'd almost gotten her to agree.

"I'm afraid tea will be impossible," she said. "I'm much too busy to get away."

His eyes narrowed at her refusal, not so much in anger as calculation. Well, he could calculate all he wanted. Roxanne didn't care if she grew a tail. She wasn't going to change her mind about having anything to do with him. She left him without a good-bye, trusting her rudeness would spur him to go.

Ten minutes later, a knock sounded again.

"Damn it," she said as she yanked the door open. "Leave me a—"

She stopped mid-curse. A sharp-faced little girl stood on the landing. She was ten or so, and wore a street-sweeper's yellow uniform. A row of shiny brass buttons marched diagonally down her narrow martial jacket.

"Message," she said curtly, her shoulders thrown back with pride. Roxie's hostility seemed not to have upset her. Perhaps she was used to it.

Nonplused, Roxie took the envelope from her out-thrust hand and peeked inside. Adrian's sketch of Tommy Bainbridge stared up from the shadows. "Can you wait for me to give you something to take back?"

"I'm on my tea break," said the girl, who looked like chances to eat didn't come often enough.

"Hm, well." She gestured the girl into the kitchen, pulled a plate from the cabinet, and began slicing bread. "Perhaps you'd consent to have a bite here while I copy these?"

One look at the spread Roxie was preparing convinced the girl the wait would be worth her while. When Roxie returned to the kitchen an hour later, the girl was regaling a goggle-eyed Max with tales of her street-sweeping adventures.

"Adrian got her the job," Max announced. "One of the sergeants threw her in a smelly old cell for stealing an orange, but our Adrian rescued her."

"Did he?" The pride in the boy's voice made Roxanne's eyes burn. How was she going to explain that "their" Adrian wouldn't be coming around?

She handed the girl a dozen neatly copied ink sketches. Subdued again in the presence of an adult, she refused Roxie's offer of payment to cover her return trip.

"Have to go back that way anyway," she said, wiping away a milk mustache with the back of her hand.

Roxie wished she could take the package to Adrian herself, but it was better this way. A clean, quick cut was always better.

⟡

Adrian was a mess. He'd just gotten back from handling a domestic disturbance in Harborside. Normally this was not his responsibility, but the argument had involved a Yamish couple fighting over their shared human servant, and it had escalated beyond what the nonenhanced sergeants could handle. Despite his implants, Adrian now sported a host of bruises and a completely wrecked tweed jacket.

The human servant didn't have a scratch, but both demons were being booked and held overnight.

The funny thing was, Adrian was grateful the call had come in. Any situation that reminded his superior why he kept Adrian around struck him as a good thing.

Clearly impressed by the damage, if wary of the fact that the demons had displayed more, the watch sergeant handed Adrian an envelope. The moment he saw the handwriting, his heart began to pound. He'd have known Roxie's penmanship anywhere: bold and sharp but with an extra sensual fillip on the capitals.

Calm down, he ordered. *She's probably just returning your sketches.* There was no reason to expect to find anything personal. Nonetheless, he didn't risk his shaky knees on the stairs to his office. Instead, he took one of the cracked leather seats across from the watch desk and cracked the seal.

Her note was disappointingly businesslike:

Adrian,

Hope you find these copies useful. Let me know if you need more.

She had signed it simply "R."

He frowned. Would he have rated a "respectfully yours" before he chose his job ahead of her? At least she was calling him Adrian—although what did that matter when he wasn't going to see her again?

He wondered how Sis and Max had gotten on. Max didn't seem to have playmates his own age. An image formed in his mind of Roxie smiling on the mismatched pair. Tall, skinny Sis. Short, sturdy Max. He could see her in that good-smelling kitchen of hers, making sure Max felt safe with the stranger, making sure Sis felt welcome. Roxie was great with children. Someday, she ought to have a dozen.

Like a dash of icy water, a realization hit. He hadn't protected her. Not even once. Nor had he noticed her taking any precautions herself. He'd assumed with her experience . . . but who knew for sure?

The watch sergeant must have heard his indrawn breath. The doleful old hound leaned forward over the high desk, eager to commiserate. His sympathy might even have been sincere.

"Bad news?" he asked.

"No." Adrian smiled in spite of his shock. "Just something I forgot to take care of."

There was no getting around it. Like it or not, he was going to have to see Roxie again.

Chapter 17

~≥~

Children are our future. We cannot allow them to run amok.

—*The Collected Sayings of the Emperor*

~≥~

Adrian expected Charles to challenge his reap-
pearance, but his mind was clearly elsewhere.

"Oh, it's you," was all he said before letting him in.
"Roxie's out back."

He mumbled to himself as he escorted Adrian through
the apartment. "Braise six minutes over a low flame," he
caught, and "Two pinches of fresh basil." Adrian coughed
into his fist to stifle a laugh. The boy must be preparing for
his meeting with Gaspar.

His attire certainly impressed. Garbed in a loose-
legged, black "city" suit, the sort favored by workers for
Sunday best, Charles looked as neat as a pin. It was hard to
believe he'd spent a day on the street. In a sense, though,

the street had represented a step up for Charles. Roxie had confided one night that, after his mother abandoned him, Charles had worked for a top hat club, a brothel catering to blue bloods. Charles had thought this would be better than throwing in his lot with the demons, and at first it was. The proprietors had fed and dressed him well, even offered some of the affection he hadn't found at home. But such luxuries came at a price. At least on the street, Charles had been able to call his soul his own.

Adrian hoped Charles would never have to make that kind of choice again. He knew his brother-in-law would offer the boy a job. Gaspar was a bootstrap success himself. Though Charles was proud and not sweet-tempered, Adrian thought he had enough self-control not to botch his chance.

A snatch of off-key music caught his ear as they passed the door to the parlor. Max was singing to himself. "The big ol' grasshopper climbin' on the wall," was how it sounded to Adrian. His steps faltered. He wanted to stop. Say hello. Ruffle Max's hair. With a grimace, he forced himself onward. For both their sakes, he had to keep his distance.

Still muttering recipes, Charles left him in the studio, where he could see Roxie through the window doors.

She sat on a stone bench beneath the rose arbor, wearing her oldest, most paint-stained blue serge trousers, a man's cotton shirt, and a shawl whose wool was so rough and mottled it might have been dragged across a cellar. The style had recently come into fashion among the city's seafarers. It suited her. Her loosely braided hair glowed like copper against the teal yarn. He paused, drinking in the sight of her.

Her gardening gloves lay idle by her hip, but a pile of discarded dead growth suggested she had at least begun her task. He supposed she hoped to coax a few more cycles of bloom out of the bushes.

Twirling one of her prized Crimson Beauties between her fingers, she stared through the crisscrossed slats toward

Little Barking. Was she thinking of him? Was she equally haunted by what they'd shared? He decided this was how obsessions were born: one small delusion at a time. But maybe the fascination was mutual. Maybe they'd both stepped into the fire.

Whatever the truth, he hated to disturb her. Even if this wasn't something he could handle through the post, he couldn't swear his motives for coming were pure.

"Roxanne," he finally said, pushing through the square-paned door.

She spun as if he'd caught her at something. One hand tugged her shawl closer to her neck. A flurry of emotions crossed her face. He was reasonably certain pleasure was not among them.

"Adrian. What are you doing here?"

He shifted from foot to foot. "I needed to ask you something. In person."

"Ah." She stood and smoothed her palms down the front of her blue trousers. The cloth fit snugly enough that the central seam divided the delectable peach halves of her sex.

He wet his lips, momentarily mesmerized. The taste of her ghosted across his tongue, the melting softness of sheltered skin, the tiny swelling that could be rolled in the mouth and suckled . . .

With an effort, he threw off the seductive memory. She was waiting for him to speak. He gestured to the pile of brambles. "I, um— Do you need help cleaning this up?"

"No." When she crossed her arms, her bosom plumped.

He remembered how she tasted there as well. When he ran his finger under his tightly fastened collar, it came away damp. *Schoolboy,* he mocked, and squared his shoulders.

"I need to know if you could be pregnant."

Her arms dropped in disbelief. "You ask me this now?"

"I know I should have asked sooner. I know I should have gone to the apothecary and bought some Jeruvian gloves as soon as I realized we might, well, become intimate, but I didn't. I need to know if pregnancy is a possibility." The speech had exhausted his breath. He pulled another into his lungs and waited for her answer.

"You've no need to worry about that. The moon wasn't right for me to get pregnant."

"The moon! Are you crazy?" He closed the distance between them and clasped her shoulders in his hands. The scent of drying roses swirled in his head, heavy and sharp.

"Let go," she demanded, shaking free.

"But, Roxie, moon watching is hardly a reliable method of contraception."

"It is the way the Bhamjrishi do it." Her eyes dared him to contradict her. "Their method, which they've spent centuries perfecting, is based on the position of the moon at the moment a female baby first draws breath, which determines ovulation cycles, which determines when you can—or even ought—to have a child. My mother didn't have one 'unfortunate mishap' once she learned their technique, and she made sure I had my chart drawn up. You have to admit Bhamjran know more about sex than anyone."

"But Roxie—" He wasn't sure what he wished to protest, only that he did.

She folded her arms again, her sleeves pushed to her elbows. She still had the muscle from her days rigging sails on the *Queen*. "If you think I've been irresponsible with regard to diseases, I had the demon who works next to Abul's free clinic check you out."

"A demon?" He squinted in confusion.

"Abul's been trying to shut her down, but his patients swear by her. She's what they call a 'sensitive' *rohn*, except she doesn't tell fortunes, she does medical aura readings."

"Aura readings!" His voice neared the range only dogs could hear. "Exactly how far out of your way did you have to go to find the two most dubious schools of human and demon philosophy?"

"Fine. Be narrow-minded." She tossed her shawl onto the bench and collected her garden tools. With shears and gloves tucked underneath one arm, she gathered the edges of the tarp on which she'd thrown her cuttings. "Just don't waste time worrying about catching anything from me."

"And why is that?" he asked, trying to ignore the lovely rear view she was presenting. The fit of her trousers taunted him. He couldn't help thinking his palms were the only objects better suited for cupping her derriere.

"Because you were my first," she said, not looking at him.

"Oh, really, I was your—" He stopped, mid-scoff. A chill, or maybe it was a thrill, expanded outward from his solar plexus, numbing his fingertips, slowing his heart. Mindless as a puppet, he followed her to the potting shed that jutted from the nearest wall. Lit by a single dusty window, the interior was dark, fragrant with damp brick and old wood. She threw her gear onto one of the shelves.

"I was your first?" he asked as she emptied her tarp into the compost box. He tried to think back to that night. He remembered she'd been tight and that there had been a moment when he thought she might not be ready. He supposed the excitement of finally being welcomed into her bed might have distracted him from the signs. Lord, what an idiot he must have seemed!

"You didn't complain," he said, remembering his ex-wife's extremely tear-filled wedding night. There'd certainly been no mistaking her virginal state.

Letting the waist-high lid slam shut, Roxie dropped the canvas and leaned straight-armed on the weathered wood. Her back was to him, but the stiffness in her body spoke volumes.

"I know you think I've been tupping my brains out for years, but, as it happens, that's not the case."

"Why didn't you tell me?" He wanted to touch her so badly his palms tingled.

"That ridiculous tone of voice is why. I didn't want you to make a blithering big deal about it. And I was afraid—" Her jaw clacked shut.

This time he did touch her, taking her shoulder into his

hand. He turned her, at least part way, to face him. "Afraid of what?"

Her eyes flashed silver fire. "I was afraid you'd change your mind. A fallen woman doesn't have to be handled with kid gloves, but if you'd known I was a virgin, you might have thought: *This poor girl, she ought to be saving it for her husband.* But I don't care about that rubbish!"

If the tears that glimmered on her lower lids were any indication, she cared a great deal. She blinked them away, too proud to acknowledge them.

Oh, Roxie, he thought. *I wish I could make all your dreams come true—and mine in the bargain.*

"I'm sorry." He squeezed the single point of contact she'd allowed him. "I wish you'd told me. I wish I could say I would have left you alone, but that probably isn't true." His voice thickened with memory. "You made me feel like I'd burst, I wanted you so badly. If I'd known, though, at least I could have taken more care. I could have tried to make your first time more special."

Her laugh was strained. "If your lovemaking had been any more special, I'd probably have slit my wrists before I let you walk away."

"The hell you would," he growled, tugging her closer.

The press of her breasts and thighs woke memories, memories he had no right to revisit. Desire drummed in his chest and between his legs. God help him, he didn't know how to stay away from her. A day was too long. An hour.

"Don't do this," she warned, but he gripped her beneath the arms and, with a soft whuff of effort, lifted her onto the age-silvered lid of the compost box.

"Adrian." She gripped his upper arms. "You have to either stay or go. You can't keep changing your mind. It isn't fair."

"I'm having trouble being fair—or rational, for that matter. My head knows what's right, but my body can't wrestle out from under your spell. It keeps prodding me to go to you, like you're the only cure for a fever. I can't even sweat it out except with you."

"Oh, Adrian." His confession weakened her. How good it would be to lean into him, to forget the world. He pressed closer like a penitent, his fingers brushing her knees.

"Please don't say anything," he whispered, lifting stormy eyes. She saw such longing there that her breath caught in her throat. "I just want . . . I need to kiss you. Just that, I promise. I'm starving for a taste of you."

Sweat prickled across her scalp. He moistened his lower lip and stared at her mouth as if he meant to devour it. She closed her eyes. Heat rose through her like steam off a boiling pot. Her chest warmed, her palms, the soles of her feet. Her secret flesh seemed to have swelled shut. The sap of her hunger squeezed through the sweet constriction, drop by silky drop. When she spoke, it was weakly.

"I don't think a kiss is a good idea."

"Probably not." He leaned forward and slid his hands down her back until they encircled her bottom. "But I'm going to take one anyway."

She didn't consciously decide to do it, but her legs parted for his approach. His lips touched hers, warm and soft, whispering lightly over the tender swells. She barely felt the first brush of his tongue; only knew it had been there from the moisture it left behind. Unable to resist, she cupped his face with both hands, savoring the subtle movements of the muscles in his cheeks. A hint of a beard roughened his olive skin. He must have come straight from work.

"Open for me," he whispered, nuzzling her cheek.

When she did, he remained just as tender, just as slow. His tongue probed deeply, the intrusion more intimate than a hard kiss. She brushed her own tongue against the silken lining of his mouth. He inhaled sharply and dragged her to the edge of the box. Though he did not crush her to him, he must have felt her heat. His cock and balls formed a warm bundle, pulsing steadily against the juncture of her thighs. More force would have been welcome, much more, but she didn't dare encourage it.

This interlude was fragile. Apparently, he knew it, too.

He clung to her mouth as she clung to his, neither of them wanting to end the gentle torture. Slipping her arms beneath his suit coat, she dragged her nails up and down his back, enchanted by his periodic shivers of pleasure. The starched linen of his shirt made a noise like bed sheets rustling.

His hands shifted to cup her breasts. He squeezed them firmly, then gentled, his fingertips circling the peaks until they'd tightened to the point of pain. She couldn't help leaning toward him to urge him on.

Heaven, she thought, running her hands over his skull and shoulders. He was here. He was in her arms. She didn't want to think about anything else.

They spun the kiss out as long as they could, but she knew it would have to end. When it did, he rested his forehead on hers. Both of them were shaking.

"So," she said, straightening his damp, disarranged collar. "We're back to where we started: a soft kiss and a trembling hand."

He surrendered a melodious breath. "Roxanne, I am sorry. About everything. Please believe me when I say I didn't mean for things to turn out this way."

"I don't doubt that." She grinned with bitter humor. "I can't imagine a man like you meets a woman like me every day."

Adrian squeezed the scruff of her neck the way one would a naughty puppy. "There's more to you than what you have to offer in bed. You're a fine woman. Any man would be lucky to find you."

"Criminy." She tried to shrug him away.

"I want you to be happy," he insisted.

She cursed him so vociferously he laughed. "Very well. I'll spare you the platitudes—though I mean them." His mouth made a teasing feint at hers. "One last kiss for the road?"

"Adrian," she groaned. "What are you trying to do?"

"I don't want you to forget me."

"I'd be happier if I did."

He drew back as her words sank in, all playfulness

gone. His eyes were very bright. "Good-bye, Roxie," he said softly, sadly. "You'll tell me if anything unexpected happens? In case the moon was wrong?"

His wistful expression made her smile. "You act as if you wish I were pregnant."

"I'd do the right thing, Roxie."

She touched the lines bracketing the corners of his mouth. He looked so serious. Did he mean he'd marry her? A plain gold ring? A little church by the sea? Temptation hissed like a wisp of opium in the dark. It would be so easy. Bhamjran had practically invented the science of conception. Want a healthy girl? A healthy boy? They could pinpoint not just the optimal day for congress but the hour. With a shudder, she pushed the smoky lure away. She knew what she wanted from Adrian, and it had nothing to do with duty or dirty tricks.

"I wouldn't let you do anything for a reason like that."

His eyes narrowed, but he refrained from making grandiose claims. He kissed the tip of her nose.

"Contact me if you need me," he repeated, then turned to go.

She watched the garden door swing shut behind him. She doubted she'd ever stop needing him. A score of heart-beats later, an uncontrollable fear overtook her. What if this was the last time she saw him? He'd seemed so sad when he said good-bye. Maybe her hopes, always thin, were completely delusional.

Shawl hugged tight against a private chill, she dashed down the hall to the front window, the one that overlooked the street. Her worn canvas shoes screeched to a halt just short of crashing. She tugged back the gauzy curtain, then pressed her nose to the panes.

One last glimpse. One last—

There he was, stepping down the front stairs in his plain brown suit. He looked small from up here but not or-dinary. Lean and tall, he held himself like royalty. When he raked one hand through his hair, the silky strands gleamed blue on black like a raven's wing. Her fingers twitched in remembrance.

How was she going to bear this? Every time she saw him, the strain of parting grew worse.

His gaze lifted, searching the front of the twilit house. She shrank behind the curtain. He couldn't possibly feel her eyes on him, unless they shared some mystical connection.

Schoolgirl, she mocked, moving back into view. He'd already turned away. He was striding down the cobbled street, no longer looking back.

Adrian didn't see the man in the navy peacoat who peeled out from a doorway after him, but Roxie did. She squinted down at his follower. Shamble-gaited and grimy, he didn't strike her as Securité material. Adrian's colleagues tended to look milk-fed. Maybe he hailed from Bow Street or somewhere even less scrupulous. Regardless, she'd bet her eyeteeth she knew who'd hired him.

"Herrington." She made the name a curse. No doubt this invasion of privacy was his warped idea of safeguarding his family blood, his precious "heritage." *Bah.* Had it been possible, Roxie would have drained it from her veins then and there.

If he made trouble for Adrian, she'd—Well, she couldn't think of anything awful enough that she'd actually stoop to do. If he pushed her though . . .

"Watch out," she muttered, her hands clenching on the sheers.

She mouthed a silent prayer that Adrian wasn't too distracted to shake his uninvited tick.

~⋙~

Herrington had come into the city from his estate both to gather and give intelligence. The first task taken care of, he was engaged in what had come to be a favorite hobby: human-watching in Queen's Park. The mile-long green space was one of Queen Victoria's less-controversial gifts to Avvar. Riding paths wound through the trees and grass, past ponds and ornamental fountains, even an electrified carousel. Though dusk had fallen, a recent bout of clear, mild weather encouraged a few working families to bring their children to play. His eye was caught in particular by a chubby redheaded toddler who kept letting a ball fall through her mittened hands. Her ineptitude seemed not to bother her at all. She was full of bounce and squeals of laughter.

Herrington had no doubt her parents hoped to fatigue the little monster before bedtime.

No matter his choice of words, he could not mistake the fondness of his own sentiments, nor the personal parallels. His reaction should have been impossible. Even if Roxanne had grown up in his care, her childhood wouldn't have been like this. Yamish parents guided their children in structured activities, in educational games. More to the point, if they were as well-born as he was, they hired someone else to do the job for them.

Though Herrington's frown of disapproval was better than a smile, it was not the expression he wished to have on his face when his handler arrived.

The man the *rohn* simply called The Dragon appeared silently. Few knew the famous doctor had been born *rohn* himself and had clawed his way up from the lower ranks with a combination of intelligence, ambition, and unwavering ruthlessness. It was whispered that he'd poisoned one of the Yamish princes he'd served as personal physician, an act that had led to the ascension of a presumably grateful rival. Because that rival was the current emperor's cousin, the whispers were very soft. Herrington was positive that, had The Dragon been able, he would have filled the stolen throne himself.

Unfortunately for Herrington, a *rohn* could only rise so high. Because of this, The Dragon was his problem.

"Worried?" his black-garbed contact asked. He stood slightly behind Herrington, his expression as serene as any royal son. His face was long and narrow, his cheekbones high. All Yama were slender, but the doctor's thinness looked starved. Like Herrington, he reported to the Under-Minister of Trade, an innocuous title that really meant spymaster. Though the doctor's voice held no inflection, his aura conveyed the slightest hint of mockery.

Herrington made no move to erase his frown. "My expression discourages the children," he said. "Otherwise, they are apt to request you throw back their balls."

This, he was pleased to see, caused The Dragon to flinch. Herrington turned to face him fully.

"I hope this meeting finds you well, Raymond," he said, purposefully using the human bastardization of his name. "Raymond's" aura flared slightly, but gratifyingly, with pique.

"I am very well," The Dragon said, "though I wonder how I find you. You led our prince to believe you would send him information about this . . . creature you have fathered."

"Our prince is everything that is gracious. However, if you will permit me to say so, he is occasionally impatient."

"It is not for *me* to permit," The Dragon responded, at which Herrington allowed himself a tiny smile. The Dragon's mouth tightened infinitesimally at the insult.

Satisfied he'd made his point about the chain of command, Herrington turned back to the young family. "The prince will have his information as soon as I've gathered it."

"You claimed you would lure her into your sphere."

"I am doing so."

"Forgive me for suggesting otherwise, *Lord Herrington*." The Dragon tried to return Herrington's favor by making an insult of his human name, but because Herrington took no offense, the attempt fell flat. Sensing this, The Dragon smoothed his straight black hair around his head. He'd been given dispensation to wear it long, but a true *daimyo* wouldn't have called attention to the honor. This time, Herrington allowed the smile to reach his eyes.

"Perhaps I am lacking in comprehension," The Dragon began again, "but it appears to me that you are doing nothing at all."

"My lures are subtle," Herrington said, "as they should be."

"The prince does not have to wait for you. He can assign

me to study the girl—to collect her, if need be."

For a Yama, this threat was crudely direct. Herrington permitted himself neither anger nor fear, but banished every shred of emotion from his face and aura, stuffing his secret hopes down in the darkness of his soul.

"You do not know these people," he said, looking straight into the doctor's deep-set silver eyes. They were of a height, both tall members of a tall race. "You have cut them open and put your toys inside them, just as you have done to your fellow *rohn*, but you do not understand what makes them tick. You do not know how to coax them onto the path you wish them to walk."

"And you do?" The Dragon's perfect mask was stiff, his hands clenched at his sides.

"I do," Herrington confirmed, allowing his fire-talk to say soothing things. He did not want the doctor to lose his temper completely. "Understanding humans is the mission to which our prince—and our emperor—set me. It is a trust I shall not betray."

"I, too, have served our emperor," The Dragon said.

Herrington accepted the reminder placidly. "I am aware of that," he said. "Alas, many of your services cannot be spoken of aloud."

As Herrington hoped, The Dragon was disconcerted by the sympathy rippling through his aura. In the proper context, conveying emotion could be useful. A *rohn* would not realize fire-talk could lie. They excelled at reading auras, not at sending potentially duplicitous messages. Herrington, by contrast, had become quite mendacious in the last few years. Beginning to like the objects of his study had necessitated perfecting that talent.

"We shall not wait much longer," The Dragon warned as he turned away.

"You will not have to," Herrington murmured.

His curses he kept even from himself until the man was gone. *Damnation.* He was going to have to pry Roxie from her sticking place, and by less gentle means than he'd tried thus far. She was too comfortable in her life, too girded about by support. She needed to understand how precarious her position was.

If that meant destroying any hope of developing a true father-daughter bond, they would both have to live with it.

Chapter 18

Every culture knows love: romantic love, parental love, even
love for ideas. To suggest a race is incapable of feeling, simply
because they express their emotions differently, is not only ignorant but dangerous. After all, if a people cannot feel, we are justified in treating them as barbarously as we wish. As the
merchant said, "If you prick me, do I not bleed?"

—*The True and Irreverent History of Avvar*

Roxanne was in the studio when Charles staggered
in, coat askew, hair plastered to his forehead by perspiration. She dropped her palette in alarm.

"Max," he gasped, sagging against the parlor arch. "Max."

She reached his side in an instant, touching his dripping
face, clutching his elbow to support him. "What happened?
Did Max get hurt at school?"

His chest heaved. "He wasn't there. The Headmaster told me someone from the Children's Ministry took him away in a van. They had official papers. I couldn't find a cab. I"—he was sobbing for air—"ran all the way here."

Roxie's blood ran so cold her fingers tingled. *Herrington.* She clenched her fists. "That bloody bastard."

Charles stared at her. She knew she should have told him, should have warned them both. Now it was too late. When he recovered from his shock at her language, he gripped her arms with the strength of the desperate. "We have to do something. We can't let them take him. What if we can't get him back?"

She closed her eyes. It took exactly two seconds to make up her mind. "I want you to change into your most conservative outfit. We'll take a cab to Little Barking. I'm not tackling those bloodsuckers without someone official to back me up."

Charles blinked. "You're asking Adrian Philips to help?" Then he nodded in answer to his own question. "Yes, he won't turn you down."

"What about me?" asked her model, a scantily clad tin peddler. His laurel wreath was drooping over one eye, but he had a wonderfully noble nose.

Roxie smiled despite her panic and tossed him two silver coins. The peddler caught them neatly.

"I'll send a message if I need you," she said and hurried off to make herself appear respectable.

~⊛~

She scribbled furiously throughout the hansom ride, aware that Charles was bursting with questions. She would tackle the challenge of answering them when she had to. Now she needed to focus on Max.

Though they'd hired an electric hansom, it was almost dark by the time they pulled up before the rough red hulk of Little Barking Station. On the street ahead, a lamplighter was igniting Victoria's pride and joy with his long brass pole, this neighborhood not yet converted to electric power. The gas-powered wicks sprang to life with a sound like pillows being punched. Roxie prayed Adrian hadn't gone home.

"You'll have to go in by yourself," she told Charles. "I don't want to cause any more trouble for Adrian. Give him this note. If you can bring him back with you, well and good. Otherwise, we'll meet him wherever he says, as long as it's soon."

Charles didn't look comfortable with this charge, but he tucked the note into his breast pocket and sprinted off. Minutes later, he returned—out of breath and alone—with the address of a tavern where Adrian promised to meet them within a quarter-hour.

"Tavern" was too kind a term. Roxie cast a wary glance around the basement barroom. Sawdust blanketed the floor. It stuck to her shoes as if it hadn't been changed recently. Fortunately, the crowd was light, a spattering of workmen's caps and humble corduroy trousers. Regulars, she judged, eating a bachelor's dinner: a roast and pickle, according to the waitress who seated them in a booth toward the back. The greasy aroma stuck in her throat. She ordered a cup of tea, more to wash down the smell than because she wanted it.

Seated across from her, Charles drummed the table with nervous fingers. Max was tough for a five-year-old, but they both knew every second they delayed was a second more of fear for him.

He didn't deserve to face that. He'd been through enough already.

When Adrian arrived, he looked harried. Though she hadn't the faintest notion whether he could help, her heart lightened at the sight of his dear, serious face.

He slid into the bench next to Charles.

"Sorry I took so long," he said, though he'd arrived almost on their heels. He flattened his hands on the battered table and drew a deep, businesslike breath. "Now. Tell me again what happened, and don't leave anything out."

When she got to the part about Herrington being her father, Charles's eyes went wide. "Herrington, the Yamish envoy? The demon who helped negotiate the Avvar Accord?"

She shouldn't have been surprised he recognized the name. Charles liked to follow current events.

"I know I should have told you," she said, covering his hand pleadingly. "Part of me kept hoping if I ignored him, he'd go away."

"But how can—" Charles leaned forward, his voice sinking to a rasp. "You're not a—"

"I am," she said when he failed to find a word. "At least, part of me is."

Charles sagged back against the booth, looking thoroughly flattened by the news. Though his mouth worked, nothing came out. His expression wasn't precisely horrified, but it was close. In spite of everything else that was going on, tears started in Roxie's eyes. Adrian looked at her, then at Charles. He put his hand on the boy's shoulder.

"Pull yourself together," he said, his tone gentler than his words. "She's the woman she's always been, the woman who took you and Max in, the woman who fed and clothed you, the woman who loves you with all her heart. She needs your support now, and so does Max."

Charles stared at Adrian, seeming almost as startled by the lecture as he'd been by Roxie's parentage. She wondered if any man had spoken to him in this fatherly way before. Hearing Adrian do it shocked Roxie a bit herself.

"All right," the boy said slowly, like someone shaking out of a dream. "What do we do now?"

The waitress clanked Roxie's cup of tea onto the table, pulled a grease pencil from behind her ear, and looked hopefully at Adrian. She was so pregnant she could balance her order pad on her stomach. Adrian stopped scratching his head long enough to smile at her, order a platter of cornbread, and inquire after the baby-to-be. Though he wasn't flirtatious, the woman was blushing when she left.

"Are you certain Lord Herrington is behind the Ministry's actions?" he asked, returning to business.

Roxie turned her cracked white cup in a circle. The warmth felt good against her hands. "It couldn't be anyone else. The babyschool never asked me for birth records, and no one else has any reason to care if I'm Max's legal guardian. I don't have many enemies or even rivals. Serious artists don't consider me a threat, and the not-so-serious ones are too fond of running up debts at my shop to risk getting on my bad side."

Adrian tapped his lips with a forefinger. "What about Max's parents?"

Charles quashed that idea. "No such people. I spent weeks trying to find someone to claim him. Far as I'm concerned, he might have fallen from the sky." Without bothering to ask permission, he removed the teaball that was threatening to turn Roxie's hot water to ink and dropped it onto the tray of a passing dishboy. He nudged the steaming cup closer to her mouth, then waited until she took a sip. "My guess is, Herrington figured Roxie wouldn't have anyone else to turn to. Whether she blamed him for Max being taken or not, she'd have to ask him for help. For better or worse, he's the most powerful person she knows."

Adrian pinched his lower lip. "I don't suppose Herrington had anything to do with the man who followed me to Little Barking the other day?"

The waitress cut off Roxie's response by sliding a platter of golden bread in front of his place. She stood a moment longer than she had to, waiting for another smile perhaps, but Adrian was too busy offering the plate to Roxie and Charles.

"Ironic, eh?" he said, unaware he'd dashed any feminine hopes. He tucked a corner of cornbread into his mouth and chewed. "When he found out what I did for a living, he must have figured I wouldn't risk getting involved."

"That could be," Roxie said, trying to act as if the thought that Adrian might refuse hadn't crossed her mind. Maybe she shouldn't have worried about coming to him. "His reasons aren't important now. All that matters is getting Max back as quickly as possible. Lord." She put her head in her hands, anger and fear sapping her strength. "What I'd really like to do is go straight to that heartless bastard and wring his neck. I'm just afraid confronting him will make it worse. If he had enough leverage to arrange this . . ."

Adrian opened his silver watch fob. "We could *try*

speaking to him. At this hour, the Ministry offices will be closed. I'm not sure we'll be able to get anywhere with them until morning."

"I'm not leaving Max there overnight. I won't have those people ruining the progress he's made this year. He'll never trust me again if I abandon him."

Adrian's eyes flicked to hers and then away. She suspected he was remembering their nights in the parlor, with Max's head resting on her knee or Adrian's. *I wish* . . . the boy had said more than once. Neither of them had to hear the phrase's end to know what Max wished. Adrian's departure had shaken his trust already. He didn't need any more blows.

"Very well," Adrian said, pushing to his feet. "They probably took him to the orphans' dormitory on High Street. That's the closest to his school. We'll start there."

⁓

To Roxie's relief, Adrian's legalistic language, coupled with a flash of his lovely smile, cozened them past the dormitory mistress. The challenge for Roxanne then was to handle what she found inside.

She froze just beyond the doors to the second floor, unable to go a step farther. She had forgotten until that moment, but now, poised in the maw of that sorry, lonely hall, she remembered being taken to a place like this herself a very long time ago.

She remembered the dingy white walls, the sound of an iron bar clanging shut, the shadowy figures of adults coming and going with their own mysterious logic. Voices had babbled in a foreign language, and the smell of disinfectant was just like this, seeped into the wool of a gray blanket.

She had refused to call out for her mother because she'd been convinced Yvonne wouldn't come. Roxie was a bad, ugly, stupid girl. Nothing but trouble. She had no right to expect rescue. When the miracle happened and Yvonne did arrive in a swirl of silk and camellia perfume, Roxie's throat was so tight with unspoken pleas, she wasn't able to talk for days.

There was ice cream then. Tea with honey. Ringed hands brushing her hair until it crackled with static and floated in the air. The brief interlude of maternal care was sweet, but far too short to erase the shadow of the cold, locked room and the sputtering tallow candle.

She'd known it could happen again any time.

Roxanne began to shake. She'd never get Max out of this terrible place. Never. She knew it.

Adrian retraced the steps he'd taken ahead of her.

"Roxanne," he said and again, louder. *"Roxanne."*

She looked at him, scarcely understanding that he was speaking to her. His face was pinched with concern. Reaching for her frozen hand, he chafed it between his own.

"What is it?" He pulled her hand between the open flaps of his coat and tucked it to his chest. His heart beat steady and warm against her skin.

"I've been here before," she whispered.

"Here?" His other hand circled her wrist, the thumb slipping into her palm to stroke it soothingly.

She drew a choked breath. "A place like this. When I was small. They said my mother wasn't fit to keep me. I thought she'd never come. I fought them. They locked me in a room by myself. The candle burned out." She shook her head in denial of the old phantom. "It was so dark."

"Shh." Turning his broad shoulders to block their escort's view, he ducked his head and pressed a hard kiss to her knuckles. She shuddered with lingering fear. "You're here now. With me. Your mother got you out, and we'll get Max out, too."

"Will we?" Her words were the entreaty of a small child.

"Yes." His eyes had hardened, but they held tears. "Yes."

His will poured into her with the word. *There's someone to help me now,* she thought. *I don't have to do it all by myself*. In truth, she sensed she was being asked to surrender this burden completely to him—at least for the moment. That request was harder to accept. She trusted him, she did, but life had pounded the importance of self-reliance so firmly into her character that it was almost impossible to exercise her faith in him. Her body quivered with the force of the struggle before her resistance crumbled.

"Yes," she said, feeling as if she were saying "yes" to something else, something from which there would be no turning back.

Adrian's lips curved softly in approval, his gaze roving her face as if to commit the moment to memory.

"Ready?" was all he said.

She felt shaken, emptied, but she nodded and renewed her grip on his hand. He let her keep it even when the dormitory mistress stared at their clasped fingers from the corner of her persnickety brown eye. Far from letting go, Adrian winked at Roxie and gave her fingers a squeeze.

"Here it is!" Charles shouted from half a corridor ahead.

He was pointing at a numbered door. Roxie quickened her stride. Charles threw up the bar and yanked the door open.

"Come on, mate," he said, crouching down to child size. "It's me and Roxie. We've come to take you home."

Her breath caught in her throat as Max tottered out, looking dazed. His face was bruised. He must have struggled when the van came.

"Charles?" he croaked, as if he couldn't believe the older boy was there.

"That's right," said Charles. He took Max's hand as gently as if it were made of glass. "And see, here's Roxie."

Roxie smiled and put out her arms.

Max hesitated an instant before catapulting toward her.

"I knew you'd come," he said. His eyes screwed shut as his arms locked around her legs. "I told them you would. They didn't believe me, but I knew."

Tears ran down her face as she lifted him off the ground. "Yes, sweetie. You're mine, and I'll always come for you. You're my baby. My sweet, sweet Max." She kissed his sticky neck. "Mm, and you taste good, too."

Max giggled, and she felt his tension ease. His arms loosened as his head sagged limply to her shoulder. His eyes were drooping in exhaustion. Charles rubbed his back, smiling like a proud uncle.

"Really!" objected the dormitory's mistress, finally making herself heard above the confusion. "I'm not sure I can allow this. You didn't say anything about removing the child. I simply couldn't permit that without proper authorization from my supervisor, even if you are Securité."

"I'm afraid there's something you don't know about this case," Adrian said in his most concerned and confiding tone. He steered the worried drone to the side of the hall. "You see, I happen to know that the person who filed the unlawful custody claim isn't the concerned citizen he pretends to be."

"He isn't!" The headmistress pressed a plump hand to her tightly bound bosom, shocked titillation flaring in her eyes.

"No, ma'am. He's . . . well, let's just say he's a very *foreign* national, hoping to take the child into his own care, for who knows what nefarious purpose. The truth could make for terrible press if it got out. Goodness knows, the Children's Ministry doesn't need any more of that."

The headmistress nodded with pretend sobriety. "My," she breathed, "that would be bad."

"It would," he agreed. "Not that I'm free to tell you any more. It's a delicate diplomatic matter."

"Well, goodness, we wouldn't want to get tangled up in that!"

"No, indeed. Suffice to say that this woman"—he tilted his head toward Roxie—"has been instrumental in preventing an international incident. I can vouch for her character . . . if I'm forced to."

He allowed the threat of possible unpleasantness to enter his voice. The dormitory mistress turned satisfyingly pale. After that, she was only too happy to let them take Max off her hands.

"You know," Roxie said as they escaped the dreary building, "for a policeman, you're pretty handy with a lie."

"Not a lie," Adrian corrected. "Just innuendo."

"Yeah." Charles laughed. "You *innuendoed* us right out of there."

"I want ice cream," Max announced, lifting his sleepy

head from Roxie's shoulder. "And Adrian has to come, too."

The invitation touched him inordinately, though he knew it put Roxie in an awkward spot. When he met her eyes to see if it was all right, they shone with gratitude. For one wonderful moment, he felt as if he could conquer not just the Children's Ministry, but the world.

"Yes," she said softly, "Adrian should come, too."

Everyone, Charles included, seemed to assume he'd accept.

The resiliency of youth went a long way toward explaining how a dish of strawberry ice cream with chocolate sauce could succeed in restoring Max to his former self. Adrian's presence didn't hurt, either. Roxanne was forced to conclude that there was no real substitute for a protective male adult. No matter how capable the female, the masculine half of the species was primally comforting.

Despite Max's obvious improvement, Roxie carried him to his room and cuddled him on her lap in the rocking chair. She'd hoped to rock him to sleep, but every time he began to drift, he'd jerk himself awake again.

"I'm here," she murmured, stroking his hair. "You can rest."

Charles lay on his back on his own narrow bed, staring at the ceiling with his hands folded over his diaphragm.

Max caught them both by surprise when he spoke. "That wasn't as bad as the dragon," he said.

"What dragon?" Roxie asked, assuming he meant some childish bogeyman.

"The demon doctor. The one who bought me from my father."

Charles's head turned toward them on his pillow. A single candle burned on the nightstand. From the way it flickered at his indrawn breath, this was the first he'd heard of Max being sold.

"A demon bought you?" Roxie asked. Though Max was too young to sell legally, she knew that wouldn't stop a truly desperate—or truly greedy—parent.

"Uh-huh," said Max around his thumb. "The dragon put me in a machine. It was supposed to stop me from feeling things."

Charles swung his legs around and sat on the side of his bed. "Is this a real story, Max? Or a made-up story like your teacher reads from a book in school?"

"It's real. The dragon said I was tainded. He said I had too many motions for dymos to feed from me."

"Do you mean *daimyos?*" Roxie tried not to let her horror color her voice. A chill swept across her shoulders. "This dragon said you had too many emotions for the *daimyo* to feed from you?"

"Yep," Max confirmed equably. "And I kept feeling motions no matter what he did. I was so tainded, he had to let me go. I couldn't find the street from when I was little. It wasn't like Avvar. But then Charles saved me, so that was all right."

Charles muttered a curse under his breath. Max waved a floppy hand at him.

"Love you, Charles," he said fuzzily.

Charles covered his mouth, but whatever sound he was muffling couldn't trouble Max. The boy had dropped his cannonball and promptly fell asleep.

"I didn't know," Charles said, coming to stand beside her as she tucked Max into his bed. "It must have been some sort of experiment. Good thing it failed."

"Yes." Roxanne gazed down at the peacefully slumbering boy. "Good thing."

Those are my father's people, she was thinking. *Those are the kind of people I come from.*

Charles laid his palm on her back. "You aren't like that," he said, knowing her well enough to guess at her fears. "You could never, ever be like that."

His words were a comfort, but not an absolute cure.

Chapter 19

Is any creature more reckless than a man in love?

—Welland Herrington, *A Memoir*

Adrian stood as soon as Roxie entered the parlor. Her expression was distracted, her curls straggling unpredictably from her coiffure. Circles of worry darkened the hollows beneath her eyes.

To Adrian, she'd never looked more beautiful.

"I didn't know if I should stay," he said. "I wanted to make certain Max was all right."

"He's sleeping." She took a seat on the settee where he'd been perched a moment ago. Seeing she expected it, he sat again. "He told me something before he dropped off, and I confess I don't know what to make of it."

He listened to her story with steadily rising brows, then

scratched his stubbled jaw. "So, you believe he was taken from another city in Ohram, brought here, and used in a secret experiment to make him fit for upper-class Yama to feed on?"

"Taking etheric-force is supposed to have significant benefits—aside from being pleasurable. As long as the *rohn* avoid becoming addicted, it's said they live longer, healthier lives. If the *daimyo* could enjoy the same advantages without suffering the taint of human emotion, why wouldn't they jump at the chance?"

Adrian rose and began to pace, absently rubbing his right wrist. He couldn't help thinking of Tommy Bainbridge— even though the boy's disappearance seemed unlinked to Yamish affairs. "Did Max mention anyone else? Any other child being subjected to these tests with him?"

"No, but we can't assume they only tried this once. Adrian." She caught his arm to stop him going back and forth. "Do you think Herrington had anything to do with this experiment?"

He considered that. "I don't know. It seems unlikely. If he wanted Max for more testing, why involve the Children's Ministry? For what it's worth, your father has a better reputation than most of the Yama in Avvar. Humans like him. With his archaeological projects, he's actually become a romantic figure."

Adrian took her hand in both of his as she made a face. "I am aware of one Yamish doctor working here, the one who put in my implants. He struck me as more than capable of doing this, but perhaps that's because his manner was so foreign. He has the Queen's seal of approval, at any rate. She appointed him to oversee the process of retraining human doctors as part of the negotiated exchange of technology." Adrian knuckled his forehead. "I can't recall if I've heard anyone refer to him as a dragon, but the *rohn* are always giving people colorful names. There could be dozens of Yama they call that."

"I could ask Abul what he's heard."

Adrian shook his head. "I'm not sure that's a good idea.

These are highly placed people, people who are adept at intrigue. Your friend could get himself into trouble without even realizing he had." He thought back to the coffee vendor outside his station, to the way she'd stared at him and the doctor, practically boring holes with her eyes. If nothing else, he knew she hated *daimyo*. *The enemy of my enemy . . .* he mused. "There may be someone I can start with more quietly, someone who won't underestimate their ruthlessness."

"Oh, God." Roxie covered her face in her hands and blew out her breath. "I don't want to be thinking about this, or making you. Right now, all I want to focus on is keeping Max safe."

Hearing her exasperation, Adrian sat again, closer this time, allowing himself the pleasure of wrapping his arm around her back. Roxie sighed and relaxed against him. Saints above, she felt good.

"I forgot to mention this before," he said, "but a former colleague of mine sits on the board at the Children's Ministry. I'll speak to him tomorrow. He owes me a favor, as it happens. Between us, we might contrive to get you official custody."

"That would be better than a dream." She twisted around to face him. "Are you sure you should involve yourself any further? Considering who I am?"

He kissed her furrowed brow. "Haven't you heard that famous Bhamjrishi saying, 'It's not who you are, it's who you know'?"

She smiled, but her eyes were shadowed. "I don't want to get you in trouble."

"I'm not sure I care anymore."

"Oh, Adrian." Her laugh was sad but not completely. "I don't know what I would have done without you tonight. You were magnificent."

He grinned. "I was, wasn't I."

She caught her lower lip between her teeth. Her hands lay flat across his chest, smoothing him through the cloth of his shirt. The gentle friction had his heart racing.

"Adrian?" she said shyly. "I'd like you to know how grateful I am."

He plucked a quick kiss from her lips. "It was my pleasure and my privilege to help you. You don't have to thank me."

She caught her breath with a little sigh. "But suppose I wanted to express my gratitude"—her fingers circled his middle shirt button—"more substantially than just saying 'thank you'? Suppose I wanted to be grateful for purely selfish reasons?"

"Ah." His heart leaped inside his rib cage. "That would be a different story."

Their eyes met and held. The memory of all that had passed between them hung in the air. *You're an idiot,* he told himself, *if you leave this woman behind again.*

Not yet ready to accept the ramifications of that, he cleared his throat. "If you're going to be, er, substantially grateful, I think we ought to move to your room."

"I don't want to force you into anything."

He laughed and placed her hand on his markedly bulging cock. "I know you're fairly irresistible, but does this feel like I'm being forced?"

"No-o," she admitted, her fingers tightening a little on their own. She seemed to want to test just how hard he was.

With a chuckle that was half groan, he wrapped his arms beneath her buttocks, lifted her off her feet, and carried her down the darkened hall to the stairs. Small brass lamps lit the turn of each flight, and the walls were lined with brick. A faded green runner, patterned with hummingbirds, flowed down the creaking treads.

He set her onto the landing so he could crush himself into the lee of her thighs. It was only one floor to her bedroom, but at that instant it seemed too far. "Why," he asked, "am I always going out of my mind around you?"

She snaked her hand between their bodies to unfasten his strained trousers. "I think we're not—goodness—" She broke off as her palm brushed his arousal through the cloth, apparently finding more than she expected. "I think we're both a little crazy because we're not doing it enough."

Her fingers slipped beneath his linens to curl around his naked flesh. He grunted with the overwhelming relief. Her hand was on him. *Her hand* was on *him*. She eased his shaft upward, measuring his strength and weight. He couldn't resist pushing himself through her hold, slowly, so he could savor the sensations, so she'd know exactly what she'd done to him. A coolness at his very tip told him he was growing wet.

She moaned admiringly at his state, her grip both torture and reward. "Maybe three, four times a day, we'd feel calmer."

"Four," he said, catching her lips for a deep, wet kiss. If she wasn't going to mention why they weren't doing this that often, neither was he. "Four would wear me out fine."

He kneaded her breasts through the conservative dress she'd donned to impress the Children's Ministry, a maneuver that caused her to wriggle against the bricks. The distention of her nipples turned the stiff navy bodice wicked. Smiling to himself, he circled each hardened tip with the pad of his thumb, then bent to suckle them through her dress. The material tasted of starch but smelled of her.

"Take me here," she whispered, releasing him long enough to hike up her skirts.

He touched one perfect thigh, spellbound, then squeezed until he could feel the long, strong muscle that lay beneath. Following it upward, he cupped her dampened underclothes.

"I want you in a bed," he said.

"You can have me in a bed next time." She caught his earlobe between her teeth. "I'm very, very grateful. It's going to take a while to show you how much."

If her mention of next times weren't enough, when she curled the tip of her tongue inside his ear, he was lost.

Immediately outrageously impatient, he ripped her underthings at the crotch. A heartbeat was enough to shove his trousers down his hips. He bent his knees to align their bodies and found her thighs already spread.

"In me," she whispered. "Oh, God, come in me now."

She was wet, quivering against his crown. The little cry she made when he pressed that part of him inside her sent icy-hot thrills skittering down his spine.

"All of it," she said, her hands urging.

He thrust without a second thought, burying himself within her sex. Her flesh fluttered around him, clinging and then releasing in quick, almost frantic alternations. Adrian thought he'd been hard before, but now his skin felt stretched enough to burst. He ground his teeth together for control.

"That's not . . . quite all of it," he gasped, swiveling his hips a fraction deeper.

"I want it," she said, one thigh rising to climb his leg. "I want it all."

Taking her at her word, he hooked her knee over his elbow and spread her wide. With one more push, he reached his limit.

"Ah," she said, her head rolling on the brick. "Yes. *Yes*."

Heat expanded in his groin, the sensation of urgency rising with her response. He braced his knees on the wall and ground deliciously in. The ache of being inside her was heaven, anticipation and reward swirling into an intoxicating mix. Everything he knew about his own body said this was going to be quick. He had just enough presence of mind to find her bud of pleasure with his thumb.

As he did, Roxanne gasped something unintelligible, then almost lost her footing as she began to climax. Not about to relinquish his precious mooring, he shoved her tighter against the brick. Then, every bit as needy as she, he drew back and pumped her onward with quick, short thrusts.

"I can't stop coming," she moaned, though it was hardly a complaint. Her hands tightened around his shoulders. "Oh, God, harder." Her pelvis arched up to help him, shifting the pressure of his strokes to the bottom side of his cock, where the nerves were more sensitive. He gasped at the change, his testicles pulling tight in preparation, his groin ready to explode.

"Oh, yes," she cried. "Faster. Yes, come with me. I want to feel you. Oh, Lord, I can tell you're close."

She muffled a scream against his neck, her sheath quivering violently around his cock.

He loved the look of her in climax, the feel, half regretting the need to come himself. Hoping to keep her in her present state as long as humanly possible, he worked her swollen clitoris beneath his thumb.

She flung her head back at the stimulation, her muscles locking in place. Her shudders deepened. Like drumrolls, they ran up and down his prick. Sucking a desperate breath, he drew out nearly to his crest, then drove in hard. He was riding the edge of his culmination, close enough to taste. One more time he pulled back against the exquisite suction of her spasms. Her body grasped him greedily beneath the crown. That was it. Muscles tightened at the base of his sex. He surged forward, jolting her into the wall with unthinking force.

She moaned his name as he burst in deep, aching pulses, pouring out the feeling in long, sweet jets. Just barely he managed to keep his feet. He came until he couldn't anymore. Then silence spread around them while he rocked her gently, thankfully, in his arms.

"Well," she said at last, rubbing her silky hair against his cheek. "I'm not sure who showed who they were grateful, but that'll do for a start."

He laughed, helpless not to. "Is that an invitation to stay the night?"

She pulled back far enough to see his face. "Do you want to?"

"Always," he said, then wondered if he should have. That word was a kind of promise. He tested it in his head, a cautious swimmer with one toe in the water. *Always*. It didn't sound as strange as he'd thought.

More skeptical than he, Roxie's eyebrows climbed her forehead. Whatever her doubts, she didn't air them out loud, just shook down her skirts and offered him her hand.

As she led him the rest of the way to her room, he tried to decide if he were relieved or sorry not to be confronted. After tonight, he couldn't doubt that risking everything for her would have extremely sweet rewards.

Chapter 20

〜

"I have lied to you," her handsome swain confessed. "I am no prince. Only a humble rag seller. It was my sturdy peasant blood which allowed me to survive the demon's attack. Alas, one such as I cannot marry you!"

"You can," cried the princess, stamping her dainty foot. "The world and its opinions can go to Hades!"

—*The Perils of the Princess,*
as serialized in the *Illustrated Times*

〜

I wonder if I ought to marry her, *Adrian* mused, squinting at himself in the bathroom mirror. He dragged Roxanne's straight razor up his cheek. Maybe it was time he admitted he couldn't stay away from her. Atkinson had to view marriage as a lesser evil than living in sin. If Adrian intended to continue the latter, he might as well propose the former. To hell with promotion, anyway.

Roxie could do worse than marrying an inspector.

Grinning, he shook foam off the blade and rinsed it under the automatic tap. Being flippant was easy when you'd woken from your first sound sleep in weeks.

As he pulled his upper lip taut to get at the stubble there, a flood of optimism buoyed his spirits. Atkinson wouldn't fire him. Not for falling in love. Yes, he'd be annoyed, maybe even disappointed, but the chief liked and respected him. Adrian had caught him off guard that night at the Astoria, that was all.

He was humming as he tilted his head and began to work on his throat.

Just think: He could sleep beside Roxanne every night, kiss her every morning, help her stuff Max into his clothes, watch her paint and laugh, and be able to reach out and touch her whenever he chose. Charles might not be enthused by the idea, but the boy no longer hated him. He might come around eventually, and Adrian did like him, prickly though he was.

This was assuming Roxie wanted to marry him.

His hand stilled at the possibility that she might not. *Nonsense,* he thought. She claimed she didn't care about marriage, but he didn't believe her for a minute. She'd almost said she loved him. She would have if he hadn't been too unnerved to let her. She'd marry him. She had to.

But maybe he ought to wait for her to start dropping hints the way his first wife had.

His stomach clenched at the thought of botching a marriage with Roxanne. He wouldn't, though. For one thing, he already knew they were compatible. For another, he wasn't the same person he'd been then. Even two years later, he knew he'd changed a good deal. His mother told him so every chance she got, though she didn't seem to think he'd changed for the better. Would she consider Roxanne an improvement, he wondered, or a sign of continuing decline? But who cared what his family thought? It was his life, his happiness.

If she'd have him.

Just because Adrian had been her first lover didn't mean she wanted him to be her last.

He frowned blackly, then cursed as the razor nicked his chin.

"Knock, knock," Roxie said, leaning against the open door. "My, Adrian, that towel becomes you."

Though her tone was light, it held a thread of tension. He hoped she wasn't worrying about his reaction to their current morning after. Banishing unpleasant thoughts, he turned to beam at her.

His face fell. "You're dressed!"

He'd been hoping to kiss her awake before he left for work, to rest his hand on her cool, soft breast and feel the peak tighten under his palm. He'd promised this to himself as a reward for letting her sleep. Now she'd deprived him.

"You don't like it?" She looked down at herself, sober as a nun in moss green velvet. The gown's long sleeves and high neck ended in half-inch ruffles of the same cloth. She'd scraped her glorious hair back from her face and contained the resulting bun with a small netted toque. The hat's matching baby ostrich feather trembled as if in alarm. The outfit was smart, but he couldn't help finding it funereal.

"It's handsome," he said, honestly enough.

She rolled her eyes, then clucked when she saw the cut on his chin. "You hurt yourself!"

She closed the gap between them and touched her finger to the wound. Despite their night of debauchery, his cock stirred slightly in interest.

"It's just a nick." Smiling, he tightened the towel and leaned forward to lick her right cheekbone. "The thought of you distracted me."

She laughed as he continued to lap at her freckles. "Adrian, what are you trying to do? See if they come off?"

"I thought they might taste like something. Nutmeg. Apricot. Something yummy for the most beautiful freckles in the world."

"You're an idiot." Playfully, she pushed his shoulder, still damp from his bath.

"No, I'm not. They're the most beautiful freckles in the

world, and they're all mine. I don't want anyone else tasting even one."

Her eyes flew to his. He forced himself to hold her stare, though he was almost as surprised as she by his vehemence. He hadn't planned on broaching the subject of fidelity in quite this fashion, but what was wrong with saying he wanted her to himself? At the least, he wanted that understood.

Roxie cleared her throat and looked at the floor, obviously taken aback. "I'm bringing Max to babyschool this morning," she said.

"Oh." He blotted the last of the soap from his face. "I guess that explains the dress. Do you want me to go with you?"

She shook her head. He was disappointed, despite having business of his own to attend to. He'd liked having her ask him for help. How was he supposed to convince her he was indispensable when she did everything herself?

"Charles usually takes him to school," she said, then grinned slyly. "Today, however, Charles is starting a new job." She nodded at his inquiring look. "Yes, at the Astoria House. For now he's on breakfast shift. Apparently, the head chef was impressed by his toasted cinnamon kirbaz. You should have seen him bouncing around this morning."

"I'm sorry I missed it."

"Me, too. That was a wonderful thing you did for him. I don't know how to thank you."

He brushed his thumbs through the baby-soft tendrils above her ears. Though his heart was pounding, he tried to speak casually. "It's not the least bit necessary, but if you wished, you could let me stay here on a regular basis. We could thank each other the way we did last night."

She opened her mouth, then shut it, then shook her head. Her response seemed more a sign of disbelief than refusal, but it disturbed him. Was she really that surprised he wanted a more permanent arrangement?

"Roxanne." He rubbed the small of her velvet-covered back, just above the bustle. "Won't you let me stay? I don't think I can stand another separation."

She buried her face in his shoulder. Her hat's little feather tickled his ear, but he didn't want to move. When she spoke, he felt as well as heard her words.

"I'd like you to stay," she said, "but I don't want you to look back someday and be sorry."

"Missing you is the sorriest thing I know."

She looked up at him, her lips caught between her teeth.

"Let me," he crooned, kissing the slant of her cheek. "I don't ever want to be away from you."

"Ever?" she said in a small, worried voice.

For some reason, her insecurity sparked his confidence. He dropped his mouth to hers, tasting her tremors and her welcome. Her arms tightened around his neck even as her mouth tightened on his kiss. When she pressed closer, the folds of her velvet skirt swung between his legs, half parting his towel. It gave him an odd feeling, as though he were at once naked and clothed.

"I could get you a key," she said breathlessly when he finally released her.

Adrian smiled. A key might not be as satisfying as a successful proposal of marriage, but it was a start.

⌐⊸⊸

Work was quiet for once. Maybe too quiet. Adrian caught more than one speculative look as he passed his fellow officers in the halls—though that could have been because Adrian was too contented to wear his usual reserve. Despite the oddness of their reactions, he saw no point in worrying what rumors might be flying. Trying to quash them was likely to make them worse.

The sphere of avoidance that surrounded him did have one positive effect. He had plenty of time to call on his acquaintance at the Children's Ministry board. Adrian had extricated the man's eldest son from a situation that, while not illegal, could have caused his family embarrassment. Happily, the father was still grateful, though he cautioned Adrian that his intervention might raise eyebrows.

Beyond caring about that, Adrian thanked him for his help.

The plan for Max's future safety set into motion, Adrian decided to act on the instinct that prodded him to speak to the station's coffee vendor. She confirmed his suspicion that the doctor who handled his implants was known as The Dragon. Though she seemed unsurprised by Max's story, she professed not to have heard of the experiment.

"We only know what The Dragon do to us," she said, her lips pursed with what, on a human face, would have signified mild disapproval. On her, it had to mean hatred.

"What did he do to you?" Adrian asked.

She turned away to serve another customer, her motions suddenly sharp. Adrian wasn't sure she'd answer when she turned back. She wiped her spotless counter with a clean white rag.

"If a *rohn* is exiled," she finally said, "no matter how small the crime, that *rohn* never have babies."

"Oh." Adrian rubbed his chin. He wanted children himself, but he could only begin to imagine what being unable to have them meant for a woman. Now he knew why he'd never seen young demons in Harborside. He'd thought they were simply kept very close.

"Yes, *oh*," said the *rohn,* her expression fierce, her silver eyes glittering. Adrian didn't think he'd ever seen a Yama this close to crying. "No babies. No grandbabies. No one to bounce on one's knee or make one laugh when one is too old to shock anyone."

"Other doctors refuse," she went on. "Say even *rohn* deserve to have their lines live on. Not The Dragon. He do whatever *daimyo* want." Her rag rubbed another furious circle on the smooth old wood. "You stay away from him, Policeman Philips. He not care about the law."

Adrian hadn't been aware that she knew his name. He certainly didn't know hers. As gently as he could, he put his hand on top of hers. Her skin was cooler than a human's—and surprisingly smooth. Her eyes widened at his touch, exposing even more silver. "I'll be careful," he assured her.

"Careful not good enough," the *rohn* said emphatically. "You be smart."

~∂~

Though Adrian's exchange with the coffee vendor had unsettled him, he managed to shake off the reaction by the time he returned to Roxie's that evening.

Charles made dinner for everyone, a truly inspired meal of fresh baked bread and greens and pepper-roasted fish with baby lemon rosettes. The four of them made a cozy group around the butcher block table in the oven-warmed kitchen. Charles looked tired but happy. Their conversation was quiet, mostly murmurs of appreciation for the food. This was a far cry from Adrian's parents' house, where the constant babble barely left one energy to think. Adrian ate everything set before him, then tucked into dessert as well.

Once the last crumbs of hot apple tart were licked from the last thumb, he pulled a document from his jacket pocket and gently whacked Max over the bristly top of his head.

"Wha-ha-hat?" he giggled.

"Wash your hands, and I'll let you read it."

"But I can't read yet!" he protested.

"Then tell Roxie to wash her hands, and I'll let her read it to you."

Max was laughing too hard to follow those instructions, so Roxie rinsed her hands in the sink and dried them on Charles's apron.

"Hand it over," she ordered, her face alight with pleasure.

Her hand flew to her chest as soon as she opened the folded document. "Oh, my goodness. 'The fifth children's court of the third district of Avvar hereby declares the male child heretofore known as Maxwell McAllister to be the true and lawful custodial responsibility of Roxanne McAllister, from this day forward until he shall reach the age of majority in the aforesaid district.' Oh, *Adrian*."

Overcome, she sank into the chair that Charles slid behind her knees.

"Does that mean I'm really, truly yours?" Max asked.

Charles ruffled his cowlick. "Really, truly."

"And Charles, too?"

Color swept up the older boy's face. Adrian's own cheeks heated. He hadn't thought about Charles.

"Actually, Max," said the boy, with a small, throat-clearing cough. "I'm only six months short of majority. I've got a good job now, and much as I appreciate having a . . . a family to be with, I can take care of myself."

His countenance was purple by the time he finished. The parlor clock could be heard ticking across the hall. With a woman's genius for deepening a man's embarrassment, Roxie assured Charles that he was family, too. "And I love you every bit as much, sweetie."

"Yes, well." Charles cleared his throat again, then popped up like a jack-in-the-box to clear the table. "Thanks."

Roxie was still chuckling when the doorbell rang.

"I'll get it," Adrian volunteered, sensing his absence could only improve Charles's situation.

Whoever had rung must have remained outside. Adrian left the door ajar behind him and sprinted down the twisting flights to the street. The setting sun filled the stairwell with dusty gold and rose. Whistling as he went, his legs felt as bouncy as Southlandic rubber. He was a hero tonight: his soon-to-be family's hero.

To his surprise, he knew the person waiting on the stoop. A full-blooded Silver Islander, Sergeant Farsi Ross had skin the color of roasted chestnuts and the curliest black hair Adrian had ever seen. His accent was melodic, serving as counterpoint to his intimidating bulk. In Adrian's opinion, he was the department's most promising new recruit.

"Sergeant Ross," he said, swinging the door open. "Has something happened with one of my cases? Do I need to return to Little Barking?"

He hoped not. Roxie deserved a bit of a honeymoon before being forced to habituate herself to policemen's hours.

Whatever the sergeant's news, he seemed more interested in tugging imaginary creases from his uniform than in sharing it.

"Would you like to come in?" Adrian offered, a prickle of unease flashing between his shoulder blades.

"No, sir. I am sorry to be the bearer of bad tidings, but Superintendent Atkinson asked me to relay the message that you need not come to work tomorrow."

Adrian fell back a step. The glass of the door was cool against his shoulder. "I'm being suspended?"

The sergeant screwed his dark, broad face into a picture of regret. "Well, not to put too fine a point on it: You're being dismissed. I am sorry, sir. It's ridiculous to dismiss you simply because you intervened with the Children's Ministry on behalf of a friend."

Adrian cursed under his breath. He'd known word would spread, but not that this would turn out to be Atkinson's final straw. He supposed he hadn't wanted to know.

"Rumor has it the superintendent was getting pressure from above," Ross said sympathetically. "But he knows you're a good man. Maybe if you talk to him?"

Adrian snorted. "And say what? That I'm sorry? I'm not sorry. Or maybe he wants me to promise not to come here again. I won't promise. I intend to see this woman as often as she'll let me."

Ross lifted his hands. Even in the fading light, his grin was brilliant. "I'm no enemy to romance. We Islanders have our priorities straight. Your gain is Securité's loss."

Adrian was warmed by his response, even if it didn't change a thing. "Somehow, I doubt Atkinson is wasting any tears on me."

Ross treated him to a true Island shrug. "So you'll work for yourself now. No more politics."

"Maybe." He picked a fleck of paint off the door, then watched an electric tram clack its way along the rails. Sparks flew off the metal wheels as it rounded the corner. *Dismissed.* This threw a proper wrench in his marriage plans. You couldn't support a wife on what he'd set aside to supplement his pension.

"You put your mind to it, sir," Ross said, "and you can do whatever you like. In fact, you ever want to hire another investigator, you call Farsi first."

Adrian smiled. "That means a lot to me. Of course, I'll be lucky to support myself as an independent, never mind hiring an employee."

"Don't count on it. You've got a way about you, Inspector. I know Securité hasn't always treated you as they should, but outside the department, people trust you. You make them want to put their troubles on your shoulder. I think you'll have plenty of work." He finished his declaration by pressing Adrian's severance envelope into his palm. The stack of notes felt thick. Atkinson must have been feeling guilty.

"Thank you," he responded, trying to hide his dejection. He wasn't sure he wanted to enter the sometimes seedy business of private surveillance. Still, the sergeant meant well. He held out his hand for the other to shake. "I'll remember what you said."

◁━▷

When he shut the outside door, he found Roxanne waiting on the last step. *So.* She'd witnessed his humiliation. It seemed inevitable, even appropriate. Her hands were knotted together, and her feet were bare. For the first time he realized how affluent she looked, despite her eccentric dress. The sheen of good health and regular meals glowed in her skin. *She owns her own business,* he reminded himself. *And she's twelve years younger than you.*

He hated the look of pity in her eyes.

"I'm sorry," she said. "You loved that job."

He shoved his hands in his pockets to hide their unsteadiness. He shrugged. "I've lost things I cared about before. What's one more?"

"One more is one more." She sounded watchful. Wary. "If Herrington was behind Max being taken, he may be behind this, too: his retaliation for being thwarted."

Adrian wasn't sure it mattered. Atkinson might have fired him anyway. He pushed his hair back from his face. He was going to have to get it cut. Then again, why worry about looking businesslike now?

"We should have talked to Herrington," she said, "as soon as we got Max back."

"We can't know that would have made a difference. Plus, your custody of Max wasn't secure."

"But if we'd given . . . my father a chance to yell at us to our faces, maybe he wouldn't have done this."

"Yama don't think that way. They prefer the indirect route."

"If I'm mad at someone, I want to yell."

"That's funny. I don't believe I've ever seen you do it."

She sighed. "I could have given in to him," she admitted reluctantly.

Adrian cocked one eyebrow. "Without knowing what his idea of father-daughter obligations involves? Assuming he was behind this—which we don't know—you couldn't have guessed this would happen. Hell, if I'd guessed, I would have done it anyway."

She took this in, her wrists twisted together between her knees. "What are you going to do?"

"I don't know. Go private, maybe. Investigative work is all I'm trained for. I'm not destitute, if that's what you're worried about."

"Adrian." One bare foot dropped to the dusty vestibule floor, but aside from that, she didn't come closer. "You know I'm not worried about your finances."

"Aren't you?" He studied the concern on her face. "Tell me you weren't wondering whether you should offer to help."

She blushed and drew a circle with her toe.

"That's what I thought."

"You're my friend. And you've helped me. Look what you did for Max and Charles."

"You're a woman," he said. "You're supposed to need help."

She drew her foot back onto the step and crossed her arms. Her expression said this was the stupidest thing she'd ever heard. "Come on, Adrian. With thinking like that, you might as well grab my hair and drag me back to your cave."

Anger heated in his veins. So what if he was stuffy and middle class? So what if she wasn't truly his to take care of? What right did she have to mock him when he was at his lowest?

Catching himself before he could say something he regretted, he forced his body to relax. He wasn't angry at her. He was angry at fate. "You feel like a drink?" he asked abruptly. " 'Cause I sure could use one."

"I don't know." She seemed startled as he caught her elbow and began to escort her back up the stairs. "Maybe you shouldn't drink when you're upset."

"Who's upset?" He stomped them forward determinedly. "We'll celebrate my freedom. We'll celebrate not having to worry about whether I'll get fired. After all, I already have been."

When he laughed at this irony, Roxie did not join in.

Chapter 21

Ironically, the *rohn*'s industrious habits did not endear them to their human hosts. Though poor compared to the *daimyo*, each exile arrived in Avvar with his royally mandated "bloodstake": a small sack of Northlandic gold which was meant to prevent him or her from becoming a drain on Victoria's purse. With this capital, far greater than most residents of Harborside would see in their lives, they began small businesses that then provided humans with employment—menial, it was true, but in an impoverished area like Avvar's slums, such jobs could not be scorned. Hole-in-the-wall restaurants sprung up, used-clothes sellers, tiny repair shops for the new technology. Harborside had never been so vibrant . . . or so divided. Envy, it seemed, was not a good basis for friendship.

—*The True and Irreverent History of Avvar*

*They started at the Book and Beer, a local estab-*lishment that was half bookstore, half public house. It boasted a mixed crowd: students, artists, even a few *rohn*. The Yama sat quietly amongst themselves, dressed in their traditional navy and gray, a small but telling distance between their tables and the rest—as if the other patrons feared the foreigners might lose control and start draining everyone's energy. Had the pub been any nicer, the Yama would have been turned away. Had it been any worse, they wouldn't have come near it. Demons were notoriously finicky about dirt.

Their coin was fine, of course. Everyone liked demon gold.

Most of the humans at the Book and Beer were drinking absinthe and smoking the strong Jeruvian cigarlings that were all the rage that year. Pungent silver-blue clouds swirled above the marble café tables. With their sensitive noses, Adrian wondered how the Yama could stand it. For himself, he hoped the fashion wouldn't last.

By the time he procured a half-pint from the tap, his determination to enjoy himself had run dry. Back at their windowside table, Roxie was reading the *Avvar Post*. Didn't want to encourage his drunken revelry, he supposed. He turned his chair backward and straddled it. The bent-cane back provided a welcome support for his chin.

He sucked the froth off his Bookman's Red. He sighed. Roxie turned a page. "Home Rule Sympathizers Dump Tea in Harbor," tattled the headline. The *Post* was staunchly pro-Empire. If Victoria sneezed, it made the front page. His mind turned in an aimless circle as he thought back to the stack of papers he'd found in Tommy Bainbridge's temporary burrow. Now that Adrian was unemployed, he'd have plenty of time to look for lost boys, just no means to support it.

The reminder stirred a wave of restless energy.

"This place is too tame," he groused.

Roxie lowered the edge of her paper. She stared pointedly at a nearby table where a young woman, probably an artist's model, sat on the lap of a delighted law student.

They were sharing smoke and absinthe without benefit of a glass.

Adrian chose not to acknowledge the refutation. He set down what remained of his beer. "Let's go somewhere near the harbor. I want to see the tea those 'sympathizers' dumped."

"Adrian." She folded her paper with a brisk rattle. "Charles says you have a portrait of the High Lady in your office, so I know you don't really want to view this outrage to the Crown."

"For your information, every Securité officer has one. Victoria's in our oath." All too easily, he pulled himself into review posture and placed his hand over his heart. " 'I swear to uphold the laws of the Aedlyne Empire and offer my undying fealty to our most esteemed High Lady, Victoria Christiana St. Steffin Faen Aedlys.' "

"Hear-hear," said one of the patrons, probably a second-generation immigrant.

Another, from the opposite camp, offered up a raspberry.

The *rohn* simply looked nervous.

Feeling bad about this and hoping to avoid a scene, Adrian stood. "I'll let you choose the spot," he said to Roxie. "As long as there's music and beer."

She considered this. "You won't argue with my choice?"

Policeman's honor, he almost said: his own personal anachronism.

"All right," she surrendered. "Be forewarned, though, the place I'm taking you isn't for tidy folk."

"Who's tidy?" he scoffed, and tugged off his cravat.

⤛⤜

Adrian's mood made Roxanne nervous. Was this brittle cheer what failure—*temporary failure,* she assured herself—brought out in a man? If so, how long would it last? He certainly wasn't behaving sensibly. First, he insisted on covering the evening's expenses, then wanted to hire an electric cab. She coaxed him onto the trolley instead. He might prefer to play the gentleman of means, but pride wouldn't protect his reserves.

Giving their seat a surly swipe with his handkerchief, he muttered under his breath about people who pinched a penny until it screamed.

Heat swamped her face at the unexpected barb. Yes, she economized, but why buy everything new when there were so many nice old things that only needed a bit of care to catch their second wind? Besides, she had two boys' futures to consider. And her own. And Adrian's, in a way. She knew it galled him to accept anything from her, but he'd gotten fired on her behalf. She wasn't about to let him swing in the wind. He'd have her support and be damned to him. Even if he wouldn't take her money.

She resettled herself on the hard wooden seat. *Stupid male.* Had their positions been reversed, he'd have sheltered her in a minute.

They debarked at Front and First. Adrian stepped onto the cobbles and inhaled deeply.

"See"—he handed her down—"you can smell tea."

"I smell old fish," Roxie teased.

They stood a stone's throw from the docks. Oil lanterns lit the pier. Between bursts of noise from the taverns, waves slurped at barnacled pilings. Her nose detected the faintest whiff of oolong. The strongest smell, however, was the aroma of fresh lager. And why not? These brews made their way to Avvar from all ports of Victoria's Empire. After a long journey spent inhaling the yeasty perfume, the sailors were understandably eager to sample the goods.

"Over there." She pointed to the sign swinging above one entrance. It portrayed a grinning terrier guarding a mug between his paws. "The Hair of the Dog serves the best beer in Harborside. And they've got a piano."

The fact that the owner was a personal friend and would make sure they didn't stumble into trouble, she kept to herself.

When they entered the noisy tavern, the piano sat abandoned. To Roxie's relief, Adrian put up no protest. Not that he had much opportunity. As soon as Genevieve Bleeker spotted her former shipmate, she let loose a whoop that rattled the bottle-bottom windows.

Built like a bulldog and twice as determined, Bleeker had been forced from the sailing life when she lost half an ear in a dockside brawl. Not only did the injury offend their captain's sense of aesthetics, the fight represented a serious breach of discipline. The heartbroken Bleeker was obliged to find a new love. Fortunately, Roxie was a well-heeled landlubber by then and could afford to stake her bar. The day Bleeker paid back Roxie's loan, she thanked her for the first time. Roxie understood. Some people couldn't rest easy until they'd paid their markers.

Sparing a brief glance for Adrian, the grizzled salt pulled Roxie into a bone-crushing hug. Her short silver hair clung to her head like a cap, beneath which her mangled ear was defiantly visible. When she pushed back, her sea green eyes twinkled like stones in a streambed.

"Long time no see, Red. Been too busy playin' Hide the Sausage with the pretty boys?"

"Get swived," Roxanne retorted, falling easily into her former foul-mouthed seafaring ways. "*Queen*'s crew always know where the sausage is."

At this, Bleeker gave Adrian a once-over direct enough to bring color into his cheeks. "Hard to lose track with a two-fister like that, eh?"

Roxie grimaced on Adrian's behalf. "Take pity, Bleeker. This one's a daisy."

"Fresh enough to pick," Adrian threw out, still red in the face. Bleeker laughed and walloped his shoulder. His good sportsmanship established, a friendship commenced. With Bleeker's help, Adrian snagged two pints and a table.

"For the sake of appearances," he said when Roxie looked askance at her brimming tankard. "Otherwise, these old salts will think I'm drinking alone."

He downed his drink with the appreciation of a thirsty man, after which he braced one hand on the smoke-blackened wall and stood.

He certainly didn't have a hollow leg. Roxie grinned into her fist as, swaying slightly, he shouldered through the crowd toward the battered black upright on the far wall. Her eyes widened when he tipped the bench down off the top, sat, and slid back the cover.

Adrian played?

Apparently so. He cracked his knuckles and rolled his shoulders in preparation. His hands descended. At first, she couldn't hear a note above the din but, gradually, as a circle of quiet spread outward from the piano, the music reached her. No childish plunking, this, but a lyrical sonata, deceptively simple, exquisitely timed. Her eyes burned, her intuitive response to artistry. Brine-tinged air gusted through the room as people on the street heard and came in. Even a few *rohn* braved the rowdy surroundings.

Roxie didn't bother to wonder why. Adrian was good: concert quality, and—unlike well-born Yama, who tended to suppress such proclivities—*rohn* were as susceptible to the enticements of human music as they were to etheric-force. Adrian's fingers must have seemed magical as they flowed over the keys. His body swayed. His eyes closed. Then, as though embarrassed by his solemnity, he broke into a champagne waltz so bubbly it made her feet itch for dancing slippers.

When the last note faded, she put two fingers to her mouth and whistled. "More," she called. "More."

Suckers for a good tune, no matter what sort, the Dog's nautical patrons seconded her.

A sheepish grin split Adrian's face. "Only if you come up here and sing," he shouted back through cupped hands.

"Sing!" demanded the crowd, lifting her bodily out of her chair. They pushed her forward until she reached his side.

Adrian thought he'd never seen anything as beautiful as the flush of laughter on her face. He might have embarrassed her, but not badly.

"How do you know I can sing?" she hissed by his ear.

He tilted his shoulders. "You've got your mother's voice."

"Well, scoot over at least." She used her hip to make room for herself on the bench. "I want to be sure you play something I know."

Elbowing his arm out of the way, she jumped into the prelude of a popular drinking song. Her style fit their surroundings better than his. Heedless of missed or ill-counted notes, her playing raced onward like a runaway carthorse. Within moments, she had toes tapping and heads nodding. She was clearly trying to stump him with her choice of music, but as the son of a ship's carpenter, Adrian knew plenty of sailors' favorites. Determined not to be outdone, he bounced an impromptu embellishment off the lower octaves. The barmaids cheered.

That'll show her, he thought. *One more pleasure we have in common.*

Roxie laughed and tossed her head. Her chest inflated with a breath. She opened her lovely mouth to sing.

Her mother's voice did not come pouring out. Roxie's was too gruff and underused to reach the diva's shimmering perfection. She had no vibrato, catch-as-catch-can volume, and an overfondness for slide. What she did possess was absolute and perfectly rounded pitch, as though the notes had been hammered into her in the cradle. And there was something about the way she sang, some quirk of phrasing, some knack for tugging the emotional heartstrings, that reminded the listener of the Incomparable One.

"La Belle's daughter," he heard someone whisper after they finished in a crash of chords.

Before they had time to think of returning to their table, a balloon of brandy was placed on top of the piano, a silent request for an encore from an extremely polite-looking Yama with his hair slicked like a seal's behind his ears. The demon melted back into the crowd before anyone could express surprise at his presence. Adrian experienced a twinge of concern for the man's well-being but supposed the music made temporary brothers of them all.

Refusing to worry, he nudged the glass toward Roxie with a wink. "Good for the throat."

She rolled her eyes, but she took a sip, and another when the *rohn*'s small table sent a second offering. The crowd began to cheer both the Yama and Roxie on, making a joke of their bowing generosity. Adrian was sober by the time Roxie slipped into a giddy sort of melancholy, crooning out a string of sailors' laments: deaths at sea, unfaithful wives, all of which she ruined by dissolving into giggles at inappropriate intervals.

The "Song of the Love-Mad *Rohn*," a god-awful piece of sentiment that for some reason was popular with both races, nearly brought down the house.

Adrian didn't care if the tune was maudlin. The sight of Roxie's glowing face entranced him. Her eyes danced with the music. Her hair spilled little curls from the edges of her sunny braid. For once, she was glad to be her mother's daughter. He wished he could surround her with adulation for the rest of her days, that he could keep her safe from worry.

In the end, he had to force her hands off the keys.

"That's enough, you drunken parakeet." He kissed her cheek. "Any more and you won't be able to talk tomorrow."

"I will," she protested, but she had to cough to get the words out.

~~~

The night was black and star-strewn, the city silent as it held a long predawn breath. They ambled across deserted Victoria Bridge, their arms around each other's waists, trying to walk off Roxie's inebriation. Adrian had no gloves, so she coaxed his hand into the pocket of her long tweed coat and slipped her own beneath it. Of his own volition, Adrian tangled their fingers together.

I love this man, she thought, knowing the ache in her throat was due to more than strained vocal chords. *What will I do if he decides I'm not worth his sacrifice?*

Given her preoccupation, it was no wonder she didn't see the danger behind them until it was too late.

The five laughing Yama appeared out of nowhere, drunk and stumbling and attempting to sing in the horribly off-key manner of their race. From their choice of tunes, they must have followed them from the Dog. Not wishing to insult them, Roxanne fought a compulsion to plug her ears.

"You!" one of them called, bumping up against her and taking her arm. "La Belle Yvonne's daughter. We throwing party. You come sing for us, and we pay gold."

A second Yama hooked her arm familiarly. She was about to offer a polite refusal when she noticed three of the others had stumbled between her and Adrian and were crowding him back into the bridge's balustrade. They were dressed like *rohn* in simple blue and gray, but their hair was not short the way it should have been. Instead, it was tied back in crisscrossed leather and fell to their waists. Her drunkenness cleared in an instant.

These were *daimyo*.

"Hey!" she said, abruptly alarmed.

Before she could shout any further warning, something cold pricked her neck. Her knees crumpled, her body going numb with what felt like a massive dose of narcophane. Paralyzed, unable to speak or fight, she struggled simply to breathe while the two Yama who had bumped her wrapped their arms around her waist. Lifting her to her feet, they started dragging her to the opposite end of the bridge.

The tall black lampposts blurred as if she were passing them at a dead run. Roxie didn't think this perception was the effect of the drug. The demon's swiftness was impressive, far greater than humans would have managed with a limp burden. Their manner, too, had undergone a transformation. Gone was the laughter and drunkenness, gone the humility. As they pulled her along, they wore the haughty masks *daimyo* preferred to expressions.

To her dismay, she recognized them as the Yama who'd bought her all those glasses of brandy at Bleeker's place. Obviously, this was a well-planned attack.

She barely had time to register the presence of the electric automobile before they shoved her into its backseat.

"Wha—" she gasped, trying to wedge her dangling foot into the open door, not an easy task when one's muscles felt like overcooked noodles.

While the Yama struggled to close the door, she heard cries back on the bridge, followed by a splash. Unable to turn her neck, she could only hope Adrian hadn't been thrown into the river.

Her captors began to argue in Yamish above her head— at least, it sounded like an argument. They threw her leg in and climbed into the seat beside her. A sixth Yama started the car, which rolled speedily into motion.

Good Lord, she thought. *I'm being abducted.*

Her body slumped half-upright against the door, exactly as the demons left it.

"Wha—you want?" she managed to ask, her tongue as thick as cotton.

Perhaps because she'd spoken Ohramese, the Yama did, too.

"How much did you give her?" the second demon asked the first, all hint of halting accent gone.

"Enough to knock out one of us," the other replied. "The man said not to give her a chance to fight. Said he didn't want damaged goods."

What man? she wanted to demand. *Who sent you to do this?*

Clearly they'd given her a larger-than-human dose of sedative. Just as clearly, she wasn't reacting as they expected. Maybe her mixed heritage made her respond differently. Maybe if she tried, she could throw off even more of the drug's influence.

They rattled past a repair shop she frequented, the "Toasters Fixed Like New!" sign wavering before her bleary eyes. Two of her fingers twitched. If she could open the door latch, she might be able to roll out of the car and scream for help.

She heard a new sound then, one that caused her captors to turn and exclaim with un-demonlike surprise.

Someone was running after the speeding car. Not only that, someone was catching up.

Adrian, she thought, anxiety and hope twisting in her breast. He must have activated his implants. That splash she heard must have been him throwing the other three into the river.

As long as her captors were distracted, Roxanne gritted

her teeth, maneuvered her tingling hands around the door latch, and pulled feebly.

Luckily, the door wasn't locked.

As her weight toppled, she fell out, hit the rushing ground like a sack of flour, and rolled into a hitching post. Her head smacked something hard, but for the moment she was free. If she could have gotten up and run, she would have felt better about her chance of staying that way.

As she'd feared, the electric car turned with a squeal of brakes and started coming back for her. Adrian was waiting. She watched, astonished, as he ripped off the door she hadn't fallen out of, yanked one of the Yama from the opening, and tossed him through a shop window. Glass shattered noisily. The car screeched to a halt.

Though the Yama wasn't as badly hurt as a human would have been and was only bleeding from several cuts, he did seem dazed as he tottered out through the shards.

Adrian didn't give him time to recover.

"Who sent you?" he demanded, grabbing the stunned *daimyo* and shoving him against a wall.

The other demon, the one still in the car, barked an order he underscored with the universal gesture for "come."

The demon Adrian held bared his teeth and stuck out his tongue. The forked marking at the end turned what would have been a childishly mocking gesture into a threat.

"Tell me!" Adrian growled.

His enhanced strength must have been fading, because the demon tore free and sprinted to the car. Adrian didn't follow, just stood there breathing hard, his neck bowed, his left arm propped against the wall while his right held his stomach as if he might be about to throw up. Despite the commotion they'd caused, not a single window opened above the shops, not even the one whose front had been smashed. Adrian didn't seem to expect it to.

He dealt with this every day, she thought, *and still loved his job.* She was marveling over that when he straightened and blew out his breath.

"You all right?" he said, turning just his head.

Roxie discovered she was strong enough to sit up. "I

think so. They gave me some sort of drug, but it's wearing off."

"You want me to find a doctor?"

Roxie didn't hold out much hope for that. "Let's see if I can stand up first."

With Adrian's help, she did, though the ground felt a bit as if she were at sea. She couldn't help being amused by the way he gripped her elbow and led her like an invalid to the circular overlook on the river side of the street. Sweet Adrian. Always the gentleman.

Sitting sideways on the bench, he pulled her back against his front. His muscles shook with the strain they'd been forced through. Comforted all the same, Roxie rested her head on his chest, gazing past him toward the water.

A barge was bearing downriver. Its running lights, a string of lanterns to port and starboard, glimmered like butter in the dark. A heap of coal rose from the deck in a small mountain, three quarters of its bulk pinned beneath a tarp. She watched the barge wallow, then straighten as it forged through the backed-up current beneath the bridge.

She hoped she and Adrian would regain their balance as easily.

"My," she said, striving for lightness, "that was amazing. You tossed that Yama through the window like he was a twig."

"The implants tossed him," Adrian said.

"I'm not so sure of that. You fought off three of them, chased a speeding automobile, then almost overcame a fourth. I thought your implants were supposed to make you *as* strong as a demon, not stronger."

When she looked into his face, he was squinting sheepishly. "Actually," he said, "when the doctor who put them in tested me, to see how much enhancement I required, I pretended to be weaker than I was. I thought I might need an advantage someday."

"How positively devious of you!"

"Yes, well, it's also true that Yama aren't used to the way humans fight. A straightforward fist to the gut will get them most every time."

"I'm still impressed," Roxie insisted, barely holding back her laugh.

Adrian shifted behind her. "I'm sorry I couldn't find out who hired them, though one would hope there'd only be two choices: your father or The Dragon."

"As opposed to a really enthusiastic fan of my singing."

"Yes," Adrian agreed, his lack of humor quelling hers.

Roxie rubbed his shoulder. "They knew who I was," she said, "and probably you, as well. They wouldn't bother to set three demons on an ordinary human male."

"Which suggests it might be The Dragon—"

"But doesn't rule out my father." Roxie shook her head, relieved that most of her dizziness was gone. "What I don't understand is what either could hope to gain by kidnapping me. If The Dragon feared exposure of his experiment on Max, why not just kill me? He has to know no one but me would take the word of a five-year-old. And how would he know Max had told the story? Does he even remember who Max is? On the other hand, if it wasn't The Dragon, but my father, trying to drive me into his company, how can he believe his behavior will do anything but estrange me permanently?"

Adrian pushed his hands down his thighs as if they were sore. "Your guess is as good as mine. Yama's minds work differently from ours."

"We have to confront Herrington now," Roxie said resignedly, the "we" coming a little too naturally. "If only to discover whether he was involved." Her face twisted at the prospect. "Lord, I hate doing that. Even if we escaped this attack, going to see him makes me feel as if he's won."

"He can't win," Adrian said. "Your head and your heart will always belong to you."

Though this was only half true, she appreciated his confidence.

Chapter 22

⥿

For an archaeologist, dawn is the magic hour. Its mix of light and shade reveals what brighter hours hide as effectively as night. Only at dawn does the day tremble with possibility.

—Welland Herrington, *A Memoir*

⥿

The last trolley was a memory and the first cab a futile hope when Adrian and Roxie rose creakily from the bench and turned to watch the sun breach the horizon. Streams of green and gold lit Avvar's largest river. Ice crusted its edges now, but come spring, snowmelt from the mountains would swell the Cheske to a tumult. The peace of the scene made their recent encounter seem unreal.

"We could walk home," Adrian suggested, reaching for her hand. "If you're up to it, it's only a couple miles."

"I don't want to stay," she said. "Even if the threat is

past, the back of my neck is creeping every time I think back."

"That's probably just nerves."

"Whatever it is, it's making me want to lock the doors and pull the covers over my head." Actually, now that she'd recovered, it was making her want to pull Adrian under the covers with her and keep him there all day. Perversely, her body was aroused by the danger they'd escaped, throbbing strongly with eagerness. She'd have given a great deal for him to pull her into the nearest alley and take her against the wall. Embarrassed, she looked away as they began to walk, hoping Adrian wouldn't spot her blush.

She knew she'd failed when he slanted a look at her and grinned. His fingers squeezed hers suggestively.

"Ah, yes," he said. "Facing death. The greatest aphrodisiac in the world."

"We didn't face death," she protested, though for all she knew they had.

"Speak for yourself. Now that the aftereffects of using my implants have worn off, I've got a cockstand as big as the Grim Reaper's scythe."

"Adrian!" She couldn't recall him speaking this bluntly before—not in public, at any rate. In spite of everything, or maybe because of it, her excitement intensified.

"I could happily keep you in bed all day," he went on, for once unabashed. "The bathroom would do as well. Or the stairwell. For that matter, the shadowed doorway of that secondhand clothes dealer seems mighty inviting."

Roxie cursed at the sudden hungry flutter between her legs. Adrian chuckled and pulled her close as if he meant to kiss her. With an effort, she held him off.

"Just get me home," she growled under her breath.

"The feeling will last," he warned. "The longer we wait, the more impatient we'll become."

"You don't have to sound so cheerful about it."

He laughed. Then he did kiss her, quick and hard on the lips. "I'm cheerful because I know you and I are going to work off this feeling the way it deserves."

His eyes were lit with joy. She knew he was reveling in

the freedom to be a sensual creature. She couldn't begrudge him his pleasure, even if she wanted more.

"You know." He hugged her shoulder as they resumed their journey. "The farmers' market should be open soon. We could grab breakfast. Although, maybe we shouldn't stop. Max will be crawling out of bed soon. If Charles is at work, he'll be alone."

Roxie's heart turned over. Sensual creature or not, he'd made her concerns his own. *Stupid man.* He behaved like a husband already. Would making it official really be that terrible? Of course, now was no time to push the issue.

"I doubt we could get home in time even if we tried," she said. "Fortunately, Max has strict instructions to knock on Abul's door if he wakes up alone. Linia will scold me up and down for staying out late, but the two of them will make sure he gets to school safely."

"Then we could have breakfast. Store up a little energy for later . . ."

Eyebrows wagging, Adrian's stride turned jaunty. She shook her head at his boyish glee. Apparently, he was enjoying bedeviling her.

They were still arguing over what to eat when they reached the open-air market. The neighboring shops were shuttered, but most of the stalls were set up. They skirted around dusty farm wagons unloading fresh vegetables, past basins of flopping fish, even a loom that had been set up beneath one of the striped awnings. Halfway through the central square, Roxie succumbed to a ruinously expensive bag of Medell cherries, which she would not let Adrian buy. The fruit was garnet-ripe. She made a game of feeding them to Adrian, giggling and whispering lurid promises each time his lips closed on her fingertips.

If she was going to be sex-mad, she'd make certain he was, too.

⌐≈⌐

Adrian knew what she was doing and didn't mind in the least. Every teasing gesture told him she was his. He was going to have her. Repeatedly. Strenuously. Endlessly. Until she lacked the strength to even dream of taking other men. Maybe he'd use his implants again. She'd seemed to like that the last time. Now that he no longer worked for Securité, he supposed the devices were his to do with as he pleased. At that moment, pleasing Roxie seemed the highest purpose he could conceive.

"You're going to pay," he whispered darkly. "I'm going to kiss you from head to toe and tup you until you scream."

"Braggart," she whispered back, her eyes twinkling merrily.

He couldn't resist. Despite the presence of watchers, he hooked one arm behind her neck and kissed her, deeply, wetly, his tongue pushing strongly against hers. Roxie moaned and began to cling. He could feel her warmth through both their sets of clothes. Abruptly desperate to plunge inside her, he wondered if they might sneak beneath the tarp in someone's wagonbed. Who cared about the risk? As far as he was concerned, the farmer could carry them back to Medell. Not that it would take that long the first time. From the feel of her squirms, minutes would be enough for them both. God, he needed to have her. His entire body pounded with lust.

Distantly, he was aware of someone calling his name. Since it wasn't Roxie, he ignored the voice. It took her taking hold of his ears and tugging to make him stop.

"What?" he asked plaintively.

Roxie tipped her head meaningfully toward the right. When Adrian saw who stood there, he nearly choked.

"Hullo, son," said his father, doffing his tweed cap and rubbing it confusedly along the part in his salt-and-pepper hair. True to form, his mother wasn't half as diplomatic.

"Well." Her hands bracketed the waist of her narrow skirt. "This must be the girl who's making you lose sleep!"

Anger set a pulse ticking in his temple. Did his mother have to let everything that came into her head burst out her mouth? Then he felt Roxie's nails digging into his coat sleeve. The evidence of her distress encouraged him to compose himself.

"Mother. Dad." He transferred a cherry pit to his pocket. The paper bag that held the fruit crackled in Roxie's hand. *Poor thing*. She could sing her heart out in front of a roomful of drunken sailors, but the thought of meeting one middle-aged couple gave her the shakes. He slung his arm around her. "This is my friend, Roxanne McAllister. Roxanne, meet my parents, Varya and Isaac Philips."

"Nice to meet you," said his father, staring pop-eyed at her ankle-baring trousers.

"Likewise," said his mother, who grinned with a bit more relish than Adrian found comfortable.

Unable to guess what that grin really meant, Roxie's tremors increased. Adrian could imagine what she was thinking. Never mind openmouthed kissing in a public place, being found in the company of a woman this early in the morning could only mean one thing—at least to people like his parents. That they were not ordinary parents went right over Roxie's head.

"Don't suppose you'd like to have breakfast with us," ventured his father, squinting vaguely at the cloud-flecked sky.

"We ate," said Roxie.

"We'd love to," said Adrian.

"We'd love to," he repeated, stroking her sleeve and ignoring her silent plea. Maybe the timing wasn't perfect, but he wanted her to understand he was ready to face a horde of parents on her behalf. He would ask her to marry him at some point. And then, God and Roxie willing, Varya and Isaac would be her in-laws. Might as well get used to the horror now.

"Wonderful," said his mother in an alarmingly pleasant tone. "I'm sure we have lots to talk about."

Oh, boy, thought Adrian. *Here we go.*

~⇒~

Roxie didn't want to think what she looked like after a night of drinking and falling out of cars. She'd never been

this aware of her difference from normal folk, which
Adrian's parents quite obviously were. Adrian's mother
made her feel like a giantess—and a demon giantess, at
that. Varya's hands were dolllike, her waist as trim as a
twelve-year-old's. And could she talk! Roxie had never
heard anyone talk as much as Adrian's mother. The woman
hardly paused for breath. Her own mother, La Belle
Yvonne, would have given much to perfect that trick.

Adrian's father, Isaac, appeared used to his wife's con-
versational habits. He gazed distractedly around the small
awning-covered eatery, smoothed his napkin, poked the
coals in the nearest brazier. Though he smiled at the rest of
the table occasionally, for the most part, he looked as
though he weren't all there. Despite this, she couldn't help
noticing how handsome he was. If this was an indication of
how Adrian would age, he'd be stirring her blood for years
to come.

Assuming he stuck around.

Needing reassurance, she slipped her hand under the
checkered oilcloth and laid it on his thigh. He squeezed
her wrist, perhaps to soothe her nerves but maybe in warning. The latter possibility put a devil into her mind. How
dare he worry that she'd embarrass him? He could do that
all by himself. In fact, he had done it. If it weren't for his
insistence on accepting his father's invitation—probably
because he was too embarrassed to refuse—they'd be
home now in her bed. Keeping her eyes on his chattering
mother, she slid her little finger into the crease between
his leg and torso, then dragged her nail over the swell of
his testicle.

His groin warmed flatteringly at her touch. Curious as
to whether his self-proclaimed cockstand had survived his
parents' appearance, she hooked her pinky to the left. My,
yes, he was definitely sporting a ridge, a ridge that was
growing bigger by the second. The fine wool that contained
him tautened until there wasn't one fold left. Feeling rather
taut herself, she added more fingers and squeezed. To her
immense gratification, he proved superior to the pressure.

His length was such that her hand couldn't cover the entire span. She consoled herself by enclosing the arch in a snug half-fist.

"Down," he hissed through his teeth, his tone a trifle too close to the way one would scold a dog.

"As you wish," she agreed and dragged her fist to his crown.

Pushed well past his limit, he coughed repressively and tried to elbow her arm away.

"Are you ill, Adrian?" asked his mother, rerouting her prattle without the least sign of strain. "I always say you don't take proper care of yourself. A winter cold is a terrible thing."

She turned to Roxie and smiled confidingly, woman to woman. "He works too hard, you know. That supervisor of his can't do without him. But I say, if he wears Adrian out, then where will he be?"

Roxie shot a look at Adrian. Did he want to break the news about getting fired? *Not now,* he mouthed, his face tightening. Roxie wasn't surprised. Could anything be harder than kicking himself off his parents' pedestal? Anxious to soothe, or at least distract him, she slipped one finger between his trouser buttons. Perspiration, nervous and otherwise, had plastered down his linens, but with a little maneuvering she managed to reach bare skin.

"Lunatic," he whispered, an inch from her ear. Roxie didn't think he meant it. In contradiction to his words, his hand now covered hers. He was, truth be told, squeezing her closer. Their eyes locked, both hot, both glittering. Adrian might not realize it, but he was daring her to go on.

"Don't," he ordered through gritted teeth, but he still wasn't pulling her off.

"Very well," she said, because even she had limits. She did, however, leave her hand where it was.

Oblivious to her son's dilemma, Varya babbled on about his lack of concern for his own well-being.

"Now, you, Roxie," she said, "you look sturdy enough to keep him in line. Not like that first wife of his, that Christine.

What a pale little flower she was! You'd have thought the first breeze would blow her away."

Varya's voice faded beneath the sudden ringing in Roxie's ears. *That first wife of his, that Christine?* Dimly, she heard Adrian choke back a protest as she clamped onto a sensitive portion of his anatomy. She barely felt him prying her fingers loose. Her attention was completely caught by her own horror.

A wife. Adrian had a wife? Was he still married? No, his mother had said his *first* wife. So that meant widowhood or divorce. Unless he was married again? With a bone-deep shudder, she shook off that alternative. Varya wouldn't have been this friendly if Adrian had another wife. More to the point, she didn't think Adrian capable of that much duplicity.

Only of failing to mention a little thing like a marriage.

But why should he mention it to her? Who was she? Someone he slept with on occasion, someone without even as formal an arrangement as most mistresses had. What if he did want to live with her? She had no right to expect him to share his past. She set the rules for their relationship the minute she let him into her bed.

Pleasure was all she'd asked for, and pleasure was what she got. In strict point of fact, she'd gotten more.

I deserve more, she protested to herself. *No matter what I said out loud. No matter if I did chase him.*

"You'll be there, won't you?" his mother was saying, snapping Roxanne's face back into focus.

Roxie stared at her slack-jawed.

"There, there, dear." Varya reached across the table to pat her hand. "There's no need to look so surprised by the invitation. I know matters are . . . somewhat irregular between you and my son, but we are on the cusp of a new century. As long as you and Adrian intend to treat each other with respect, I don't see why his father and I can't attempt to be modern. After all, there's no telling whether you'll want to do it up proper someday. Don't you agree, dear?"

On being addressed directly, Adrian's father turned his

weather-worn blue gaze toward Roxie, his smile both un-demanding and kind. Under other circumstances, it would have warmed her. This morning, she was so distressed she could scarcely comprehend what his wife had said.

"That's enough, Mother." Adrian's voice was soft but firm. He laid his hand on Roxie's neck beneath her braid and squeezed the knotted tendons there. He might have been strangling her for all the good it did.

"Did I say something wrong?" Varya's eyes were glint-ing with sudden tears.

"I think Roxie is a bit overwhelmed."

"Yes," she agreed faintly because she knew she couldn't sit there like a stone, even if her tongue did feel as thick and slow as when she'd been drugged. "Just a bit."

"But you'll bring her to the baby's welcoming, won't you?" Varya's mouth quivered as Adrian tugged Roxie from her seat. She looked genuinely stricken. Roxie was confused by a sudden urge to comfort the woman. "You know everyone would love to see you. I'm sure they'd do everything possible to make Miss McAllister feel at home."

"We'll see," Adrian said, hugging Roxanne protectively to his side.

But it wasn't his mother she needed protection from. She felt numb as he led her back to the market square. She'd thought she was coming to mean more to him. He'd as much as said he didn't want her seeing other men. He'd lost his job over her, over Charles and Max. Sadly, his feelings appeared to run just so deep and no deeper. He didn't want her in his parents' house. He didn't want her meeting his siblings.

Frowning, she let him steer her to the stone jetty behind the spice carts. He urged her to sit. The crowds were begin-ning to thicken with wives and servants. Here, behind the business side of things, no one would pay them any mind. Heaven forbid they should make a scene.

Clearly, Adrian had had enough of doing that.

He stood before her, stroking her cheek with his knuck-les. "I'm sorry, Roxie. My mother rarely thinks before she speaks. I hope she didn't embarrass you too badly."

Roxie looked at her hands. *That other woman wore his ring,* she thought. *She was Mrs. Philips.*

"I'm afraid she is usually like that," Adrian said, "but you'll get used to it eventually."

"Will I?" she asked, surprised by how calm she sounded. "And will I get used to the fact that you were married, too?"

"Roxanne." He sat beside her on the wall and wrapped her hand between his own. "Let me explain."

"No." She pulled her hand away. "I don't want to hear. It's perfectly obvious I'm not important enough to be entrusted with the most basic facts of your personal history."

"That's not true!" He circled her with both arms. "You're very important. You're everything to me." His voice sank, roughened by emotion. "I love you."

She wanted to believe him, but who knew what he meant by those words? As far as she could tell, the only thing he stood to lose was an interesting bed partner.

Her thoughts must have shown on her face, because his mouth tightened with anger. "It isn't fair of you to doubt me," he said. "I might not have told you all the gory details of my past, but I never gave you reason to question my word."

"Haven't you?"

"No, I haven't. Everything I've ever promised I've done. My failure to be completely forthright might prove I'm cowardly, but not that I'm dishonest. For God's sake, I *wanted* you to meet my parents. Would I have done that if I weren't serious?"

"You wanted me to meet them? I thought you were just too dutiful to refuse."

"Hardly," he said with a muffled snort, "as you'll discover once you get to know me a bit better."

"But—"

"You're arguing," he said, the corners of his mouth beginning to turn up. "You shouldn't do that with a man in love."

She pressed her steepled hands to her lips, feeling dangerously close to tears. Before she could collect the power to speak, Adrian stiffened.

"Hell," he said, his gaze narrowing at something on the lower end of the street. "Our little demon friends are back."

Chapter 23

When Roxanne would have turned, Adrian caught her arm.

"Don't look," he cautioned, low and steady. "I don't want them knowing they've been seen."

Not turning seemed the hardest thing she'd ever done, but she forced herself to hold Adrian's warm gray gaze. "How many are there?"

"Four." As if nothing were wrong, he stood and smiled down at her. "Unfortunately, I can't guarantee the other two aren't around somewhere. I'm going to help you up now. It's broad daylight, and there are plenty of witnesses. You and I are going to stroll calmly to the next watch post, where we'll enlist the aid of the sergeant on duty."

"What if no one's there?" Roxie asked as he tucked her arm through his and began to walk.

Adrian's smile twisted grimly. "If no one's there, we'll throw caution to the winds and run."

Roxie didn't want to remind him only one of them could outrace a demon, not when he was working so hard to calm her. But perhaps he planned to throw her over his shoulder and carry her to safety like the fire brigade. The thought tweaked her humor, though she was too uneasy to laugh. Her neck felt stiff, her hands icy.

They turned up a narrow street, one that led away from the river. The pavement was worn but swept, kept clean by the local shopkeepers. Every window they passed tempted her to check for their followers' reflections. As they passed one filled with sausages, Adrian hugged her arm.

"They're still behind us," he murmured, though she couldn't tell how he'd seen. "They're holding back. They must not know we've spotted them."

A dog barked territorially from an alley, not a stray but a good-sized pet, straining to the end of the rope that held it bound. Its teeth looked sharp. Roxie wondered which species the canine would prefer to bite. Whichever was closer, most likely.

"Just a bit farther," Adrian said. "Then we're home free."

His claim had no chance to be tested. As they approached the next cross street, an electric automobile rolled slowly into the intersection, its engine eerily silent. Once there, it stopped. Long as a hearse and just as black, the car's soundless appearance filled Roxie with foreboding. The car did not look like a vehicle human hands had made. It was too shiny and perfect, too regular and smooth. In place of windows, its sides had small round mirrors. Whoever sat inside could not be seen.

Adrian stopped and rubbed his chin, obviously stymied by this behemoth blocking their way.

"This isn't good," Roxie said.

"Don't panic," Adrian said. "We'll try going around."

He was beginning to peer down the cross street when a

hollow sound brought both their attention back. A door had opened in the black car's previously seamless side. Her father's leonine head leaned out, his hair blazing incongruously in the sun. His face was blank but oddly urgent, or perhaps Roxanne imagined the urgency. No doubt she felt enough of it for them both.

"Hurry," Herrington said, gesturing. "Get in before they catch up."

Roxie retreated instead, looking back the way they'd come. To her dismay, the other *daimyo* were at the bottom of the street, still wearing their navy and gray *rohn* robes. They had stopped in their tracks, not speaking, not reacting. Perhaps they couldn't decide what to do any more than she.

"Don't be stupid," her father said, actually sounding angry. "They mean you no good."

Roxie was far from prepared to assume any different of him, but another head leaned around his too-broad shoulder. This time, she gasped in horror. Charles was with him, looking pale but more or less calm.

"It's all right," he said, though he didn't seem quite convinced. "Max and I are both here."

A rage of almost frightening strength surged through her veins, all the more intense for being impotent. Herrington had her boys. Herrington was using her boys to get to her.

"We have to go with him," Adrian said, caressing the fist she hadn't known she'd made. "If he has the boys, we have to go with him."

"Damn it."

"I can't fight him," Adrian said. "Not in that car."

She went, though she didn't want to, because she knew Adrian was right. The demon car might as well have been a fortress. All Herrington had to do was shut the door to keep them out. To her surprise, he was driving, with Charles on the seat next to him. Max sat on one of a pair of padded leather benches in the cool, cavernous back. From inside, the funny round mirrors were transparent. The windows at the front and rear were larger, but, aside from that, they were enclosed in unnaturally smooth black metal. Lights whose purpose she could not fathom blinked on the strange instrument panel. As soon as she slid across the rearmost seat, Max clambered into her lap.

Knowing he was safe made her feel a fraction better.

"It's all right," he whispered, his little hand patting hers. "We're going to swim in your papa's pool and look at statues."

Roxie didn't know how to respond to what must have been the bribe that disarmed Max's natural distrust. Hugging him close, she kissed his bristly hair. The car rolled backward with the same uncanny silence of its approach, then began to turn. Roxie tried to stop shaking.

"I can't believe you'd involve Max in this," she said to the back of her father's head, her tone not quite as level as she wished. "He's a little boy. What if they try to take him again?"

Her father jerked. *"Again?"* Something in his inflection told her once and for all that he'd been behind Max's removal to the Ministry. "Those men aren't after him," he said, his hands working the leather-wrapped wheel around. "They're after you."

Roxie fell back against the seat, shocked by his words, though perhaps she shouldn't have been.

"You know who they are?" Adrian asked, almost as composed as her monstrous sire.

"They're agents of an associate of mine. I expect they want to take her in for medical observation."

"An *associate?*" Roxanne repeated, bubbling with outrage.

"Perhaps you would say a rival. I regret I couldn't warn you sooner. I only received word that he was planning to abduct you an hour ago."

So not last night, Roxie thought, wishing that didn't mean anything to her. He might have used Max as a pawn, but if what her father said was true, he couldn't have warned her and Adrian of the first attack against them.

"Your daddy is going to protect you," Max announced in a whisper everyone could hear. "He says our home isn't safe."

Roxanne's sole response to that was a curse.

"Shush," said Charles. "We're rolling by them now."

They were indeed. The four demons watched impassively as Herrington eased past them at a leisurely, horse-carriage pace. Though she knew little of Yamish ways, their progress felt like a ritual, a parade to mark a bloodless victory. The car was impregnable, the enemy outmaneuvered. To drive away any faster would have been undignified.

Either that, or Herrington wanted to rub the demons' noses in their defeat.

She clenched her jaw as four pairs of all-silver eyes followed their departure. The last flickered his tongue in parting. Roxie shuddered and turned away.

"You might say 'thank you,'" Herrington suggested.

"Ha," she said. "Don't hold your breath."

⌐≥⌐

His daughter's retort was to be expected. She was half-human and, consequently, had not been raised to perceive the currents that could lie beneath a seemingly smooth surface. She believed Herrington's methods had put Max at risk and didn't think to wonder what end he'd been working toward—if it might not be for the good of all. She believed him heartless and did not imagine her words could hurt. Perhaps they shouldn't have hurt. Sadly, Herrington could not deny they did.

Wanting her to be his daughter in truth had made him vulnerable. He wasn't the least bit certain he liked the effect.

At least her lover deigned to speak to him. Possibly, the prejudice he'd been subjected to following the installation of his implants had made him less judgmental of others. Herrington had been quite interested to unearth this detail of Philips's past, had hoped it might mean his daughter was broad-minded, had even regretted the necessity of getting Philips fired so as to make Roxie less reliant on his support. That the ploy had not worked only increased his respect for the man. He had not thought a human capable of his loyalty. Had Roxie been a member of a lesser bloodline than his own, the former policeman would have been an adequate candidate for marriage.

Not that his daughter was likely to ask his approval.

Herrington fought a grimace as they followed the sandy coastal road toward the Downs. Philips was leaning over the front seat, watching the landscape. That was fine with Herrington. He preferred the man not read his inner turmoil.

"When you mentioned 'medical observation,' " Philips said now, "I gather you don't mean The Dragon wanted to run a few tests and then let her go."

His knowledge startled Herrington. "How do you know about The Dragon?"

Adrian's shrug was admirably unrevealing. "People talk."

"So they do." Herrington steered his lovely Yamish saloon car around a hole in the road. Seated up front, the older boy, Charles, watched the procedure with interest. Herrington could catch hell for driving this car in public— it was beyond the technology humans were supposed to be aware they had—but Herrington sincerely doubted he cared. The thing was a bloody tank, and the only vehicle fast enough to have gotten him to Avvar in time to help.

"Well?" said Philips, still waiting for his question to be answered.

"The examination would not be brief," Herrington conceded, though it went against his nature to answer directly. "Chances are, if she fell into The Dragon's hands, she wouldn't be seen again in Avvar."

That she might not be seen again anywhere he kept to himself. No need to frighten the girl.

"Why?" Roxie said, making his heart leap at the sound of her voice. He risked a glance at her in his back view mirror. For an instant, her eyes were wrenchingly familiar, despite their human surround of whites. She could have been his sister, Louise, staring at him in challenge. *Why can't I?* she'd liked to say. *Don't you think I'm as clever as you?* Herrington hoped his daughter was clever enough to reach a loftier age than Louise. The little boy was half asleep on her shoulder, the trust between them tightening his throat. When she caught him staring, the frown she shot at him was dark. Quite clearly, she begrudged the need to have anything to do with him.

"Why would anyone care enough to study me?" she asked more insistently. "I'm not that different from other humans. A little stronger maybe, but that's it."

"Knowledge is power," Herrington answered. "To the Yama, the fact that you exist, when truthfully you should not, makes you interesting enough. Plus, you might be more different than you suspect."

"Then why not ask permission to examine me? See if I'd cooperate. Surely encouraging the abduction of human citizens isn't your government's policy."

Herrington almost had to clear his throat. "Not its official policy, no." He succumbed to the need to sigh. After this morning, he was entitled. "The problem is, unofficial or not, The Dragon can't be doing this alone. There's organization behind this, and money. I don't know if the person backing him is someone I can counter, or if his support comes from the highest ranks."

"Like your prince," Philips suggested, surprising him again.

"He is young," Herrington admitted. "And lamentably malleable."

"Then we'll go to our government," Roxanne said. "Ask them to protect me."

Thankfully, Philips countered that. "They might not want to protect you," he said. "You are only one person, and the Avvar Accord is crucial to the Empire's security. I hate to say it, but if The Dragon does have high-placed allies, our government might prefer to look the other way."

Roxanne huffed and shifted Max on her lap, her hand cupping his head protectively. "There must be something we can do. Begging your pardon, Lord Herrington, but I am not hiding away on your estate for the rest of my life. Frankly, I'd rather not go there at all."

Her plea for pardon was hardly heartfelt, but the manners

she felt obliged to put on for the children caused the ghost of a smile to tug at Herrington's mouth. Perhaps he should have involved Charles and Max earlier. "We'll think of something," he said. "In the meantime, I hope my hospitality won't prove onerous."

Roxanne's sigh was far gustier than his own. "Thank you for that," she said, then muttered, "assuming you haven't engineered this whole thing."

Her addendum took a bit of the shine from his pleasure. He dreaded her response to his solution of last resort. Alas, with The Dragon fully on the move, he saw no way to avoid it.

⟶⟶

Much as Roxanne wanted to hate her father's estate, she couldn't deny it was magnificent.

His land hugged a rolling stretch of coast halfway between Avvar and Downingdale. Set on a rise of wildflower-dotted grass and shaded by large maples, the three-story mansion had been built a century earlier of buttery brick and fine Ka'arkish glass. A spearhead fence girded the main grounds, its martial air softened by a cloak of blood-red ivy. Viewed through a mid-morning fog, with tapers glowing gold behind the tall arched windows, the house seemed a place of magical antiquity. It might have been the home of a well-heeled human aristocrat: the very best of old Ohram.

The butler who opened the tall double doors was all starched collar and snow-white hair, as if he'd stepped out of a picture book. His manner toward Herrington was proper in the extreme. No one would guess his master was a demon.

Inside, the house was much the same, conservatively beautiful. She found herself wondering if her father liked human furnishings or if he hadn't cared enough to change them. Perhaps, to a Yama, surroundings didn't matter. As he led the way up the grand staircase, however, his hand caressing the glossy mahogany rail, she rather doubted that.

He assigned them a suite of rooms that interconnected on the third floor, a home within his home. As gracious as anything they'd seen yet, the rooms smelled of a recent airing and were decorated with fresh flowers—tiny arrangements of hothouse lilacs and snowbells. The manner in which he adjusted the little vase on the mantle created the impression that, despite his army of servants, he had selected the blooms personally to please her.

As if to prove her an overimaginative fool, when he spoke, his voice was as cool as ever. "I trust you'll be comfortable here. I'll have Cook pull together a spot of tea."

She couldn't do anything but nod. Confusion had stolen her voice. As soon as he was gone, Max wriggled down from her hip. For the first time, Roxie registered the fact that he was still wearing his pajamas, his favorite footed pair with the leather soles. She was oddly reassured that getting one small boy into streetclothes had been beyond even Herrington's manipulative skills.

"I'm going to pick a room for me and Charles," Max yelled at full volume as he scampered off. "Then I'm going to write my book."

"Well, he seems fine," Adrian said. "But what's this about a book? I thought Max couldn't read yet."

Charles sighed like a long-suffering older brother. "His latest enthusiasm. He had Roxie bind a bunch of pages together, and now he scribbles in it and pretends it's a history of Avvar. He's actually memorized a list of kings and queens."

"What an, er, original occupation for a five-year-old."

"Don't encourage him," Charles warned. "He's liable to quiz you and see if you know what you should. Since he makes up half the stuff, it's pretty hard to answer correctly."

Their conversation was so normal, Roxie had to sit down. What was she doing here in her father's house? Demons were trying to kidnap her, were hoping to study her as if she were a two-headed cow. Her father had as good as admitted to getting the Ministry to take Max. They couldn't turn to her government for help, or to his, because neither could be trusted. She could trust Adrian, she supposed, as long as she didn't ask him about his past, and—for the life of her—she couldn't see how to squirm out of any of these fixes.

"What's wrong?" Adrian asked as she pressed her aching temples between her hands.

"Oh, nothing," she said, not knowing whether to cry or laugh. "Everything is right as rain."

Adrian knelt beside her and squeezed her knee. She was sure he only meant to comfort her . . . and he did. The problem was, if they'd been alone, she wouldn't have wanted to worry about anything but him.

When his eyes met hers and went abruptly hot, she knew he was thinking the same thing.

Chapter 24

〜

Some say knowledge is power, but for the Yama it is an addiction. The more they learn, the more they wish to know. In truth, it is difficult to blame them when this attitude has taken them so very far.

—*The True and Irreverent History of Avvar*

〜

With his maddening knack for guessing where her weaknesses lay, Herrington gave Roxie the key to his archaeological gallery, then sent her and Adrian there alone.

"Albert and I will take care of the boys," he assured her, Albert being his starched butler. "Max has requested a swimming lesson."

Roxie would have liked to object but could find no good reason to, especially when Max hung on her arm and said, "Please, please, please." Whatever fear the boy might have felt toward her father had disappeared. She hoped the cause was childish intuition rather than being dazzled by their grand surroundings.

Herrington's pool was heated, it seemed, and bore on its vaulted ceiling a painted version of the cosmos. Five-year-old Max wasn't sure what a cosmos was, only that his life depended on seeing it.

"They'll be fine," Adrian had coaxed quietly. "You know you'd rather see the Boral Lake collection for the first time on your own, without little voices interrupting."

So now she and Adrian toured the meandering rooms of a large sandstone building behind Herrington's mansion, marveling at the implements of long-ago life his team had dug up and fanning their faces at what her father called "climate control." However the system worked, it succeeded admirably at re-creating the hot, dry atmosphere of Southland. Defying the fog outside, a golden glow shimmered through the space, the effect of his nearly hidden electric lights. Even the scent of the enclosed air, a mix of sand and coffee and spice, called up memories of Bhamjran, the more explicit of which were making her more aware of her body than she had any wish to be.

She didn't need images of naked demon dancing boys to heat her blood. Adrian accomplished that by peeling off his jacket and rolling up his sleeves. His forearms were wonderfully corded, his back broad beneath his snug waistcoat. The narrow streak of damp at the center of the silk in back did nothing to calm her urge to tear it off. She told herself she was a woman, not an animal. Nothing forced her to attack her lover in her dastardly father's house—no matter how appealing her lover was.

All the same, she didn't dare sneak a look at Adrian's trouser front. Better not to know if he shared her dilemma.

Leaving the baskets and pottery behind, they passed into a skylit chamber in which an ancient house had been reconstructed block by block. Roxie thought the concept very clever. Desert grasses had been planted, and tools were left lying out, enhancing the impression of forgotten ages brought back to life. The garden held a crumbling fountain. When she peered past it, she saw the room that overlooked it contained a low stone platform for a bed.

That spurred thoughts best avoided.

"My," she said, turning away from the deep window, "wasn't that a spread Herrington's cook laid out for tea?"

Adrian smiled and drew the tip of one finger down her cheek. His touch made her shiver. "Yes, it was," was all he said.

"And how about when Max shouted, 'I could get used to this!' "

"He did catch everyone's attention."

Roxie should have evaded the thumb Adrian was using to stroke her jaw. Instead, she nattered on nervously. "I'm sure I should be grateful. Max barely spoke when he first came to stay with me. He's finally beginning to act more like an ordinary boy."

"I doubt Max will ever qualify as ordinary, but he does seem resilient."

Roxie put her hand over his to stop it from edging beneath the collar of her man's-style shirt. When she had been washing up, one of Herrington's retinue of maids had brought her a fresh outfit, a beautiful blue plaid gown with all the appropriate underthings. The dress would have flattered her coloring immensely, but, perceiving it as one more form of pressure, Roxie hadn't been able to bring herself to put it on. Now she wore the same tired clothes she had the night before.

"He heard me, didn't he?" she asked.

"Hm?" said Adrian, engrossed in watching her pulse beating in her throat.

"My father. When Max said, 'I could get used to this,' and I muttered, 'Yes, well don't.' "

Adrian's soft gaze met hers. "Your father's people do have sharp ears."

Unable to face his kindness when she might not deserve it, Roxie looked at her feet. "I might have accidentally on purpose muttered it too loud."

"You might, but only you can answer that."

"Adrian," she said with a hint of exasperation for his mild response.

His gentle smile became a grin. "I don't feel right judging you, Roxie. Plus, you appear to be working this out perfectly well on your own."

"I'm mad at him," she admitted. "I don't care if he rescued us, or that he's being an annoyingly considerate host. He probably got you fired, and I'm positive he was behind Max being taken by the Children's Ministry. And don't say I can't be, because I think I am. You know that thing the Yama do, that fire-talk? I think I can read it. I wasn't sure at first because it was so vague, and his face never shows anything, but now I'm almost certain I can feel what he's feeling sometimes. When he questioned my statement that demons might take Max again, he gave off a definite whiff of guilt. There." She blew out her breath. "I've admitted it."

To her surprise, Adrian didn't seem the least bit shocked. His hands moved to her shoulders, smoothing the now-creased cotton down her arms. "Why shouldn't you admit it?"

"Because I don't want it to be true. When I was a child, all I wanted was to be like other people. To put down roots in one city, to have a house, to be able to rely on my family. Now, every time I turn around, I find I'm even stranger than I thought."

Adrian reached behind her and gave her braid a tug. "Being strange, as you put it, doesn't mean you can't have those things. You can't deny some of your Yamish qualities are useful. Being strong, being smart—"

"—knowing what my father's feeling without him saying a word?"

"Well, that is a bit awkward, but perhaps you'll learn to block it out."

Roxanne made a face, then felt bad for having done so. "The worst thing is, I think I hurt him. I think . . . I think he really cares about me, Adrian. When I'm around him, I start having this sensation like I used to when I was little and I'd see other children with their families." She pressed her gathered fingers to her breastbone. "It's a little ache, right here, and I'm pretty sure it isn't mine."

"Ah."

"Yes, ah." The confession was hard to get out, but she pushed. "I think, maybe, I've been crueler to my father than he deserves."

"And maybe you haven't," Adrian said just as gently as before. "He could care for you and be completely horrible otherwise." He smoothed her curls back from her temples. "One thing I know about the Yama is that they're an extremely patient race. Even if you have been unfair to your father, he won't expect your actions, or your feelings, to change overnight. He'll wait until you're ready to accept him."

"That just makes me feel worse!" Roxie exclaimed, giving in to the temptation to rest her head on his shoulder. "Are all families like this?"

"All the ones I know have their challenges. I love my parents, but that doesn't untangle the complications of being their son. Sometimes, it makes them worse."

"Wonderful. Another treat to look forward to."

Adrian chuckled and rubbed her back obligingly. As if magnetized, her glance lit on the window to the ancient bedroom, now directly behind his shoulder.

"Hell," she said, pushing determinedly back from his hold. "Let's see what's in the next gallery."

⤙⤚

To Adrian's amusement, the next room was no improvement. Here statues of satyrs in states of high arousal intermixed with couples twisted into copulatory postures that would challenge the most limber of human beings. Some were diminutive, some nearly life-size, but all were graphically sexual. Adrian tugged his suddenly tight collar. He could see why their Ministry of Culture might not object to leaving these objects in Herrington's care. Any one of them would cause an uproar if displayed in Avvar's museum. He craned his head in an attempt to decipher the activity of a small stone woman who was balanced in a handstand in front of her slightly crouched partner.

"Hm," he said. "She must get dizzy trying that upside down."

"Dizzy!" Roxanne exclaimed. "It's a wonder she doesn't choke. His thing is half as long as my arm."

To Adrian's relief, she began to laugh. Sensing her resistance crumbling, he pulled her into his arms.

"I wasn't going to do this," she protested.

"Laugh?"

"Make love to you in my father's house."

Though he'd known what she meant before he asked, the words sent a pulse of feeling through his already straining sex. He locked his arms behind her waist and squeezed her close enough to know what she'd done. "Strictly speaking, we aren't in your father's house. We're in his archaeological annex."

Her moan of answer combined temptation and regret.

"What do you say?" he teased, rolling his hips a little harder into the softness between her legs. "Want to see how long *you* can stand on your hands?"

He knew she desired him. He'd known it since he touched her knee in their rooms. Nonetheless, her reaction took him by surprise. With a muted growl of impatience, she ripped his waistcoat open, undid the fastenings of his trousers, and—in a single motion—sank to her knees and took his aching hardness in her mouth.

Then he was the one who moaned. Her lips and tongue were completely fearless, her hands a sweet torment. They scratched up his exposed shirtfront, kneaded his thighs, then his buttocks, then the swiftly tightening sac between his legs.

He found her aggression unexpectedly exciting.

"Roxanne," he gasped, his eyes tearing up with pleasure as she found a particularly sensitive spot to suck. If she kept that up, this wasn't going to last long.

He gasped again when she let him go, despite his relief. The beat of the blood surging through his cock felt hard enough to shake the ground.

She rose and backed a step away, beginning to wriggle out of her white trousers.

"Keep yourself warm," she said with a pointed look at his shuddering sex.

His mind couldn't quite keep up. "It's sweltering in here."

"With your hand," she specified, sounding oddly fierce. "I want to see how you pleasure yourself."

He couldn't restrain the impulse to glance back the way they'd come.

"We have the key, Adrian. No one's going to interrupt us."

Though he had no way of knowing if they had the *only* key, at that moment, he didn't care. He wanted her enough to throw every shred of caution to the winds. They needed each other. They'd been through too much not to take advantage of this temporary privacy.

"Fine." He tore off his ripped waistcoat, then his shirt. "Let's do this."

"Take yourself in your hand," she repeated, removing her shirt with a bit more care than he'd shown. "You're supposed to be staying warm."

He forgot to be embarrassed when she bared her breasts. She was naked then, more beautiful than a statue, more alluring and womanly. Her nipples were the same flushed color as her lips. His fist tightened on his shaft and pulled toward the crown without thinking. His palm was sweaty, his sensations sharp. Performing this personal act in front of her felt both strange and natural.

When she licked her lips and looked at his sex, he knew he had to have her soon. He went to his knees, the same position she'd held before, thighs spread, still working himself up and down. He hadn't had a chance to remove his trousers, and he stroked himself through their opening. She watched the way his fist twisted slightly on the shaft, the way his left hand tugged his scrotum down when the right went up. He swelled beneath her close attention, almost more aroused than he could stand.

"Come here," he ordered, his voice as rough as the unpolished sandstone pavers beneath his shins.

"I want to see," she said, her tongue creeping out to wet her lip again.

"I want to be inside you. I want to feel your heat on this skin." Beyond inhibitions, he pulled his shaft out hard enough to stretch the ligaments at its base. He hadn't meant to shock her; he'd simply needed his tightest grip. Her blush of reaction made his own face heat. His next words came out a growl. "I want to watch your eyes flutter when you spend."

He released himself, holding the same hand out to her that he'd used to rub himself. She jerked at its heat, then accepted its support to join him on her knees.

Looking down between them, she touched her index finger to the small clear bead that welled from his tip. "There's a little drop."

He flinched at the contact, then wrapped his hand around her wrist to keep her from pulling away. "There's more than one. I've been wanting you like this for hours. When you started watching me stroke myself, I thought I'd explode."

Her gaze rose to his and held. Too emboldened to hesitate, he guided her finger around his crown. From rim to rim he drew her, then around the center opening. A fresh wash of rose stained her cheeks. She could feel how slippery he'd grown.

"I want you," he said, for the pleasure of saying the words. "Let me come inside you before I die."

"Adrian."

His name was a rush of breath. Taking this as permission, he clamped his hands on her waist, lifted her, then let her weight ease her down his shaft. Feeling his hardness reach its limit was pure heaven. She was wet for him, and hot. Her thighs gripped his hips and held tight.

"God," she said, her head thrown back. A droplet of sweat rolled down her graceful neck.

He loved the look of her, the feel, but they couldn't stay like this for more than a few heartbeats. They had to rock their hips together, then pump them, then twine their fingers into knots of strain. Everywhere around them, statues flaunted the shapes of sex. Breasts and bellies. Mouths and cocks. Stone hands locked in seductive rituals of lust.

Adrian tipped her back onto the heated floor and worshipped her living flesh.

"Oh!" she cried as he lowered her, her hands sliding greedily up his ribs. He had more purchase then, and he used it. Her body shook with the increased strength of his thrusts. "Oh, Adrian, *yes.*"

Even this approval wasn't enough. He changed his angle, running his crown and shaft across the tender upper wall of her sheath, over and over, steadily, firmly, taking care to jar the bud of her pleasure each time he sank home. With every stroke, she tightened around him more, intensifying his pleasure as well. Neither of them could bear so much sensation. Her eyes slid shut as he lengthened dangerously inside her. Her teeth bit her lower lip. Then she caught her breath and came.

Her climax triggered his like flame set to a trail of gunpowder. His thigh muscles locked him in as deep as he could go. His buttocks clenched, the air kicking from his lungs in a rumbling groan. He came with a force he thought she must feel, hot pulsations that didn't seem to want to stop.

They did, though, and that was a pleasure, too: a release even from release. He eased free and lay on his back on the hot dry stone, deliciously replete, wonderfully calm, though he knew every challenge they'd faced before they'd come here remained.

In unison, he and Roxie sighed, two notes of a single chord. She chuckled softly, then rolled toward him and put her head on his chest. Her fingers played with the hair just above his heart.

"I love you," she said, and that was the nicest finish of all.

～⁂～

Roxie found her shirt again and pulled it on, though she wasn't ready to get up yet. The world and its problems waited outside this golden oasis. A few more moments of peace were irresistible.

As she settled back against him, Adrian stroked her hair. "I know you're curious about Christine."

"You don't have to tell me about her now."

"Maybe not, but I doubt you'll trust me until I do."

He was rubbing his wrist against his ribs as if it itched. Roxie stopped him, turned his forearm over, and kissed the spot where his implants lay.

He drew a lengthy breath and let it out. "When I first got these," he said, "the men at the station took to calling me demon boy. 'Where are your horns, demon boy?' they'd ask. 'Better watch your tail in that door.' I tried to ignore them, but sometimes my face would give me away. They'd scold me for being annoyed, tell me it was just a bit of friendly teasing, that I ought have a better sense of humor.

"I was still a sergeant then, a uniform. We had lockers to store our civilian clothes. The men liked to jam mine shut with all sorts of things, hoping for a show of demon strength. Finally, I got tired of calling the janitor to unscrew the hinges and ripped the door off myself. Then, for good measure, I threw a bench across the room with one hand.

"That stopped the teasing, but not the fear that lay behind it. From then on, men who'd trained with me from my first day found it impossible to meet my eye. I'd never been one to spend hours at the pub with my associates, but after that I might as well have been a leper. When I was promoted to inspector, it got worse. Jealousy was no cure for suspicion."

"I'm sorry."

Adrian's chest moved with his sigh. "There's nothing to be sorry for. I made my choice, in part because it seemed the quickest route up the ladder. I didn't have friends in high places. Hell, I barely had friends in low ones. I don't . . . have a gift for that."

Roxie kissed his shoulder, though she wasn't sure he wanted sympathy.

"The thing is," he went on, "after dealing with my fellow officers all day, I'd come home to Christine. Her family was poor gentry, mine middle working class. She'd married down for me—not a lot, but enough to matter. One of the things I'd hoped my promotion would do was salve her pride. She didn't complain, but it wore on our relationship. We didn't have much to hold us together. She wasn't comfortable with my family, and she'd never been interested in sex. She didn't want me to try to make it pleasurable. When I realized this wouldn't change, it disappointed me, but I concluded she was too refined to want what other women did. In a lot of ways, I wasn't much more worldly than she was.

"After I got my implants, she couldn't even stand to kiss me. Said she couldn't help thinking about demon tongues. Yama were depraved, according to her, and she couldn't believe I'd done what I did without asking her."

This made Roxie lift her head. "You didn't discuss it with her beforehand?"

"I wasn't allowed to. The procedure was untried and extremely controversial. I was their test case. If anything went wrong, Securité wanted to be able to deny they'd had anything to do with it. Even now, I doubt there are more than a dozen of us on the force."

"Did you ever try to contact the others?

Adrian shrugged. "I don't know who they are. After my experience, Securité took more care to keep their identities secret. I guess I knew Christine might object at first, but I never imagined how deep her aversion ran. I thought she'd adjust when she saw how much better our life could be on an inspector's pay. At last, she could have some of the luxuries her friends took for granted."

Roxie rubbed her cheek against his chest. His heart beat steadily, only a little faster than normal. Maybe, after all they'd been through, he was too tired to worry what she'd think. "When did you finally decide to end the marriage?"

"The day she told me she didn't want to have my children, that she was afraid they'd be tainted, too. I should have ended it sooner. I knew being around me made her miserable. She was relieved when I let her go. I simply couldn't bear to admit I'd failed."

"I'm not sure you did fail, Adrian. I think perhaps she did."

"Oh, I failed," he said, certainty in the words. "I failed the day I asked her to be my wife. She was a pretty girl, and sweet-natured, but looking back I'm not sure how much of my choice was love and how much was prideful pleasure that a gently bred girl like her would want to marry me. She'd never made any secret of her feelings. Chased me a bit, God help her."

"I'm sure you're weren't a bad husband."

He shook his head. "I was a bad husband for her. That's all that mattered in the end. To tell the truth, I don't know if I could stand letting anyone down that way again."

You don't have to, she wanted to say. *You can choose a wife who's strong enough to stand on her own no matter what you do.* It seemed too forward, too much like she assumed he would marry her. She wished she could make that leap of faith but, as yet, he'd hadn't given her a reason to.

Christine had chased him, and so had Roxanne. The parallels weren't pleasant to contemplate.

Chapter 25

❦

The press are a scourge to any thinking society. If they didn't occasionally amuse me, I'd ban them all.

—*The Collected Sayings of the Emperor*

❦

Through a fog of sleep, Roxanne was muzzily aware that the door to her room was creaking open. Adrian lay beside her, warm and quiet, so it wasn't him returning from the bath.

A maid? she wondered, but after a brief pause, a small—and in no way light-footed body—hurtled itself across the carpet and onto the bed.

"Wake up, wake up!" Max squealed as every nerve Roxie possessed jumped beneath her skin. "Roxie's in the paper."

"Stop bouncing," Adrian said in a soft, if froggy, morning voice. He had jolted up as soon as Max landed. "Let Roxie rest."

At this, Max switched to his most ear-splitting whisper. "What are ya doin' here, Adrian? Didn't Grandpa give you a bed?"

"Oh, God," Roxie groaned into her pillow. She needed only one guess to know who'd suggested Max call Herrington that.

"Roxie and I thought we'd share," Adrian said calmly enough. "Since we like each other so much."

"Oh," said Max, sounding oddly satisfied with that answer. "Want to see the paper?"

Roxie was doing her best to squirm into a silk-lined robe while still under the covers. She was glad now that the maid had left it. When she wriggled over and sat up, she was decent.

She found Charles standing awkwardly in the door. Even wearing pajamas, the boy looked as crisp as a new pound note. Though he must have known what was going on between her and Adrian, he appeared more discomposed than Max.

"Sorry," he said, raking back his smooth fair hair. "He got away before I could stop him."

"That's all right," she tried to say with Max flapping a newsprint sheaf in her face.

"Read," the little boy insisted, forgetting not to bounce. "There's a picture and everything."

Roxie exchanged glances with Adrian over the boy's bristly head. Adrian's grimace of response could have meant anything. Resigned to seeing for herself, Roxie unfolded the paper.

"Long Lost Daughter Found," screamed the *Courier*'s front-page headline. "Explorer-diplomat claims he couldn't be happier."

Pictures did indeed accompany the story. A playbill sketch of La Belle Yvonne sat next to a grainy daguerreotype of Herrington. In it, he stood among the diplomats who'd negotiated the Avvar Accord. A more heroic image was provided by a pen drawing of him swathed in desert robes as he trekked through the rocky pass toward Boral Lake. There was even a recognizable picture of herself, though the Lord only knew how they'd obtained it. She was gazing at the unknown and unremembered artist in supercilious amusement.

The mattress shifted as Charles sat hesitantly at her hip.

"The article *is* rather flattering," he said as Roxie turned. "Intrepid orphan snatches herself from the jaws of poverty. Redeems her unsavory past with hard labor. Makes you sound better than a two-penny heroine. Everyone knows what muckrakers the *Courier*'s writers can be, but this almost obscures the fact that you're, you know, half-demon. Lord Herrington must have paid a pretty penny to have the story go out like this."

"I'm half-demon, too!" Max chortled, obviously overcome with excitement. He had rolled onto his back and was waving both arms and legs.

"You're not a demon," Charles said. "I explained that."

"Am, too," Max shot back with a stubbornness that made Roxie roll her eyes. "I don't care if I'm only 'dopted."

He crawled into Roxie's lap, looking for support, but she was too befuddled to referee the boys' dispute.

"Why would he do this?" she asked Adrian. "The press will be all over it for weeks. You'd think he'd be embarrassed. *Daimyo* are supposed to be above consorting with humans. Being caught fathering a daughter with one must be a disgrace."

Adrian dragged his knuckles along his shadowed jaw. "I expect he wanted the attention. If the world knows who you are, and anything happens to you, it won't happen unnoticed."

"Hmph," Roxie snorted, her regret at having been cruel to Herrington swept away. "If that was his motivation, why not warn me ahead of time? I expect he's hoping to get more influence in my life. Aedlyne law gives fathers certain controls over their daughters, even when they're adults— especially if those fathers are filthy rich and famous."

"Maybe," Adrian conceded, but Roxie doubted *maybe* had anything to do with it.

Herrington wasn't sure how his daughter got past Albert, but she confronted him in his private office, wading through the clutter with surprising precision. He shut the almanac that hid his communicator screen. The call he'd just received had his nerves stretched thin.

Hell, he thought. Though he'd been expecting this, he didn't feel prepared.

Roxanne's face was flushed with fury as she slapped a copy of the *Courier* on his black marble-topped desk. Even after thirty years among the humans, the strength and openness of their emotions hadn't lost its power to shock.

"I presume," she said in a low, tight voice, "that you fed this story to the rags."

"I did," he said.

"Because your associate—pardon me, your *rival*—The Dragon is after me."

"It will be more difficult for him to act if your existence is public knowledge. I know you might find the process repellent, but I advise you to speak to any members of the press who ask. The more sympathetic a figure you become, the less likely your government will be to disown you."

The supremely practical counsel did not calm her. She was wearing the blue plaid dress he'd told the maid to leave, but the acceptance of his gift gave him little pleasure. Her shoulders went up and down with her shortened breaths until he feared the outfit's corset might induce her to faint. He needn't have worried. Far from being overcome by feminine weakness, a second later, she let loose a string of oaths he would have been hard-pressed to translate into his own, more decorous language.

He had spread his hands on the polished stone of his desk on either side of his almanac. He'd meant to appear calm and nonthreatening, but at some point during her tirade, his pose became more like a fisherman who grips the sides of his boat to prevent it from capsizing. Her anger made him feel disturbingly off balance. When she finally slammed her hands beside his, the break in tension came as a relief.

"That man," she said, "that Dragon should be brought to

justice, not maneuvered around as if this were a game of chess. What he tried to do to Max, and perhaps to other children, was unforgivable."

"I agree," Herrington said.

"Then do something!" She grabbed the newspaper back off his desk and flung it against his bookshelves. A small volume of sonnets thunked to the parquet floor.

"I do what I can," he said, pulling his framed portrait of Louise farther out of reach. As he recalled, Roxie's mother had had a fondness for the music of shattering glass. "I'm simply concerned—"

"You're concerned with protecting yourself," his daughter accused, a barb he supposed she couldn't know how little he deserved. Sometimes he thought all he'd done since meeting her was endanger his standing—maybe even his life. Despite his innocence, his face felt curiously hot and stiff. "You're concerned with controlling me!"

"I'm concerned with protecting my power," he said evenly. "Without that, I cannot ensure anyone's safety. If my government suspected the respect with which I regard your race—"

"Respect!" Her laugh was sharp with disbelief. "You abduct my ward. You probably got my lover dismissed from his job—or helped it along, at the least. Adrian's superintendent might not have fired him if he hadn't been getting pressure from 'higher up.' And now you don't even do me the courtesy of warning me I'm about to become the public's latest penny-dreadful heroine."

"I hardly think—" he began crisply, then surprised them both by not finishing. She'd guessed more of what he'd done than he expected. Perhaps he'd underestimated the subtlety of her mind. If he had, the situation demanded— no, *deserved*—a change of tactics.

"You're right," he said. "I should have consulted you before going to the papers. I know it is the human way. Though I'm obliged to convince my superiors I find your existence distasteful, if I wish you to regard me as your father, I must make concessions to your upbringing."

She leaned closer over the desk, her body vibrating with

passion. "You need to stop interfering with those I love. People have a right to chart their own course."

He disagreed with her in more ways and for more reasons than he could enumerate. Those with power had the privilege and the responsibility to exercise it on behalf of those in their care, especially family. Herrington had grown up with those beliefs, had accepted them into his bones, and yet . . . how often had he seen those tenets abused or even ignored in the name of ambition or expedience? He knew some humans—male ones, anyway— believed precisely as he did. He also knew that the most private, least-disciplined reaches of his heart thrilled to the implication of her claim.

Didn't he secretly wish to be free?

"Perhaps I shouldn't have suggested your friend ought to be released from his position," he admitted gruffly. "I will try to refrain from similar acts from now on."

His words made her step back. She pressed her hand to her chest, as if to protect the organ that beat within. The gesture made him wish he were as adept at reading human auras as some of the *rohn*.

"You're serious," she said, her rage replaced by slow wonderment. "You'd compromise your 'superior' Yamish traditions to have me in your life." She pulled a nearby chair to his desk and sat, her blue dress a striking contrast to its yellow silk upholstery. "You really do care about me."

"I thought I'd made that clear."

She put her chin in her hand and smiled. "You made it clear you cared about your bloodline."

"There's no shame in caring about that."

"There's no shame in caring about me as a person."

He found himself tugging his waistcoat defensively, exactly as a human would. "You have an admirable amount of spirit. From the first, you reminded me—" He stopped, unable to say the words.

"Reminded you of what?" she asked softly.

He did not have to be a *rohn* to hear her tenderness. It washed over him as sweet as a robin's song, undermining his natural caution.

"Of her," he said and handed her Louise's portrait. "My sister. I lost her two years ago in an accident. A runaway carriage."

She stroked the protective glass with her fingertips, her expression as gentle as it had been when she held Max in the car. "Now I understand how the *Courier* got a sketch. She looks just like me."

"Louise's nose was bigger. And you outweigh her a bit."

"An even trade, I hope," she said with a little laugh he didn't understand, probably some female mystery. When she looked up, her eyes glimmered on the verge of tears. "You know I can't replace her."

"I know," he said through his tightened throat. "But meeting you, hoping we could eventually become a family, did take away a bit of the pain. I miss being able to confide in her, sharing the burden of living in strange surroundings. Louise was an extraordinarily trustworthy sibling. I imagine you'd say she was my best friend. I look at you, at your beautiful human eyes welling up, and I think maybe you can give her the tears I could never shed."

As his daughter pressed her lips together, a shining droplet rolled down her cheek.

Herrington stiffened. "I didn't mean you had to do it in front of me."

To his amazement, she laughed outright.

⤙⤙

It wasn't fair of her to laugh at him for being alarmed by her emotion. Plenty of human men would have reacted the same. Knowing this, Roxie attempted to compose herself. As he waited, her father drew his hands around the edges of the heavy book that sat on his desk.

"Why do you have that?" she asked, noting that it was a *Farmer's Almanac*. "I didn't see fields on your estate."

"Cultural artifact," he replied, carefully layering his hands on top. "It's part of my job as envoy to investigate all facets of human society."

Roxie squinted at him. She wasn't skilled enough at

reading Yama to be sure, but she could have sworn this wasn't the whole story.

"Since we're being forthright with each other," he went on, almost making her laugh again, "there's something you need to know."

"Yes?" She smoothed her skirt over her knees, feeling oddly armored in her feminine clothes.

Whatever had unsettled her father, he was shielded again as well. He pushed the almanac to one side. "I received a communiqué from the Prince of Narikerr, the administrator of my home city. He has become aware of the story in the *Courier*."

"Already?" Roxie exclaimed. "That only came out this morning."

"We have . . . private means of sending messages."

" 'Private' like that fancy car you used to rescue us?"

At her shot in the dark, Herrington gave the impression of wincing without a muscle of his face having moved. Then again, maybe she was picking up his discomfort through his energy. At once, she saw the usefulness of the skill. As if aware of her attention and wishing to avoid it, he turned his gaze to his well-kept nails.

"It would be better," he said, "if you didn't mention seeing that vehicle to the prince."

"Understood." She leaned forward. "Does this mean I'm going to meet the prince?"

"It would appear so. He has decided to pay me a visit tomorrow night, to 'assess conditions for himself.' Most likely, he's only bored, and the visit will be brief. His presence, however, will necessitate a small gathering, which you—as the object of his interest—will be expected to attend."

"Whether I want to or not, I take it."

Herrington inclined his head in a gesture she found peculiarly Yamish: a combination of respect and drollery. "Princes do not wait on others' convenience."

"Is he a good prince or a bad one?"

Herrington thought before he answered. "That's difficult

to say. He's flighty and, as I mentioned, easily bored. When he speaks to you, as I'm certain he will, you'll need to be careful not to react."

Roxie's eyebrows rose. "Not react?"

"He's not the brightest of Yamish lights. Too much inbreeding, I suspect. But that doesn't mean his temper can't be dangerous. He has a history of—one presumes—inadvertent rudeness. Since he doesn't have direct experience with humans, he's liable to put his foot in it with you. It's important that you not betray if he gives offense."

"Because that would make him angry."

Herrington spread his hands, palms up. "I know it isn't fair, but he doesn't like being embarrassed. Whatever his private agenda, we don't need him as an enemy."

Roxie nodded, then rubbed her chin. "I don't think I can guarantee the boys' behavior."

"We can keep them out of the way. Young people aren't expected at these events."

"Good," she said. "Because I'm not sure I want Max anywhere near your prince."

"Perfectly understandable," Herrington assured her. "Even wise." He relaxed in his dark tufted-leather chair. She sensed the change of posture was an act of trust, that Yama didn't often let down their guards. "Thank you for agreeing to my request."

Roxie hid her mischief by gazing at the hands she'd laced modestly in her lap. "I can be extremely sensible when I understand the reasons why."

"Hm," was Herrington's dry response.

"So," she said, letting a hint of her grin show. "You're from Narikerr. You must have seen the famous DuBarry expedition."

"I was a young man and not yet involved in government, but, yes, I was residing there when humans first arrived." He hesitated, his pale, blunt hands slowly smoothing the edge of his desk. "Possibly, someday, I could tell you about those days."

When his all-silver eyes met hers, they seemed strangely vulnerable, as if he were braced for a blow.

Why, he's afraid I won't be interested, Roxie realized. The Great Herrington was feeling shy.

"I'd enjoy that very much," she said, "as would Max. For the moment, at least, he's fascinated with all things historical."

"Ah," said Herrington with an unusual twinkle in his eye. "Perhaps that explains his fascination with me."

Then, to her astonishment, her father smiled.

Chapter 26

Once upon a time, when her baby's birth was mere weeks away, a queen of the far north land chanced to gaze into a mirror made of ice. Hearing news of this ill omen, her king requested that the child-to-come be slain. Alas, the queen was too tenderhearted. Thus was born the fabled Prince of Ice.

—*Tales of the Northland*

Roxie was a passable seamstress, but the gown the maid hooked her into was a marvel: the stitches invisible, the intricate cutting of the pattern calculated to perfect the fit. Roxie could well believe the race that had fashioned this creation was superior.

"*Rohn*-made," the maid informed her, noting her dazzled look.

Roxie stroked her hand down a skirt that flowed like water

to the floor, the cloth a rich indigo velvet that made her want to purr. "This fabric . . ."

"That's *rohn*-made, too, miss." The maid adjusted the gathered straps on Roxie's upper arms until their height matched the low straight line of the neck. "Whatever else you might say about those demons, they do lovely work."

"It must have cost the moon!"

"If you'll pardon me for saying so, I don't think your father'd feel it even if it did."

The maid's saucy grin told Roxie something she hadn't known. The servants might be respectful of her father, but they weren't afraid. They seemed, in fact, to relish working for their foreign employer.

"Lord Herrington wants you to look nice," the woman went on, shaking the complicated train that waterfalled down the dress's back. "He wants you to do yourself and him proud."

A day ago, Roxie would have remarked on the chances of the latter greatly outweighing the former. Now she merely gazed in mute amazement at her image in the full-length mirror. Though she didn't often fuss over her looks, she thought she'd known how to bring out the best in them; thought she'd mastered those secrets at her mother's knee. The miracles the maid and this dress had wrought taught her differently.

Her skin was porcelain next to the purple cloth, almost as pale as a full demon. Cosmetics enhanced her features, making her eyes seem huge and her lips dewy. Her hair was caught into a complicated arrangement of braided loops, gleaming after a long brushing. With the corset cinched, her figure could have been a queen's.

She looked, for once, as arresting as La Belle Yvonne.

"You'll do," said the maid just as someone knocked.

When she opened the door, Adrian came in. "Lord Herrington sent me with a gift." He lifted a jewelry box. "He thought you might refuse it if he brought it himself."

"Don't kiss her," the maid ordered as she left. "You'll ruin my good work."

Adrian watched her go, blinking slightly at her imperti-
nence. Then he stepped farther in.

"My *Lord,*" he said, getting his first good look. "It's almost worth everything we went through to see you like
this."

Roxie took a breath and felt her bosom swell over the
bodice. "I think the maid laced me too tight."

Adrian circled her halfway round. "I think the maid is
my new best friend. You look exquisite. A lady from head
to foot." As if he'd been kicked in the gut, he pressed his
hand to his white waistcoat. "No wonder she warned me
not to kiss you. You make me want to peel you out of that
bit by bit."

His awe was flattering, especially when he looked so elegant himself. His shirt was starched within an inch of its
life, and his black trousers and tailcoat seemed tailor-made
to show off his honed body—a body that was, in its way, a
weapon. Perhaps it was childish, but ever since she'd seen
him tossing demons over bridges and ripping doors off au-
tomobiles, she'd found him even sexier than before. That
being so, it was no wonder the sight of him in his dress
clothes went to her head.

"You'd better stick close tonight," she teased giddily.
"Given how devious my father is, he may be angling to find
me a high-born spouse."

Adrian's gaze came up startled. "Yes, I—I wouldn't be
surprised if he had ambitions along those lines."

His tone was odd enough to make her regret her words.
"I didn't mean—"

"Hush," he said, touching one finger very lightly to her
painted lips. "You can mean what you choose. I believe
that's a woman's prerogative. As for your father, if he
thinks you're too good for me, he could be right."

She wanted to protest, but every way she thought of doing so seemed awkward, either a suggestion that his pride
needed coddling, or that she, at least, had marriage on her
mind.

"Where's my gift?" she asked instead.

Adrian didn't hand it over immediately. "Your father

warned me you'd cast dishonor on his family by appearing in any less."

"You're quoting, I assume."

"I am. He also said to tell you this wasn't Louise's. He thought you wouldn't be comfortable wearing her jewels. Do you know what he meant?"

Roxanne nodded but was unable to explain because he'd opened the flat, hinged box and stolen her breath. An extravagant necklace lay inside, structured like a chandelier but made of diamonds and sapphires rather than glass. No stone was smaller than her fingernail, and quite a few were larger.

"Good Lord," she said as Adrian shifted behind her to do the clasp. His breath stirred the tiny hairs on her nape. As if wriggling might break the bauble, she felt quite afraid to move.

"Naturally," he said, "I'd be enjoying this more if I were remotely capable of buying it for you myself."

Roxie barely registered what he said. The longest sapphire brushed her cleavage, glowing mysteriously in the muted light. "My father *was* involved in having you dismissed," she said dazedly.

Adrian dipped his head to kiss her shoulder. "Is there a purpose in bringing that up?"

Her fingers disobeyed her will to stroke a glittering diamond drop. "I'm reminding myself to stay on my guard with him."

Adrian laughed and straightened, his face beside hers in the mirror, his hands warm on her shoulders. "I have a feeling we'll have to be on our guard with everyone we meet tonight."

Roxie shook herself from her jewel-induced haze. "Are the boys safe?"

"They're spending the evening in the butler's pantry with a strapping young man named Keane. He has strict orders not to let them out of his sight. Charles will probably be more use for keeping Max from running off, but Keane had some practical-looking brawn."

"Good." She frowned at herself in the glass. "God, I hate this."

"Dressing up?"

"Playing demon games."

"Your father's been at this for thirty years. I expect he knows what he's doing."

Roxie drew and released as deep a breath as she could, considering the snugness of her corset. Oddly enough, Adrian gave the impression of being energized by the challenge. Perhaps it seemed a return to his lost duties.

"Yes," she said, "we ought to be able to trust my father to be the most devious demon around. And if he's not, well, God help us."

"God help us anyway," Adrian said with a smile. "It never hurts to have influential friends."

❧

Roxie and Adrian were separated almost immediately by the crowd—a large one, she thought, for a supposedly small gathering. Perhaps one couldn't throw a modest party for a prince.

The attendance was split between human dignitaries and *daimyo*. She assumed they were *daimyo,* at any rate. They were extremely opulent of dress: human styles, for the most part, but richer in fabric and decoration. Evidently, there was no reason to sew a bit of beading onto a sleeve when a line of emeralds would do. By comparison, Roxie's outfit looked sedate. All the female *daimyo* were slender, haughty, and beautiful—enough to make the humans who passed them occasionally catch their breath. Almost without exception, and regardless of the hue of their gowns, the lady *daimyo* wore long red leather gloves extending up their arms. They did not remove them even to pluck hors d'oeuvres from the plates her father's army of footmen were circling with.

Feeling lost in the milling ballroom, Roxie tugged her own cream kidskin gloves above her elbow. The color difference must mean something. She wished her father had explained before he sent them as accessories.

"Quite a crush," said a cheerful human voice at her side. "And what a glittering picture those Yama make!"

Roxie turned to find a bookish young man in the bright green uniform of the Jeruvian embassy. He was inches shorter than her but comfortingly cheerful. Once he'd brushed pastry crumbs from his palm, he bent in gentlemanly fashion over her wrist.

"Rinaldo Nazaire, from the embassy." He waved at his chest ribbons to demonstrate. "Naturally, I know who you are, though that engraving in the *Courier* didn't do you justice."

"Er, thank you," Roxie said as he snagged a flute of champagne and presented it to her.

"It's Jeruvian," he said, urging her to take a sip. "A special favor from my superior. Hard to pull a party like this together on short notice." He nodded approvingly as she swallowed. "So, enjoying your notoriety?"

Maybe it was the bubbles tickling her nose that made her laugh; she should have been too nervous. "I had some notoriety already," she admitted. "Just not among this lot."

The junior ambassador, or whatever he was, smiled at her wit. Because he seemed at home in this milieu, she decided to ask him her question. "Mr. Ambassador—"

"Rinaldo," he insisted, though it probably was not proper.

"Rinaldo, why are almost all the Yamish women wearing red gloves?"

"Ah, that." The faintest blush belied his worldly pose. "Means they're available for, well, anything."

"Anything? Even . . ." She hesitated, but she needed to know. "Even drinking etheric-force?"

"They won't take it without a willing partner, but, yes, that's precisely what most of them are interested in. The diplomatic circuit tends to draw a fast crowd. The more forbidden the pleasure, the more it attracts their type. Conservatives stay at home. They wouldn't touch a human if you paid them." He peered at her through his round-lensed spectacles. "I hope you don't mind my being frank."

Roxie's hand was at her throat. Inexplicably, her concerns for her and Adrian's safety while in this throng were joined by a bit of fear for the Yama themselves. When a

society's elite became more interested in self-indulgence
than government, could that be a good sign? Worse, did the
fact that she cared mean she wasn't thinking of herself as
wholly human anymore?

With an effort, she shook off the strange worry. "I don't
mind you being frank at all. In fact, I thank you for answering honestly. I had no idea my father was being so considerate when he sent me these."

She turned her cream-gloved hands back and forth.
Smiling gently, Rinaldo offered his arm. "Why don't you
let me introduce you around, since you know you're not
sending the wrong message."

He was as careful of her comfort as if his government—
or her father—had ordered him to the task. The more she
thought about it, the likelier that option seemed. If her father wished his superiors to believe he found her existence
distasteful, delegating such chores would be appropriate.
Happily, Rinaldo was a fine stand-in, steering her toward
those individuals who would behave themselves in her
somewhat scandalous presence. Without taking a single insult, she met a number of human diplomats, one grand
duke from a tiny Silver Island, two Ohramese earls—both
of whom had bought her paintings—and even a few lady
daimyo whose exquisite manners put her on her mettle to
be as polite.

"You're a quick study," Rinaldo praised her jovially.
"Perhaps the Queen should put you on staff."

Before she could respond, her escort caught sight of
someone behind her shoulder who made him purse his lips
ruefully.

"Brace yourself," he warned in an undertone. "I'm
afraid I can't wiggle you out of meeting this fellow."

Not surprisingly, *this fellow* turned out to be Narikerr's
prince.

Their guest of honor was an exceedingly elegant and
languid young man, gliding through the crush as if his
pointed slippers didn't touch the ground. As beautiful as
any of the women, with straight, hip-length black hair and
slightly tilted eyes, he wore traditional silver-on-white

Yamish robes. The garment's shoulders were unnaturally broad, their pale embroidery designed to resemble a long-tailed phoenix rising from a fire. His skin very nearly matched the white of the cloth. Strikingly, the only color on his person was the belt that wrapped his narrow waist, a tasseled silk so deeply red it put Roxie in mind of a slash of blood. A single faceted diamond, as large as a pigeon's egg, hung from his neck.

Even without such dramatic garb, he was worthy of a stare. Roxie was obliged to remind herself to shut her mouth.

The junior ambassador bowed low as the prince approached. "Your highness," he said in a deeply deferential tone. "Might I have the honor of introducing Miss Roxanne McAllister?"

"You might," said the prince with a nearly invisible Yamish smile. When he turned his lazy silver gaze to her, she saw his brows were slanted like his eyes, giving him a faint—and possibly misleading—expression of surprise. Taking his time, he perused her up and down. When he finished, she had a feeling her every measurement had been committed to memory. She was grateful she'd been cautioned not to betray offense.

"Your highness," she said with a small curtsey.

Perhaps he had expected a deeper obeisance. When she rose, his glimmer of a smile was gone.

"You favor your father's family," was all he said.

Though his voice held no inflection, she sensed this was not a compliment. "Many children do, your highness."

He blinked at her temperate response. Perhaps he thought she ought to wish she were prettier. Genuinely unmoved by the implication, she noticed his pupils were large and black, as if he were under the influence of a stronger substance than champagne. She must have said something wrong in a way she didn't understand, because Rinaldo's formerly gentle fingers were digging into her arm.

"Yes," mused the prince. "Many children do take after their parents." Suddenly, he smiled, a dazzling exposure of snow-white teeth. "I wonder that your father didn't mention your resemblance to Louise. What a gift from heaven you must have seemed, as if his darling sister had returned from the grave."

"I regret I cannot satisfy your curiosity on that score," Roxanne said, hoping she sounded suitably respectful. "Lord Herrington keeps his feelings to himself."

Again the prince gave a single blink. His smile had disappeared as quickly as it came. "Of course he does. He's a deep one, your father."

As this seemed to have no answer, Roxie inclined her head. She was beginning to feel very uncomfortable, in a way she hadn't with the other Yama she'd met. Peculiar prickles were crawling down her spine, and she wondered if there might be something odd about the prince's energy, something only a half-breed like her could sense. No one else was looking askance at the prince, and if her father had noticed the effect, surely he would have said.

"My, it's stuffy in here," the prince commented in his languid way. "Why don't you and I stroll toward the orangerie for some air?"

Rinaldo uttered a soft protest, but the prince flicked his fingers to shoo him away. "No need to tag along," he said. "Miss McAllister and I shall enjoy getting acquainted."

When they reached the cooler air of the conservatory, the prince seemed unable to look away from her eyes. Dwarf orange trees blossomed all around them, smelling as sweet as spring, but her companion spared them not a glance.

"So strange," he murmured, his hand lifting slightly without coming close enough to touch. "Seeing those human eyes in a Yamish face. I wonder whether the world looks different from behind them."

"I couldn't say, your highness, not being able to see the world through yours."

The prince's almost-smile appeared again, curling just the corners of his mouth. "You are cleverer than I expected. I suppose you get that from your father."

Roxanne offered a tiny shrug. "People say my mother knew how to land on her feet."

"Like a cat," said the prince.

Though his amusement remained in place, Roxie was unable to restrain a small shudder. She couldn't help thinking she might have caught the response from him, that her reminder of her human mother had repelled him. If it had, his outer manner didn't show it. Looking beyond her, he pressed two fingers to his lips.

"Oh, look," he said. "I believe one of *my* cats has caught a mouse."

Roxie looked. In the arch that separated the crowded ballroom from the conservatory, she saw one red-gloved female *daimyo* leaning close to Adrian. She was the tallest Yama Roxie had seen yet, so slender she seemed spindly. She was beautiful—as they all were—but with looks like that, her nonhuman nature shone undisguised. Though Adrian appeared to be holding her off adequately, he must have been unnerved by the way her glove-clad fingers caressed the whorl of energy above his heart. The *daimyo* looked as if she longed to drink him down then and there.

What disturbed Roxanne more was the man in black who was even then slipping furtively behind the pair, a figure whose appearance caused Adrian to tense like a hunting dog. The figure seemed more startled to see the prince. As he passed, his eyes went as round as silver coins. If he'd been human, they would have been showing whites.

"Oh, dear," said the prince. "I'm certain I didn't request that *he* be added to the guest list."

Roxanne didn't stop to ask what he meant.

"Excuse me," she said, forgetting in her dismay to add *your highness*. "I believe I must go rescue my friend from yours."

Chapter 27

To keep a friend close is pleasant. To keep an enemy close is wise.

—The Collected Sayings of the Emperor

"*Was that him?*" Roxie demanded, taking Adrian's arm and forcing the hovering lady *daimyo* to step back. She lowered her voice until she was only moving her lips. "Was that The Dragon?"

"Yes," he said, then strained to watch the black-clad figure wend toward the door. "That exit leads to the servants' quarters. I should go after him."

"I'm coming with you."

"No," Adrian refused. "I'll take care of it."

She was about to tell him he was crazy when the prince joined her in the arch. The smile she was beginning to hate was painted on his lips.

"You two look worried," he said. "Might I be of assistance?"

Adrian glanced at her, but she gave her head a tiny shake. In no fashion were they going to trust this Yama. Whether his involvement with The Dragon was real or merely speculative, she had no desire to have him know what was going on.

"Go," she said reluctantly, knowing every second they delayed gave their enemy a better chance of accomplishing whatever he'd come for. "See if you can find my father to help."

Adrian didn't bother to ask if she'd be fine. He knew he had to move quickly to be sure of Max's safety. Giving the prince a single doubtful look, he pressed through the party-goers toward his quarry.

"How nice," said the prince, forcing her to turn back to him. "Now you have more time for me."

"Forgive me, your highness," she said, adding a curtsey for good measure. She looked around for possible distractions, but the woman who'd been trying to work her wiles on Adrian seemed to have melted into the crowd. "I'm sure I shouldn't be monopolizing your company, certainly not at such a splendid gathering."

"Nonsense," said the prince. "I see this lot all the time." He gazed at her with an odd approximation of paternal care, as if he'd been practicing human expressions in front of a mirror and hadn't quite got them right. She knew Yama lived longer than humans, but if he was trying to treat her like a daughter, she had to wonder what age he was. He didn't look a day older than her. Now he spoke again. "I couldn't help overhearing you mention wanting to find your father. I believe I saw him go upstairs a short while ago."

"Thank you!" she said, forgetting herself enough to touch his shoulder. "I'll run up and get him now."

"If you wouldn't mind taking me with you . . ." the prince requested before she could slip away. "I'm feeling a trifle overwhelmed by the heat."

For God's sake, Roxie thought impatiently, but he did

look pasty—even for a Yama. His brow was slightly blueish, and his pupils glittered in his silver eyes, larger than the last time she'd noticed them. Perhaps he was having a bad reaction to whatever substance he'd imbibed. She wished she could ignore him or pass him off to someone else, but for all she knew her refusal would cause an international crisis. It wasn't as if she knew what sort of deference was due a prince.

"I'd be happy to escort you to a quiet room," she said as amiably as she could. "Perhaps you'd like a moment to lie down."

"You are graciousness itself," the prince praised weakly, taking the arm she hadn't thought to offer.

His grip was heavier than she expected. She doubted she'd be able to shake him off even if she threw caution to the winds and tried. As they climbed the grand stairway to the second floor, much too slowly for her peace of mind, she attempted to resign herself to having him along. Maybe it was just as well she knew what one of their possible suspects was up to.

"I'll stop in his study first," she said, because that door came after the landing. She received no answer when she knocked, but when she tried the knob it was unlocked. From her previous visit, she knew the room was big enough that her father might not have heard. To her dismay, though she'd meant for the prince to wait in the corridor, he followed her inside.

Well, fine, she thought. Completely uncaring of how it looked, she hiked up her skirts to wade through the stacks of books and papers that formed a maze on the carpet.

An electric light with a deep-blue glass shade burned on her father's desk. Other than this, the room showed no signs of occupation.

"Hello," she called, hoping against hope that she'd missed some concealing nook. Didn't wealthy people love putting secret passages in their mansions? Couldn't Herrington be hiding away to escape his guests? "Father?"

It wasn't a sound that made her turn, but an awareness

that the atmosphere in the study had suddenly grown thicker than it ought to be. Her ears felt as if they'd been stuffed with cotton.

She found the prince affixing a palm-sized silver disk to the heavy wooden door. Whatever the device was, she knew it was the source of the change in the atmosphere. The air directly around it shimmered like summer heat. Her heart began to hammer in her throat.

"What are you doing?" she asked.

The prince spun back to her, his black hair fanning out from his hips. "I'm guaranteeing our privacy." He indicated the thing on the door with a graceful hand. "This mechanism blocks both sound and pressure. No one will be able to hear us, and not even a Yama will have the strength to break in—perhaps not even a group of Yama."

Knowledge dropped into Roxie's mind like a pebble hitting the bottom of a well. She leaned back against the front of her father's desk and gripped its marble edge. Though the prince remained by the door, the distance to where he stood seemed far too small. His smile was gone, as if it had never been. He watched her with the unemotional interest of a naturalist studying a bug.

"You planned this," she said, fear roughening the words. "You wanted us to catch sight of The Dragon so Adrian would be drawn off."

"And your father as well, apparently. My friend, Vyineyri, must have caught up with him after all."

"Your friend?" Roxie said, because she couldn't have repeated his pronunciation. Maybe it was a good thing the Yama took human names.

The prince stroked the corners of his mouth as if to smooth away any possible return of his smile. "The tall woman with the long red gloves. I needed help to ensure that all the pieces of my game fell into their proper place."

"But why?"

"Because *Raymond*"—he said the name with an edge of mockery—"has become dispensable. Constantly importuning me to raise him up from the *rohn*—as if he were the only low-born doctor willing to work for gold. True, there aren't many as brilliant as he is, but I think I'll be content with his replacement."

"The Dragon is a *rohn?*"

As he came closer, the prince swept a stack of books aside with his foot, a gratuitous bit of destructiveness. "Oh, yes," he said. "I don't think you realized how lucky you were when you didn't know who your father was. Such trouble parents cause their children—either dragging them down or setting a standard the world refuses to believe they can match. If I had one of your human pennies for every time I've been called a pale shadow of my sire, I'd be twice as rich as I am."

His grin was not a human gesture, more like a baring of fangs. Roxie began to edge toward the other side of the desk, wanting to put it between them. With a flash of unnatural speed, the prince blocked her way, a stream of toppled books and papers settling in his wake. The maneuver was so swift, it stole her breath. While she was still too stunned to move, he took hold of her throat in a cross between a threat and a caress.

"I showed them," he said. "Even as they whispered insults behind my back, I proved I was more cunning than anyone. Your own father, the great Red Fox, was fooled. He thought I couldn't tell how much he treasured you from the start, how he'd do anything to keep you safe." The prince shook his head and clucked. "Blood ties can be the most seductive set of chains."

Roxie struggled not to show weakness by shrinking back, but the place where he gripped her neck was buzzing unpleasantly. "Are you trying to get back at my father by hurting me?"

"Nothing of the sort," demurred the prince. "That's simply an agreeable side effect. No, what I want from you is exactly what my hopefully soon-to-be-departed employee did."

"To study me," Roxanne said.

The prince's thumb followed the line of her throat to the first curve of her necklace. Roxie couldn't tell whether he was more interested in stroking her skin or her father's finely polished sapphires.

"What I want," he said, soft and intimate, "is to drink you down, drop by drop, without fear of being tainted by undiluted human energy. I want no risk of addiction. No nasty, uncontrolled emotions. Nothing but strength and pleasure and longer life. Through me, my dear, you will have the honor of serving the Yama's greater good."

The prince's touch made it hard to swallow. Her instincts screamed for her to fight him off, but she feared he'd do even worse if she tried and failed. "You were behind The Dragon's experiments on children."

The prince shrugged one slanted eyebrow at her guess. "I funded them. Regrettably, they were unsuccessful but a worthy effort all the same."

"A worthy effort!"

"They were only *human* children. Plentiful as rats, and all bought fair and square with demon gold. If you want to be outraged, blame the parents who sold them to Raymond. Those children were lucky to have done their small part to advance etheric science—as you shall also do soon enough."

Roxie struggled to contain her rage. Succumbing to it wouldn't help her escape. "You're forgetting I can taint you exactly as those children did," she said, unable to resist bracing her hands against his chest, even if she wasn't able to push him off. "Half-demon or not, I have emotions."

"Everyone *has* emotions," he said, condescension coloring his tone. "The question is, how strongly do they infuse your etheric-force, and how much of them cross over in a transfer. If your energy isn't perfect for our purposes, we can always breed you until the mix is right. Perhaps a quarter-human would be better. Or an eighth. I'm a patient man, Miss McAllister, despite my reputation. I'm more than willing to try as many times as it takes. In fact"—he rolled his pelvis tellingly against hers, trapping her between him and the desk—"if more demon blood will improve your strain, I'd happily breed you myself."

The ridge that dug into her abdomen left no doubt as to

what he meant. He wasn't as hot as a human would have been in that stage of arousal, but he was warm enough. His pupils were huge circles of black, as large now as her own irises. Finally, she understood that no drug had swelled them, but rather excitement at what he planned. He'd been anticipating having her at his mercy all night.

As if he knew the moment she comprehended, he opened his mouth and let his tongue flick out, curling the dark, forked marking over his upper lip. "What's the matter, Miss McAllister? Never seen a demon in rut?"

"I disgust you," she gasped, pushing futilely against his chest. For all his slightness, the prince's strength was greater than hers. "I know you can hardly stand to look at me."

This claim surprised him, but whatever perplexity she might have caused, he shook away. "Of course you disgust me. The mixing of a lower race's blood with ours is abominable. What my body desires, however, is a separate matter." His gaze narrowed as he studied her, his now-black eyes glittering. "I'm intrigued that you read my fire-talk that well . . . unless your father has been instructing you?"

If he didn't know the answer, she wasn't going to supply it. "I'll kill you before I cooperate."

The demon blinked, his only sign of reaction. "You can try," he said and pressed his mouth over hers.

For one astonished moment, she couldn't believe what he'd done. Did he honestly think he could seduce her? Then, as her knees threatened to give way and the front of her body suddenly went cold, she realized there was a different, and far more pernicious purpose to his kiss. He was feeding from her. His hand had slipped between them as she tried to push him off, and he was now drawing energy from the swirling center above her heart.

"No," she said against his mouth, sickened by the numbing dizziness. Her protest did her no good. Her legs turned to rubber, and she fell.

The prince didn't bother to hold her up, but simply caught her beneath the arms and followed her down to the paper-strewn parquet floor. He was strong enough to make their descent graceful. At the bottom, his body settled between her sprawled thighs, his hips rolling pointedly against hers.

"That's it," he praised, as if she had welcomed him there intentionally. "Give everything up to me."

She struggled under his weight, wishing her father *had* instructed her so she'd know how to stop what he was doing. His hand was on her breastbone again, sucking her energy. She couldn't comprehend how other humans could stand this—even for money. The sensation was horrible. She could feel her strength throbbing out of her with every beat of her heart, or maybe with every beat of the prince's heart. He, by contrast, was energized, lengthening as he rubbed her with greater and greater force, digging his erection into her mound. His whole body writhed against her, as if he wanted to bathe in her etheric-force. His breath came quick and fast.

"This won't hurt you," he panted. "I'm only taking enough to make you faint. Then I'll carry you out of here with no trouble. Come on, girl. Give yourself over to your prince."

"Not . . . my . . . prince," she said. Her hand was between them just as his was. She shifted it to cover his heart as if somehow that would help her lift him off. "Never . . . my . . . prince."

Something rose inside her in frustration at her helplessness, an anger that went deeper than flesh and bone. She couldn't let him take her. Wouldn't let him rob Max and Charles and Adrian of her care. Never again would she let him hurt a child, whether it came from her womb or another's. She didn't care if The Dragon had done the dirty work; the prince had been the mastermind. This man who crushed her deserved to be crushed himself, deserved to be torn apart limb from limb.

"NO!" she said, the strength of the word buoying her spirit.

She shoved, but not with her hand. With some knowledge she'd held unsuspected in her half-demon blood, some method of focusing the will, she pushed the black rage from her body and into his. He stiffened, but she didn't care. *No,*

she said again with her mind. *You are not my prince.*
The blackness swallowed him and her, shrieking like a ban-
shee, tossing the tiny spark of her soul inside its whirlwind.
The immensity of her anger frightened her, the violence that
seemed to have no limit. In that moment, she did not see a
vast distance between the prince and herself. In that moment, they might have been one. *Back,* she thought in a
panic. *Pull back.*

The blackness obeyed her call. Back it rushed, to her
skin, to her heart, forcing it to pump so hard each com-
pression hurt. To her surprise, the blackness came back
crammed with rainbow gleams of light, beautiful corrusca-
tions of energy. Force was force, she supposed. No matter
its source, it could have no ugliness. This force made her
skin prickle as if tiny wires were running over it. She flung
out her arms, trying to ground herself. Then she lost consciousness.

She couldn't have been insensible for more than seconds, because when she jerked back to awareness, her hair
hadn't stopped standing on end. The prince lay completely
limp on top of her. Repelled by the contact, she pushed
him off. Far from resisting, he rolled just as limply onto the
floor. His appearance shocked her. His face was blue, his
silver eyes wide and staring. His pupils were shrunk to pin-
pricks. He seemed not to realize a book was digging into
his cheek.

"Oh, God," she said, struggling to sit up. She pressed
one hand in horror to her mouth. She was both blazing hot
and shivering, as if she had reversed what he was trying to
do to her, then magnified it twentyfold.

Long before she dared to touch him, she knew the
prince of Narikerr was dead.

Chapter 28

❧

The Yama have had their own internecine struggles, about which
we know little. Suffice to say, they haven't become so good at intrigue by accident.

—*The True and Irreverent History of Avvar*

❧

Adrian wouldn't have guessed a dead body could be
this heavy, even one rolled in a strange cold tarp—a 're-
frigeration sheet,' according to Herrington. Obtained from
the fruit cellar, the rubbery black cloth smelled of the ap-
ples it had been keeping crisp. As he and Adrian lugged it
through the secret passage's twists and turns, Adrian was
grateful one of the guests had alerted Roxie's father to The
Dragon's presence. With his strength burned to its lowest
ebb from using his implants, Adrian doubted he could have
managed alone. As it was, his shoulder burned from the
scoring it had taken.

"Almost there," Herrington said, his face dripping sweat. He was carrying the body's shoulders and, hence, most of its weight, though his Yamish muscles were up to the challenge. The sweat was the result of the hot steam pipes that ran through the tunnel, which seemed to affect him more than Adrian, perhaps because of his colder national origins. Tiny electric lights lit the walls at meter-long intervals, like fireflies that didn't blink. The way the illumination glistened on the signs of Herrington's exertion almost made him look human.

Exhausted beyond logic, Adrian decided this was as good a time as any to make his stand.

"Your daughter . . . isn't marrying . . . that Jeruvian diplomat," he said between pants. "He's far too short."

Despite the perspiration running down his face, Herrington's response was cool. "Are you suggesting my daughter has a height requirement for a mate?"

"No, sir. Just stating that I don't intend for her to marry anyone but me."

"Might tell her that," Herrington muttered as they maneuvered their burden around a last bend. He set the body down with a sigh and wiped his forehead on his sleeve. Adrian let the feet fall, too. "Lord," said his future father-in-law, "I must be getting older than I thought."

He gazed at Adrian in the dim yellow-white light. Adrian had a feeling Roxie's father had done—or at least seen—skulduggery like this before. Herrington's face was oddly relaxed for a man who'd recently witnessed, then helped cover up a killing. "Are you prepared for this?" he asked Adrian.

This seemed to be passing through a door in the tunnel wall, presumably back into the house somewhere.

"Yes, sir," Adrian said, though he did give in to the urge to blow out his breath.

Herrington's ghost of a smile felt like the equivalent of another man's shoulder clap. "I'll go first," he said, "to make sure it's clear. I didn't get a chance to lock up before I left."

Adrian leaned against the peeling wall as Herrington

pressed a secret latch to slide the paneling aside. The older man stiffened at what he found.

"Roxanne!" he said in a startled voice, which brought Adrian to alert as well.

When he saw her for himself, he understood the reason for Herrington's surprise. Roxie looked as if she'd been through the proverbial wringer: her face pale and smudged with dust, her hair falling every which way out of its coiffure. She must have been more worried than he'd realized. When she spotted Adrian, she pressed her hands to her mouth.

"Oh," she cried, her eyes welling up with tears. "You've been hurt!"

"Just grazed," he said, touching the bullet wound on his shoulder without turning his gaze from hers. Luckily, he wasn't bleeding anymore. Her concern for him filled him with a longing only holding her would satisfy. If her father hadn't been there, he would have gone to her straightaway. "The Dragon had an odd sort of gun."

"A gun!" she exclaimed, even more horrified.

"Automatic pistol," Herrington corrected as he lowered himself into his big leather chair. He didn't groan, just looked like he wanted to. "It fires without being—Oh, never mind. They're quite illegal, I assure you, here or at home. Civilians aren't allowed to possess firearms."

In light of what they'd been doing, Herrington's legal quibble was humorous. Adrian only wished he had the energy to laugh.

"Max is all right," he said, propping his hips on the corner of Herrington's solid desk. "Charles got him away before anything happened. The Dragon shot at us while we were chasing him across the grounds."

"The wonder is that you caught him," Herrington said in the manner of one man congratulating another on a tricky billiards shot. "Those implants are impressive. It must be divine justice that you wouldn't have apprehended the man who installed them if he hadn't designed them so well." He rubbed his jaw in an unwittingly human gesture. "Hopefully, someone can reverse engineer them, and the Securité program will be able to continue."

Whatever that means, Adrian thought. He was too weary to ask, even wearier than his post-implant crash could account for. This was only the second man he'd killed in his life, the first that wasn't in the line of duty. Mixed in with his relief at being alive was his awareness that he'd done something he truly wished he hadn't had to. Unfortunately, The Dragon hadn't given him a choice.

He was wiping his hands up and down his face when he noticed the body lying half hidden by Roxie's skirts, a body in an unmistakable silver-on-white outfit. The pointy-toed slippers clinched the matter.

"Criminy," he said. "What happened to the prince?"

Roxie's cheeks flared cherry red. "Um," she said. "I accidentally killed him while he was attacking me."

It wasn't the least bit appropriate, but Adrian couldn't keep a laugh from snorting out his nose. "My, what a murderous bunch we are!"

"Bunch?" Roxie repeated. "I thought you said you *apprehended* the doctor."

"Apprehended with lethal force, I'm afraid. I had a choice of breaking his neck or letting him shoot me again. We left him in the passageway until we can figure out what to do with the body. Bodies now, I suppose. Lord. How are we going to explain a missing prince?"

"I don't understand this," Herrington said as if it pained him to admit. His elbows were on the desk, his head wagging like a bear. "Why did The Dragon try to take Max? From what you say, he already knew the boy was no use to his experiments. And why on earth would he bring a gun?"

"The prince must have led him to believe he'd need one," Roxie said, then explained what had passed between her and the ruler of Narikerr. Adrian listened with growing shock. Here he'd thought she'd been pacing the floor over them, when in truth she'd been fighting her own demon. Even with the editing Adrian suspected she was doing, the story appalled.

She seemed rattled to tell it, but not hysterical. Out of

respect for that, Adrian tried to respond calmly. "In other words, whatever reason he gave the doctor for taking Max, what he really wanted was a clear field to get to you."

The sound of glass smashing on the wall brought both of them around to stare at Herrington. The tumbler that had sat on his blotter a moment earlier was in pieces.

"Sorry," he said, on his feet with his hands clenched on the edges of his desk. Considering the force with which he gripped it, Adrian half expected to hear marble crack. "Sorry. I just . . . If that bastard wasn't dead already, I'd kill him myself." He released one side of the desk to squeeze his temples and shade his eyes. After a few more ragged exhalations, he composed himself and stood straight. "You're sure you killed him by taking his energy? He didn't perhaps hit his head?"

"I don't think so," Roxie said.

Piqued by Herrington's question, Adrian followed him to the corpse.

When he saw the gaunt, blueish features, he couldn't suppress a low whistle. "Boy," he said. "He looks bad."

Herrington knelt down heavily and felt for his pulse. Adrian could have told him not to bother—the prince was deader than dead—but Herrington seemed to need to check. When he looked up again at Roxie, a very definite emotion had gripped his face, an emotion Adrian could only specify as dread. Meeting it, Roxie looked as if she longed to crawl under the carpet.

"This isn't possible," her father said. "Yes, maybe being half-human gives you the power to feed off us, but you can't kill a person by draining their etheric-force. Not like this. A human would go catatonic before you could finish, and the only time I saw an energy death imposed on a Yama was during the intercity wars. The process took three priests working on the prisoner in shifts and lasted nearly a week. This must have happened in minutes."

"Maybe less," Roxie admitted, then pressed her thumb to her teeth.

"Maybe less," he repeated and breathed a very human curse.

"If it makes you feel any better," she said, "I've no idea how to do it again."

⇌

"Believe me," her father said, pushing to his feet as if he'd aged a hundred human years, "once is more than enough."

She thought he was going to berate her. Instead, he took her face in his hands, his touch so tender it tempted her to cry. The expression in his eyes was frightening. It was naked with emotion: love, fear, a determination so deep it seemed boundless. Until she saw the look, she hadn't truly known what she, what *family* meant to him. Despite what his eyes were saying, when he spoke, his voice was pure demon ice.

"I want you to listen to me very carefully. You must never tell anyone you did this, no matter the provocation. If anyone, human or Yama, imagined you had this power, the prince's interest in you would seem like child's play."

"But how can we hide it?" Roxie exclaimed. "Look at him!"

Her father didn't look, simply held her worried gaze with his steady one, as if he could force her to do as he wished by will alone. "I know he appears strange to you, but these symptoms aren't unheard of for a Yama who's had a heart attack."

"Surely he's young for that," Roxie protested.

"Yes," Herrington agreed, "but he led a less-than-wholesome life. Who's to say he didn't have a hidden weakness? Fortunately, what you did to him left no marks. If pressed to explain his condition, we'll tell my government the prince tried to rape you. When Adrian walked in on the heinous attempt, the prince's shock and humiliation must have been too much. Even if they don't believe us, the chance that we're telling the truth will discourage them from asking more questions."

"You can carry that off?"

"I can," said her father, "and I will. He got what he deserved. No one needs to know how."

When he released his clasp on her face, Roxie's knees

were so wobbly she had to sit. She barely noticed the discarded papers crinkling in the chair she chose. Her skin
was prickling again, as it were about to shoot sparks, despite which she felt as if she could have slept for a week.
She pressed her hand to her breast. She was having trouble
catching her breath.

Seeing this, Herrington turned to Adrian. "She drank a
lot of power," he said. "Take her to your suite before she
swoons."

"I can't leave you with this mess," Adrian said, then
added, "sir."

His politeness in the midst of chaos made Roxie smile,
but her father's response was stern. "The less you know
about how I handle this, the better."

To her surprise, Adrian didn't accept his pronounce-
ment. "I know someone who'll take the doctor's body off
your hands, a *rohn* who has more reason to hate him than
we do. I suspect she can make his death appear as accidental as you wish."

Her father stared at him narrow-eyed, then inclined his
head. "You may tell me how to contact her," he conceded.
"For now, you will take care of my daughter."

This Adrian did not argue. He bent to her chair and
scooped her into his arms. Though his body shook with
weariness, his hold was wonderfully secure. He squeezed
her for a moment, as if to let her know he felt the comfort,
too.

"Come on, my demon killer," he whispered fondly
against her hair. "I'm giving your father an address, and
then I'm getting you to bed."

⥤

She cried a little as he tucked the covers around her, claiming the cause was the ruination of her new purple gown. To
hear her tell it, that dress had been the only garment ever
capable of rendering her beautiful.

"Of all the demon families to be half-born into," she
sniffed, "I had to pick a homely one."

"Hardly that." He smiled down at her from his seat beside

her hip. "Or do you think I'd prefer you look like that spider-woman?"

"She *was* pretty," Roxie sighed.

Adrian laughed at her seemingly willful misreading of his meaning. "Her breath smelled funny."

"No-o," she said, scandalized.

He nodded. "Just a bit like flies."

She smiled at his foolishness and touched the single clean spot in the center of his shirt. He could tell she was sleepy. "You're a nice man, Adrian Philips."

"I'm a smart man. Look who I finished the night with."

Her eyelids closed as he stroked her brow, her lashes golden in the candlelight. Circles as purple as her gown curved underneath. "I think my father likes you."

"I got that glimmer of an impression, too. In fact, I think he may be ready to jettison his plans for the Jeruvian diplomat."

"Who?" she asked drowsily.

"Precisely."

He caressed her face and hair until he thought she slept, but she murmured "Stay," when he would have left.

He peeled off his bloody shirt and curled around her on top of the blankets. She hugged his arm under both of hers.

"I didn't like that feeding thing," she confessed, sounding like his nephews when they were fighting the need for a nap.

"Probably just as well. I don't think many Yama will be lining up for the experience."

He sensed she was smiling even though he couldn't see. "Maybe humans taste better to them than they taste to me."

"Maybe they taste like cinnamon kirbaz," he teased next to her ear.

She hummed with pleasure and wriggled her bottom closer to his groin. "I'm sorry you had to kill that doctor."

"I'm sorry you had to kill that prince."

"Will you be here tomorrow?" she asked.

His eyes stung without warning, his soul overwhelmed with love for this salty, regicidal, dress-mourning, beautiful-homely woman. He had no doubt the love he felt would fill the rest of his life.

"I will," he said hoarsely. "I promise. For as many to-morrows as you want."

"That could be a lot," she warned.

"It had better be," he warned back. "I fully intend to keep you around till death do us part."

"Need a ring for that," she said muzzily.

"So you do," he agreed. "I'll see to it first chance I get."

⤙⤙⤚

He drowsed with her, sleepy but not asleep, listening to the house grow quiet as one guest after another left.

He wondered how Herrington had managed breaking the news of the prince's death, if he'd told everyone or only the prince's closest associates. Adrian wasn't worried, merely curious, an unusual state of affairs for a man used to having, and taking, complete responsibility. Herrington had weathered political intrigues the likes of which Adrian could not conceive. Until his own aid was needed, he was content to leave the details in expert hands.

He had better things to think about.

He wasn't completely certain, but he believed he'd proposed to Roxanne. Even better, he was pretty sure she'd said "yes." Never mind she'd been half-awake at the time, he smiled to himself all the same.

Implied or not, he knew he could hold her to her promise. Roxanne McAllister was a woman of her word.

Chapter 29

∼

"We *shall* live happily ever after," declared Princess Hyacinth.

Her husband hadn't the slightest wish to contradict her, not when she clung to him and kissed his lips.

—*The Perils of the Princess,*
as serialized in the *Illustrated Times*

∼

The snow had ceased, and the sky glowed a deep velvet gray. Roxie caught her breath at her first glimpse of Adrian's family home. Abruptly nervous, she wiggled her new ring around the finger of her glove. Adrian had given it to her this morning at breakfast. He'd slid it between their plates with no more fanfare than a smile and a comment that now their engagement was official. Until she saw the gleam of the little sapphire against the gold, Roxie had been thinking she might have dreamed his proposal.

Their engagement might be official, but it hardly seemed

real. It certainly didn't seem real enough to announce to his
family. Why, she hadn't even told the boys!

"This is it." Adrian reached across her to unlatch the
hansom door.

She stepped out with her hand pressed to her throat.
"Look at the icicles on the eaves. It's straight out of a fairy-
tale."

In truth, the scene could have been taken straight from
her childhood fantasies. The front windows shone so
brightly they cast squares of molten gold on the snowy
lawn. Someone had shoveled a winding path to the door, a
convenience ignored by a number of small-booted children. Their laughter, blown in swells and ebbs on the leaf-
scented air, escaped the house's thick stone walls. She
experienced a fleeting sense of perfection, of God come to
Earth in simple human ties. Her eyes stung as Adrian embraced her from behind.

"You grew up here," she said. "In this beautiful place."

He kissed her ear. "Want to petition to make it a national landmark?"

Before she could answer his teasing, he straightened. A
big electric Falkham had pulled onto the shoulder of the
road, its deep-grooved tires flinging snow and gravel in its
wake.

"That's my father's automobile," Roxie said, recogniz-
ing the crest emblazoned on the boot. Without even thinking, she hid her ring beneath her cloak. She wasn't sure
what Yamish fathers expected, but by human standards,
she and Adrian should have consulted him. Now she regretted their rebellion against familial expectation. She
might have no wish to let any one control her life, but she
dreaded him taking insult. As she chewed her lip over this,
a boy in dark livery scampered out of the car and threw a
blanket over the hood, the way one would a horse left in
the cold.

"My mother must have invited Herrington," Adrian
said. "She probably read about him in the rags. She has
definite ideas about family, and I'm afraid advance warning isn't always involved." His thumbs soothed the bare

strip of skin between her chignon and collar. "I hope this won't upset you."

"No," she said slowly. "If my father wanted to come, I have no business objecting. We owe him a lot."

They owed him their freedom, if not their lives. Just that morning, the papers had reported on a famous Yamish doctor being fished out of the river. The city coroner surmised he'd slipped off an icy bridge a few weeks earlier and broke his neck. Despite Roxie's reasons for wanting her father to feel welcome, she was surprised Mrs. Philips wanted that, too. Perhaps Adrian's folks were more broadminded than she'd been herself.

Adrian hugged her as Herrington stepped out. Roxie was glad for the support. She still wasn't used to the idea of liking him.

Herrington seemed as awkward as she was. His big hands smoothed his scarf as his eyes shifted from her face to Adrian's, quite the nervous gesture for a Yama. "You look well," he finally said to her.

If she did, it was due in part to him. A *rohn*-made dress had arrived by messenger that morning, this one a delicious apple green. It was more modest than the gown her fatal struggle with the prince had destroyed, but equally irresistible.

"Thank you for the present," she said.

"You're exceedingly welcome," he replied stiffly.

Adrian laughed at them both. "It's good to see you again, Lord Herrington. I applaud your courage at being willing to meet my family."

"Your mother was . . . most insistent."

"Yes, sir. She has that gift."

The great Herrington was at a loss to answer this. It remained to Herrington's butler, Albert, doubling as chauffeur this evening, to rescue the awkward moment by suggesting they step inside where it was warm. As they moved ahead, the butler bent to whisper some direction to his youthful aide, who nodded earnestly. Herrington dressed his grooms well. The boy's burgundy coat matched the car, and he was equipped not only with a dashing gold scarf, but with cap, gloves, and boots. Still, it wouldn't be pleasant to sit in the cold all evening.

Adrian thought the same, apparently.

"Hey, there," he called, crunching toward the boy through the snow. Though Adrian's tone was kind, he recoiled slightly. "How would you like a job taking coats tonight, and a break for dinner after that?"

"That's all right," the boy demurred with a wary glance toward his employer. "Gotta watch the car."

Adrian stepped close enough to put his hand on the boy's shoulder. "It's a cold night. I'm sure you could dart out now and then to check on the— Good Lord!" In a flash, his hand shifted to the scruff of the boy's neck. "It's Tommy Bainbridge!" He gave the boy, who looked quite wretched, a shake. "Your parents and I have been searching for you for the past two months."

"Don't be ridiculous," said Herrington. "That's Rodrigo, my new mechanic."

"Mechanic, my foot. I know that face better than I know my own. He may be good with cars, but he's twelve years old. Didn't you think to check whether someone might be missing him?"

Herrington's chest expanded beneath his huge bearskin coat. "That's hardly my responsibility. The boy wanted a job, and I gave him one. He said he was an orphan. I trust you're not suggesting he came to any harm in my care."

His tone was as aristocratic as his blood, his silver eyes as cool as the fallen snow. When Adrian began to bristle, Roxie knew she had to smooth the waters fast.

"Father," she chided, laying her hand on his thick fur sleeve.

Herrington opened his mouth to take offense, then snapped it shut. "You never called me that before."

"Well, I'm calling you it now," she said briskly. "So you can just get used to it. And don't be yelling at Adrian. He saw how worried Tommy's parents were. Wouldn't you have been worried in their place?"

It might have been a trick of the winter light, but she thought Herrington blushed.

"But I'm fine," Tommy declared, trying to squirm free of Adrian's grip. "I read about Lord Herrington in the rags and thought I'd hitch up here to get work. At first I just wanted to pay back for the car I accidentally crashed, but then I saw what was in his barn. Lord Herrington promised I could learn to drive them all. Why should I go home anyway? I'm nothing but trouble to my folks."

Heedless of the snow, Adrian hunkered before the boy and took his arms. "I understand how you feel, Tommy, maybe better than you think, but your parents were afraid something bad had happened to you. You're a bit young to be running your life by yourself. When you're older, you can work for Lord Herrington."

"But I'll miss the expedition!" Tommy wailed. "I'm supposed to keep the trucks running."

Herrington clapped his arm around the boy's shoulder. Roxie suspected no apology for his behavior would be forthcoming. Nonetheless, the gesture tugged at her heart.

"Don't worry, Rodrigo, er, Tom," he said. "We'll work something out. I'll run you back home tonight and talk to your father. Maybe he'll let you spend summers with me, and you can catch all the good expeditions." Giving the boy a last squeeze, he indicated the house. "Shall we?"

His hand settled between Roxie's shoulder blades as they advanced down the shoveled path and up the steps of the porch. Her skin prickled strangely under the contact, as though her nerves had been thrown into confusion.

She didn't want to let him take charge, and yet she couldn't help but sympathize with his need to. She'd seen the man he was underneath his demon mask. She couldn't claim to understand everything about him, or to approve, but she couldn't deny they shared a similar loyalty to family. Knowing they'd both protect those they loved, even to the death, was oddly—and perhaps dangerously— comforting.

⤚⤙

The house surrounded Adrian in warmth and light.

"They've put up the Solstice decorations," he said, eyeing

the garlands of holly and bay spiraling down the staircase. He inhaled deeply, then turned to help Roxie with her cloak. She fussed a bit with her gloves before handing them and her reticule over.

"Rum punch," he confided, smiling as the smells and sounds of childhood celebrations washed over him. How different this homecoming was. How long it had been since he'd allowed himself to enjoy one. He was so caught up in remembering, it took him a moment to realize how nervous Roxie was.

"It's crowded," she said in a low, startled voice. "I thought you said only family was coming. These can't all be your relatives."

"I am," piped the chestnut-haired girl who was struggling to heft Herrington's bearskin coat over her shoulder.

"Hello, Amanda," Adrian said, the smile coming as naturally as the name, though it had been years since he'd seen Alice's oldest.

"Hello, Uncle Adrian." She goggled at Roxie's bright hair. "Your sweetheart is pretty."

Herrington's butler choked on a laugh. He covered the lapse by nudging Tommy forward to help Amanda with her burdens. Then he followed the young people to the back of the house.

Herrington turned a distinctly wistful eye on their disappearance. "Where's the receiving line?"

Adrian bit back a grin. "I'm afraid my family doesn't go in for receiving lines."

Herrington leaned closer. "Are they really all related to you?"

"Mostly." Adrian raised a hand to greet an aunt he'd been convinced was dead. "The rest are neighbors. This is Mother's idea of giving the new baby a proper welcome."

"A proper welcome," Herrington repeated. Before he could investigate further cultural differences, Adrian's sixteen-year-old sister, Beth, came barreling down the hallway.

"You're here, you're here," she cried, flinging herself into Adrian's arms. Going on tiptoe, she buried her nose in his neck. "And you smell heavenly! Oranges and ginger."

Adrian's face heated as he realized his scent and Roxie's must have combined from stealing kisses in the cab. Charles and Max had taken their own hansom. The boys considered this a special treat and, although Roxie had ordered them not to ask the driver to race every vehicle they met, Adrian had no doubt they'd beaten his and Roxie's cab by miles. Not that it mattered. His family was good at making rambunctious boys feel at home.

No slouch herself when it came to being rough-and-tumble, Beth let him go. "You must be Roxanne!" she chortled effusively.

"I am," Roxie said unsurely. "Pleased to meet you, too."

"Hah!" Beth barked, punching Adrian's shoulder with enough friendly vigor to make him wince. He'd forgotten what a boisterous puppy she could be, though if her manners could put Roxie at ease, it would be worth it.

With a complete disregard for the honors due Herrington's rank, his sister waved at him, grabbed Roxie's hand, and started tugging her down the hall. "Come on, Roxie. I'll take you to the tower. They've got the latest baby in Mother and Father's room. Everyone's dying to meet you. Do you know that divine blond boy of yours chased Mother out of her kitchen! Said she wasn't basting the squabs properly. Mother near about popped."

Adrian turned to an endearingly lost-looking Herrington. "Why don't I introduce you to my grandfather? He's always saying he'd love the chance to chat with a diplomat. Besides which, he's got the key to Mother's brandy store."

"Ah, er, very good. Always ready to sample a home cordial." The hesitation in Herrington's voice told Adrian he suspected what he was in for but couldn't think how to evade it.

⟡

The round master bedroom, where the new baby was purportedly being shielded from too much excitement, reminded Roxie of a lighthouse. Tall, deep windows ringed it, between which brass ship's lanterns glowed. The air smelled pleasantly of baby talc. Despite its size, the room was crowded. Both Adrian's parents were there, though Varya was chatting too busily to do more than wave. All four of Adrian's sisters and their assorted husbands were ranged about the walls: the plain and placid Alice, the breathtaking but highly strung Marianne, Beth, of course, and Adrian's oldest sister, Julie, the voluptuous new mother.

Appearing perfectly content with the attention, Julie sat cross-legged on the bed in the curve of her dapper husband's arm, her baby cradled in her lap, her skirts spread across the counterpane. Though the styles of their dresses were different, and hers had a clean nappie thrown over one shoulder, hers was the same apple-green as Roxie's. Julie laughed delightedly at the coincidence, her cheeks glowing milk and pink with motherhood.

"Here she is, Gaspar. Guardian of your most treasured new employee."

"Hush," the restaurateur scolded without the slightest ire. "That boy's got a big enough head."

Julie patted the bed in front of her and, before Roxie even had time to say hello, a bright-eyed, squirming baby was ladled carefully into her arms. She gasped at the feel of him. He was so warm, so little, but so strong in his kicks and wriggles. With no more shyness than if she'd been a lifelong member of the family, Gaspar's hand came under hers to help support the baby's head. Julie leaned forward to coo at her infant son.

Before she could adjust to this unexpectedly warm welcome, Gaspar was calling out a greeting to Adrian, apparently shed of the burden of entertaining her father.

Even here, in the midst of his family, Roxanne's heart beat more forcefully at his approach. His smiling eyes locked with hers as he shouldered through the gathering, barely responding to his family's greetings.

"Hello," she said nervously as he stood beaming down at her, at the baby in her arms, at Gaspar's hand curled so naturally beneath her own. She shouldn't have been tense. Everyone was being extremely nice, but part of her couldn't believe they'd really let her belong. Damn Adrian, anyway, for not telling them about the engagement ahead of time. She, for one, could do without the suspense.

"You look good with a babe in your lap," he said, not helping matters at all. He sat behind her on the edge of the bed, close enough that his chest warmed her back. When he reached over her to brush the baby's plump cheek, he noticed the omission on her right hand. Overcome by anxiety, she'd slipped his ring into her reticule.

"Ahem," he said, tapping the offending finger.

"I couldn't," she whispered back pleadingly. "Not by myself!"

"Is something wrong?" Julie asked.

"No, no," Adrian assured her, clearly amused. "Roxie's just a little shy in this chattering horde. Gaspar, do you think you could do the honors and quiet the room?"

The honors turned out to be an earsplitting whistle.

"Thank you," Adrian said as everyone settled. "You know I'm not much for speeches, but I have a few things to say. I'd appreciate if you'd refrain from rushing us until I'm done. First, and most important, this lovely woman has agreed to be my wife. Second—" He broke off laughing to let them exclaim while Roxie covered her blazing face.

"Second," he continued with no sympathy whatsoever for her embarrassment, "since Roxie didn't grow up in a big, noisy family, I ask that you treat her gently for a while. Give her a chance to get used to your insanity."

"Adrian!" Roxie cried. "Don't make them think I consider them insane!"

Though her protest went unheard, it didn't seem to matter, because his relatives were indeed rushing them, surrounding them with too many hugs and kisses to tell who each belonged to. The effect was both alarming and wonderful. This was better than the family she'd dreamed of having as a child—messier, maybe, but a hundred times as warm.

"Well, that's nice," Adrian's mother chirped through the hubbub. "A wedding. And here I thought he was only going to tell us she was with child."

Judging she'd had enough of his relatives, Adrian helped Roxie escape to his old bedroom, now a sewing chamber. Though outwardly sentimental, his mother had made no shrines to her children. The moonlit room held few signs of its former use. He thought Roxie would find it peaceful enough to brace for the second wave. After all, the other half of his family—the cousins and aunts—still awaited downstairs.

"Whew," she said now. "I thought they were going to follow us."

He didn't tell her they would have if they weren't just a little intimidated by his sternness. "I hope I didn't embarrass you too much."

She shook her head shyly. "Now it's real," she said. "Before it wasn't, but now it is."

"Hm," he said. "Suddenly, I have the feeling my proposal should have been a bit more formal—not to mention romantic."

He expected her to smile, but instead she worried her lip. "Are you certain about marrying me, Adrian? Your folks seem understanding, but you'll never be respectable. And there's Max and Charles to think about. You're wonderful with them, but two boys are a lot of work. Plus, you might not know this, but I've got a good bit of money. You'd have to come to terms with that. If you marry me, the law will say it's yours."

Adrian was still smiling when she rattled to a halt. "There's only one thing you have to ask yourself. Do you love me enough to share the rest of our lives?"

"Yes. More than anything."

"Good." He held her face for a serious perusal. "Because I want us to be together, you and me and Charles and Max. I want us to be a family. Maybe have a few of our own when we're ready."

She closed her eyes at the gruffness of his tone, but she didn't tell him to stop. She wanted—no—needed all the words. Needed them to wash her clean of the last vestiges of doubt.

"As for the money, I plan to ask your father to undo

whatever he did to get me dismissed from the Securité. I'm going to see if I can get reinstated on my own, now that the superintendent has had a chance to cool down." His lips whispered across her brow. "Whatever happens, I promise you'll never be sorry you accepted me. Given our history, our life is bound to be eventful, but we love each other. We can make a success of this."

"I believe you," she said just as earnestly. "Oh, Adrian. This is all the romance I need." She tugged his hands down to her bosom. Her heart was pounding, and he smiled slowly, sleepily as he spread his fingertips across her soft flesh, drinking in the furious vibration of life and love.

When he laughed, she heard joy in the husky sound.

"Can't back out now," he warned. "I know your secrets."

"As I know yours," she reminded.

Fortunately, his kiss ensured her silence.

⤛

Charles guessed what had happened the moment he entered the cloakroom; didn't even need to see the ring she was slipping on. They locked gazes, and then she smiled, her eyes crinkling, her mouth curving softly. She glowed with a new inner certitude. He'd never seen her look this beautiful except once, when she glared down at him on a dirty Avvar street, challenging him with her outthrust hand.

Take a chance, Charles. Take a chance.

Something sharp and hot stabbed the region of his heart, but he couldn't hold out against her when she opened her arms. They embraced amid the smell of rock salt and damp wool, neither wanting to let go.

Charles thought of the position Herrington had offered him earlier this evening, to serve as cook on his next expedition to Sammerhorn. He'd been leery of working for a demon, but he knew now that he'd accept. No matter how much he admired Adrian and loved Roxie, it would be better for him if he weren't around to witness their newly wedded bliss. He was almost a man now. He hadn't wanted to face it, but sometimes it was hard to think of Roxie as a sister.

Happily, lots of things could happen in a summer. When he returned, he'd find a way to love more than her.

"He asked you then." He pulled back, made a separation between them. "I'm glad."

It was almost true.

Then Adrian was there with Max flopped in sleep over his shoulder. Max looked as if he belonged there, like Adrian's son. Charles told himself he was grateful there'd be someone to care for Max when he was gone, but in truth, it seemed a betrayal of all he'd done for the boy.

He forced himself to face Roxie's fiancé. It wasn't easy. Adrian was smiling softly, his eyes filled with a terrible understanding, as if he'd looked into Charles's soul and seen all its dark corners.

"She told you?" he said, rubbing a slow circle on Max's back.

Charles nodded, jaw tight to keep his emotions checked. He moved to shake the man's hand, but Adrian pulled him into his unoccupied shoulder and kissed his hair with surprising affection. No grown man had ever held him this way. Other ways, but not that. Adrian was tall. Charles only reached his shoulder. Something tensed and strained inside him as he suffered the embrace, clenching his throat and making him tremble, making him feel young.

"Don't worry," Adrian whispered fiercely. "I want to give you more, not take anything away. You're as dear to me as Max."

Charles pushed away from him, the confusion of strong emotion making him dizzy. He hardly heard the women flutter into the coatroom, too eager to wait for Adrian and Roxie to emerge. They filled the space between him and the couple, laughing and wishing them well.

He braced a hand on the coat-padded wall, too weak to leave, though he felt a tear rolling down his cheek.

"Lord!" said a disgusted female voice, breaking his solitude. "Don't let them see you dripping like a faucet. Silly cows are liable to call the whole thing off. I'm counting on my mother being distracted for the next six months."

It was the funny-looking girl they called Beth, the one who acted like a boy in a dress. She was shoving a hand-kerchief in his face as if it were his sacred duty to use it.

"Bugger off," he said as soon as he'd blown his nose sufficiently to speak.

"Hah!" she said and punched his shoulder hard enough to hurt.

Charles surprised himself by laughing back. When he did, he knew he'd survive.

Epilogue

Since I have stated on numerous occasions that I abhor gossip, you may rely on what I tell you now. Yes, the unlamented Prince of Narikerr did meet his end in a woman's arms. Yes, Adrian Philips rose to lead Securité's Department of International Affairs. Roxanne McAllister bore four children by him—despite many bitter people's claim that she would have none. It is also true that she was the first human artist to show her work in the Northland. I have it on good authority that every piece she brought past the border sold, though naturally none of the Yama would later admit to buying them.

More to the point, if my esteemed readers followed the *responsible* news outlets as they should, they would know Lord Herrington was awarded both the Distinguished Victoria Cross and the Yamish Order of Valor. The services that earned him these honors remain open to debate. Diplomacy is a tricky matter, and trickier still when royals are involved. One never knows when one will accidentally end up on the winning side of a family feud.

—*The True and Irreverent History of Avvar*

⊂≥

How about June?" Roxie asked dreamily, smoothing her hand down his sweat-slicked chest. Adrian was still breathing hard, and she loved the sound.

"I was thinking more along the lines of next weekend," he replied, then jumped as her fingers swept past his navel. With the flat of her hand, she stretched his sated organ gently toward its head. He should have been exhausted, but he stirred.

"I couldn't get a dress that soon," she said reasonably, going up on one elbow to examine his progress. She repeated the stroke, incrementally increasing the pressure as her palm dragged toward his tip. A strange caress, it was nonetheless arousing.

Amused by his own susceptibility, he looked up at the absorbed expression on her face, still flushed from their last lovemaking. Her hair hung in streamers of red-gold satin across her breasts, her nipples peeping through the waves. He rolled closer to kiss one peak, coaxing it with lips and tongue until it took on the sharpness of a beginning rather than an end. He trailed his fingers down her arm, pleased when she shivered.

"I take it you want a real wedding," he said. "A fancy dress and a veil? A wide gold band and a seaside chapel?"

"We-ell," she admitted and blushed delightfully. The heat of it suffused her breasts. "Only if you wouldn't mind."

"The only thing I'd mind"—he snaked his arms around her back—"is waiting until June. I give you a month and permission to ask my interfering sisters for all the help they're no doubt chomping on the bit to give."

She laughed, then sighed as he tangled their legs together. Her insides fluttered with arousal, quickly dampening the thigh he'd wedged considerately against her mound.

"Greedy creature," he said and jerked his hips closer.

She ignored the mock scolding. "We could ask your sister Alice to sing. And perhaps Linia Rahasanchez would agree to do the dance of the thousand veils, though that might make your mother nervous." She laughed. "I can hear her now: 'Oh, Isaac, please tell me she's got something under that last scarf!' "

Her hand smoothed down the furrow of his spine, calling a lovely noise from the back of his throat. Clearly wanting the upper hand, he rolled her beneath him. His erection flattened between their bellies, hot and long once more. When he spoke, his voice was rough. "It would be an interesting crowd. My family. Your father. Your sailor friends. A few reporters from the rags."

"Better make that a few dozen. My father schooled me on the necessity of sending an invitation to the Queen."

"The Queen!" He started up in alarm.

"I can't help it," she said, her heart dancing with laughter. "My father is a very important demon."

Adrian settled back warily. As he did, his shaft slid between her lips, gathering up praise and calling forth more. "Most likely she wouldn't come."

"Most likely," Roxanne agreed, "though we could elope."

For a moment he looked tempted, then squared his jaw. "That won't be necessary. It makes me proud that you want a proper wedding. We've done everything else backward. We may as well do one thing right."

Roxie's smile was pure feminine mischief.

"Oh, no," she said, her strong hands easing him home. "That will never be the only thing we've done right."

Turn the page for a special preview of
Emma Holly's novel

Strange Attractions

Available now from Berkley Sensation!

"Come closer," B.G. Grantham said to his employee.

Though Eric Berne was dressed, his boss was not. The notoriously reclusive physicist lay face down on a black leather massage table—his long, lean body gleaming with oil. Eric knew it didn't bother B.G. to be naked. His employer's reserve had never been physical. It didn't need to be. From his broad, straight shoulders to his narrow feet, his every sinew was perfectly conformed. Had B.G. wished, his image could have been used to hawk men's cologne.

He's the Greek ideal, Eric thought, flashing back to his days at U.C. Berkeley, *mind and muscle both at their peak.*

Because he was an avid swimmer, B.G. had taken to removing his body hair. As Sylvia, the pretty blonde masseuse, pushed her hands slowly down his spine, nothing spoiled his sleek, athletic lines.

Eric fought an urge to lick his lips.

"Yes?" he said, shaking himself from his fugue and stepping within arm's reach. "You have an assignment for me?"

"Of a sort," B.G. said, then groaned as Sylvia took his butt in her hands and squeezed.

The masseuse was his latest find, hired away from an exclusive spa in nearby Victoria. Though B.G.'s staff usually went through a longer vetting process than Sylvia had, Eric could understand why he'd made an exception for her. Her hands were magic, her gift for intuiting what sort of touch would spur the greatest pleasure formidable. It was as if she'd been born to please. Naturally, this fascinated B.G., whose lifelong study of pleasure—what caused it, what heightened it—neared obsession.

Now his legs shifted slightly, languorously, betraying his enjoyment as much as his groan. The change in position bared the lower bulge of his balls, full and sexually flushed. For the last three months, B.G. had withdrawn from everyone on his staff, devoting himself to mental labors until he had to be reminded to eat and sleep. Eric could tell that phase was over and that B.G.'s appetite for sensual indulgence—always considerable—had been heightened by abstinence.

Once again, B.G. was taking his place as the erotic fulcrum around which Mosswood revolved. Once again, he'd decide who would be pleasured and who would not. Sylvia seemed to sense the change, her body humming softly with interest. She stood at the head of the table, and her front brushed B.G.'s back as she reached down.

She was a lovely woman—naked, of course—with slight, high breasts and nipples as tight as pencil erasers. Her hair was so short it clung to her head like a feathered platinum cap. Eric had reason to know those locks were just as soft as they appeared. She was an odd creature in bed, more comfortable with giving pleasure than in taking it. The few times they'd had sex—while B.G. was caught up in work—she'd given the impression that she wasn't completely there, as if she were perpetually waiting for someone else to appear. The effect was disconcerting, and

explained why her status had been so quickly changed
from plaything to staff. Competence was what B.G. valued
most in an employee. In a sexual partner, however, a desire
for the rewards he meted out was all important. Ironically,
Sylvia wasn't greedy enough to suit B.G.—a problem Eric
suspected he'd never have to worry about.

He did wonder, though, if he'd ever get used to being
able to desire a woman even as his mouth was watering for
a man.

Eric had been attracted to both sexes since he was
young, a quirk in his makeup he'd been lucky enough to
accept almost as soon as he'd figured out what it was. His
parents had been open-minded, his circle of friends liberal.
Before taking this job as B.G.'s sexual major domo, he'd
thought attraction ought to be a one-gender-at-a-time affair. Serial mono-sexuality, so he thought, would keep his
feet on the ground.

He should have guessed his old friend would be beyond
any rules at all. The world of the quantum, B.G.'s favorite
playground, knew few limits. Consequently, B.G. saw no
reason why he should invent limits for himself.

"You've been here, what, three years now?" B.G. asked,
his voice altered by a combination of sensual enjoyment
and the pressure of stroking hands.

"About that," Eric agreed.

"And we've met in this chamber at least twice a year."

Reflexively, Eric looked around. The room in which he
stood was shaped like a pyramid, great blocks of softly
polished graywacke narrowing rank by rank to a central
point. Blue pinprick lights underlit each level, enhancing
the impression that this place was both old and new, a jux-
taposition B.G. loved.

The quantum realm, he liked to say, *can't tell the difference between all times and none at all.*

Then again, since some of his employer's beliefs verged
on the crankish, he might have been trying to test the valid-
ity of "pyramid power."

"Yes," Eric said, fighting a smile, "we always start our
adventures here."

Despite the chamber's familiarity, or perhaps because of it, merely opening its heavy door had the ability to disengage Eric from his normal self. His inhibitions fell away, along with his preconceived ideas of what sensible people did. Here, where each new round of play began, his desires spoke to him in the clearest possible tones.

Though it disturbed him sometimes, he was beginning to think the person he became within these walls was the real him. Regardless of whether that was true, his skin tightened in anticipation as his employer drew breath to speak.

"I want you to choose," B.G. said, startling Eric enough to rock him back on his heels.

Abruptly, he was aware of what hung beneath the lining of his trousers: the thickening weight of his cock, the tensing power of his legs. Eric was bigger and stronger than B.G., not stupid, but more of an athlete than a brain. B.G.'s mental charisma was the force that kept him in check. On his own, Eric wouldn't have had a fraction of the experiences B.G. made possible. Because of this, as well as his debt of loyalty, Eric chose to indulge the other man's whims, to wait however long it took for permission to sate his desires—which didn't mean the reins never chafed.

That was the idea, of course: that no one around B.G. be able to predict when release would come, that the possibility it would be withheld would make them desperate. In that state of suspended frustration, the smallest erotic reward gained intensity.

Blinking sleepily, B.G. turned his head on his folded arms. His face was as attention-grabbing as the rest of him—quirkier perhaps, narrow and olive-skinned, with a long, curving nose and a mobile mouth. His hair was straight and black, cut short except for a shock that hung over his dark-brown eyes. On anyone else, these features would have been expressive. On B.G., they gave away virtually nothing. His emotions were hidden, as was usual, behind a wall of lazy calm.

Only a long-time associate like Eric could tell how jazzed he was.

"Did you hear me?" B.G. asked patiently. "I said I want you to choose our next candidate."

The candidates' files sat open on the granite tiles beneath the table where B.G. lay. One candidate was male, the other female. These reports were part psychological profile, part personal history. Eric had not only directed their compilation, he had summarized them for his boss. It wasn't standard procedure, but Eric himself had taken the long-lens photos for one. That being the case, he knew the files' contents intimately.

"I heard you," he said to B.G. "I'm just not sure which option you'd enjoy more."

This spurred a reaction. Like a leopard waking from a nap, B.G. rolled onto his back and pushed up on his elbows. His chest bore creases from the table's leather seams. Though the marks cut enticingly across his nipples, Eric's eyes drifted farther down. B.G.'s cock was swollen and straight, flushed like his scrotum but not lifted yet. Because his hips were slender, his shaft seemed larger by comparison. With painful clarity, Eric recalled the silkiness of its skin.

As B.G. undoubtedly intended, remembering the pleasure they could share made the waiting worse.

B.G. and Eric had known each other since they were boys, thrown together by well-meaning parents who thought the oddball genius needed a friend his own age. Eric sometimes wondered if the Granthams and the Bernes had suspected what they'd begun. From the time he and B.G. were teens, it had been like this between them, a game of do-we-dare and Lord-I-can't-resist. Losing touch for a while hadn't changed their chemistry. B.G. was still the partner Eric couldn't get out from under his skin.

Similarly drawn, if not for the same reasons, Sylvia reached for her client's burgeoning erection. To see a need and not satisfy it at once went against her nature. B.G. held her off by spreading his hand across her diaphragm. Though his touch was gentle, it made her flinch. No more than that was needed to make her stop. Sylvia might believe in instant gratification, but like everyone at Mosswood, she knew who was boss.

"I want you to choose the candidate *you* would enjoy," B.G. said, his gaze intent on Eric's face. "I want you to consider no one's desires but your own."

"My desires?" Eric repeated. The hair at his nape prickled in a wave. He had to take a step to keep his footing, more off-balance than he could account for by the surprise. Without exception, B.G. always set the rules. He bore the ultimate responsibility for the end result. Changing that seemed vaguely dangerous, as if the haven Eric had found here could be threatened by what he chose.

Why B.G. would want to do this was beyond him.

Watching him, B.G.'s fingers played idly across the shaven skin of his own abdomen. "Yes," he said. "I want to know which of these people you could get most enthused about having. Who would frustrate you more to be deprived of? Who do you wish to help me drive to their brink?"

Eric knew the answer, and had known it even before he passed the name to their investigator to start the file. He'd never had such a strong reaction to a candidate. The thought of having this person here, at B.G.'s estate, under their conjoined control, thrust through his body like a velvet hammer blow. Goose bumps swept his scalp as he hardened with a swiftness B.G. seemed mysteriously able to suppress.

"You know you can't lie to me," B.G. said at his hesitation. "I've known you too long, and I'm too good at reading how you feel."

The knowledge that this was true freed him to respond.

"This one," he said, stooping to pull a picture out of the pile. His hand shook slightly as he held it out.

B.G. nodded, smiling faintly as if the decision was expected. "Good," he said, settling back against the table. "I appreciate your honesty."

B.G. beckoned to Sylvia, who moved eagerly forward and took his shaft between her well-oiled fingers. B.G. was human enough to shudder at the first contact. Given her personal predilection, the reaction encouraged her to even more exquisite care. She stroked him hand over hand, from root to rim, the rhythm slow and hypnotic while his cock wavered back and forth at each pull—the tides of his blood a force both Eric and she could see.

This time B.G. didn't stop her, though his eyes, glittering within the spikes of his dark lashes, remained on Eric. As if he'd given himself permission to be aroused, he rose to full erection, his veins filling darkly, his untouched crown as taut as a drum.

The visual he presented was tempting in the extreme— and not only to Eric.

"Do you want me to suck you?" Sylvia asked breathlessly.

B.G. reached out but not toward her, the back of his hand brushing the front of Eric's thigh. Trembling now, Eric tried to breathe as steadily as his friend. His own erection felt like a club, hot behind the cloth B.G.'s feather-light caresses tugged. His employer was always gentle, always careful not to hurt. It was the only complaint Eric ever had. Right now, Eric wanted a good, firm grip so desperately he could have screamed.

Images streaked through his mind of taking someone against a wall, of pounding recklessly into them until he came. Who it was he hardly cared, though he couldn't deny the phantom had a face.

The guilt this specificity inspired didn't weaken the fantasy.

"What do you think?" his old friend asked. "Shall I have her take me in her mouth?"

Eric shivered, his inner vision seeing someone besides the masseuse performing the task. Unused to having the power to choose, he took a moment to decide. He had no doubt what Sylvia wanted the answer to be. "Yes," he said, "but don't let her bring you to climax."

B.G.'s hand shifted sideways, his palm closing gently over Eric's crotch. "If I can't come, neither can you."

Eric gritted his teeth. B.G. was already rubbing his erection, probing for vulnerabilities, stretching him impossibly

inside his skin. When his longest finger dragged toward the
nerve-rich flare, Eric couldn't repress an anticipatory twitch.

His zipper was a barrier he wished his heat could melt.

"Agreed," he gasped, knowing his employer—his rescuer, truth be told—would make it as difficult as possible
to comply.

"I want us all to wait," Eric added impulsively. "Nobody
gets off until our candidate arrives."

B.G.'s brows quirked in surprise—this edict was more
his style than Eric's—then relaxed as his eyes briefly
closed. Sylvia had bent to surround the upper half of him
in her mouth. She held him for a moment, her tongue
working against the cap, before beginning to move up and
down. As before, her pace was languid, her suction strong.
A sheen of sweat broke out on B.G.'s face as his now-rigid
cock grew wet.

Sylvia would get him off if he wasn't careful. Then
again, "Careful" was pretty much B.G.'s middle name.

Despite the battle for control he must be going through,
when he spoke, his voice was only a little husky. To Eric's
relief, he did not seem angry at his demand.

"This," B.G. said, "should prove more entertaining than
usual."

Eric got the distinct and somewhat unnerving impression that, in addition to making his own choice, he had vin-
dicated B.G.'s.